CARE TO DIE

First published in 2017 by Bloodhound Books

www.bloodhoundbooks.com

Print ISBN: 978-1-912175-28-4

This novel is dedicated to my wonderful mother and to Agnes and Miller Brown.

PRAISE FOR TANA COLLINS' ROBBING THE DEAD

"A finely plotted mystery. Tana Collins racks up the suspense on this one. DI Jim Carruthers is a cop to watch."

Peter Robinson Bestselling author of the DCI Banks series

An author to keep an eye on and a series that will be one to watch in the future. Another well-deserved five stars from me and a story I will highly recommend to all.

Gemma Gaskarth BetweenThe Pages Book Club

"This book forces the reader to hit the ground running as the story unfolds. There is a lot of character building as I would expect from the first book in a series. The author manages to build in depth characters while telling the story and has successfully avoided large chunks of descriptive text."

Jill Burkinshaw Books 'n' All

"I read this story in one and I hadn't a clue where it was going to go but it mixed history with modern day and came up with a belter. I felt so emotionally involved with all the characters both good and bad, you had to feel for them all. A heart breaking story from the past that just continued to claim more innocent lives. I am so looking forward to more books in this series."

Susan Hampson Books From Dusk Till Dawn

"I'm already a fan of this series and as Collins as a debut writer and am anxious for the next book to be released."

Amy Sullivan Novelgossip

"Collins's strength is in her characterisation, and I look forward to another one in the series. This is a good, very promising debut."

BA Steadman author of the DI Dan Hellier series

PROLOGUE

The old man lies on his back, head turned towards her. His left arm thrown out in front of him, right leg bent beneath him. A pool of something dark stains the snow. But it's his eyes that frighten her most. Wide open and terrified. She takes off a red mitten. Tentatively touches his hand with her bare skin. It feels as cold as ice. Now she knows she is staring death in the face. And not just death. Something worse.

The wind picks up; a sudden rushing noise. The tops of the trees sway. Scrambling to her feet she screams – a loud lingering scream that pierces the stillness of the woods. Then she turns and runs. Icy air hits the back of her throat. Her mouth feels dry. Sheer terror makes her heart hammer in her chest.

She tears through the silent woods. Adrenaline carrying her forward. Ghostly branches whip her face, ice from an elder tree cascades down her back. Her foot catches on something. She is propelled forward, her face slamming into the frozen earth. She feels the skin on her chin graze. She smells decaying leaves and earth. Her leg hurts where she has hit it against a tree stump. Whimpering she scrambles to her feet and runs.

Her bare hand is cold. The taste of blood in her mouth where she's bitten her tongue. It's only now she realises she's left the mitten behind.

Breathless, she stops and squeezes herself through a gap in the old stone wall beside the Pink Building. She feels the heat from the run in her cheeks. The strap of the rucksack she carries over one shoulder catches on the jagged wall and with a huge effort she finally shrugs it loose.

Her cry comes out in ragged sobs. The breath visible in the freezing air. Nearly out of the woods. Almost safe. Safe from whatever evil lurks in the forest. She still sees him. Bloodied, mutilated. Lying on the ground. Unmoving. Unimaginable horror etched in his dead eyes. She will never go back and play in the woods again. Never.

Beyond the Pink Building her house is now in sight and she limps and cries towards what she knows will be the protective arms of her mother.

CHAPTER ONE

The hard ground crunched under foot and the air is so cold that DI Jim Carruthers felt it hit his throat, then lungs. He saw a knot of people up ahead and recognised Dr Mackie, the pathologist. As he put on his latex gloves Carruthers looked around him cataloguing the details. The corpse was lying on its back under an ancient oak. The whole front of the chest was a mass of dried blackish blood. The left arm was stretched out at a right angle to the body, hand clenched. The victim's right hand was lying across his chest. Carruthers' eyes narrowed as he observed the darkened ground where the man had bled out.

The scene of crime officers had already taped off the area. Carruthers started to stoop to duck under the red tape but Mackie stopped him.

'You'll have to stay behind the tape. Liu hasn't finished photographing the body yet. He's just away for a piss,' said Mackie. Carruthers craned his neck to look at the corpse better and took in the mop of thick white hair, the whiskery chin that ended a long angular face, which was already starting to mottle. He turned to Mackie. 'What can you tell me?'

'We'll know more with the PM, laddie. All I can tell you at the moment is that he sustained a stab wound to the chest, which could be the cause of death. Certainly deep enough.' Dr Mackie shifted his weight from one knee to the other. It was accompanied by a noise somewhere between a sigh and a groan. 'In terms of a weapon you'll be looking for a knife, kitchen or hunting, with a serrated edge. You'll notice how the wound's jagged.'

Carruthers tried to peer at it from behind the tape. 'Just one puncture wound?'

'Aye, and done with some force, I'd say.'

DS Andie Fletcher sneezed and tucked a tendril of dark hair behind her right ear. She was standing just outside the taped-up area. 'Unlikely to be suicide then. And no weapon's been found, Jim.' Her breath was coming out in gasps and a gravelly voice hinted at a head cold. She was blowing on her hands and stamping her feet. 'Christ, it's parky.' She dived in to the deep pocket of the coat she was wearing and put on her own latex gloves.

A white flash startled Carruthers. 'It's January in Scotland. What do you expect?' Both he and Fletcher looked up as the clipped voice of Liu announced the return to the locus of the police photographer.

With difficulty Dr Mackie got up from the kneeling position and put his hand up to stop Carruthers from asking his next question. He placed his hands on the small of his back and straightened up.

'Not as young as I used to be. My knees are the problem. Well, that and the hips.'

'What do they say? Old age doesn't come by itself. How long dead?' said Carruthers.

'Wouldn't say that long. Rough estimate between twelve and twenty-four hours. Any longer and the body would start to freeze.'

Carruthers could well believe that. Despite it being only January it had already been one of the coldest winters on record in Fife.

'We need the PM to be definite,' continued Mackie who was peering at the corpse. 'There's already been some evidence of animal activity. Possibly foxes. Poor buggers. They'll be hungry.' He licked his lips. 'Reminds me we've got a nice bit of roast beef for supper tonight.'

Carruthers shuddered. He observed Liu taking a series of photographs of the body from different angles, the constant flashing like strobe lighting. The watery sun was low in the sky and cast long dark shadows across the wood.

'Your nose been in a fight with a cheese grater?' asked Liu of Fletcher. 'You look awful.'

'Thanks for that.' She blew her nose furiously.

'He's right,' said Carruthers.

'You're all heart,' she said.

Carruthers turned to Dr Mackie. 'Was he killed here?'

'Every indication. There's a fair amount of blood.'

Fletcher angled her head to the side so she too could get a better look. 'Appears to be in his late seventies.'

'Any ID?' asked Carruthers.

'This'll be what you're looking for,' said a young female officer. 'The SOCOs have already bagged his effects.' She gave a package to Fletcher who opened it and examined the contents before placing them back in the bag and throwing the bag over to Carruthers, who caught it deftly.

'Wallet. Found in his back pocket. His RBS card says Ruiridh Fraser,' said the officer.

'And you are?' asked Carruthers, appreciatively noting her natural white blond hair and fair looks. He wondered if she was of Scandinavian descent. More than likely if she came from the far north of Scotland. Her Shetland accent hadn't escaped him.

'PC Hutchison, sir. First on the scene.'

Carruthers arched an eyebrow at her. 'Don't suppose we've got an address for him?'

'We do, as it happens. Two Bridge Street, Cellardyke. Handy letter with him about overdue library books.'

Carruthers looked over at the young officer, noting her wide eyes and earnest expression. He wondered if this was her first dead body.

'Who found him?' asked Fletcher.

'Twelve-year-old girl, out playing, ma'am. Being interviewed at the moment. She's in a bit of a state. Wouldn't come back out to the woods to show us where she found it. But we've found this. Think it's hers.' She pointed to a child's red mitten.

'She being interviewed at home, then?' said Carruthers. 'I take it she's local?'

'Yes, sir. Ten minutes' walk from here.'

'Unlike Ruiridh Fraser, if that's who our body is. Cellardyke?' said Carruthers, turning the package over. 'That's eight miles away. I wonder what he was doing here? There's no sign of a car so how did he get here?'

'Bus or a lift?' said Fletcher.

'Braidwood is part of a nature reserve so maybe he was out for a walk,' said Mackie.

'I thought this land was owned by the University of East of Scotland?' said Carruthers.

'It is. Well, the university owns the buildings, the meadow and the woods but there's always been public access.' Mackie gestured around him to the great sweep of land beyond the wood upon which stood several huge Victorian institutional stone buildings. 'This is one of the places I go walking.'

Carruthers knew Mackie enjoyed his exercise. He turned over the plastic-bagged library letter and looked at the address again. Since moving back to Scotland he had been living in Anstruther, a fishing village on the east coast of Fife, a stone's throw from Cellardyke. They were practically neighbours. He took another long hard look at the man's lined face, noting the white beard and still thick mass of wiry white hair.

'Anything else on him?'

'Twenty-five pounds, couple of bank cards, library card for Cellardyke library, organ donor card, and, like I said, a letter about overdue books,' said PC Hutchison, tucking a stray strand of blond hair behind her ear.

'We can rule out robbery then,' said Fletcher. 'Unless they were after his library books. Did you find a mobile or set of house keys?'

'No,' said Hutchison.

'Pity.' Carruthers scratched his eyebrow.

'There's something you'll want to see in the wallet. Inside left,' said the blonde officer.

Carruthers flipped open the wallet. There was a passport-sized photograph of a child. The photo was old, the child blond.

Carruthers studied it then closed the wallet and dropped it in to the plastic bag along with all the other effects.

'We almost done here, laddie?' Mackie asked Liu.

'I'm finished.' Liu slung his camera over his shoulder. 'Got everything I need.'

'Right, let's get the body back to the mortuary,' said Dr Mackie.

Fletcher sneezed again.

Carruthers handed her a tissue. 'Look, I wouldn't normally say this, but if you're feeling really bad get yourself home. That's an order.'

'OK, I will do, but only after I visit Bridge Street. Find out if there's a Mrs Fraser.'

'Are you sure you're up to it? Could give someone else the job.'

'I need to do this. It'll keep me sane.' Fletcher's face was set like granite. Carruthers knew when she got into this kind of mood, there was no point in arguing with her, even for her own good. It wasn't just Fletcher's cold that was bothering him. Four months ago she'd lost the baby she'd been carrying and was still finding it hard to settle back in to work.

'Do you want me to come with you?' he asked.

'No, I'll be fine.'

'Well, take DS Watson with you, will you?'

Fletcher nodded. 'I'll organise for a couple of uniforms to go door-to-door around Braidwood too.'

'In that case, I'll accompany Dr Mackie back to the mortuary. Keep me posted.'

***

Fletcher parked her car in one of the two public car parks overlooking Anstruther harbour. As she opened her car door an icy gust coming straight off the cold North Sea wrenched it from her hand. A blast of freezing air hit her full in the face and she gasped. Getting out of the car with difficulty, she managed to finally shut the door on the second attempt. She turned up the collar of her coat. She knew she was just going through the motions at work. She felt dead inside. Had done ever since she'd lost the baby and Mark had left her.

From there she set off on foot for Cellardyke. It was a five-minute walk from the harbour to Bridge Street. It hadn't been hard to find. She knocked on the door of number two. There was no answer. She knocked again. Still silence. She took a couple of paces back, stepping into the road, craning her neck so she could see the upstairs windows. Bridge Street was a typical quaint Cellardyke street, narrow pavement, squashed together tall stone buildings. She took a throat sweet from her pocket, unwrapped it and popped it in her mouth. Placed the wrapper into her coat pocket.

The front door of a house two doors along opened and a middle-aged woman came out. She was muffled up against the cold.

'Havenae seen him for a couple of days. You're after Mr Fraser?'

Fletcher nodded. 'That's right. Who are you?'

'Mrs Walker.'

Fletcher showed her warrant card.

The woman studied it. 'Cannae be too careful.' She sniffed. 'Is this to do with the break-in? You're a bit late. Happened last week. Didnae think he was going to report it.'

'Break-in? When?'

'Last Friday, I think.'

'Much taken?'

'I dinnae ken. He wouldnae tell me. Told me to mind my own business.' She sniffed again.

'Is there a Mrs Fraser?'

'No. Lives alone.'

'When did you last see him?'

'Thursday, I think. He's alright, Mr Fraser, isn't he? I mean, nothing's happened to him?'

'So, no children then?'

'Not as far as I know.'

'You wouldn't happen to have a key to the house, would you?'

'I asked for one in case of emergencies, but he said there wasnae any need. Probably thought I'd be having a good poke about.'

You probably would, thought Fletcher.

'What can you tell me about him?'

'No' much. Keeps himself to himself. Doesnae have many visitors.'

'Do you know how long he's been here in Cellardyke or what he used to do for a living?' said Fletcher.

'No, like I said, he isnae much of one for talking. And I've only been here five years.'

Fletcher nodded, imagining that this could be the type of place that you would have to be living at least twenty years before you were accepted as a member of the tight-knit community. She made a mental note to ask Jim about that.

Fletcher fished her black spiral notebook out of her pocket. 'Can you give me a description of him?'

'Now you have got me worried. He's awful crabbit but I wouldnae like to think of anything bad happening to him. He is alright, isn't he?'

'Just routine enquiries.' Fletcher sneezed again and fished out a tissue. Her cold was starting to get the better of her. She felt as if she was wearing a snorkel.

'This isnae much of a job for you, love. Do you no' fancy getting married and settling down?'

Fletcher stiffened. 'You can be both married and in the police, Mrs Walker.'

'Any kids?'

She didn't like the way the conversation was going and decided to head it off at the pass. Said through gritted teeth. 'You were going to give me a description?' She crunched rather than sucked her throat sweet.

Fletcher listened politely as Fraser's neighbour described the dead man. Thanking her she then bid a hasty goodbye. She knocked on the door of number one and a few other houses but there was no response. She returned to her car, sat behind the wheel with the engine off and allowed herself a little cry. Sleet was starting to lash the windscreen and the visibility across the harbour was poor. She could just make out the boats bobbing up and down. Told herself she was emotional because she was feeling lousy due to the cold but knew that wasn't the real reason. She looked at her watch. There were a couple more jobs to do, including giving Carruthers a ring, then she could get back home, go to bed with some pills and block out reality for a few hours.

***

'This is interesting,' said Mackie.

Carruthers peered over Dr Mackie's shoulder. 'What is?'

'Tweezers please, Jodie.'

Dr Mackie's assistant handed over the tweezers without making eye contact with Carruthers. There was no reason why she should, but he had noticed that she hadn't looked at him at all since he had arrived. Carruthers didn't blame her. Months ago he'd told her he'd call with the promise of a drink and hadn't. Life had got in the way and, if he was being honest, he had been holding out for his wife to take him back. That hadn't happened.

'This was what I was after,' said Dr Mackie, his glasses perched on the bridge of his nose. 'Aha.'

He extracted a piece of white material from the open mouth of the corpse and examined it closely before dropping it into a stainless steel dish.

'What is it?' asked Carruthers, craning to take a look.

'Looks like some sort of cloth. Pushed to the very back of his mouth. Almost down his throat.'

'To keep him quiet, perhaps? Could he have choked? That caused his death?'

'Hmm. Let's find out shall we?'

Carruthers took a deep breath as Mackie made a Y-incision from the sternum down to the pubic bone. Never a favourite pastime of his, going to post mortems. Carruthers was starting to feel sick. Of course, it could be due to the final nip of Talisker the night before. When he overdid the whisky it always gave him a queasy stomach.

Mackie moved the skin and underlying tissues aside and removed the front of the rib cage to expose the organs. Carruthers tried to ignore the sawing sound Mackie's work made, concentrating instead on the technical aspects in order to control the nausea. *No more drinking on a school night,* he told himself, but knew that was going to be a tough call at the moment. He was still smarting from his demotion from DCI back to DI after the punch up he'd had at the station with Alistair McGhee. He was lucky that he was still in his old office until they found a replacement for him. The stench of death was overpowering and Carruthers found himself craving a cigarette, normally a rare thing for him.

Mackie was leaning over the stab wound. 'Pierced him a good six inches. In terms of weapon, as I said at the locus, you're looking for a sharp object with a serrated edge. Possibly a kitchen knife.'

Mackie took off the clear protective shield he'd been wearing, cleaned it with a cloth he fished out from his pocket and replaced it.

'Ah. I can see again. Always helps. Occupational hazard, getting splattered with blood and guts I'm afraid.'

Carruthers felt the bile rise in his throat. He swallowed it back down. Opened his mouth. Took a deep breath. Best not do it through his nose. He'd much rather be at a safe distance behind the observation window but it wasn't his style. He was a hands-on man. Always would be. In his book the moment he stopped wanting to be hands-on would be the day he quit the police.

'I wonder what the significance is of the gag to the back of the throat?' said Carruthers.

'Well, it's certainly interesting. I'm surprised I missed it at the scene,' said Mackie.

The deep husky tones of Jodie Pettigrew, the assistant ME, interrupted his reverie. 'I would say it was symbolic, wouldn't you? I think you're probably looking for someone who knew the victim. Where did you say you found the body?'

'Up at Braidwood,' responded Carruthers, happy that Jodie was back talking to him, even if her comment did show her to be a little naïve.

'The Old Mental Institution,' said Dr Mackie.

'Was it?' asked Carruthers.

'Amongst other things, Mackie continued. I believe it was originally built in the early 1800s, apart from the Pink Building that dates back to the mid-1500s. Architecture is a hobby of mine, Jim. As you know it's now part of the University of East of Scotland. Well, if you're going to die somewhere I can think of worse places.'

'Time of death?' asked Carruthers, watching Mackie as he cradled the heart in his hand.

'I wouldn't say he's been dead any more than twenty-four hours. If pushed I would put his time of death at between 6pm and 9pm last night. This is probably what killed him though. See?'

Carruthers did indeed see. He angled his neck so he got a closer view. The heart had a puncture wound to it.

'Knife went straight in to the heart. That stab wound was almost certainly the cause of death, barring something like a fatal administering of poison.'

'There are no defensive wounds,' said Carruthers, picking up the hands and examining the palms. 'I know no weapon's been found. But humour me for a moment. Theoretically, could it have been suicide?'

'He only has the one stab wound. Murder victims often incur multiple defensive wounds and a single, deliberate wound may be self-inflicted – but no, he couldn't have done this to himself, not even theoretically.'

'Anything else I should be aware of?'

'From the angle of the wound, your murderer was a left-hander. There is one other thing.' Mackie examined the heart more closely. 'Heart was in an advanced state of disease. See these vegetations, or masses, that have formed? Endocarditis.'

'Eh?'

'It's an infection causing inflammation of the endocardium which in turn causes damage to the heart valves. In other words, he was a very sick man.'

Carruthers took in another sharp intake of breath as Mackie placed the heart in a metal container. It had been three weeks since his own brother had had a heart attack. The fit, non-smoking teetotaller. At the mention of another sick heart Carruthers felt his own chest tighten. He was two years younger than his brother, Alan. They weren't close but Alan's heart attack had hit him hard. Thankfully his brother had survived.

'Going soft, Jim?' asked Mackie.

Ignoring him Carruthers once more focused on the ritual of the post mortem, watching as each organ was weighed and measured. Once the contents of the stomach had been dealt with, Dr Mackie picked up a small saw walking towards the victim's head. Carruthers excused himself, citing a weak bladder. It was more than he could manage.

Mackie chuckled. 'Cigarettes are in the top pocket of my jacket, laddie,' he said to Carruthers' vanishing back. 'After this we're pretty much done. I'll ring you if we discover anything else and as soon as we've got the toxicology test results back. I'll leave Jodie to show you out.' Carruthers lifted his hand in acknowledgement.

Carruthers stood, back to his car, cigarette between thumb and forefinger. He saw Jodie walking towards him. 'Look, Jodie, about not calling you…'

Having taken great lungfuls of fresh air and now smoking the cigarette, he was feeling much better and rather foolish for leaving when he did. If truth be told, he was also a bit embarrassed to be seen smoking when he was usually so anti the habit. But since

Alan's heart attack he found himself craving all the things that were bad for him.

'Och, it's fine. It was just if you were at a loose end, that's all. And obviously you weren't.'

'It's not that. I wasn't long out of my marriage.' Deciding to keep the knowledge to himself that he'd been attracted to the girlfriend of a murder victim, he stubbed the cigarette out. He went towards the litter bin by the side of the building, placed the butt in it then looked at Jodie. Really looked at her, taking in her oval face, deep blue eyes, dark hair and sexy black eyebrows. He was starting to wish he had said 'yes' but the time hadn't been right. He'd already had two women on his mind back then. There hadn't been room for a third.

'Oh, I didn't realise. Mackie never said.'

Carruthers, who'd started walking back to his car, stopped abruptly in his tracks and turned round so he was now facing Jodie. 'Is it too late for us to go out for that drink?' he asked. Jodie looked taken aback. 'I know it was six months ago,' Carruthers continued. 'What I mean is, are you seeing someone else?'

'Not at the moment.' There was a pause. 'Are you over your wife?'

'As I'll ever be.'

A half smile played on her lips. 'Honest answer. Any chance you'll get back together?'

'None whatsoever. Let's just say it wasn't an amicable separation. We haven't stayed in touch,' he added.

She fell silent for a few seconds, then shrugged. 'OK, why not?'

'Great. What are you doing tomorrow? Do you fancy a quick bite to eat?'

Jodie looked surprised. 'Won't you be caught up now you've got a murder on your hands?'

'I still have to eat,' he said, thinking of the endless nights he would be spending eating nothing more than pot noodle and sausage rolls and wanting to stave it off for as long as possible.

'I can't afford any more than an hour and I'll most probably have to stay dry as I might need to get back to the station after. Do you want to come over to Anstruther? There's a nice pub there called the Dreel Tavern. Serves good food. Or do you want to go somewhere else?'

'Anstruther's fine with me. See you at the Dreel at 7:30pm. Don't be late.' She smiled and turning walked back to the building. Carruthers watched her go.

***

After spending several more hours at the station Carruthers started to head home. The wind had picked up and as he walked to his car he was buffeted by the gusts coming straight off the North Sea. Once he left the police station on the outskirts of Castletown he drove home through the inky darkness. There had been no fresh snowfall but the plummeting temperatures were starting to turn the wet snow to ice and he took extra care, mindful that the smaller country roads may not have been gritted. Silhouettes of trees cast ghostly shadows and an owl flew across the path of the car startling him.

Once back in Anstruther he parked outside the famous Anstruther Fish Bar and joined the inevitable queue that had spilled outside the restaurant. The salt air mingled with the smell of batter and vinegar. The queue moved quickly and it wasn't long before he was back in his cosy cottage enjoying the crispy batter and tender flakes of white fish washed down with a cold beer. As he licked the grease off his fingers and picked up a chip that was almost too hot to handle, he started thinking about the brutal end of an old man in a nature reserve. He glanced at his watch. Too late to phone his mother to ask how his brother was doing. Taking a finger of whisky up to bed with him, leaving the remains of his chips to get cold on the table, his final thoughts that night, as the wind buffeted against the windows of his bedroom rattling the panes, were of a woman with sexy dark eyebrows leaning over a corpse.

CHAPTER TWO

Carruthers arrived at work early the next morning to find Fletcher was already at her desk. He stopped in his tracks. 'You well enough to be here?' he said.

She looked up from her paperwork. 'Feeling much better now, thanks. How's your brother?'

Carruthers shrugged. 'I don't know. I was too late to phone last night. And I forgot to do it first thing this morning.'

'Oh Jim. Forgot? Really?'

He waved her away. 'I'll do it later.' He drew in a deep breath. Of course he hadn't forgotten. The simple fact was that he didn't know what to say. What do you say to a fit forty-one year old brother who's just had a heart attack?

'How did the post mortem go?' she asked.

'Looks like he was killed with a single stab wound which pierced the heart,' Carruthers said, taking his jacket off and shaking off the rain. 'Toxicology isn't back yet, of course. One interesting thing though: looks like whoever did it shoved some sort of cloth to the back of the throat.'

'To stop him crying out for help, perhaps?'

'That's what I wondered but Mackie thinks it was done after he was killed.'

'After he was killed? Now that is interesting.'

Carruthers placed the jacket over his arm. 'How did the door-to-door go with Watson?'

'Found out Ruiridh Fraser lived alone. Couldn't gain access. I called out a team to search his house. Nothing obvious to report. We've got some files – telephone bills etcetera to sift through. But nothing out the ordinary. I spoke to a neighbour, a Mrs Walker at number four. Right nosy cow. Apparently, Fraser got broken into last Friday.'

He frowned. 'I don't remember hearing about that.'

'You wouldn't. He didn't report it. I've already checked. Did it first thing. She didn't know what, if anything, got taken. There were brand new locks on the doors and windows though. There is one thing,' she continued. 'Like I said, I've been through the incident book…'

'Yes?'

'Well, here's something. Fraser reported his next-door neighbour's teenage son for harassment back in September. In fact, looks like there's been at least three incidents, ranging from shouting obscenities at him in the street to putting dog dirt through his letterbox. I'm just double-checking the incidents now.'

'Which neighbours?'

'The Hunters. They're at number one. I tried them last night but they weren't at home.'

'Who investigated the original complaints?' asked Carruthers.

'Dougie. He's not back from leave until tomorrow.'

'Well, we've got a suspicious death. Get him back in today.'

'He's abroad, Jim.'

'Shit, I'd forgotten.' Carruthers then thought about the lazy, overweight DS and wondered if his absence was such a loss. He picked up some of the paperwork on Fletcher's desk and examined it. It was a bunch of Ruiridh Fraser's telephone bills.

'So, what do we know of Ruiridh Fraser?' Carruthers said.

Fletcher shrugged. 'To be honest, not much. The man obviously kept himself to himself. According to Mrs Walker, didn't have many visitors. Didn't go out much.'

'A man of mystery.'

'Seems that way.'

'And who's this, I wonder?' said Carruthers, picking up the photograph of the little boy found in the old man's wallet.

'That photo must be forty years old,' said Fletcher. 'My guess is a son?'

'A son who's now in his forties,' said Carruthers. 'So where is he?'

'Perhaps they're estranged.' Fletcher took the photo out of Carruthers' hand. 'Or the kid's dead. Maybe the son died in childhood?'

'OK, well you know the drill, Andie. Get the team to start putting together a picture of the man– hobbies, friends, last known movements– that type of thing. Brief me when you have something. I'll be in my office.'

Fletcher nodded. Starting to walk away from her desk, Carruthers hesitated and turned round.

'Oh, and Andie? We need results, and fast. You need to be top of your game. If you're not up to it, I can give the lead to Gayle.'

'Don't even think about it. This is mine.'

'OK, just don't screw up. A lot's riding on this one. For both of us.'

'Jim?'

Carruthers looked up.

'Ring your mum.'

***

'Briefing session in five. Spread the word.' Superintendent Bingham appeared at the office door, mobile in hand.

Carruthers looked across at Fletcher.

'I'm on to it,' she said. Standing up, she smoothed her navy skirt, grabbed her notepad and headed to the newly set up incident room. She put her pad down at a table in the front of the room and then rounded up the staff. As the room started to fill she glanced around her. With all the staff squeezed into the office the air was fugging up. Detective Constable Brown was perspiring, fiddling with his tie as if his collar was too tight. DS Gayle Watson, taking a seat to Fletcher's left, joked about something with Carruthers. Jealousy shot through Fletcher, surprising her. Several DCs filed in. Superintendent Bingham was the last to enter. He cleared his throat as he shut the door. Silence descended.

'Right, tell me what we know about Fraser,' said Bingham.

'Lived alone at two Bridge Street, Cellardyke. Retired,' said Fletcher.

'Do we know what he did for a living?' asked Bingham.

'Not yet, sir.'

'What *do* we know?'

Fletcher swallowed hard. Hands perspiring, she said, 'I've spoken to the neighbours. He was quiet, kept himself to himself. Didn't go out much. Not many visitors.'

Bingham cracked the knuckles on his left hand. The sound, like pulling chicken joints apart, made Fletcher wince. 'Has the investigation team recovered much from his house?'

'The usual phone bills, files, what looks like an appointment book,' said Fletcher. 'He didn't have a computer.'

'Pity.' Bingham started to crack the knuckles on his right hand. 'We need results on this one. I don't need to tell you that. Apart from anything else I have the Chief Super breathing down my neck. I can do without it.' It was no secret that the two of them didn't get on. Addressing Carruthers he said, 'What do we know about his death, Jim?'

Carruthers stood up and walked over to the incident board. On it was pinned a photograph of the body of Ruiridh Fraser.

'Killed by a single stab wound to the chest. Pierced the heart. Done with a degree of force. Mackie says assailant was a left-hander. Oh, and he was definitely killed at Braidwood.'

'No chance at all it could have been self-inflicted?' asked Bingham.

'Suicide, you mean?' asked Carruthers.

'What else would I mean, man?' Superintendent Bingham hated suspicious deaths on his patch. Took it as a personal affront.

'None whatsoever. No weapon's been found,' said Carruthers. 'Anyway, with the force inflicted and the angle of the thrust there's no way he could have done it himself.'

Bingham rubbed the side of his whiskery chin. 'Pity. So far we've got precious little to go on, then. Bugger.'

'There is something, sir,' this from DS Gayle Watson. All eyes turned to her, Fetcher's narrowed. 'I've been looking at previous incident reports. There was some trouble a few months ago involving his neighbours,' she continued. She read from her black notebook. 'On 25th September Fraser made a complaint against the son of his next-door neighbours, the Hunters. Said the boy had used abusive language on him in the street. This after reporting his tyres slashed the week before. Apparently, according to Fraser, this teenager was waging a personal vendetta against him.'

'Teenager's name?' asked Bingham.

'Jordan Hunter,' said Watson. 'Detective Sergeant Harris, Dougie, attended.'

'What came of the complaint?'

'Dougie spoke to both parties involved. No evidence was found that the tyres were slashed by Jordan Hunter. We threatened to charge the boy with breach of the peace. The abuse was overheard by another neighbour, Mrs Walker. As it was a first offence he got a verbal warning.'

Bingham scanned the room. 'Where's Harris?'

'On holiday, abroad. Be back at work tomorrow,' said Fletcher.

'Good work, Watson.'

Watson beamed, showing her dimples.

Fletcher cursed under her breath. *One–nil to Watson.*

'Did you speak to the Hunters during the door-to-door yesterday?' Bingham directed his question to Watson.

She pulled a face. 'No. I wasn't there. I believe Andie attended.'

All eyes on Fletcher. She was biting her lip, aware of Carruthers' steely gaze. She studiously avoided eye contact. 'They weren't at home. I've made that a priority for today.'

'OK, let's crack on,' said Bingham. 'You all know what you've got to do. Get someone to ID the body. We need a request for information printed up – distribute to local shops; pubs and community notice boards. Jim, I want you to get a team set up to sift through Fraser's paperwork. Start with interviewing this boy, Jordan, again. Find out where he was at the time of the murder.

And we also need to speak with the media.' Superintendent Bingham turned to Carruthers. 'Just do what it takes to keep that scrawny little Yorkshire man off my back, will you.'

'You mean Chief Superintendent Greenwood, sir?'

'How many other scrawny little Yorkshire men do you know living in Fife, Carruthers?'

Turning to the windows he made an exasperated clicking noise with his tongue and drew in a deep breath. 'Need to do something about that condensation.'

Carruthers followed Bingham's gaze, noticing the pooling on the windowsills.

Bingham turned his attention to Fletcher. 'Get on to the cleaners, will you? Make sure they mop up.'

'It's not my—' she bit her lip in a bid to remain silent. She was aware of Carruthers taking a keen interest in her. Not just Carruthers. Watson as well. Too early in the investigation to be disobeying orders. What had she been thinking excluding Watson from the door-to-door? She glanced over at her. If she was going to stay ahead she'd just have to outsmart her and show Carruthers she was indispensable. *Damn the bloody woman.* Why did she feel like this? Why did her return to work make her feel so insecure? In the last couple of weeks before her return she'd been champing at the bit to get back to the fray. Now she was back she was riddled with anxiety. She swallowed hard trying to push the heavy sick feeling away from the pit of her stomach.

'I'll get on to it,' she said.

'Good girl,' replied Bingham.

***

Carruthers followed Fletcher out of the incident room. Catching up with her, he took her arm and guided her out of hearing. Turning to face her he said, 'I'm heading over to Cellardyke to interview the Hunters. I'm sorely tempted to ask Gayle to accompany me after the stunt you pulled yesterday. What the hell was that all about?'

She hung her head. 'Don't ask her. I'm more than up to the job.' She snapped her head up. 'By the way, how long's she staying at the station? We don't need another DS.'

'It's not just whether you're up to the job, Andie. I need to know the team's going to pull together– forget the petty squabbles, the jealousies. We've got a murder to solve. You can't let your personal feelings about DS Watson get in the way of the investigation. Just out of interest who did you take with you if it wasn't Gayle?'

There was silence from Fletcher who seemed to be staring at a spot beyond Carruthers.

He exploded. 'Jesus Christ, Andie, don't tell me you went on your own? It's against procedure. You know that. Whatever made you do it?'

'I'm sorry. I don't know. I can't talk about it right now. I'll see you in the car park,' she said and strode away before Carruthers was able to say anything else.

***

The police station was on the outskirts of the historic town of Castletown, six miles from Anstruther. The sun was shining and the Fife fields and farms that dotted the countryside lay under a thin covering of snow and ice. Ice crystals glittered in the sun. Carruthers turned to Fletcher. 'You've lost your confidence, haven't you?' he said as they climbed into the pool car. 'That's why you went to conduct the interviews alone. And you feel threatened by having another female DS here who stepped in for you when you were off work.'

'If you're done psychoanalysing me.'

'You're a good cop. Don't overthink it,' he said. 'But don't ever flout procedure like that again. Next time, I won't cover your back.'

Fletcher stared straight ahead of her but the look on her face wasn't lost on Carruthers. He knew he'd hit home.

***

The door was opened by a woman in her early fifties with ash-blonde shoulder-length hair and eyes the colour of cornflowers. She was wearing a pale blue cardigan and a multi-coloured print dress over black leggings.

The two officers produced their ID. 'Mrs Hunter?' said Carruthers.

'Yes.'

Carruthers noted that she didn't seem surprised to see them.

'You'd better come in.'

As Carruthers and Fletcher entered the hall Carruthers noticed a dark-haired teenage boy skulking on the stairs. He looked watchful, sullen. He didn't move, but followed them with his eyes.

'This is my son, Jordan.'

The boy mumbled something. Carruthers didn't catch it.

'You'll be here about Mr Fraser's disappearance,' she said.

'Why do you think he's disappeared?' asked Carruthers.

'One of my neighbours told me. Funny, you never think of anything like that happening to someone you know, least of all your neighbour.' The woman suddenly shivered as she said this. She wrapped her cardigan protectively around herself.

Taking them in to the lounge, she shut the door. Jordan had still been rooted on the stairs. Carruthers wondered if he would creep down and eavesdrop. He wouldn't blame him if he did.

'What do you know about Ruiridh Fraser?' asked Carruthers.

'Must be late seventies, early eighties. Not over friendly. Please have a seat. Would either of you like tea? Coffee?' They both declined, although looking at Fletcher's pale face and watery eyes Carruthers bet she wouldn't have minded a Lemsip.

'Do you know if he had any family?' asked Carruthers. 'A son perhaps?'

'Never seen him with family. A son? No. Don't think so. Why?'

Suddenly the door was flung wide open and a young girl of about fifteen wearing headphones burst in. 'Mum, have they found the old paedo yet?' She stopped short as she caught sight of

Carruthers and Fletcher and took the headphones off in surprise. She had the same blonde hair as her mother and was wearing a short skirt and T-shirt. The contour of her young breasts was just visible through the top. Carruthers did a double take, he couldn't help himself. The girl was going to be a stunner. Mrs Hunter drew in a sharp breath.

'Don't talk about Mr Fraser like that, please.' She turned to Carruthers and Fletcher. 'Sorry. This is my daughter, Rachael.' She caught the girl by the shoulders, held her close stroking her silky-looking hair.

'Why did you call him a paedo, Rachael?' asked Carruthers.

'It's what Jordan calls him.'

'You know what teens are like, inspector. They call everyone a paedo. It doesn't mean anything. Have you never watched *The Inbetweeners*?'

Carruthers hadn't heard of *The Inbetweeners*. He didn't watch much TV – just *Newsnight*, sport and the occasional Bond movie on DVD.

'Were you aware Mr Fraser had a break-in last week?' continued Carruthers.

'Yes, we heard from Mrs Walker. It was her who told us about his disappearance.'

'It's actually your son, Jordan, we'd like to speak with, if you can call him in?' said Carruthers.

'Why? Jordan hasn't done anything wrong.'

'Well, then he hasn't got anything to worry about, has he?' Carruthers grabbed his mobile out of his coat pocket and put it on silent.

Fletcher addressed her next comment to Mrs Hunter. 'We know there was some trouble a few months back involving your son.' She read from her notebook. 'On the 18th September Mr Fraser reported Jordan for slashing his tyres.'

'Now just a minute. He never got charged. There was no proof it was him. You're not telling me you think my son's responsible for his disappearance?'

'This is just a routine enquiry, Mrs Hunter,' said Carruthers. 'Can we see him please? Now. We can do this here or down at the station.'

'If you really need to speak to him, I'll go and get him.'

A few minutes went by then the door opened and in walked Mrs Hunter. Jordan slipped in behind her a few seconds later like a shadow. He stood hovering by the couch. His eyes shifted from his mother to the two detectives with very little movement of head. His gaze eventually settled on Fletcher's chest. She folded her arms.

'Jordan, where were you between the hours of 6pm and 9pm Monday night?' asked Carruthers.

'Here.' He looked surprised.

'Why do you want to know that?' asked Mrs Hunter.

'What were you doing?' asked Carruthers.

Jordan tore his gaze away from Fletcher and glanced over at his mother who had taken a seat opposite.

'Don't look at your mother. I asked you the question,' said Carruthers.

'I was in my room.' Jordan was looking down at his feet, not making eye contact.

'Doing what?' said Carruthers.

'Playing computer games.'

'For three hours?' said Fletcher.

Jordan shrugged. 'I had my tea, too. Downstairs.'

'What time do you eat tea?' Carruthers addressed the question to Anne Hunter.

'About seven.'

'Did Jordan eat with you?' said Fletcher.

'Yes, he was here all evening.'

Carruthers turned to Fletcher, 'When do we think the old man got broken into?'

'Last Friday between 4pm and 7pm, according to the neighbour.'

'Well, it couldn't have been Jordan. He was abroad on a school trip. You can check,' said Mrs Hunter.

Rachael had crept back into the room.

'Why did you call Mr Fraser a paedo? Your sister said you called him a paedo,' said Carruthers, glancing at the girl.

'Because he was one.'

Fletcher studied Jordan as he answered her question.

'Jordan,' cried his mother.

Rachael looked on the verge of crying.

'Mr Fraser told police that on September 18th last year, you slashed his tyres,' said Fletcher.

'I never!'

'He also alleged the week after, that you shouted abuse at him in the street. I believe you got a verbal warning?' she continued.

'I might have shouted at him, but I never let his tyres down … or broke into his house. I was playing football when his tyres got slashed. I told the police that at the time.'

'Why did you shout at him?' said Carruthers.

'He's a perv. He—' Just as Jordan opened his mouth to answer, the door flew open and in walked Mr Hunter. He threw his briefcase on the couch followed by a packet of Camel cigarettes and strode over to his son. He put a protective arm round him. 'Don't answer any more questions until we get my lawyer. What are you accusing him of now?'

Jordan's sister started to cry. Her mother rushed to her side. 'Now look what you've done. She's only thirteen and easily upset. I want you to leave. Now.'

Carruthers eyeballed the dark-haired man, judging him to be in his late forties, early fifties. He couldn't help but notice the pronounced scar on his chin. 'I need to know why Jordan called Mr Fraser a paedo.'

'You're upsetting my family. I want you to leave.' Mr Hunter stood, hands on hips.

Carruthers looked at Jordan who had a scowl that resembled a storm brewing sky. He had his hands shoved so far in his jeans pockets that it looked like he might go through the fabric at any minute. He was scuffing the carpet with the heel of his right shoe over and over again looking very much like a teenage nightmare – all mood, attitude and hormones.

'I asked your son a question and I'd like an answer,' said Carruthers.

'And I asked you to leave my house,' said Mr Hunter.

Carruthers signalled for Fletcher to get up. 'Right, we'll see ourselves out.' He addressed Mrs Hunter. 'I'm sorry if you feel we came across heavy-handed with your son, but we're just doing our job. One final question before we leave, Mr Hunter. Do you know if Jordan was in between the hours of 6pm and 9pm Monday night?'

'I couldn't tell you. I didn't get back from work till 10pm.' He looked over at his wife. 'Was he in?'

'Yes,' she said simply.

'There's your answer. Now get out. You know where the door is.'

***

'What do you think?' asked Carruthers as they walked away from the house.

'Pretty obvious Mrs Hunter phoned her husband whilst she went to fetch Jordan. All I can say is he must have been damn close by to get here that quickly. Well, the boy's got an alibi for the murder, although it's pretty weak. Plenty of mothers would lie for their sons. Says he's also got one for the housebreaking.'

'Get that checked out, will you?'

Fletcher nodded. She turned to Carruthers. 'His mother *could* have lied for him. And the father couldn't vouch for him being at home.'

'What does he do again?'

'Works for a pharmaceutical company. Jim, did you notice how protective Mr Hunter was of his son?'

'Hardly surprising. Parental instinct,' said Carruthers.

Fletcher turned to him, 'Jordan could've nipped out whilst his mother's back was turned. She might've assumed he was in his room.'

'Bit more than nipping out. Braidwood Nature Reserve is miles away. Anyhow, how would Jordan have got him there? He's too young to drive.'

'So are half the joyriders we've nicked,' said Fletcher.

'True. However, his alibi about being at the football when Fraser's tyres got slashed checked out. It's in the earlier report.'

'Well, it'll be interesting to see if he's got a solid alibi for the housebreaking. See if Jordan *was* on this school trip.'

'We're still no further forward knowing anything about Ruiridh Fraser – our mystery man,' said Fletcher.

'We're talking to the wrong people, Andie. We need to find people who can shed light on what sort of man he was. People who were close to him. Friends, former work colleagues…'

'If they're not all dead.'

'Why would they be?'

Fletcher snorted. 'This is Scotland we're talking about. Lower life expectancy than most of the countries in Europe.'

'Even so, they're not all going to be dead. Anyway, you're making a big assumption that all his friends are going to be his own age. He might run around with a younger set.'

Fletcher raised an eyebrow. 'Unlikely. After all, according to neighbours, this is the man who hardly ever left his house. And I don't really see him running anywhere at his age.'

'Don't take that literally. You know what I mean. There's got to be somebody. We just have to find them.'

As they approached the car Carruthers frowned. There had obviously been escalating issues with Jordan Hunter, but could they have ended in an old man's murder? Was the Hunter boy even capable of murder? The fact was someone had killed the old man. If not the boy, then who? As Fletcher opened the driver door and climbed in to the car Carruthers pulled his mobile out of his jacket pocket and finally rang his mother.

***

'Andie, can I have a word?' Fletcher swung round to face DS Gayle Watson.

Fletcher appraised the other woman as she spoke. Wearing one of her trademark suits the DS was powerfully built. She had the sort of broad shoulders better suited to a prop forward, in Andie's opinion, and short cropped spiky hair. She had kindly hazel eyes and a mouth that dimpled when she smiled which made her very attractive. Her smile wasn't in evidence now.

'What's the big idea?' said Watson.

'What are you talking about?'

'This murder case. Ruiridh Fraser? You're shutting me out.'

'No, I'm not.'

'Aye, you are. I've just found out we were supposed to have conducted yesterday's interviews together. Brown told me. Overheard you talking to Jim.'

Inwardly cursing, Fletcher shook her head, grabbed her handbag and walked off.

Watson caught up with her. Grabbed her arm. 'Have you got a problem with me?'

Shrugging her arm off, Fletcher said, 'Of course not.'

'Then, like I said, what's the big idea?' The silence stretched. 'You don't want me here, do you?'

Fletcher sighed. Kept walking. Shouted over her shoulder, 'It's nothing personal.'

'So what is it?'

'I can't do this now.' Fletcher pulled open the front door of the police station and walked out in to the cold air. Watson strode after her, catching the door as it swung back.

'I heard about your miscarriage. And I'm sorry. But I'm here to do a job. Let me do it,' she said.

Andie Fletcher walked on without looking back. She heard Watson cursing. Language, in Fletcher's view, better suited to a naval dockyard.

She threw her handbag on to the back seat of her green Beetle. The light had already faded and she'd missed the pink hues of the sunset that often follow a bright sunny winter's day. Feeling as if someone had tied weights to her legs and arms, she climbed in to the driver's seat, started the engine and switched her headlights on. The bright beams pierced the gloomy darkness. Letting out a deep sigh she drove out of Castletown Police Station to the sound of the wheels crunching on spitting gravel.

Her shoulders sagged as she let herself in to her flat and dumped her handbag on the purple couch in the sitting room. The phone was winking at her. She played the message wondering if it was from Mark. It wasn't. It was from her mother. Returning the call could wait. She trudged in to the kitchen. After making herself a pot of scalding tea, she took a couple of paracetamol. She kicked off her shoes and changed out of her skirt and blouse into jogging bottoms and T-shirt. Sat down cross-legged on the couch.

She tried not to think of the purple couch. It was where she and Mark had last made love, just before she'd had her miscarriage. How everything had changed in the shortest of time. Six months ago she was pregnant, getting ready for motherhood and had a boyfriend who loved her, or so she thought. She swallowed hard.

As she grabbed her laptop, the phone rang. She let it go to answer machine as she switched her computer on. She heard her own voice telling the caller that neither she nor Mark could get to the phone and would they please leave a message. The message would have to be changed to say 'I' instead of 'we'. She was loath to do it feeling that she would be announcing her single status to the world. A lot of her friends still didn't know that she and Mark had split up. It was too much to cope with at the moment. She was still trying to come to terms with her miscarriage.

When she heard the voice on the other end of the phone she felt sick. It was Mark. 'Er hi, Andie. It's me. God, I hate these machines. If you're there pick up.' There was a pause then he continued. 'I've got some stuff I want to collect from the flat. I'll come round tomorrow about six. It would be good if you were there. We need to talk.' There was a tightness in her chest and she felt she couldn't breathe. What a bastard he was. There was no hint of concern in his voice for her – no question of whether she was OK. In fact, apart from the hesitancy, he sounded like he was in a business meeting. Well, to hell and back with him. She was better off without him, the shit.

She tried to concentrate on catching up with her friends' lives on Facebook but hearing his voice had really unsettled her. She set the laptop aside and padded through to the kitchen. Pulling open the fridge door she rooted around for some food. There wasn't a huge amount in it, but she did find eggs and mushrooms. She decided to make herself a mushroom omelette and have it with a glass of orange juice.

Feeling better after eating, she settled down with a small whisky. Told herself it was for medicinal purposes. In the mood for some Scottish folk music she put on a CD by King Creosote, and as the first few notes started playing, she settled the laptop back on her knee and tried to focus on the constant stream of mostly mind-numbing nonsense on Facebook.

Picking up her whisky glass, she swirled the glass around, coating it in the viscous amber liquid, before she downed it in one. Replacing the glass on the table she frowned. Her thoughts turned to Jim. What had he said? 'A lot's riding on the case, for both of us.' What had he meant by 'both?' Well, it was obvious what was riding on it for him. Perhaps bloody DS Watson was here to stay after all, and, if Golden Tits out-performed her she'd be the one booted out to another station. She couldn't let that happen. She and Jim worked as a team, he was Batman to her Robin and he was a great boss to have. She knew they complimented each other. She groaned. What had she been thinking, going alone to Cellardyke? Although she was loath to admit it, he was right. She was lacking in confidence. She'd been off work for three months. It was a long time to be out of the field. But with a murder investigation there was no time to ease herself back in gently. There was only one thing for it. She'd have to find a backbone.

CHAPTER THREE

Carruthers ran his hands through his short greying hair. He sat staring at the phone. He was worried about his brother, wondered if he was at risk of a second heart attack. According to his mother one of the arteries was still blocked.

DC Brown put his head round the door. 'That's me away, boss.' Not one to normally say goodnight, Carruthers wondered what Brown really wanted. He looked up to find Brown still loitering at the door. 'Was there anything else?' he asked.

'You missed the makings of a good cat fight earlier.' Brown's face lit up as he said it.

Carruthers raised an eyebrow.

'Andie and Gayle going head-to-head. Could have been a fair old stramash.'

'Carruthers' heart sank.

'My money's on Gayle,' continued Brown. 'Definitely a heavy-weight to Andie's bantam. Ha ha. Na. Seriously. You should have seen them.' He jumped about on his toes and did a bit of shadow-boxing. Rubbed his hands together. 'Thought I was going to have to throw a bucket of the wet stuff over them.' He grinned. 'Pity Fat Dougie missed it. He loves to see girlies scrapping. Still, back from hols tomorrow, eh? Sure he'll have plenty of stories.' His eyes were twinkling. 'Reckon we'll see round two soon enough,' he said with relish. Not waiting for a response, Brown disappeared.

Carruthers heard the door slam as he threw his pen down and thought about the evening ahead. He'd been looking forward to meeting with Jodie immensely, but suddenly his mind strayed to Fletcher and it had taken some of his appetite away. It wasn't like her to deliberately disobey an order and a repeated one at that. He was worried about her and, in her current mercurial mood, wasn't looking forward to having it out with her. He looked at the time, tidied his paperwork away and made a move home. There would be time for a shower and shave if he was quick.

***

He stooped as he entered the front door of the Dreel Tavern. These old doorways didn't suit his tall frame. He walked to the bar where he ordered a pint of Shipwreck IPA. After passing the time of day with the barman he took his drink over to one of the scuffed wooden tables in the corner by the piano and waited for Jodie.

There was a smell of fish and chips in the air. He sniffed appreciatively. The truth of it was that he was starving. Now he came to think about it he couldn't remember eating lunch. As he looked around him he noticed a group of people sitting eating at a table close to the window. At least three of them had the fish. Their English voices rose above the sound of the music being played. It was the Beatles 'Strawberry Fields'. They were rather well dressed for the pub, but from the babble of noise and hearty laughter coming from their direction, they seemed to be enjoying themselves immensely.

Glancing around him he noticed this popular pub was busy. Although there was no shortage of drinking houses in Anstruther, this and the Smugglers Inn were his two favourites. He liked a good old-fashioned pub with a bit of atmosphere and the Dreel Tavern had atmosphere in spades.

Reputed to be the oldest pub in Anstruther, with a back room dating from the fourteenth century, it had characteristic low ceilings, wooden beams and stone walls. The huge fireplace looked original. The pub was lit by yellow glass lanterns, which bathed the pub in a golden glow. From the piano in the corner to the bass guitar propped against a wall, it had the cosy comfortable feel of a welcoming pub where a good time was had on a fairly regular basis.

There were one or two men at the bar who had come in for a quick pint after work. Carruthers recognised one face and nodded a greeting. There were a couple of old boys with weather-beaten faces, looking like characters from the past, propping up the far end of the bar. Probably fishermen. Picking up his menu he was starting to study it when a cold gust of night air greeted him as the front door opened.

He almost did a double take. It was Jodie. She looked completely different. Gone were the over-sized glasses and white lab coat. Her hair was shoulder length and loose, and it had been styled so that she had a side parting with a partial fringe. It suited her, as did everything else about her. She was wearing a fitted black belted coat over a bronze woollen dress and black knee-length boots. She looked sensational.

'Wow.' He got up and almost knocked his drink over. She laughed.

'I take it I meet with your approval?'

'You look absolutely stunning.' He was serious. He couldn't take his eyes off her. There was an awkward moment whilst he decided how to greet her. In the end he kissed her lightly on the cheek. Her hair tickled the tip of his nose and a delicious citrus scent filled his nostrils.

'What's your poison?' he asked.

She looked over at his glass. 'Thought you weren't going to drink.'

'I changed my mind,' he said, thinking about Fletcher.

'Well, seeing as you're having a pint, I'll have a rum and coke, please.'

'Be back in a minute.' He studied her from the bar when he thought she wasn't looking and hurried back with the drink.

He put her glass in front of her on a stained and tatty beer mat.

'How've you been?' he asked.

She laughed. 'You only saw me yesterday, Jim.'

'Of course I did. Sorry. Feels longer. Must be the investigation,' he added quickly.

'How's it going?'

Carruthers debated telling her about his brother.

'Any developments?' she prompted.

He realised she was talking about the case. The moment had passed. Her voice was deep and husky. Carruthers was reminded of a well-aged malt.

'Very few. The old man seems to have been pretty reclusive; although he's had a few run-ins with the son of the people next door... Boy's only fifteen... That's one line we're pursuing.'

'What triggered that?'

'Not sure. Looks as if the old man had an eye for the boy's sister.'

'It's not a crime if he's only looking.'

'She's only thirteen.'

Jodie picked up her menu. She looked over the top of it at Carruthers. 'Do you think the kid's capable of murder, though?'

'I really don't know, but somebody is. Anything new turn up at the lab?'

'Not yet. We're still awaiting toxicology.'

The conversation was put on hold as they studied their menus.

'What would you recommend?' she asked.

'What would you prefer? Meat or fish? Or are you vegetarian?' Even asking the question made him realise how little he knew about her, apart from what she did for a living. He hoped that he would have a chance to get to know her better.

'No, I'm not vegetarian.'

Carruthers was relieved. 'They do great fish and chips here.'

'So I can see,' she said, as a waitress sailed past, weaving in and out between the wooden tables carrying two plates of fish and chips high above her head. 'OK, you sold me.'

Carruthers caught the waitress's eye and ordered fish and chips for Jodie and a steak and ale pie for himself. Just as the waitress put her pen away, the door of the pub opened with another blast of cold air and a boisterous group of arty looking men and women spilled in. Most of the men had beards and some of them had long hair.

Jodie leaned forward and whispered, 'They look interesting.'

'They are. They're folk musicians.'

'You can tell that just by looking at them?' Her mouth dropped open.

'I'm a detective, but I'm not that good. Na, I know them.'

They both laughed.

'I've been thinking about your case,' she said. 'The thing that makes it so interesting is the gag in the back of the throat. Uncover why he gagged the victim and I reckon you'll have your motive…'

'That's a bit of a leap.' He paused. 'You said he.'

'Did I?'

'Yes. You said uncover why *he* gagged him. Do you think it's a he?'

'I don't know. I guess I must do. I don't know why. Anyway, find out why he was gagged and I reckon you'll discover why he was murdered.'

'If only it was that easy.'

Their conversation was interrupted by a young waitress in black jeans and T-shirt bringing over two plates of steaming food. Carruthers fell about his steak pie greedily, approving of the way the rich and aromatic gravy oozed out when he cut the flaky pastry. 'This is really good. I can taste some sort of herb in the gravy. Think it's thyme.' Between mouthfuls he said, 'This case has got me thinking. Why gag him?'

Jodie laid her knife and fork down and looked at Carruthers intently. 'I have no idea. But we see all sorts at the mortuary.'

'I'll bet,' he said, hoping she wasn't about to elaborate. Carruthers also put his knife and fork down for a moment. Jodie leaned forward. 'You told me the old man had been broken into the week before, but hadn't reported it to the police.'

'That's right.'

'Any theories on why he didn't?'

Relieved they weren't about to start talking dissections, Carruthers speared a succulent looking piece of meat. 'An awful lot of victims don't report burglaries. Maybe he thought the robbers would never be caught?' He shrugged. 'Or maybe they didn't get away with much.'

Jodie shook her head. 'If you ask me, he's got something to hide. Doesn't want the police sniffing around. Why else would you no' report a break-in?'

Carruthers was silent for a moment wondering if Jodie could be right. He suddenly smiled and leant forward. 'So tell me something. What's a nice girl like you doing as a pathologist's assistant?'

***

They finished their evening together by taking a stroll down to the picturesque cobbled harbour. Jodie said something as they looked towards the murky depths of the sea, but it was taken away by the sea breeze. Carruthers leaned in to hear her better and she placed his arm around her shoulder. Despite the coldness of the night he could feel the warmth of her body through her thin coat. She made a comment about not coming prepared for a walk in winter and they embraced whilst she laughed, shivering. Carruthers traced his fingertip over one of her rough sexy eyebrows feeling the coldness of her cheek.

To the sound of the moored boats bumping against each other and the harbour wall they had their first tentative kiss. Carruthers tasted salt on her tongue, which wasn't unpleasant and smelt the faint scent of her perfume. He knew then that whatever the future held for him and Jodie, he would cherish this evening for a long time to come.

***

Carruthers was at his desk at seven the next morning, a little tired but clearer headed than usual. He really should stick to drinking whisky at the weekends. Managing to keep to his quota of only two pints last night and no whisky hadn't been easy but at least he found it achievable. He liked achievable targets. Realised that as he climbed higher in rank there would definitely be fewer of them. At least he knew that if he was in control of his drinking, it wasn't a serious problem.

Glancing out of his window he noticed the change in weather once again. A steady drizzle had given way to persistent rain sometime in the night. The temperature was warmer than the last two days. The trees and hedges dripped with rain and a small stream ran down the guttering of the station roof. He was glad of the romantic walk by the harbour with Jodie before the rain had set in.

At nine he walked into the next station brief. The first thing he noticed was Fletcher. She looked awful. Drained of colour with dark circles under her eyes. He wondered if her cold had worsened.

'OK, listen up people,' he said. 'We're conducting this brief without Superintendent Bingham so let's get on with it. Quick recap for those dozing in the last brief. And for Detective Sergeant Harris who's just back from his holidays.'

'Tenerife,' he shouted. 'Check this bad boy oot.' He rolled up his shirt sleeve to reveal his latest tattoo. It was of a rooster. 'I was blootered. It was supposed tae be a stallion.'

'Good choice. You've always been a bit of a cock.' This from Brown. He roared. Harris looked at Brown as if he wanted to deck him.

Carruthers put his hands up. 'Settle down. Settle down. Right, from cocks to corpses. This is what we know so far.' He strode over to the incident board and pointed to the photograph of the body of Ruiridh Fraser.

'Seventy-eight year old Ruiridh Fraser killed by a single stab wound to the chest somewhere between the hours of 6pm and 9pm three nights ago. No murder weapon found, no fingerprints so far. Murdered at the scene and a gag was forced to the back of his throat after death. Why? Ruiridh Fraser's a bit of a mystery man. Doesn't seem to have any family, although an old photo of a child was found in his wallet. We want to know who that child is. Very few visitors. Neighbours say he was reclusive. None of them knew of his hobbies or even what he did before he was retired. We're currently thin on the ground for suspects. The only suspect so far is fifteen-year-old Jordan Hunter, son of Fraser's next-door neighbours.' Carruthers pinned a photograph of a young-looking Jordan Hunter next to Fraser. 'He seems to have had a vendetta against Fraser. Jordan admitted that he shouted abuse at Fraser in the street a few months ago, but not the other crime Fraser accused young Jordan of, namely slashing his car tyres. Jordan's alibi is that he was at home with his mother and sister on the evening of Fraser's murder. His mother said he spent the evening in his room apart from when he came downstairs for tea at seven. Let's not forget that Fraser was also broken into the week before his murder, but didn't report it. Andie, did Jordan Hunter's alibi pan out?'

'Yep,' she said with a sniff, 'school trip to France. Spoke to the school. There's no way Jordan could have been responsible for the break-in.'

'OK,' continued Carruthers. 'We need to find out what Jordan Hunter had against Ruiridh Fraser. One possible theory is that Fraser had an eye for young girls. Previously Jordan called him a paedophile. Jordan's sister is a bit of a looker. Some might say provocatively dressed. Looks older than her thirteen years.'

'What do you think, Gayle?' Carruthers asked.

'I think we're getting off the point,' she said. 'We need to find out more about Ruiridh Fraser.'

Carruthers nodded. 'I agree. We also need to think about where the body was found. Is there any significance? He was murdered at the scene, according to Dr Mackie. What was he doing there? It's a local beauty spot but hardly local to him. Was Fraser in the habit of taking a stroll there? It's eight miles from where he lives, not exactly at the end of his street and his car was back at Cellardyke. What, if anything, is his connection with Braidwood? We also need to keep in mind the fact that a bit of cloth was shoved down his throat. Why? Does it have any meaning?' Carruthers paused, then looking over at Fletcher said, 'Has there been any joy with the door-to-door?'

She shook her head.

'I can't believe there wasn't a single person who saw anything. It's a nature reserve, for Christ's sake. I want Dougie and Gayle to conduct door-to-doors starting at Cellardyke. See if anyone knows the victim. We need to piece together his last few days. Sounds pretty reclusive, but *somebody* has got to know something. What were his hobbies? Was he much of a drinker? If so, find out which watering hole he drank in, speak to his drinking buddies. I also want a door-to-door done over a wider area around Braidwood. And let's not forget we still haven't got to the bottom of why Jordan Hunter called Fraser a paedophile. Is it because the man was looking at his little sister? I also want to find out about Jordan's dad, Malcolm Hunter. If Fraser has been sniffing round his daughter then he'll have a motive for wishing the old boy harm. Andie – I want you on that. Who have we got going through Fraser's paperwork?'

'Support team's going through it. Nothing as yet,' said Fletcher.

Harris leant over to Fletcher and hissed, 'Desk duties? What have you done to piss off Jimbo?' He rubbed his hands together, his face wreathed in smiles.

'Oh, fuck off,' she growled.

'OK, well let's go, people.' Carruthers clapped his hands together. 'We have a murderer to catch.'

***

Back in his office Carruthers picked up the phone to make the long overdue call to his brother. He figured he'd feel better when he heard Alan's voice. Just as he was punching in the numbers Fletcher walked in.

'Why have I been side-lined? It's humiliating,' she demanded. 'Even Dougie has noticed. It's because of what happened yesterday, isn't it?'

He put the phone down with a sigh. 'What are you talking about? You haven't been side-lined. And by the way, have you never heard of knocking?'

'Why have I been put on office duties when I should be the one to go door-to-door?'

'I would have thought you would be glad of not having to go door-to-door in this weather with your cold. Anyway, as you know fine well, going door-to-door is a job for a DC not a DS.'

Fletcher snorted. 'Since when did you ever stick by the rules? Why is *she* going instead of me?'

'By "she", I assume you mean DS Watson. She's going because I need you here.'

'You don't think I'm fit for work, do you?' Fletcher's eyes glinted dangerously. 'And I don't mean because of my cold.'

'Oh for God's sake. If you really want to know, I think you're a raging torrent of hormones and I—'

Fletcher marched across the room; body-swerved the big desk and slapped Carruthers round the face. The noise of the slap echoed around his office. She then left the room slamming his office door as she went.

***

Keeping her head down Fletcher stormed to the ladies' toilet. Grateful it was empty she went to one of the cubicles and pulled handfuls of toilet roll. She found she was shaking. Walking out and looking at herself in the mirror above the basins she dabbed at her stinging eyes and inhaled a few deep breaths. When she felt composed enough she left, got herself a strong mug of tea and sat down at her desk. Her hand stung from where she had slapped Carruthers. She put her head in her hands. She was furious for herself for losing her temper. Just as she was about to pick up the phone, it rang.

Automatically she picked it up. 'DS Andrea Fletcher,' she said.

'Andie, it's me.'

'What do you want?' she hissed at Mark.

'I thought you might have returned my call last night.'

'Why would I want to do that?'

She heard an impatient sigh. 'Don't be like that.'

'Like what? Upset my boyfriend walked out on me just after I've miscarried?' She hissed this down the phone, looking around to see if anyone was listening. Harris was on another call and Brown had his head stuck in a file.

'I'm sorry. Look, is it OK if I come over and pick up some of my stuff later today?'

'What time?'

'Sometime after work. I'd really like to see you as well. We need to talk.'

'Knock yourself out, but I won't be there. Just be out by eight.' She hung up. Hearing a noise behind her she swung round to see Carruthers. His right cheek was red from the slap. Fletcher put her head in her hands. 'Christ, do you usually creep up on people? How much of that did you hear?'

'Enough. Why didn't you tell me you were still having problems with him?'

She shrugged. Suddenly she was full of remorse and something else. God, she was not going to cry at the station. She just wasn't. She felt her lips quivering dangerously so she said through gritted teeth, 'Look, what happened back in your office… I'm really sorry.'

All the whispering had alerted Harris who having finished his call was watching them intently through narrowed eyes.

'You can't go on like this,' said Carruthers.

'I know.'

'What time is he getting his stuff?' Carruthers looked over at Harris who made no attempt to get on with his work and was just staring at them. 'Look,' said Carruthers, 'it's too public here. My office.' Fletcher got up from her desk.

With the door firmly closed behind him he said, 'What time's Mark coming round?'

Fletcher sighed. 'He said after work. Told him to be out by eight.'

'Damn inconvenient time.'

'Tell me about it.'

'What are you going to do whilst he's there?'

'Haven't thought that far ahead yet.'

'Come and have a bite to eat with me. Can't promise gourmet food but I'm pretty good with pasta.'

Fletcher hesitated.

'Oh for God's sake. If it makes you feel any better we can discuss the case.'

She managed a feeble smile. 'OK, you've got yourself a date.' Suddenly serious she said, 'Are you going to suspend me?'

Carruthers didn't hesitate. 'No, I'm not.'

She let out an audible sigh of relief.

'However.' He put his hand up. 'Have you had any form of counselling since you lost the baby?'

Fletcher shuddered. 'No, I'd rather poke my eye out with a sharp stick. All that navel gazing. No thank you.'

'It's not a request, Andie. I want you to get some help. You slapped me in my own office. Another DI and you could be up on a charge for that. Also, you should know your altercation with Gayle yesterday was seen by Brown, who's by now probably told the whole station.'

Fletcher swore under her breath.

'You're losing control, Andie. I'm going to give you the number of our counselling services and I want you to call them.'

'And if I don't?'

Carruthers shrugged. 'You'll be off the case and back on sick leave. Your choice.'

Fletcher was silent.

'Christ, we all need to accept help from time to time,' he continued.

'Did you have counselling when your marriage broke down?'

'No, I didn't. You know I didn't, but now I wish I had. I might still be a DCI.'

Fletcher nodded. She thought back to the summer. It already seemed like a lifetime ago but in reality was only a few months. It had been their first real case together. They'd had to enlist the help of the anti-terrorist squad which had brought Carruthers back in to contact with an old adversary, Alistair McGhee. She'd been worried then that her boss had been drinking too much.

As if echoing her thoughts he said, 'Apart from hitting McGhee in the station, for which I got suspended, I also had a drink problem that nearly got out of control. Don't go down the same road.'

'Is it under control now?'

'What do you mean?'

'Your drinking? Is it under control? It's just I couldn't help but notice… Jim, are you back on the booze? I'm not judging or anything… the demotion, your brother…'

Carruthers ran his hands through his hair. 'I'll admit there's been a couple of nights recently where I've had more than I should, but it's under control. Anyway, we're not talking about me. We're talking about you.' He handed her a little red card. 'Ring them.'

She popped the card in her shirt pocket. 'On one condition. Let me go with Dougie.'

'You're not in any sort of position to start bargaining, Andie.'

'I need this, Jim.'

He turned away. Thought about it. Turned back to face her. 'OK. Just don't make me regret it.'

She gave him a half smile, turned and walked away. Looked round at the door. 'You sure you're OK? It's just that I've smelt whisky on your breath a couple of mornings this week.'

'I'm fine.'

CHAPTER FOUR

'OK, let's start by finding his local,' said Harris, rubbing his hands together gleefully. 'It's nearly lunchtime anyway.'

Fletcher gave him a look that could have withered a plastic plant.

'What?' said Harris. 'I'm starving. I could eat a scabby dug.'

She glanced sideways at him. 'What if he doesn't have a local?'

Harris snorted, looked at her as if she'd just added up two and two and made five. 'Everyone has a local.'

She rolled her eyes. 'No. We'll start with some door-to-door. And let's get a move on.'

It was now just spitting with rain, but the sky was heavy with dark cloud that threatened to bring a further deluge. Fletcher neatly sidestepped the pools of water, which gathered in the car park. Harris, unconcerned just strode straight through them. The spray of dirty water flecked the bottoms of his navy blue trousers.

***

'So, what's the story with Mark?' asked Harris. She and Harris had interviewed three local residents in Antigua Street and drawn a blank. They were now standing on the doorstep of the fourth. Fletcher rang the bell.

'Cellardyke is so wee you'd think everyone would ken everyone else but they clearly dinnae,' Harris grumbled. 'We could be doing this all fucking day.'

'Maybe Fraser liked his privacy,' said Fletcher. She stepped up and pressed the bell again.

'You were going to tell me about Mark?' said Harris.

'No, I wasn't.'

'I heard you and Carruthers whispering earlier. He's left you, hasn't he?'

Fletcher stayed silent. Harris shrugged. She turned her back to him.

A sudden blast of icy wind whipped in and, despite her black coat, Fletcher shivered. As she turned to Harris the front door was opened and a large framed woman, leaning heavily on a walking stick, looked down on them.

***

The call came in just as Carruthers was leaving the gents'. A uniformed PC approaching his desk caught sight of him in the corridor. Slipped him a piece of paper. 'That was DS Fletcher on the phone, boss,' said PC Dix. 'They've just finished interviewing a woman in Cellardyke who knew the deceased.' Carruthers nodded his thanks. In seconds Watson was at his side.

'I need to talk to you,' she said.

He handed her the scrap of paper after reading it.

Her eyes narrowed. 'He has a son,' was all she said.

Carruthers nodded. 'So it would seem.'

'Well, it's a start at least. I'll get the support team to chase it up.'

Carruthers turned to her. 'How are you getting on?'

'Just ringing the numbers in his appointment diary.'

'Anything?'

She shook her head. 'Barber; GP; bank. Nothing interesting yet. And before you ask, nothing for the day he died. The page has been torn out.'

'Damn. Well, keep at it. What did you want to talk to me about?' He led her towards his office.

'Why did you change your mind and send Andie out today instead of me? Dougie and I, well, we've been working well as a team but, now Andie's back…'

Carruthers ran his hands through his hair, feeling it stubbly. He thought about overweight misogynistic Dougie Harris. Who would have thought he'd get on so well with no-nonsense lesbian, Gayle Watson. He turned to her, 'You don't know where you fit in?'

'Exactly.'

'There's room for both of you on this team. Sorry if you felt side-lined. Just try to cut Andie some slack, will you? She's going through a tough time.'

***

Fletcher and Harris were sitting by the window in the Ship Inn. Fletcher had her hands cupped round a strong coffee. Harris was slurping a pint of Guinness. He managed to slop some over his black trousers. He pulled a face and stood up. 'Pint's aff.'

Fletcher looked up at him quizzically. 'Can't be much that's wrong with it. You've had half of it.'

Harris stood up. 'Willnae be a tick.' Gave her a wink. 'Watch and learn.'

Sighing, Fletcher watched the retreating back of her colleague and strained to hear the conversation between him and the disgruntled looking bartender. She glanced outside the window to see the choppy waves slapping against the harbour side. The Ship Inn was right on the corner of Shore Street, overlooking the harbour. Today low cloud and spitting rain obscured the Isle of May that sat six miles off the Anstruther coast. Fletcher had promised herself a visit to the fascinating little island but, as excursions only ran in the summer months, she'd have to wait until the long winter was over first. She'd read that it was an important nature reserve and was longing to visit. She dragged her gaze away from the window back to the pub, noticing how every so often an enormous silhouette of a seagull would cast its shadow over the cosy room and all who were in it. Harris, she noticed, was still arguing with the bartender. She decided to let him get on with it, craning her neck so that she could examine the fading black and white photographs of the ships and rugged looking fishermen that adorned the walls.

'You're looking very smug with yourself,' she said after Harris had ambled back with a full pint. She watched the bartender polish the brass fixtures and fittings. 'There was nothing wrong with that pint, was there?'

'Way I look at it, got myself a top-up and dinnae have to pay for it.'

'Do you always do that?'

'Do what?' Harris managed to look smug and innocent at the same time.

'Play the cop card?'

He beamed at her. 'Only when it works. And the beauty of it is that I dinnae even have to tell them I'm a cop. Do it by pure menace alone.'

'I'm sure there's a word for people like you,' she said looking at Harris critically. With a slow, deliberate movement Fletcher picked up her coffee cup again and inhaled the steaming aroma. It was clearing her sinuses.

'It's not a bad cup of coffee for a pub.' She looked up at Harris, who was drinking his pint with a look akin to ecstasy, almost as if he was having a religious experience. 'It felt good today, getting a positive lead,' she said, 'An estranged son and an ex-wife. As good a place to start as any.'

Harris swallowed two or three mouthfuls of foaming liquid. 'Aye,' he said, wiping the back of his hand over his mouth. 'Let's face it, most families have skeletons in their cupboards. Mebbe we've just uncovered two of Fraser's.'

'She didn't say it outright but I got the impression Fraser used to batter his wife. Maybe that's why she left him. Did you notice how evasive she was when we pushed her on it?'

Harris shrugged. 'Most folk dinnae like to get involved. Anyway, my maw used to get a battering every now and then. My daw used to say it kept her in order.'

This was the first bit of personal information Harris had offered up since they'd started working together, other than the fact he was married.

'What did he do for a living. Your dad?'

'No much. Mostly drinking.' Fletcher watched Harris staring into his pint. 'In his spare time he was a bare-knuckle fighter. Made money out of it too.' He took another slug. 'Most of it went straight down the pub.'

'Did he ever hit you?' she asked.

'Got belted a few times. Didn't everyone?' He stood up. 'Right, I'm away for a piss and then to check on those pies. I'm dying of hunger here.'

Fletcher couldn't swear to it but she thought she saw tears clouding Harris' eyes.

***

Fletcher sat tapping her pen against her teeth back at the station continuing to stare at the slip of paper. Ruiridh Fraser – son, Paul. Born approximately 1965. Current whereabouts unknown. Catching a movement, she looked up to see Superintendent Bingham striding towards her.

'Where's DI Carruthers?'

'Back in his office?'

'Ask him to see me, will you?' He started to walk away, hesitated, then half turned round. Fletcher wondered why Bingham couldn't put his head round Jim's office door. After all Jim's office was closer to the superintendent's than theirs.

'Busy this afternoon, DS Fletcher?'

'No more than anyone else,' she answered carefully, thinking there wasn't much left of it. It had already gone 4pm.

'I want you to go over to Braidwood. Interview the little girl who discovered the body. I've got uniforms already going door-to-door there, but I want someone with specialist training to talk to her. Mother's worried about the police talking to her again.

Says she's fragile. You've done that course on negotiating with children, haven't you?'

Fletcher's heart sank. She was doubting anything further could come of a second interview.

'Yes, sir.'

'Good. Right girl for the job, then. I'm aware it might be difficult after–' Bingham coughed. 'You know. But best get back in to the saddle. Think you can handle it?'

'I can handle it.'

Bingham nodded. After he'd left the room Fletcher sighed in frustration. How typical that the minute they had their first breakthrough she was likely being sent on what would most probably be a wild goose chase. She grabbed her purse and headed to the canteen for a bar of chocolate.

***

Fletcher looked at her watch. She was early for her meeting with the Heatons. Parking up in a space three doors down from them she glanced up at the sky to see a chink of light between the grey clouds. Decided to chance it. She unbuckled her seatbelt and in one fluid movement got out of her car and shut the door. Throwing her coat on, she deftly fastened the buttons and turned up her collar. She started walking up the quiet, narrow lane outside the row of terraced Victorian homes on Cults Road that led to a footpath to the University of East of Scotland's Braidwood Campus and the nature reserve.

As she passed the Pink Building she glanced up at the narrow prison-like windows and shuddered. In the distance she could see other university buildings dotted around the landscape – all similar Victorian-looking institutions and at odds with the character and architectural style of the Pink Building.

As she slipped through the gap in the old stone wall, her thoughts drifted to the old man's violent death. He'd been killed with a single stab wound to the heart. There had been no defensive wounds on his body. The most likely scenario was that the victim knew his attacker. That way the perpetrator had got close enough to kill him before he had a chance to react and raise his hands and arms. Of course, they all knew that most murders weren't random; that victims were most often killed by those closest to them. The fact Ruiridh Fraser had an estranged son made everything all the more interesting.

Fletcher sidestepped a puddle, glancing down at the boots she was wearing. So why did she intuitively feel that this case was going to be complicated? She stood opposite the tree where the body had been found. There was nothing to mark the spot where he had died except the fluttering yellow police tape. She frowned and blew her nose, wondering who or what had brought him out to this spot. And the most interesting thing, as far as she was concerned, was that there had been no attempt to bury the body. Why?

She scuffed the hard earth with her foot, smelling dirt and dead leaves. Despite a recent thaw, it would still take some effort to bury a body in woodland. In the dead of a Scottish winter. Ruiridh Fraser had been murdered on one of the coldest nights of the year so far. If the murder had been premeditated, the murderer would surely have brought a spade with him, or some digging implement. Or at least made an effort to cover the body in mulch and leaves. But if he'd wanted to keep it hidden, would he have even brought it to a nature reserve and walker's paradise? It just didn't make sense. Unless it wasn't premeditated – or the murderer didn't care about getting caught. She shook her head, perplexed and walked round the old oak tree with its gnarled branches. She breathed in the decay. Shivering, not just from the cold, she turned and swiftly headed back to conduct her interview.

***

'We really don't want her to go through this again. She's already been questioned once.'

This from Eva's father, a slim built man in his early thirties with round glasses and wavy shoulder-length chestnut hair. Fletcher was in the family's big kitchen, one hand leaning on a large heavy built oak table, her other hand wrapped around a welcome cup of tea.

'Is it OK if both myself and my wife sit in?' Mr Heaton pushed his glasses back on to the bridge of his nose as he said it.

'Of course, Mr Heaton. Look, I know this is really unpleasant for your daughter but I'll be as gentle as possible. It's surprising what somebody can remember a couple of days later, however insignificant it may seem.'

'I take it you suspect foul play, otherwise why would you be back here? Was he local?'

The man had been stabbed to death, she thought. *Of course it's foul play.* 'Cellardyke.'

'That's a good few miles away.' Eva's father stood up. 'OK, I'll bring her in. She's up in her bedroom.'

Fletcher took a seat and shifted some unopened post and coloured crayons so she would have somewhere to put her cup. Her eye caught a leaflet. The words on it jumped out at her.

'Stop the developers ruining Braidwood!'

Fletcher frowned and picked it up. The door opened and Eva's father came back in. He was alone.

'Sorry. She's being a bit difficult. Says she won't come out of her room. Lesley, my wife, is with her. Can you just give them a few minutes?'

'Of course.' Fletcher held up the leaflet. 'This looks interesting.'

He pulled up a chair opposite and sat down. 'Yes, the Friends of Braidwood are really good at giving us regular updates.'

Fletcher raised an eyebrow. 'Friends of Braidwood?'

'Oh. I assumed you knew. Braidwood Campus has been sold to property developers. The Friends of Braidwood are a local campaigning group.'

Fletcher's brows knit together. 'Oh? I didn't know the university had sold up? Anyway, I thought Braidwood was a nature reserve. Can it be bought by property developers?'

'Apparently, developers are now deliberately targeting protected green space.' Fletcher was all ears as Mr Heaton continued. 'If they can get planning permission to build, they stand to make a fortune. You'll have seen for yourself. Site's stunning.'

Fletcher was curious now. 'And if they get planning permission what do they want to do?'

'Conversion of the existing buildings and a hell of a lot of new build right across the existing orchard.'

'And I'm guessing that it's the idea of new build that's proving unpopular?' said Fletcher. 'Is there a lot of local opposition?'

'Let's just say opposition is gathering momentum. You should go to this evening's meeting. In the church hall. Seven o'clock. It's open to the public. Both the developers and the Friends will be there. Strength of feeling being what it is, I reckon half the local community will be there. Locals have got a lot of questions that need answering.'

'I'm assuming one of them being how property developers were even allowed to purchase land from a university when it's a nature reserve with no existing consent to build?'

'Yes, although interestingly the university has now become part of the consortium.'

Fletcher was digesting all this. 'So the university stands to get a kick-back?'

Fletcher turned the leaflet over but it was blank on the other side. Might be worth a visit. She could go, under the guise of appealing for information, but at the same time observe the loyalties, rivalries and jealousies that were part and parcel of a small community. She knew that there was a lot of money at stake in a proposed development and if developers had bought a nature reserve in a conservation area, then they meant business. But how *had* they got permission to buy the land in the first place? She was so absorbed in her thoughts she didn't hear the door open as a frightened little girl entered the kitchen clutching her mother's hand.

CHAPTER FIVE

'Jim, do you mind if we take a rain check on supper tonight?'

Looking up from his paperwork Carruthers frowned. 'No, of course not, Andie. What's up? You OK?'

'Yes, I'm fine. I found out there's a Braidwood Community Council meeting tonight.' Fletcher filled him in. 'To discuss the issue of the campus. It's been sold to property developers.'

Carruthers picked up his coffee cup, realising it was empty, set it back down on his desk. 'And I'm guessing that's not a popular decision given the fact it's a nature reserve.'

'Got it in one.' She showed him the flyer. 'Thought it might be a good chance to talk to both groups and members of the community. See if anyone knew Fraser.'

His eyes scanned the flyer. 'That's an excellent idea. What time's it start?'

'Seven at the church hall, Braidwood Road.'

He gave her the flyer back. 'You got time to go to the meeting? It's six now.'

'I'll be fine. I'll get something to eat after.'

'Do you want me to come with you?'

'No. I can do this on my own.'

'Well, it should be done by eight thirty latest. Come to mine afterwards. We'll have a late supper together. That way you'll be out of your flat all evening, if that's what you want?'

'Are you sure?'

Carruthers smiled. 'Yeah, it's fine. We can catch up on the case. Gives me a chance to do some paperwork first. See you the back of half-eight. If you're gonna be later than that, just text.'

'Thanks, Jim.' Fletcher was touched by this little act of kindness and, not for the first time, thought what a great boyfriend her boss would make.

***

The hall was packed with people sitting on tight rows of plastic chairs. Fletcher managed to find a spare seat on the edge of the room and sat down. She was aware of people coming in behind her having to stand.

A silver-haired woman wearing cream blouse and brown tweed skirt stood up at the front of the hall and addressed the crowd.

'As you know, this is no ordinary community council meeting. We'll be having that next Tuesday instead, same time and place. Tonight we're here to discuss the future of Braidwood Nature Reserve. I'm delighted to say we have both the developers and members of the campaigning group, the Friends of Braidwood with us. We would also like to welcome Detective Sergeant Andrea Fletcher from the Fife Constabulary. As you will no doubt be aware, a man was been found dead on the site in the last few days. Before we proceed, I would like to give DS Fletcher the opportunity to appeal for information about this suspicious death. I'm sure any information you may have will be dealt with in the strictest confidence.'

Fletcher stood up. She got through her speech and finished by giving out a phone number for anyone who had information on the deceased. It became apparent, from the silence that followed, that neither the developers nor the Friends knew Ruiridh Fraser. At least, if they did, they weren't admitting it in public.

As she retook her seat she glanced at her watch. On schedule. She settled comfortably back in her chair and listened as the immaculately dressed developer stood up and pitted his charm against what she expected to be the passion of the local campaigning group.

He was introduced as Edward Buchanan, a slender, not unattractive man whom Fletcher judged to be in his late forties. He spoke as if he had a plum in his mouth. Fletcher couldn't tell if he was English or very posh Edinburgh. He also exuded a natural charm and not a little arrogance. He outlined the ambitious plans he had for the site, detailing how the new build would pay for the sensitive conversion of the Grade A listed buildings in to luxury flats.

All of this sounded quite reasonable to Fletcher and she was starting to wonder what all the fuss was about when an attractive, dark-haired woman in her late thirties stood up and spoke.

'I think we need to be very clear what you're proposing here. Let me get this right,' she said, brushing back a lock of unruly black hair which had fallen over her face. 'You're wanting to place eight new development sites on this land.'

'Yes, that's right.' The developer was smiling.

'The whole site of Braidwood sits within a conservation area.' The woman addressed her comments not to the chair but to the public. 'The amount of new build proposed ignores all the planning protections on this site.' She jabbed a finger towards the developer. 'This is not a brown field site, nor is it detailed in the Fife Local Plan as an area proposed for building.' There were murmurs from the audience.

'Now look, Alison,' said the chair standing up, 'the Friends of Braidwood' will get their chance to speak later. 'Let Edward talk.' She promptly sat down again with a flourish. The woman, Alison, remained standing.

'We all know it is a heavily protected site,' said the developer, his crocodile-like smile having evaporated. He took off his dark blue tailored jacket and hung it carefully on the back of his chair.

'That's just my point though,' continued the dark-haired woman. 'We wouldn't know that by looking at your website. Nowhere on it do you mention the fact that it is protected green space.' The developer was momentarily quiet. 'Well, do you?' the campaigner continued, completely ignoring the chair.

A sheen of perspiration was starting to appear on Edward Buchanan's forehead. His cheeks flushed. At last he spoke. 'Look, as I said, we all know that this land is heavily protected.'

'Not from your website,' the dark-haired woman continued. 'In fact, from reading it we would think there was already planning permission to build on the site.'

'There is.'

'There is NOT!' The woman was controlling her temper but it was obvious to Fletcher from the spontaneous cheers and claps from the crowd that feelings were running high and this feisty woman who was clearly the spokesperson for the Friends of Braidwood was stirring them up in to somewhat of a frenzy.

Fletcher noticed that every so often Buchanan would glance down at two men to his left. They were both smartly dressed, in suits. The man to his immediate left was clearly a body-builder, the shirt straining over his torso and pumped up arms. He looked menacing, even in a suit. Fletcher wondered if he was there for protection, should things turn nasty. She then reminded herself that this was a community council meeting in a wealthy part of Fife.

The second was a ferret of a man with shrew-like eyes. He was taking notes on a tablet. There was a shiftiness about him that Fletcher didn't like. She was sure she recognised him from somewhere. He met her gaze and hastily looked away. She was convinced that he'd recognised her. She couldn't place him and that frustrated her.

The dark-haired woman faced Edward Buchanan again. 'What you are alluding to on your website is planning permission that expired in the mid-1990s.'

'Well, I—' he said.

'That planning permission was overturned when this whole area was made a conservation site, with all its attendant protections. I have to tell you, I find your website very misleading. You don't care about this land at all, despite what you say. For you, it's all about making a profit. It's greed, pure greed.' The woman sat down to cheers.

'Right, that's enough,' roared the chair. 'The Friends of Braidwood will get your turn to speak. And *you* have had more than enough speaking time, Alison Stephens. Sit down. I want to hear from someone else who hasn't spoken and who isn't a member of the Friends.'

'Let her speak,' shouted a young woman from the back. 'This is supposed to be a public meeting and the Friends are members of the public.'

The chair clicked her tongue in annoyance. Fletcher wondered if she'd been a schoolteacher.

'Look, as I said, we all *know* there are numerous designations on this site,' the developer continued, his smile fixed firmly back in place.

Like a jack-in-a-box Alison stood back up again. 'Perhaps you would like to list them for us?' she said with a sweet smile. Buchanan threw her a look of such hatred that Fletcher was starting to wonder whether her role would develop into a peacekeeping one. A UN hardhat would come in useful.

'I have no problem talking about the protections.' He reached out and poured himself a glass of water from the jug on the table in front of him. Fletcher wondered if this was a stalling technique.

'We all know, for example, that this is a local nature conservation site. Do you not think I would rather keep this site as it is and just develop the listed buildings?' At this Buchanan picked up his pointer pen and waved it at the overhead projection of the image of Braidwood on the wall behind him. 'Of course I want to preserve the beauty of this very special site and we will; but sadly, financially, we also need to do some new build. It's inevitable, I'm afraid, and the only viable way forward.' At this, Buchanan coquettishly turned his head to the side, in a manner that reminded Fletcher of the footage of Lady Diana when she talked about the failure of her marriage to Charles.

'I mean, nobody wants to see the Grade A listed buildings fall into disrepair, which is what will happen if the new build is axed. Now.' He paused. 'Let's move on, shall we?' The developer lifted an eyebrow in a sardonic look. 'Look, the new build takes only three per cent of the site and most of it is through scrub. Nobody can possibly have an issue with that. It's of no use to anyone.'

'I think you'll find, if you actually bothered to read the Fife Local Plan,' continued Alison, 'that the scrub at Braidwood is valid in its own right as a natural habitat for some of the site's protected species. You do *know* that there's both bats and badgers on the land you bought, don't you? Both of these are highly protected by law.'

Buchanan spoke to the woman as if he was talking to a rather bothersome five-year-old. 'Of course, but rest assured we will be doing a full and impartial environmental impact assessment that will accompany our plan.'

The chair once more rose to her feet. 'Now I have a question of my own. I would like to ask Edward about his *financial* justification for what some people here obviously see as excessive new build.'

'Yes, certainly. What I will tell you is that full disclosure of the financial arguments will be available to the public in due course.'

'When? When?' shouted Alison. 'We have been asking for them for a year. A year! I put it to you,' her arms were flailing wildly, 'that there is no financial *justification*.' She almost spat the final word. 'And that is why the figure hasn't been disclosed.' There were cheers and some individuals got to their feet during the applause.

'Now, Alison, really, would you please sit down.' said the Chair. 'Can I have comments please from people who are *not* active members of the Friends of Braidwood.'

An elderly silver haired lady stood up. 'I would like to know how many mature trees the developers propose to axe to make way for this development. I have a serious worry about increased flood risk. My home got flooded three years ago. We're on Allen Street.'

A young harassed woman stood up to speak. 'I have a three-year-old daughter and I would like to ask about schools. The schools in this area are at maximum capacity already. Will a new school be built?'

Fletcher listened to Buchanan carefully as he answered the questions. She realised that he was skilled in the art of evasion. He should have been a politician, she thought. But she also realised that members of the public weren't buying his claims. There was, however, one older, attractive, well-dressed lady sitting in the front row with her legs crossed. Every so often Buchanan would catch her eye and smile at her. Was he flirting? She must be a good twenty years older than him. Fletcher glanced over at her. She was sitting coyly, eyes batting madly at him, seemingly hanging on his every word.

The public were starting to get angry at his evasive answers. The obvious tension in the air had started to give way to a low murmuring. Mutterings were growing louder and jeering was growing in its intensity. One man in particular was causing a disturbance in this way.

'If you carry on like this, I shall have you ejected,' said the Chair. 'The public want to hear Edward.'

A man stood up with such force his chair would have gone flying had it not been boxed in by other seats. 'I've heard more than enough. This man is nothing but a liar.' He started to shout. 'If the council let this development go ahead it will be a travesty.' He pushed past his fellow neighbours and left the room to thunderous applause.

For the next ten minutes Fletcher watched as Buchanan navigated his way through some stormy community waters. He sounded smooth and confident, but there was evidence of a nervous twitch in his perspiring face, the only outward signs that the man was under any pressure. Clearly he was a man of immense wealth and power. Fletcher wondered just how many toes he'd stepped upon to get in to his position. And how ruthless he could be, if pushed.

The dark-haired spokeswoman of the Friends of Braidwood resumed speaking, directing her next comment to Edward. 'We would like to know of any private meetings between yourselves and the council, and between the developers and the university. We will be putting in a freedom of information request. We've also noticed that since the university sold the land they've become members of the consortium. It'll be interesting to know how big their financial kick-back will be.'

'I'm afraid that we don't have the council here to comment,' said the chair, 'but I would like to ask Edward to briefly discuss the style of new build. Is it in keeping with the conservation area?'

Finally, the meeting drew to a close. Members of the public filed out, many still muttering. Fletcher approached the chair.

'Well, that went better than expected,' she beamed. Fletcher wondered if the woman had attended the same meeting as her.

'Tell me, who is that rather attractive lady with the silver hair sitting at the front?' Fletcher realised, as she was speaking, that the lady in question had made a beeline for the developer and that they were locked in deep conversation.

'Oh, that's the chair of Fife Heritage.'

That would be a good person to get on side, thought Fletcher, watching Buchanan in particular. He had his hand on the lady's shoulder and was leaning in towards her. She was laughing girlishly.

'They look as if they know each other quite well,' said Fletcher.

'Oh indeed they do. Edward became a trustee on the board of Fife Heritage about a year ago.'

'Really?'

'Oh yes, he's also a member of the Scottish Wildlife Trust. I don't think he's a trustee, though. It's wonderful isn't it? I do think he's much maligned, you know. He really does have a genuine interest in both nature and conservation.'

My arse he does, thought Fletcher. *He didn't even know that scrub was a valid habitat.* 'I would have thought it would be deemed a conflict of interest for a property developer to become a trustee on a heritage board?'

Fletcher never got an answer as the chair was already speaking to someone else behind her, who was asking about wheelchair access.

She left the building wondering exactly when Edward Buchanan had become a member of the Scottish Wildlife Trust and a trustee on the board of Fife Heritage. Call her cynical but she strongly suspected it might have been around the time that he'd first started showing an interest in the acquisition of Braidwood Nature Reserve.

***

Carruthers watched Fletcher as she left the classics and crime novels in the bookshelf to take a wander over to his CD collection. She took a sip of the glass of mineral water she'd been handed. 'You've got a very eclectic taste in music, Jim. Did anyone ever tell you that?' Selecting a CD by Neil Young she turned it over to look at the back before replacing it next to one by Iron Maiden. 'By the way, when did you start drinking sparkling water? Somehow I don't think having bottles of sparkling water in your home goes with the image of you as an Iron Maiden fan.'

He laughed. 'I got it for visitors, then started drinking it myself. I found I liked the taste. Come on. Take a seat. Supper's nearly ready.'

'This is really good,' said Fletcher, tucking in to her pasta a little while later. 'It's lovely being cooked for again. It's like being back at my parents. Jim,' she said looking round her at the décor, 'I really like what you've done to the cottage. Have you been decorating?' She looked at the cappuccino feature wall above the fireplace, warm against the cream of the rest of the living room.

'Just a spot of paint here and there. I haven't done much.'

'Well, the feature wall really sets it off. Goes well with the brown leather sofa.'

'Do you think so?' He smiled. It had taken him a while to decide on the colour, which he judged to be between grey and brown. It was a soft natural colour and his initial fear that it would make the room appear smaller had been misplaced.

'Who decided that it would work well with pine blinds?'

'My mother.' Carruthers took a sip of his water.

'How's she bearing up?'

Carruthers ran his hand through his bristles. 'In a state of shock. Like the rest of us.'

'Will your brother, you know, make a full recovery?'

'He's had stents put in one artery. The second's still blocked apparently. He's waiting for an assessment.'

'Shit. I know we agreed no personal questions but do you want to talk about it?'

Carruthers shook his head.

'You might feel better if you do,' said Fletcher.

He laughed. 'I could say the same to you.'

'Ouch.' Fletcher returned his smile. She took a hanky out of her pocket and blew her nose.

Carruthers leaned forward. 'Feeling better?'

'Yes, much.'

He set his glass down. 'Up to talking about work?'

'Of course.'

'How did the meeting at Braidwood go?'

Fletcher shook her head. 'Certainly interesting.'

'You got me intrigued. Spill.'

'Well, I knew local feelings were running high, but that meeting was something else.' She forked a spiral of pasta. 'Let's just say the developers aren't exactly flavour of the month. There's a lot of bad feeling between them and the local residents. I thought there was going to be a punch-up at one point. I tell you, if you're spoiling for a fight, a community council meeting's definitely the place to go.'

Fletcher took a sip of her mineral water. 'It had everything. A bullish community council leader; an arrogant, untrustworthy developer, and some fiery local campaigners.'

'Not that you're biased or anything. Untrustworthy developer? One to watch?'

'Could be.'

'Who are the developers, anyway?'

'It's a consortium called Buchanan and Associates Heritage Development or BHD, led by a developer called Edward Buchanan.'

'Haven't heard of them.'

'Buchanan had a couple of henchmen with him. I'm pretty sure I recognised one of them but can't remember where from. Anyway, the meeting wasn't boring, that's for sure. Only disappointment is that nobody seemed to know Ruiridh Fraser.'

Carruthers took a glug of water. 'Well, maybe someone will come forward. People don't always like to be put on the spot in a public meeting.'

Fletcher licked her fork. 'I wish I could remember where I know Buchanan's "associate" from though. It's really bugging me.'

'It'll come back to you. Tell you what, let's put the development on the backburner. How did you get on with Fraser's files? Had a chance to look through them yet?' Carruthers reached for the grated parmesan and liberally sprinkled it over his pasta.

'I'm still going through the last three months of his bank and phone statements,' said Fletcher.

'Anything interesting?'

Fletcher tilted her head to the side, considering this. 'Bank statements pretty much what you'd expect. A few direct debits going out; TV license, gas and electricity. The usual. He's had his phone bill itemised, which is handy.'

'Turn up anything?'

'Several local calls in the last couple of months; library, chemist, GP, barber's. There's one thing though. A few mobile numbers keep coming up. Calls seem to last five or so minutes.'

'Do you know who they belong to?'

'I've still got a couple to chase up. But there's one in particular. The number's been discontinued, which is a bit odd. I'll get on to the phone company first thing tomorrow to see if I can find out who it was registered to.'

'Good job. Find out the date it got discontinued.'

'Oh, and one other thing. There's been a few calls to another mobile number. I found out today the number belongs to Malcolm Hunter.'

Carruthers, who had brought his glass of water up to his lips, put it down promptly again. 'That's interesting. I wonder what he's doing ringing his next-door neighbour. Especially on the mobile. They both have landlines, don't they?'

Nodding, Fletcher opened her handbag and took out a notebook. 'I've also managed to get some background on Malcolm Hunter.'

'Go for it,' said Carruthers reaching for the pepper pot.

Fletcher flipped her notebook open. 'OK, so Hunter's worked nine years as a medical rep for Moncrieff Pharmaceuticals. It's an English company with a head office in Hertfordshire. His territory covers Scotland, Northern Ireland and northern England. I guess that explains his travelling. Before he joined Moncrieff Pharmaceuticals he was a hospital-based sales rep for Louden Pharma.' She licked her index finger and turned the page over. 'In terms of personal life, he married Anne in 1990 and, as you know, they've got two kids.'

'What are your impressions of Jordan Hunter?'

Fletcher picked up her serviette and dabbed her mouth. She shrugged. 'I don't know the boy, but he gave me the creeps. Can't put my finger on it but I found him disturbing. All dressed in black, the way he locks himself in his bedroom.'

'Let's face it, dresses in black, stays in his room. You could be describing teenage boys up and down the country.'

'I don't know. It was the way he was scuffing the carpet with his foot. Did you notice that? Just seemed to be so much pent up aggression. I get the feeling that if he ever lost it, he'd lose it big time.'

Carruthers nodded. 'His father's obviously quick to temper. Perhaps his son's inherited the trait.'

Fletcher locked eyes with Carruthers. 'Makes them both dangerous, if he has.'

'What's your gut feeling on this, Andie?'

'I honestly don't know. I don't know whether Jordan's capable of murder, but the logistics are against him doing it. I mean, how did he get himself and Fraser to Braidwood? Like we said, he's too young to drive and it's a few miles away.' She mulled it over for a few moments. 'I don't think he did it. I have to admit, it's got me baffled. Why kill an old man, dump him without burying him and shove cloth down his throat to boot?' She reached across the table and picked up the pepper pot. 'Have you managed to find any contact details for Fraser's son yet?'

'Still working on it. You've really got the bit between your teeth on this one, haven't you?' said Carruthers. 'Perhaps it's just as well we've got a case to solve at the moment.' He reached over and patted her hand, resting his on top for a moment. 'Don't shut everyone out. I know you like to be self-sufficient but no man's an island.'

'Ditto, Jim. Works both ways.' She leaned closer in to him, saying through narrowed eyes. 'I'm worried about you too, you know. Have you spoken to your—'

'My mother? Yes.'

'Was going to say brother.'

Carruthers shook his head. 'Not yet. I don't know what to say to him.'

'Well, just ask him how he is. Can't be that difficult, can it?'

Carruthers remained silent.

'So all communication's going through your mum, then?'

Carruthers nodded. Once again Fletcher was right on the money. She really was uncanny the way she seemed to understand him. 'Often the way, isn't it? Look, I will ring him. In fact, I've told my mum I'll visit.'

'Where is he?'

'Glasgow.'

'Not too far away then,' said Fletcher. 'You might feel better once you've seen him. But you are OK?'

'There's nothing for you to worry about. I haven't been sleeping too well. That's all. Nothing a good night's sleep and a bit less to drink wouldn't cure. Now I know you may not want to talk about it, but do your friends know about Mark leaving?'

She shook her head.

'Parents?'

'They'd only worry.'

'You need to tell them.'

Suddenly it was Fletcher on the defensive. 'I know and I will.' She scraped the remainder of her uneaten pasta to the side of her plate putting her knife and fork down. Sighing, she pushed her plate away. 'I guess I hoped it would be temporary and he'd come back.'

'And it isn't?'

'No, it isn't. The funny thing is that I don't even know why he left. Not really.'

Carruthers listened quietly knowing that, now Fletcher was finally opening up, it would do her good to talk.

'We didn't really talk about it. The baby wasn't planned. I didn't know what Mark felt about my being pregnant. I didn't know how I felt about being pregnant. But I started getting used to it and then losing it was traumatic. One moment it was alive and then…' Fletcher hesitated, her voice grew suddenly quiet. 'I couldn't feel it move any more. We went to hospital but it had already died. Because I was so far gone the labour had to be induced, and I had to give birth to a dead baby. The pain was horrific and afterwards Mark was great. Really supportive. But a week later when I was back home it was like I was living with a totally different man. One morning we woke up and he announced he couldn't do it anymore. I watched him pack a suitcase and then he left. Just like that.' A single tear escaped and rolled down Fletcher's cheek. Carruthers leaned over the table and squeezed her hand.

'I'm so sorry. I don't know what to say.'

Looking away from him she said, 'I don't expect you to say anything.' She took her hand away.

'I can't believe you went through all this alone.'

'Well, I didn't though, did I? I went down to my parents. And you kept in touch by phone.'

'You didn't return many of my calls.' His forehead creased. 'Mark didn't contact you in all that time?'

'Well, I had a missed call on my mobile about ten days into my stay with them. It was from him. He didn't leave a message. I didn't call him back. I just didn't expect that returning to Scotland, to the flat, our home, would be so difficult.'

'The constant reminders?'

'Yes, although once he's taken his stuff out it'll be easier I guess. It's a lot easier to be at work at the moment than at home.'

'That's how I felt when my wife left.'

'Then you understand. Do you ever hear from her?'

Carruthers stared in to space. 'No.' Carruthers still felt a wrench when he thought of his ex-wife but it wasn't the raw agonising pain that used to course through him.

'What about Siobhan Mathews?'

Carruthers shook his head. Mathews had been the girlfriend of a murder victim during that first case they'd worked on together. He'd allowed himself to get too personally involved. His inappropriate feelings for her had clouded his judgement, something he deeply regretted. It had been a difficult time for him personally and professionally. And then there had been Alistair McGhee, of course. His old adversary had been shot and almost killed saving his life. He wasn't sure, if truth be told, had the situation been reversed, he would have done the same thing. Perhaps after all, Alistair McGhee was a better man than him.

He had tried to contact Siobhan but after her rape ordeal she'd given up her studies moving away from Castletown, back to her parents. He thought of her now with her glossy black hair, green eyes and bohemian dress sense and felt a moment of immense sadness. He'd often wondered what might have been if they'd met under different circumstances.

Fletcher reaching over for her glass of water knocked over the pepper pot and the clatter broke the spell. Carruthers looked up at her, seeing a similar sadness in her eyes, said, 'Perhaps you should take a leaf out of my book.' Fletcher raised her eyebrows. 'Maybe redecorating the flat would help?'

She grinned. 'That's a great idea. The first thing to go will be the purple couch.' She put the pepper pot upright again and refilled her glass from the water jug.

'Purple couch?'

'Yep. It's definitely gotta go. Reminds me of him. Parents bought it for us when we moved in together.'

Carruthers cleared away the plates. 'Would you like coffee?'

'Coffee would be great if you've got decaf.'

Carruthers smiled. 'Coming up.'

'I do feel so much better talking to you, Jim. Thanks for listening.'

'My pleasure. But you know you still have to see a counsellor, don't you?'

'Is that an order?'

'Yes. Phone them tomorrow. But if there's anything we – Anything I can do to help at the office then let me know.'

'There is one thing.'

Carruthers looked up.

'I need to be active. Doing things. That's why I lost it at the station. And yes, if I'm honest, I do feel I'm being pushed out by Gayle Watson. She's a good detective.'

'So are you. Don't doubt yourself.' He made eye contact with her, managed to hold her gaze. 'The problem is that Gayle's now feeling pushed out, too. I had a word with her. Got her and Dougie to go back and conduct some more interviews. And before you say it, I wasn't checking up on the work you and Dougie did. This is a murder investigation. Someone interviewed may have remembered something later. Seriously, Andie, don't let a bad experience with a Grade A shit-bag erode your self-confidence. And like I said before, Gayle's not there to replace you.'

Fletcher smiled. 'Look, Jim…' She looked at her watch. It was ten. She stood up. 'I didn't realise it was so late. I'm going to head home.'

She was at the front door and grabbing her coat before he could think of something to say.

'Thanks for this evening. Good night.' She kissed his cheek. The one she had earlier slapped.

'Oh by the way, I'm glad the date with Jodie went well.'

His mouth fell open. 'How did you…' But she was already gone. He shut the front door, and leaving the dirty plates on the table, walked in to the kitchen. He looked in the cupboard at his whisky selection and took out a bottle of Highland Park and a glass. He opened the bottle and took a deep sniff of the smoky, peppery whisky. He opened the fridge door and selected a blue cheese, sniffed it appreciatively. Picked up the glass and cradled it in the centre of his hand. He hesitated then sighed and changing his mind, placed the bottle back in the cupboard and the cheese back in the fridge. He hadn't told Fletcher, but he'd been told to get his cholesterol checked. Looked like heart disease ran in the family.

***

The earlier rain had finally stopped falling. Standing on her boss's doorstep shivering with the cold Fletcher looked up at the night sky, watching as a thick band of cloud pushed its way across. Without looking back she walked over to her parked car and drove off as the streetlights cast their yellow glow over the slick wet roads and pavements.

Driving in to her street, she became aware of a light on in her sitting room. She was sure she'd switched it off. She took a sharp and anxious intake of breath. Her heart was hammering in her chest. Hairs prickled on the back of her neck. She then chastised herself for getting worked up. No self-respecting burglar would leave the lights full on. With a groan she remembered that Mark was collecting his stuff. How could she have forgotten? The little shit must have left them on. How typical, especially as she would be paying the bills on her own now.

As she looked for a place to park she noticed the dark blue Mondeo a little way up the street. Mark's car. She swore. What the hell was he still doing here? With a sick feeling in her stomach she let herself in to the flat. Without taking her coat off or putting her handbag down, she marched in to the living room. Mark was sitting in the middle of the purple couch, smoking a cigarette and drinking her whisky. The air was thick with the stench of cigarette smoke, and by the number of discarded butts in her favourite glazed soap dish, it looked like he'd been in the flat all evening. She wrinkled up her nose in disdain. He turned to face her.

'Thank God. I've been really worried. Where have you been? Didn't you get my messages?'

Fletcher dumped the handbag on the dining table and searched through it for her mobile. She couldn't find it. Then remembered that she'd left it in the pocket of her coat, which had been hanging at the front door in Carruthers' flat, out of earshot. She fished about for it, found it and found she had six missed calls, all from him.

'No, I didn't get your calls. I've been at a friend's. What are you still doing here?'

'Which friend?'

'It's a bit late to start getting jealous, isn't it?' She marched over to him, taking the cigarette out of his mouth and grinding it in to the soap dish. 'And since when did you take up smoking? You've never smoked.' She had her hands on her hips. 'And you're stinking the place out.'

'You're not making this very easy.'

'What am I not making easy?' She was confused. She looked around her and realised that the cardboard boxes she'd found in the attic for him were still empty. Her eyes darted to the CD stand and she saw with a sinking feeling that his CDs, DVDs were all still stacked in the racks.

Her brow knitted in a frown. 'What the fuck are you still doing here? I thought you were coming round to collect your stuff? Instead I find you still here drinking my whisky and smoking.'

'Oh for God's sake. Do you have to be so petty? It's not your whisky.'

'I think you'll find it bloody well is. I won it at the work raffle if you remember.'

'You don't even drink whisky.'

'And you don't smoke. But that's not the point. You haven't answered my question. What are you still *doing* here?'

Mark shifted uncomfortably on the couch. He swallowed the drink in one, placed the glass down carefully on the coaster and stood up to his six foot one inches.

'Look, the truth is. I've been thinking…' He shifted awkwardly from one foot to the other.

Fletcher raked her hand through her dark hair. 'Just get to the point. I'm tired. I need to go to bed.'

'I made a mistake. I've changed my mind. About us.'

'WHAT? Since last night?' she stared open-mouthed at him.

'I want to give it another go. I need you.' He walked round the low glass table over to the window and put a hand on Fletcher's shoulder. He dipped his head, angling his face to move in and kiss her. She could smell the Laphroaig on his breath. She swept his hand away and turned her face to the wall.

'Why?' she asked.

'What do you mean, "why"?'

'Why do you need me? I'd like to know.'

'I can't put it into words. I just need you.'

She wondered if staying with his mum and dad was beginning to lose its appeal.

'And where were you when I needed you the last few months,' she said quietly. 'How many times did you phone me? Text me? Email me?' A moment elapsed. She shook her head. Her eyes were downcast. 'No.'

'No? What do you mean, no?'

She snapped her head up. Her blue eyes were blazing like the flame in a gas fire. 'Do I have to spell it out? I don't. Want. You. Anymore.'

'You can't mean that?'

'Yes, I can and I do.'

'Look, I'm sorry I wasn't there for you. I needed time apart. To get my head together. I lost a baby too, remember.'

'Is that going to happen every time we face a crisis? You're going to run off to your parents?'

'I wasn't at my parents. I've been with Dave and Stacey.'

So Mark had been staying at his best mate's.

'My parents actually thought I should be with you. They were on your side, so I moved out. They didn't understand that I needed space.'

In that moment Fletcher could see Mark for what he really was: immature, selfish and cowardly.

'Get out. It's over.' She made a grab for his jacket and threw it at him. 'Go back to Dave and Stacey.' The jacket ended up on the floor. He bent and scooped it up. His face was flushed.

'I can't. Stacey's mum has taken a fall and is moving in with them for a while. They can't put me up anymore. They told me to come home to you.'

Disgusted, she opened the living room door. 'But this isn't your home anymore, is it?'

Fletcher knew Mark was defeated. Shoulders slumped forward he walked to the front door.

'Where am I supposed to go?'

'Not my problem.' She could feel tears glinting in her eyes. She turned her head away from him. 'Just go.'

Out of the corner of her eye she could see him turn towards the door. He hesitated. She didn't look at him. Waiting until she heard the front door shut she went back in to the living room. Picking up the heavy crystal whisky glass, feeling its weight cradled in her hand, she hurled it against the mantelpiece. It exploded into a thousand silvery shards.

CHAPTER SIX

Given the drama of the night before, Fletcher had slept surprisingly well. She'd changed the message on the answer machine and a collection of Mark's belongings was already sitting in bin bags in the boot of her car. She'd had a late night but it had certainly been worth it. Now all she needed to do was to get a locksmith. That way she wouldn't have to ask for her key back.

A plummeting overnight temperature meant a hard layer of frost coated the ground. De-icing the car was a job that normally frustrated her, but today she found it oddly soothing. She went back inside to retrieve her mobile but then had difficulty locking the front door with the mortise as her hands were so numb.

She swung by a locksmith's on the way to work. It had just opened.

'You're bright and early.' She looked up to find a young man smiling at her whilst speaking. Deciding she liked him on sight she smiled back.

'Thought I'd call in before we become too busy at work,' she said. 'Just wondered how quickly you'd be able to get my locks changed?'

'You haven't had a break-in, have you? We're a bit pushed at the moment.'

'Oh no, nothing like that. I, er…' What on earth could she say other than she was trying to keep her ex out?

'No need to say any more.'

He looked down at her, his eyes, she noticed, full of mischief. She felt like she should pat her hair or something. Grief. Was he flirting with her?

'Live locally?' he asked.

Cat must have got her tongue. She could do nothing but nod.

'If you give me your phone number I'll check the diary and get back to you. I won't be able to make it for a couple of days though. Is that OK?'

'Yes,' she squeaked, wishing it was sooner.

'We've got a lot of work on just now. John's hurt his back so it's just me. If you do need it done quicker there's another locksmith in the next town.'

'No, I can wait a couple of days.' She wrote her phone number down for him feeling shy and awkward. In her haste to leave she nearly tripped over a draught excluder that was lying on the floor.

Arriving at the station, she sat at her desk and steepled her hands. Looking around her at the hustle and bustle of the already busy office she knew this was where she was meant to be. It was a good feeling. For the first time in months she felt, well, better. Comfortable in her own skin. Yes, life had certainly been a bitch but she was strong enough to cope.

Picking up the phone she grabbed the file so she could ring Fraser's phone company. A good a place to start as any. As she punched in the first couple of digits the door opened and a red-faced Harris entered. He was breathless and his mouth was open. She stared at him noticing his cheeks were a mass of broken blood vessels and for the first time that his bulbous purple nose gave him a look of Alex Fergusson. His white shirt was straining over his belly where a couple of buttons looked as if they were about to pop.

'Andie, you're needed.'

She looked up, surprised at the urgency in his voice.

'Now.'

'What's up?'

'Another body's been found up at Braidwood.'

'Shit.' Fletcher grabbed her jacket and car keys. 'Has anyone phoned the SOCOs?'

'Already on their way. Boy Wonder's leaving in the next couple of minutes. Wants you with him.'

Standing up swiftly, she almost knocked her chair over. She wanted to get outside before Carruthers changed his mind and invited Golden Tits along instead. She headed out of the office. Meeting Carruthers in the corridor she fell in step with him. 'What the hell's going on, Jim?'

He shook his head, running his hands through his short hair. She noticed the tightness around his mouth and the concern in his eyes. 'I wish I knew. Look, we'll travel together.'

'OK.'

A watery sun sat low in the sky, casting a weak early morning light across the car park. A light frost crunched underfoot and Fletcher rubbed her red hands together.

'Who's driving?' she asked.

'You are.' Carruthers opened the car door stretching his long frame across to reach into the glove compartment for the de-icer. Threw it to her. She caught it cleanly. Noticed his breath coming out in short bursts of vapour. Turning his back to her he fumbled in his jacket pocket for his mobile. 'I'm just going to give Dr Mackie a call.' He pointed to the windscreen. 'Look to it. We haven't got all day.'

***

Even though the temperature was beginning to rise, the air was clear and sharp enough to make Fletcher's eyes water. Her boots made a noise as they squelched through the wet brown leaves. There was a smell of decay in the air.

'Body's been found in the grounds. Not in the wood. Boiler houses to the east of Queen's Braids,' said Carruthers, taking his bearings.

'Shit. I should have worn different boots,' she said, looking down at her already muddy Timberlands. 'Thought everything would still be frozen.'

Approaching Queen's Braids with the sweeping vista of meadow behind them, Fletcher took in the sculpted trees on the edge of the park, the abundance of Scots pine, holly and rhododendron. She eyed a couple of SOCOs striding across the meadow. The low sun threw their shadows fifty feet in front of them making them look like aliens on giant stilts.

As they drew closer to Queen's Braids, Fletcher and Carruthers veered off to the right taking a dirt track that skirted Braidwood Woods. Trailing branches of ivy clad the trunks of ancient trees. As the woods came in to view Fletcher's ears tuned to the birdsong. Shafts of sunlight suddenly pierced through the dark catching the dew on silver cobwebs.

Fletcher stepped gingerly over a tangle of weeds and half-hidden tree stumps. The undergrowth was thick with ivy and brambles. She slipped on some wet moss and Carruthers caught her arm in a firm grip.

She turned to him. 'Watch it. I bruise easily.'

'What would you prefer? A bruise or broken arm? You nearly took a tumble. And look. There's some broken glass there.' She followed his gaze to a half hidden broken green bottle wedged in the earth, its jagged edge ready to inflict a seriously nasty wound.

'Shit. Well, if you put it like that.' She offered him a small smile, thanks and apology rolled into one.

As they cautiously approached the boiler house, they caught sight of Dr Mackie, already kneeling by the body, which was half obscured by thick undergrowth.

'Only been dead a few hours by the looks of it,' he said, straightening himself up.

The corpse was lying on its front, a dark stain pooling by the side of the body. Fletcher felt the hairs prick up on the back of her neck. She could only make out the legs, which were encased in grey slacks. The top half of the torso was within the open door of one of the old disused sheds behind the boiler house.

'Male or female?' asked Carruthers, flashing his badge and stepping inside the cordoned off area. He lifted up the tape so Fletcher could duck underneath it.

'Male. Looks to be in his seventies, Jim,' Mackie's voice was low. 'He's got a stab wound.'

'Jesus. Cause of death?'

'Could be.'

Fletcher stepped up to get a better look, noting that one foot was shoeless. 'Any ID on him?'

'Nothing's been found,' said Dr Mackie. At that moment one of the SOCOs shouted over to him. Addressing his comment to Carruthers, Dr Mackie said, 'I'll be right back.'

Stepping further into the gloom of the shed, Fletcher brushed a cobweb and a dead spider from her coat. As her eyes adjusted to the dark she looked around and slipped her right hand into a latex glove.

'Be quick and don't let Mackie catch you,' hissed Carruthers in her ear. Keeping one eye on Mackie, Fletcher half knelt down close to the body and put her hand into each of the corpse's pockets. She glanced over at Carruthers and shook her head.

'Nothing.'

Carruthers touched Fletcher's arm. 'He's coming back.'

Straightening up she removed her hand from the glove, which she put into a plastic bag she kept in her coat pocket.

'Had a good feel about have you, lassie? Honestly, do you think I was born yesterday? Been doing this job for thirty years. Know all the tricks.'

Fletcher reddened.

'Will you move away? I don't want my scene contaminated.' Mackie held Fletcher back with his arm. 'Ahh. Here comes Lui. What held you up?'

'Traffic. What have we got?' The diminutive Chinese man appeared, camera slung over shoulder. 'Keeping me on my toes, I see.' He peered in to the gloom of the boiler house.

'Don't want you to get rusty.'

'Nae chance of that. See you got another stiff for me. Hey,' he jerked his head at Carruthers and Fletcher. 'You two are in my road.'

Carruthers guided Fletcher away by the arm and from a distance they watched Liu angling his body in a number of different positions to get the photograph he wanted. He took a series of shots, not just of the body, but also of the boiler house and scrub area just outside the boiler house. Carruthers looked at Fletcher. Between flashes of light from Liu's camera Carruthers asked, 'What do you think?' The sun had hidden itself behind a cloud and another flash of light lit the gloom.

She shook her head. 'Two men, similar age, both with stab wounds. Got to be a connection. Too much of a coincidence otherwise.'

'Have you received any calls since your community council meeting?' Carruthers asked.

Shaking her head she said, 'Not a single one.' She took a few steps back. Surveyed the scene.

'Assuming it's the same person who's killed both men, why dump a couple of bodies in a nature reserve full of runners and dog walkers? No attempt at burial. It just doesn't make any sense,' said Fletcher.

'Let's try not to make any assumptions until we get the results of the PM.' Carruthers turned to Fletcher, 'Don't forget, Fraser was *killed* here. Not dumped. But I take your point about the dog walkers and runners.'

'He was found quickly enough though and let's face it, dogs are always rooting around,' she said. He called to a nearby SOCO.

'Who found him? Was it a member of the public?'

'One of the university groundsmen, sir.' She jerked her head in the man's direction. 'Over there talking on his mobile.'

Carruthers and Fletcher looked across at a man in his mid- to late-fifties clad in a dark blue boiler suit. He had long greying hair and the ruddy complexion that comes with working outdoors.

Carruthers nodded his head in greeting as a second SOCO walked by. He glanced over at the groundsman again who'd just finished his call. 'Andie, take his statement.'

'Right, boss. Will do.'

'Also, phone the station and let them know what's going on. And get a briefing set up, will you? Sometime later this afternoon. While you're at it, get Colin Jones over. We'll need a sketch to go to press.'

Striding back in the direction of Dr Mackie, who was busy getting a thermometer out of his bag, Carruthers shivered. The old saying came to mind that somebody had just walked over his grave. 'How fast can you do the post mortem?' he asked.

'I'll get it fast-tracked, laddie. We'll get it done this afternoon.'

'OK, unlikely I'll make it. Ring me with any findings as soon as you have them, will you?'

Dr Mackie saluted.

***

'Jim, have you got a wee moment?' asked DS Watson. She was carrying her jacket over her arm. Carruthers turned round.

'Coming in or going out?' he asked.

'In.'

'Good. Be quick. Brief's in five minutes.' Watson nodded. Carruthers jerked his head towards her. 'Walk with me whilst I get a coffee. Bloody freezing out there. Need something to get the circulation going again,' he said, striding towards the canteen rubbing his hands. Watson fell in to step with him. She referred to her notebook as she walked.

'We've found two people who knew Ruiridh Fraser. John Cameron, a regular from the Ship Inn, and a Mrs Gordon from Antigua Street in Cellardyke. According to Mrs Gordon, Fraser's been married. Long-time divorced but he's got a son.'

Carruthers stopped and faced her. 'Yes, I know. Give me something else.'

'According to Mrs Gordon the two had a falling out. A big one. The son moved out well over twenty years ago.'

'Now that's interesting. Do we know what the falling out was about?'

'No, but Mrs Gordon said the son was never seen again after that.'

'How would Mrs Gordon know all this if she lives in Antigua Street?'

'Her sister used to live in Bridge Street. Anyway, as far as Mrs Gordon knows, father and son didn't remain in contact, so whatever it was, must have been big.'

Carruthers scratched his nose. 'Good work. Did you get any sense from speaking to either of the two people who knew him that Fraser was into young girls?'

'None whatsoever.'

Carruthers drew in a deep breath. 'Pity. Exactly what Andie said.'

Watson looked at him aghast.

He held his hands up. 'Not saying I want a paedophile on our hands but it would have given Hunter Senior a strong motive for murder.' He started walking again, opening the door to the canteen for Watson. 'Anything else?' He held the door open whilst a couple of uniforms walked out.

'Not a huge amount. Cameron only knew Fraser since he'd been retired. Said they didn't tend to talk about the past. Fraser wasn't forthcoming talking about himself. That's borne out by what the neighbours say about him.'

'Still a man of mystery, then?' said Carruthers joining the queue.

'Aye, seems that way.'

'Do we know how long he lived at his current address?'

'Mrs Gordonhas stayed in Cellardyke for twenty years. Says Ruiridh Fraser was already living there. There is one thing though, and it might be important.'

'What?'

'Fraser knew Braidwood.'

Carruthers stopped in his tracks. 'Did he? How well?'

'Apparently over a drink he and John Cameron started talking about new developments in Fife. Fraser knew that the university had sold Braidwood to property developers. Apparently, there's a contested area of land called the orchard that the developers want to build new homes on—'

'Get to the point, Gayle.' Carruthers looked at his watch, and then at the tray of doughnuts behind the counter that seemed to be rapidly disappearing. 'I don't have time for a lesson in local planning issues right now.'

'My point, is Fraser told Cameron he remembered the orchard when it was a meadow before the university took over the buildings.'

The queue shuffled forward. There was one doughnut left. Carruthers licked his lips.

'And that would have been mid-1990s,' said Carruthers.

'Aye, but Cameron got the impression Fraser had fairly detailed knowledge of the site earlier than that.' Watson referred to her notes. 'University bought the site in 1995.'

'And before that? Who owned the site?'

'It was a drug rehab centre in the eighties, a children's home before that.'

Both fell silent. Carruthers let the pause stretch whilst he took in the latest bit of news.

'What would you like, hen?' This from the middle-aged dinner lady behind the counter.

Carruthers turned to Watson. 'So Fraser knew the site well in the past. Don't suppose we know whether he was in the habit of taking walks up at Braidwood since it became a nature reserve?'

Watson shook her head. 'No idea. And we don't know how Ruiridh Fraser felt about the proposed development, either.'

'Pity. From what Andie tells me it's definitely an angle worth exploring.'

The dinner lady cleared her throat. 'There *is* a queue.'

Carruthers looked at Watson who shook her head. 'Nothing for me, ta.' She patted her stomach. 'On a diet.'

'Coffee, black, and a doughnut, please,' said Carruthers.

'Coming right up.'

Carruthers chewed his lip, paid and cupped his coffee tightly as they left the queue. He turned to Watson. 'Did you interview anyone who had any knowledge of the proposed Braidwood development? According to Andie, local opposition's huge. Just wondered if what's going on at Braidwood had filtered to areas further away in Fife.'

'We had a slow start with the interviewing but did speak to a couple of locals in Cellardyke who knew about the development. One man in particular. Nature lover. Told me the Friends of Braidwood are a very determined campaigning group –a real thorn in the side of the developers. They've got a petition with 5,000 signatures on it. He's signed it. Knew all about it 'cos his sister lives near Braidwood and had sent him the petition online. According to his sister, there's a lot of tension between this group and the developers. He certainly didn't want the development to go ahead. Apparently, it's got pretty nasty between the two groups. There's been threats made.'

'Threats?'

'Letters from lawyers telling the protestors to back off. Threatening them with court action. That sort of thing.'

He took a sip of the scalding coffee, tasting the richness of the beans, his mind wondering just how far either group would go to get what they wanted. 'OK, good work, Gayle. I'll see you at the brief.'

***

There was a heightened air of expectancy as officers gathered in the incident room. A hush descended as Carruthers strode in. He was greeted by the smell of coffee and sweat. In the background he could hear a ringing phone. In silence he pointed to a photograph of the dead man on the incident board and turned to face his colleagues.

'As most of you know a second body's been found over at Braidwood,' said Carruthers. 'Post mortem's being done at the moment so we're still awaiting cause of death.'

'Are we dealing with a serial killer?' asked Brown smoothing his thin and rather puny looking moustache. His hair, like his 'tache, was thin and he had the rather unfortunate habit of combing it over his near-bald head like Bobby Charlton.

'Far too early to jump to that conclusion, although I would agree there's very similar MO. Both male; similar age; both sustained stab wounds.'

'And both found in the same nature reserve,' said Fletcher.

'We're still no closer to establishing why Ruiridh Fraser was killed. We now know he's been married and has a son. What we don't know is where the ex-wife and son are. Apparently, there was some sort of falling-out and it's possible they lost or cut contact with him. Could this be relevant? We need to discover whether there's anything in his background that's led to his murder. And we need to locate his family.'

'Could it no' be possible that these are just the random killings by a deranged madman?' asked Brown, picking up his mug of steaming black coffee.

'Possible but unlikely. You and I both know that most murder victims are killed by someone they know, often someone close to them. Let's just say we haven't ruled it out. In fact, we haven't ruled anything out yet. In the meantime, we need to find out who this second man is. Is he local? Did he know Ruiridh Fraser? What were they both doing at Braidwood? Fraser wasn't known to the locals near the site. We don't think he was in the habit of taking a stroll there; however, he does seem to have had intimate knowledge of the site in the past. Is this significant? According to his neighbours in Cellardyke, he was reclusive, hardly ever leaving his house. So what was he doing at Braidwood eight miles away? How did he get there? It wasn't by car. At least not his own. Had he arranged to meet someone? And if so, who and why?'

Carruthers picked up his coffee cup and drained it. 'We've now got a second suspicious death within days. You know what I'm going to say next. I'm afraid all leave is cancelled.'

There were a few groans from around the room. The loudest from Brown who'd been looking forward to a cheap holiday in Tenerife the following week. 'We also need to deal with this sensitively. With two dead bodies, the press will have a field day. We don't want to alarm the public. Right,' Carruthers grabbed his coat and shrugged it on. 'I've decided to head over to see Dr Mackie after all. See if I can chivvy him up. I'll be on my mobile.' He called over to Fletcher, 'I'll see you later,' said under his breath, 'I want you and Gayle to play nicely together. Get it?'

***

Fletcher was sitting at her desk flicking through Fraser's diary, which she'd retrieved from under a pile of Watson's paperwork. She fingered the rough edge of the stub of the ripped-out page. There were a number of reasons it could have been ripped out but being a copper she had developed a suspicious nature. Her first thought was that there was something written on it that he didn't want other people to see. Ridiculous given that he lived alone and didn't know he was about to be murdered. The more likely case was that it had a name or address on it. The page after it was blank. Holding it to her desk light she could just make out faint indentations. She reached forward to her penholder and grabbed a pencil. Lying it flat she started shading the paper. Worth a try. Held it up to the light but the indentations were too faint to make the letters legible.

'DS Fletcher? Ma'am?'

Fletcher looked up to see a young blonde woman in front of her desk.

'Thought you'd want to see this. It was almost missed. Wedged right at the bottom of the box. Knew you'd have our guts for garters if it wasn't brought to you right away.'

'What is it? And how could you miss a blue file that size?'

'Not the file, ma'am. What's in it.'

The girl, whose name was Glenys or Gladys, slipped her hand in to the file and brought out a smaller envelope.

'I've kept them all together in this envelope.'

'Them?'

'The photographs and newspaper cuttings.'

'Sorry, you've lost me.'

Fletcher opened the envelope and took out the first photograph.

'Retrieved from Ruiridh Fraser's home, ma'am.'

It was an old photograph showing four figures, two men and two boys standing close together in front of an imposing Victorian building. She didn't recognise any of the people in the photograph but she did recognise the building. The second photograph was of the two men and a boy. One of the men had been in the first photograph but this was a different boy to the two in the first picture. She then unfolded the newspaper article. There was no doubt that it was an article that was linked to the photographs. Her eyes widened in disbelief when she read the disturbing headline. She picked up her phone and made the call.

***

As Carruthers entered the mortuary his mobile started ringing. It was Watson.

'Boss, we've just had a phone call from a woman in Cupar. She's reported her husband missing. He's been missing since last night. He's about the same age as the man we've found at Braidwood.'

'OK, go and interview her, will you? And take Dougie with you. Get on the phone to Colin Jones and hurry him up for that sketch? Take it with you to show her. Keep me posted.'

'Aye, boss. Jim.'

He put the mobile away to see Jodie hurrying towards him. She was in the process of taking her lab coat off. Since last he'd seen her she'd had her hair cut. Her straight dark fringe was short across her forehead accentuating her striking eyebrows even more. Her hair was tied back out of her face and she was wearing her glasses. Carruthers fought an urge to remove them from her face and kiss her.

'Jim, Dr Mackie wants to speak with you. We've just finished the post mortem.'

'Where is he?'

'Just getting cleaned up. I need to tell you something.'

Carruthers looked at Jodie expectantly. He didn't have a chance to find out what she wanted to say as Mackie appeared. 'Jim, good timing. Come through to my office. We need to talk.'

Carruthers touched Jodie's arm. 'Will I see you later?'

She shook her head. 'I doubt it.'

'What did you want to tell me?'

'It'll keep.'

'OK, well, keep in touch.'

'Will do. You too.' He gave her the lightest of kisses on her cheek.

Carruthers hurried down the corridor after Mackie. As soon as the door was shut Mackie got straight to the point. 'He was killed by a single stab wound to the chest. Also by a left-hander. Either with the same knife or one very similar to that used to kill Ruiridh Fraser. In my professional opinion, I would say the same person's killed both men.'

'How can you be so sure?'

'There's something else.' Dr Mackie produced a clear bag, which he passed to Carruthers. Carruthers frowned. It contained a ball of white cloth.

'Extracted from the back of the victim's throat. Inserted after death.'

'Shit. Can I see the body?'

'Come this way.'

At that moment Carruthers' mobile rang. It was Fletcher. 'Jim, how's it going?'

'I'm just about to view the body. Mackie's convinced it's the same killer. Exactly the same MO.'

'OK, that doesn't surprise me.'

'Second victim was killed by a single stab wound to the chest by a left-hander, just like Ruiridh Fraser. The victim also had a piece of cloth shoved to the back of his throat.'

Fletcher whistled. 'So do we have a serial killer?'

'I honestly don't know. It's still too early to say. And we've only got two corpses.'

'Two too many. Are you coming straight back to the station, Jim?'

'I wasn't planning to.' He knew Jodie would most probably be having a cup of tea. He was hoping to join her for a quick break. 'Why?'

'There's something I need you to see. One of the support staff found it in Fraser's flat. An old photograph, and a newspaper clipping. I think they may be important.'

Carruthers grimaced, hope of a coffee with the lovely Jodie fading fast. 'OK. I'll see you shortly. I'll leave as soon as I can.'

***

Pushing a stray tendril of dark brown hair out of her face, Fletcher said, 'OK, this is what I want you to look at.'

The images were black and white, grainy. They showed a pale building surrounded by a wild flower meadow. There were more trees framing the building than the present day. To Fletcher the building itself was little changed. In front of it stood three figures – two men and a boy. The boy was about twelve years old wearing shorts and a T-shirt. One of the men, who looked about forty, had his arm round him. He was standing close.

Carruthers wondered if it was a relation. From the wide collars that the men wore and the longer hair Carruthers guessed that this photograph had been taken in the mid-1970s.

'What am I looking at?' he asked. 'This is Braidwood, isn't it?'

Fletcher nodded. 'I've been doing some digging on its history since I was given this photograph. It was retrieved from Ruiridh Fraser's home.'

'That's interesting. So in some way he must have a personal connection to the site if he's kept photographs. And?'

'The buildings on the site date back to the 1800s. Built as a private mental institution to house the wealthy of Fife.'

'I know all this, Andie.'

'All except this building known to locals as the Pink Building. It was the original building on the site and built as a private residence in the mid-1500s. It only became part of the mental institution in the 1800s.'

'What's your point?'

'Did you know that its use changed in the 1970s? For about fifteen years it was used as a children's home.'

He nodded. 'Gayle told me.'

Carruthers examined the photograph more closely. 'This photograph looks to have been taken in the 1970s, so this boy could have been a resident.'

'Very likely.'

'Do we know who he is, or who the two men are?' Carruthers turned the photograph over, but if he was hoping for a date and names, he was disappointed. It was blank.

'No, we don't, but I should imagine the two men might have been members of staff.'

He studied the figures in the photograph again. 'What were these photographs doing in Fraser's home?'

'No idea. But like you said, it does prove he had a connection with Braidwood. Take a look at this.' Fletcher handed him a sheet of paper. 'Copy of an article written for *The Fife Courier*, 25th September 1975.'

He studied it in silence. 'There were allegations of sexual abuse at the care home,' said Fletcher.

'Was there a police investigation?' asked Carruthers.

Fletcher shook her head. 'Don't think so. Certainly wasn't reported to the Procurator Fiscal.'

'Yet it got in to the papers.'

'There's some damning things said about the Chief Superintendent at the time.'

Carruthers skim read the article reading words such as 'cover-up' and 'incompetence.'

He frowned. 'Who was the chief super?'

'Man called Bob Marshall. No longer alive. I found his obituary. Died in 2001, apparently after a long and distinguished career, if his obituary is to be believed.'

'Name doesn't mean anything to me.' He took a closer look at the photograph. Fletcher saw him frown.

'What are you thinking?' she asked.

'I'm not sure. Something's not right.' He tapped the photograph. 'At first glance this looks pretty innocent, doesn't it? See the man whose arm is placed around the boy's shoulder? It looks protective. At least that's what I first thought.'

'Now?'

'In light of what you've just said now it seems possessive, proprietorial, almost creepy. Depending on how you decide to interpret the photograph you can see it in a whole new light.'

Fletcher leaned over. 'Yes, I see what you mean. The man's standing too close. He's invading the boy's personal space.'

'Look at the boy's eyes,' said Carruthers. 'They're wide and full of fear.'

Fletcher took a closer look at the boy's face. 'Poor lad. He looks terrified.'

'Of course, this photograph on its own isn't evidence of sexual abuse,' said Carruthers giving back the photo and news cutting to Fletcher, 'but there's something about it that makes me feel uncomfortable.'

'Wait,' said Fletcher. 'There's a second article you need to see.' She handed it to him.

Carruthers looked at Fletcher. 'It's a retraction of the earlier article. Been written by the editor-in-chief of the paper.'

'And an apology to Bob Marshall,' said Fletcher.

Carruthers tapped the photograph with his index finger. 'Find out if there's anyone alive who was in the job in the mid-seventies who remembers the allegations of abuse at Braidwood. Also, see if you can track down anyone who worked for *The Fife Courier* at the time. We need to interview them.'

'Right, will do, boss.' Fletcher looked up at Carruthers who had an unreadable expression in his blue eyes. She said, 'If we could find the journalist who wrote the original article before it was retracted, it would be a start.'

'And a good one.'

'What are you thinking?' said Fletcher.

'What I'm thinking is that the two men in this photo are in their late thirties to mid-forties by the looks of it which means if they are still alive today they would be in their mid-seventies to early eighties. In other words, they would both be old men. Keep digging, Andie. Great job. With a bit of luck we'll have a name for our second body soon. We'll see if he's also got any connection with Braidwood, other than spending his last few moments there. By the way, we're still trying to trace Ruiridh Fraser's ex-wife and son.'

'What about Jordan Hunter? Do we still keep that as a line of enquiry?'

'Yes we do. He may not have broken into Fraser's home or been responsible for his tyres being slashed, but he still subjected the old man to a catalogue of harassment and we still don't know why. We also need to find out why Malcolm Hunter's phone number appears on Fraser's phone bill.'

Fletcher nodded. 'Leave it with me,' she said. She watched Carruthers walk off, knowing that his mind would still be on the photograph of the boy and the two men. Like her he'd be wondering who they were and what exactly the connection was between Ruiridh Fraser and Braidwood.

Fletcher's attention was caught by a movement at the door. She turned and saw the same dark-haired PC who had given her the cuttings and photos.

'It's PC Glenys Palmer, ma'am.'

'Of course it is. Don't be shy. What have you got for me?'

'PC Miller found it, ma'am, in Fraser's personal effects. It's a letter. Thought it might be important.'

Fletcher raised her eyebrows. 'You've read it?'

Glenys nodded. 'Written to Ruiridh Fraser from his son, Paul.'

She handed it over to Fletcher, who struggled to recognise the stamps on the envelope. She angled it so she could see the postmark. 'It's been sent from Reykjavik,' said Fletcher.

'Yes, ma'am, that's in Iceland, ma'am.'

'I know where Reykjavik is, Glenys.'

Glenys' face fell. Fletcher retrieved the letter from the envelope. It had been written three months before the old man's death. It was short and to the point, leaving Fletcher in no doubt as to how Paul Fraser felt about his father. And from the contents of the letter there was every chance Jordan Hunter was no longer the main suspect. She downed tools and went in search of Carruthers.

CHAPTER SEVEN

The following day was crisp and clear but raw, the temperature having plummeted overnight. As Carruthers hurried from his car to the station, the wind bit his face, making his cheeks feel as if they'd been skinned.

Ten minutes later he was sitting at his desk deep in conversation with Fletcher about the letter the team had unearthed the day before. 'I know this now makes Paul Fraser the main suspect,' she said, handing the letter once more to her boss.

He scanned each line, his keen blue eyes missing nothing. Having left the whisky alone the night before he felt much clearer-headed this morning than he had on previous mornings. He vowed once more not to drink during the week. And, mercifully, his sleep had been dreamless. But he still hadn't plucked up the courage to call his brother. He was starting to detest himself for his cowardice. He'd had friends who'd been ill before but it hadn't been like this. It was all just too close to home. If he didn't think about it, perhaps he could pretend it wasn't happening. He forced himself back to the contents of the letter. Scratching his chin he looked up at Fletcher. 'He hated his father. That much is clear.'

'It doesn't get much more explicit than this.' Carruthers pointed to a line three quarters of the way down the first page. 'He says he'll kill his father if he ever tries to contact him again. But he doesn't say why.'

'There's certainly a lot of anger in the letter,' said Fletcher, 'but we all say things in the heat of the moment we don't mean. That's the problem with the printed word. Once it's written down it can't so easily be taken back. Perhaps he was having a bad day when he wrote it.'

'Or maybe he meant it.' Carruthers dropped the letter to the table. 'We need to interview him. Find out if he's got an alibi.' Carruthers straightened up from his position leaning over Fletcher's desk. 'I'm going to fix myself a coffee. Get you one?'

Fletcher shook her head, picking up the photographs that had been found alongside the letter. 'No, I'm good, thanks.'

***

As she stared at the photograph she and Carruthers had been looking at the day before, she absentmindedly began to tap it, a curious expression on her face. There was something fundamental she was missing. What was it? She ceased tapping and brought it up closer, scrutinising the faces of the two men and boy. The boy was dark-haired, like Jordan Hunter, but that's where the similarity ended. The boy in the photo must have been about three years younger.

'Christ, why didn't I see this before?' She stood up abruptly, went in search of Jim. Found him thumping the coffee machine.

'Frigging machine. Just eaten my money.'

'Jim, can I talk to you for a moment. I know Paul Fraser's now most likely our prime suspect but say that letter *was* nothing but an empty threat. If we factor him out for a moment–' She looked up at her boss, her words tumbling out in a rush. 'What if we got the wrong kid, Jim?'

'What do you mean?'

'Just that the photographs I saw of Braidwood have made me think. That's all. What if Ruiridh Fraser *did* have an eye for one of the Hunter kids, but what if we got the *wrong* kid? What if it wasn't the girl but the boy? That would explain Jordan's hostility towards the old man. And say Fraser's interest in boys goes back several decades, it would explain why he has those newspaper cuttings *and* would also give him a direct connection to Braidwood.'

Fletcher watched her boss process the information. 'Reckon we need to talk to the Hunters again,' said Fletcher. 'We need to speak to Mr Hunter, anyway. Perhaps he's been warning Fraser off Jordan.'

'Hold that thought, Andie. I've a meeting in five with Bingham.' He bashed the machine with his fist one last time, to no effect. As he walked away he threw the next words back over his shoulder at her, 'I can't help but think Paul Fraser's relationship with his father is still key in all this.'

The machine sprung in to action and Fletcher watched as it dispensed a double espresso.

***

'I want to fly out to Iceland so I can interview Paul Fraser.' Carruthers was standing in Superintendent Bingham's office, having waved aside the hard-backed chair he'd been offered. He'd rather stand than be at an inferior height. Always felt he was being interviewed for a job when he sat in that chair. He gripped the edge of Bingham's mahogany table tightly.

Bingham shook his head. 'We don't have the budget, Jim. You can't go over on a whim.'

'With all due respect, sir, it's hardly a whim.'

'At the moment, we have no evidence whatsoever that links Paul Fraser to his father's murder.'

'Except the letter. A letter written by Paul Fraser threatening his father with physical violence should he ever try to contact him again. That's enough for me.'

Bingham banged his fist down hard on the table, spilling his own milky coffee. His penholder rattled. 'Bugger,' he said mopping up the spillage with a hanky from his pocket. He looked up at Carruthers with a frown. 'You're not a DCI anymore, Carruthers, and you've got to stop acting like one. You're lucky you've still got your old office. That is, until a new DCI is appointed.'

Carruthers flinched.

Bingham continued, 'It's not a DI's business to go flying all round Europe.'

Carruthers bristled. Straightened up but dug the nails on his hands in to his palms. Steadied his breathing before speaking. 'There's a connection between the death of Ruiridh Fraser and the relationship he had with his son. I know there is. I want to talk to him.'

'I'm sorry, but like I said, the answer's "No". We've got people over there who can do that.'

Carruthers turned, taking a step towards the door. Turning back, he said 'I'll fund myself.'

Bingham's lips pursed in a slash across his face.

Carruthers continued, 'And take annual leave.'

Carruthers' boss shook his head. 'You know all leave's out of the question during a murder investigation. Anyway, your best line of enquiry from this end is that Jordan boy.'

Shaking his head Carruthers said, 'Look, I might be going out on a limb here but I don't believe Jordan Hunter murdered Ruiridh Fraser. For a start, he's a minor who doesn't drive.'

'There's plenty of teenage killers out there,' said Bingham, dropping the sodden coffee-stained handkerchief in to the bin. 'So do you think it's the father, then? Malcolm Hunter?'

'We'll be checking alibis. But it's something Andie said that's got me thinking. She thinks Ruiridh Fraser may have been a serial sexual abuser of boys.'

Bingham's eyes narrowed. 'A paedophile?'

'It would explain the rift in the relationship with his son.'

'You're telling me you think Fraser sexually abused his own son?'

'Why not? He wouldn't be the first perverted father.'

'And the link with Jordan Hunter would be?'

'It's simple, sir. Jordan Hunter's an attractive teenage boy who lives next door to a possible paedophile. Fraser put the moves on him, comes on to him, made a pass at him, whatever you want to call it. And it also ties Fraser in with Braidwood.'

'So who killed him?'

Carruthers shrugged. 'Well, if it's not Jordan or Malcolm Hunter, perhaps one of the care home residents he abused tracked him down.'

'Forty years later?'

'Why not?' said Carruthers. Bingham remained silent, running his top lip over his bristles. Carruthers continued, sensing a change of heart, and a weakness he could exploit. 'We originally thought Fraser'd put the moves on Jordan's sister. But the more I think about it, well, Andie might be right.'

'All this is guesswork, Carruthers. Pure guesswork.'

'Not completely. You're forgetting one thing.'

'What's that?'

'The photograph and newspaper cutting found in Fraser's flat. The article was about allegations of sexual abuse against the boys in the home. What would Fraser's interest be in that? Why would you keep a newspaper article for over forty years on such a sordid subject?'

'Christ, Carruthers, I've got articles at home on the Dambusters. Doesn't make me one. See my point?' Bingham shook his head. 'That is *not* proof he was a paedophile or had an interest in teenage boys, as well you know. Perhaps he was an amateur local historian.'

Carruthers snorted. 'No, it isn't proof, but it certainly makes a lot of sense. Give me a chance to hear what Paul Fraser has to say about his father.'

'A phone call would achieve that.'

Carruthers shook his head. 'A phone call's not the same. I want to interview him face to face. At the very least he'll be able to shed some light on what sort of man his father was. If neither he nor the Hunters are responsible for Fraser's death, it might point us in the direction of the person who is. We now have two men dead, most likely killed by the same person. I think Ruiridh Fraser's past life might just be key.'

Bingham remained silent.

'I'll only be gone a couple of days.'

There was a laboured sigh across the big desk. 'Christ. You'd better bring me that bloody travel requisition form before I change my mind.'

Carruthers headed straight back to the coffee machine. Would risk giving it another try. He punched in his request for a black coffee and heard the machine spring in to action. No sooner had his hand wrapped round the scalding cup when Fletcher appeared behind him.

'Call's just come in from Dougie, Jim. There's been a positive ID on the second body. His name's Henry Noble. He stays in Kirkcaldy. They can't interview the wife yet, she's collapsed. GP's in attendance, had to give her a strong sedative.'

'Shit,' said Carruthers, 'OK, tell Dougie to stay with her. She needs to be interviewed as soon as possible.' He turned to Fletcher. 'Speaking with the Hunters will have to wait. I'm going to head over to Kirkcaldy myself. Stay here, will you? Find out if Malcolm Hunter's got an alibi?' He gave Fletcher his coffee, jerked his head towards the cup. You might want to put some milk in that.

He was half way to Kirkcaldy when he remembered he hadn't picked up a travel requisition form.

***

'Fletcher tried and failed to reach Malcolm Hunter either on the mobile or on his house phone. However, her research paid off. She found out that the editor-in-chief of *The Fife Courier* in the mid-1970s had been Alan Stewart. Unfortunately, her research also revealed that he'd died the year before. More hopeful was finding that the reporter who'd written the original piece about child abuse was still alive and living in Fife. She'd found his home phone number and left a message on his answer machine. The gruff voice had been of a man, possibly in his sixties.'

Peckish, Fletcher headed to the canteen for a quick snack. Her thoughts turned back to Jordan Hunter. They should interview the boy again. This time asking some searching questions about his relationship with Ruiridh Fraser.

She bolted her sausage roll, burning her mouth on the coffee she had to swill it down. She was only gone ten minutes but on her way back to her desk found Watson approaching her.

'Andie, you've just had a phone call from a Mr Dawson.'

Fletcher's expression was blank, her mind still on the Hunters.

'He used to work for *The Fife Courier* in the 1970s?' continued Watson. 'You left a message for him?'

'Oh, of course,' said Fletcher. 'Yes, I did.'

'He's willing to meet up. Said it's time. Does that mean anything to you?'

Fletcher shook her head.

'Here's his number anyway.'

Fletcher thanked her and phoned the number she'd been given. It was engaged. Swearing, she replaced the receiver and spotted Glenys heading towards her. The younger girl's cheeks were flushed.

'Ma'am. They've found the death certificate of a Margery Fraser, wife of Ruiridh Fraser.'

'Right, thanks for letting me know Glenys.'

'Is there anything else I can do for you?'

'No, I think that's well, actually, you drive don't you Glenys?'

'Of course, ma'am.'

'And you live near Cupar? Am I right?'

'Yes, actually in Cupar itself.'

Fletcher rifled through her desk drawer, making a grab for her car keys. She gave them to Glenys. 'Look, you'll be doing me a huge favour. Can you drop off the contents of the boot of my car to this address on your way home?' She scribbled the address of Mark's parents on to a Post-it note.

'Sure, ma'am. I'll just transfer the contents now, if you don't mind. I'm on a break.'

'Actually, I've changed my mind.' Fletcher grabbed the piece of paper out of Glenys' hands, crumpled it and dropped it in to her wastepaper bin.

'You don't want me to take the stuff out of the boot of your car?' The girl was all for giving the keys back to Fletcher.

'No, no. I do. But I don't want them delivered to that address.'

'Where then?'

'Take them to the nearest charity shop,' replied Fletcher.

***

Having debated whether to interview the Hunters again or to return to Braidwood, Fletcher opted for the latter. Carruthers had already disappeared and she was loath to take Watson with her. Harris was on another job. However, there was no way she could pitch up on her own again without getting into serious trouble.

Instead, Fletcher headed for the local library at Braidwood. She knew this wasn't a job for her rank but felt it was something she needed to do herself. And if Carruthers was at Henry Noble's house ready to interview the man's widow, then that was that base covered. She'd also managed to touch base on the phone with Angus Dawson, who, once he'd heard about the death of his old editor-in-chief at *The Fife Courier* the year before, had been surprisingly willing to talk. In fact, he'd been more than happy to meet up to discuss the article he'd written about allegations of sexual abuse at Braidwood. Allegations he had maintained were true and for which, he'd told Fletcher, he got sacked.

Speaking with Dawson, Fletcher had the impression the man had been threatened as well as sacked, so she was looking forward to the interview and, she hoped, getting one over Watson, as well as furthering the investigation. As she drove in to the main street and looked for a parking spot, she thought what a pity it was that the earliest he could make it was seven that evening.

Parking her green Beetle in the main street by the church tower she entered the old stone library, previously the village school, according to the stone inscription above the front door. She spotted a librarian– a rather buxom lady in her fifties who wore a pair of old fashioned looking spectacles on a chain round her neck.

'Can I help you, dearie?'

She was taken aback by a Nottingham accent in the heart of Fife but felt strangely comforted. One of her best pals from uni had the same accent. She thought of Kim now and wondered how she was doing.

'Yes, please. How would I access local newspapers from the mid-1970s? Would it be by CD or microfiche?'

'Well, we certainly don't have newspapers going that far back on CD yet. They're all still on microfiche. Are you familiar with how to use microfiche, dear?'

'Yes I am. Can you let me know where they are?'

'Certainly. Come this way.'

After an hour Fletcher still hadn't found anything on Braidwood. She sighed and stretched her arms behind her back in a cat-like pose. Her whole body felt tense from a mixture of bad posture and concentration. Her neck muscles ached. She gave them a rub.

'No joy?' asked the lady, who was now putting books back on the shelves behind her.

'Fraid not.'

'What is it that you're looking for?'

'I'm interested in the history of Braidwood.'

The lady frowned. 'That's strange. I've had two other enquiries this week about Braidwood. It must be because of the murder.'

News of the second murder clearly hadn't yet reached her. Fletcher's ears pricked up. 'Two other enquiries? Who from?' Fletcher fished out her ID. The woman put her glasses on and leant forward to study it.

'Both men.' She bent over her trolley and put another book back on the shelf. She straightened up and looked at Fletcher again. 'Honestly, I didn't pay much attention. One man was in his mid-fifties, early sixties and the other was younger, perhaps in his mid-forties.'

'Can you describe them to me?'

'Well, the older man was kind of nondescript, you know – medium height, brown hair, although he did have a big build. I remember that.'

'What about the other?'

'The younger guy had a narrow face, eyes close together. He was sort of shifty. He looked like some sort of wild animal, like a weasel.'

Fletcher frowned. It sounded like the librarian was describing the man she'd seen at the meeting sitting next to Buchanan. Told herself it wasn't surprising that the developers would be doing research on the history of the site they'd purchased.

'Do you think you'd recognise them if you saw them again?' said Fletcher.

'I honestly don't know. Maybe.' The librarian bent over and picked up another couple of books. One fell out of her hands and Fletcher bent down to retrieve it. 'Thank you. You might want to try the campus up at Braidwood. It has its own library in the Old Braids building.'

'That would be the Pink Building?'

'That's right. The university's moving out in the spring, but they still have all the inherited archives from when it was a private mental institution.'

'Would I also find information about when it was a children's home?'

'That's really odd. That's exactly what the older man asked.'

'When was he in?'

'Two days ago. He seemed in a bit of a hurry. He wasn't too polite, if I remember rightly. There's no call for bad manners, is there?'

'Did you give them the same information you gave me?'

'No, I didn't. It's strange. I'm not usually unhelpful but there was just something about him… I didn't feel like giving him any extra information.'

Fletcher had fished out her notebook and opened it up. 'Did they both have local accents?'

'No, just the older man. The younger man had a southern accent.'

'Southern? Can you be more specific?'

'I s'pose you'd call it "Home Counties", dearie.'

***

As Fletcher drove through the gates she took in the lay of the land. The Victorian buildings of the old mental hospital dotted the landscape. There was a glorious open feel to the nature reserve. She parked at the bottom car park. From there it was less than a five-minute walk to Old Braids. The light was already fading and a low pink sunset provided a stunning backdrop to the rough rose coloured sandstone of the sixteenth century building. She could see why it was known as the Pink Building. With her back to the old building she took in the sweeping vista of the area of land known affectionately as The Orchard and marvelled that anyone would be callous enough to want to build on it.

Fletcher had called ahead, spoken to Sarah Harrison, a member of the Fife university staff, who was to meet her at the entrance. Standing by the original wooden front door, Fletcher looked up at the enormous mansion with its tiny windows and slanted slate roof. There was a Latin inscription in stone above the doorway. She wondered what it meant.

'I was coming down to greet you,' the voice belonged to a pretty girl Fletcher estimated to be in her early thirties. She was wearing knee-length black boots, a plaid mini skirt and plain white blouse. 'When I saw the car, I wasn't sure you were the lady I was supposed to meet.' She laughed. 'I can't imagine many police officers drive green Beetles. It's very distinctive.'

'No, well, officially we're meant to drive a car from the car pool. But I'm rather fond of driving her. So, what gave it away? Do I look like a police officer?'

'No, not at all. Sorry I don't mean for that to sound rude. It's just I expected you to be wearing a uniform.'

'We don't wear uniforms in CID.'

'Of course not. I'd totally forgotten I'd be interviewed by CID. Look, sorry, I don't want you to be kept standing out in the cold. Please come in. I'm Sarah Harrison, by the way.' She put her hand out and Fletcher shook it. 'I'm a little nervy about spending time outside since the murders. I get my boyfriend to drop me off and pick me up. He sees me right to the door.'

'Very sensible. Detective Sergeant Andie Fletcher.'

'Andie? That's a boy's name.'

'Not the way I spell it.'

Fletcher followed Sarah Harrison up a steep flight of stairs. 'Horrible to think there's a murderer on the loose,' said Sarah.

'If it's any comfort, it's highly unlikely the public at large are at risk.'

'You mean he would have known both the victims?' asked Sarah.

'That's a line we're pursuing,' said Andie. 'I mean, it's more likely, yes. Most murders are committed by people the victim knows.'

'I understand you're interested in the history of Braidwood?' said Sarah.

'Yes, I am,' said Fletcher, noticing the smooth worn tread in the stairs. The stairwell was narrow and uneven. If she reached her arms out, she could have easily touched both stone walls.

Sarah talked over her shoulder as she climbed. 'Well, you won't be disappointed. It certainly has an interesting one. For example, this building's the oldest on site, dating back to 1537. It replaced an even earlier building that got burnt down during the time of the "Rough Wooing".'

'Rough Wooing?' repeated Fletcher. 'What was that?'

'Lovely name, isn't it? It marks the time of the conflict that took place between Scotland and England. Dates were about 1543–1550.'

'Crikey, you've got a good memory.'

'Almost photographic, I'm afraid. Great for exams but can be annoying at other times.'

Fletcher had never really met anyone with a photographic memory before and wondered at what times it could be annoying, but she kept quiet.

They reached the top of the stairs and Fletcher paused to admire the thick embossed flock wallpaper. She ran her hand over it, liking the feel of its velvety contours and the look of the still bright colours. She turned to Sarah. 'This looks old.'

'It is. We think it dates back to the 1850s. We've had folk come in with cameras and take photographs of it.'

Fletcher raised an eyebrow. 'Rough Wooing?' she asked.

'Oh yes, war was declared by King Henry VIII in an attempt to force Scots to agree to a marriage between his son Edward and the infant Mary Queen of Scots. The Scots refused. Wouldn't be bullied into love, you might say. In 1544 major hostilities were declared. The Earl of Hertford was sent up with an army to destroy Edinburgh and places across Fife. They were heading to Castletown but never got that far. They burnt towns and cities right across Lothians and Fife. Old Braids was one of the last properties that got burnt to the ground.'

Fletcher was fascinated that the very building she was standing in had been the site of such violence.

'Bloodthirsty time,' said Sarah, 'but I understand you're interested in a more recent time in our history?' She took a key out of her pocket and unlocked a door to the right of the landing. She led Fletcher in to a small, low-ceilinged room with a tiny east-facing window that looked out across the car park and meadow. 'Watch your footing,' said Sarah, 'Flooring's uneven.'

'Right. Will do. Yes, I am. Specifically the time it was a children's home in the 1970s. Don't suppose you've any records or photographs of the children in its care, or of the care workers?'

'Well, all archived material on Braidwood is kept in those boxes over there.' She indicated several large boxes on the floor underneath the narrow window. 'As you can see, I've already got them out for you. Not much of a system, I'm afraid. We were going to sort through them and get them in to hanging files but we just never got round to it. Seems rather pointless now the university'll be moving to Dundee. My uncle, on my father's side, was in care for a short time here. I guess you could say I've got a personal interest.' She bent down to pull the large cardboard box in to the centre of the room. 'Funny to think forty years later I'm working at the same place.'

'It's quite a coincidence,' Fletcher agreed.

Sarah turned to go and said, 'If you have any questions just ask.'

Fletcher nodded her thanks, and once Sarah left the room, she stepped out of her heeled shoes, hitched her skirt with her hands and knelt down by the box Sarah had pulled out. She began to rake through it, removing a couple of heavy-framed photographs and several smaller black and white ones. She studied each in turn. One was of the inside of a building, an enormous ornate wooden hall. It looked as if it would be used for assemblies, or as a refectory. The ceiling was domed. Definitely a room from a bygone age.

The door opened a few minutes later and in came Sarah carrying a mug. 'Thought you might like some tea.'

'That's really kind of you. Thanks.'

'You do take milk?'

'That's fine.' She took the mug from Sarah and held out the photo to her. 'Tell me, where is this?'

'It's a beautiful room, isn't it? It's in New Braids. The building next to this one.'

'What's it used for?'

'It's not often used nowadays. It used to be a dining room. I don't know what will happen to it when the flats are developed. Bit of a shame, really. There's such a sadness attached to this place. Past and present. When you think about all those broken lives...'

'You mean when it was a children's home?' asked Fletcher.

'Not just that. Also when it was used for caring for the mentally ill. You know the second body was discovered in the old Victorian vegetable garden?'

Fletcher raised her eyebrows. 'Go on. I'm intrigued.'

Sarah continued. 'The residents were encouraged to grow their own fruit and veg. Braidwood as a mental hospital in the nineteenth century was a very progressive place. Even then it was realised tending the land was good for one's mental health. Did you know New Braids was deliberately built so it was south facing to maximise the light coming in through those enormous Victorian widows.'

'We could learn a lot from them,' said Fletcher.

Sarah retreated to the door. She laughed. 'I've bored you enough. Anyway, better get back to it. You know where I am if you need me.'

Fletcher placed the photo carefully on the carpet. She picked up another one. Again, it was black and white. It had been taken in the grounds of Braidwood, another imposing Victorian building as backdrop. In its centre were five figures, three men and two boys. Her heart started racing. It was very similar to one of the photographs that had been found in Fraser's flat. Same boys. She was sure of it. Same two men… but wait. Who was the third man? And there was another difference. A big difference. One of the men was wearing a uniform. A police uniform. Fletcher frowned. She turned the photograph over. Overleaf it read: SE Hinton, JF Milne, HJ Noble, William Rutherford and Superintendent Bob Marshall, 1973.

Her heart jumped. She felt a sharp nervy feeling in her chest. HJ Noble? Could it be a coincidence? If this was the same man who'd been found dead at the nature reserve, then this was the connection they were looking for. And what would the superintendent be doing there? She studied the photograph more closely. Brought out her black notebook from her briefcase. Briskly turning the pages until she found what she was looking for. Muttering to herself said, 'Allegations of abuse reported in *The Fife Courier* on 25 September 1975.'

As she got up her knees cracked. She slipped her heeled shoes back on, smoothed her skirt and left the room, photo in hand. She tapped on the next door and stuck her head round. Sarah was typing away at her computer.

'I just wondered… if you knew anything about this photograph?' asked Fletcher.

Sarah held out her hand for it. She studied it, turning it over as she did so, reading the back. 'All I know is the name William Rutherford. He was head of the children's home here. I remember my grandmother talking about him. Of course, he must have been fifty-odd in this, so he might be dead by now. Apparently, he was well known in the local community… Did a lot of charity work.'

'You don't know either of the other two men? Ever heard of an H Noble?'

Sarah shook her head. 'No, sorry.'

'So this photograph was definitely taken when Braidwood was a children's home?'

'Yes, absolutely. Look, do you see the two kids in the photo?' She gave it back to Fletcher. 'They're wearing a type of uniform, aren't they? They were sticklers for rules at the home apparently, one of them being that the boys had to wear uniform.' It was true. Both boys were kitted out in almost identical grey trousers and white tops. 'I've done a bit of research on Braidwood. But don't get your hopes up if you have lots of questions. I probably won't know the answer to most of them.'

'It's interesting that the head of the home's standing with a police officer. What do you know of allegations of child abuse from the time?'

'I know there *were* allegations of abuse at Braidwood but that's about *all* I know. Sorry.'

'Did your uncle tell you?'

Sarah shook her head. 'No, he didn't like to talk about his time here. I was sorting out some archived material and came across an old newspaper article. Should be in the box.' Fletcher wondered if it was a copy of the same article she'd read. If Sarah's uncle hadn't talked about his time at Braidwood, and Sarah had read the same article as her, then she probably knew no more than Andie did. She felt a momentary pang of disappointment. The photograph at least was proof that Superintendent Marshall had visited Braidwood at least once and that an H Noble had been present. But was it the same H Noble? She wondered what Carruthers had found out talking to the widow. But from the broad smile on the policeman's face it looked more like an exercise in PR than a visit to talk about alleged child abuse. Of course, the dates were all wrong. Allegations of abuse had appeared in the newspapers two years later. So what was Superintendent Marshall doing at Braidwood? Fletcher frowned.

'Can I borrow this photograph?' asked Fletcher.

'Would you mind taking a photocopy of it?'

'Yes of course. Would I also be able to speak with your uncle?'

Sarah shook her head again.'Fraid not. He died in 2008. Suicide.'

'I'm sorry.'

Both women were silent for a moment.

Sarah took a deep breath in. 'He had a history of depression. I often wonder if it came from his time in care…'

'So you never got to speak to him about it? His time in care, I mean?'

'No. I didn't. It's not the sort of thing a niece would ask an uncle about. My father tried to speak to him but it was hard to get him to open up.'

'I'm sorry to be asking so many questions, especially as they're clearly bringing up painful memories.'

'Not too much for me, but they would be painful for my father.'

Fletcher turned to Sarah. 'From what little you've been told, do you know what Braidwood would have been like as a home in the 1970s?'

Looking at her through narrowed eyes Sarah said, 'You think the bodies found here are related to its time as a children's home, don't you?'

'It's a possibility. We just don't know. But it's definitely an angle worth pursuing.'

Sarah shook her head. 'I'm sorry I can't be more help. I really don't know very much. I meant to do some research and find out more… even bought a book on it.'

'On Braidwood?' Fletcher's voice showed the hope she felt.

'No, no not Braidwood. But about what it was like to be in care. I was trying to understand whether my uncle's depression and suicide could be linked to his time here… I never read it. The blurb on the back was enough to put me off. Too close to home after all, I guess.'

'Don't suppose you've still got the book?'

'On my shelf at home. Couldn't bring myself to read it or give it away.'

Feeling a ray of hope that she might glean something Fletcher said, 'Would you be able to dig it out for me?'

Sarah smiled and nodded. 'Sure.'

Fletcher looked at the photograph again. Both boys were standing ramrod straight. Neither was smiling. This in marked contrast to the men. These were the same boys she had seen in the earlier photograph. There was the same kid with the dark hair that had reminded her of Jordan Hunter.

Pointing at one, she said to Sarah, 'You don't know what happened to any of the kids?'

She shook her head again. 'No idea. Don't think there are any records. At least none I've come across. Won't be anything in the boxes anyway.'

Fletcher looked thoughtful. 'Thanks, Sarah. That's really helpful. Do you think there's anyone in your family I could talk to about your uncle's experience here? I know he didn't exactly open up, but any information at all might be useful.'

'Well, there's my mum. I lost my dad last year.' She turned to Fletcher, 'I'll ask her.'

'Oh, I'm sorry to hear that. You said the head of the home was known for his charitable work. Would your mum know what charities he supported?'

'She might. Like I said, I'll ask.' Sarah looked shy. 'If you've got any more questions just pop in. I don't get many visitors up here so it's rather nice to chat.'

'Nobody recently?'

'No, I think very few people realise this is a public archive.' At that moment, Sarah's phone rang. She gave Fletcher an apologetic look and picked it up. Fletcher crept out of the office, shutting the door on the way out. She went back to the room with the archive and took her phone out of her bag. No reception. She went downstairs, out of the front door, mobile in hand. Walking away from the thick-walled stone building she watched as the phone showed two then three bars. Punched in Carruthers' mobile number. Stood shivering, she waited for the connection, speaking as soon as she heard his voice.

'Jim, it's Andie here.'

'Andie, where are you?' There seemed to be a lot of interference on the line. She could hardly hear him. He sounded as if he was on a train.

She shouted, 'I'm up at Old Braids, the Pink Building on Braidwood. I've just been going through the archives.'

She heard him say something but couldn't make out what it was as his voice kept cutting out. 'Jim, I can hardly hear you. Look, will you meet me later? Say in a couple of hours. I'll be back at the station. I've come across—' She suddenly realised that the line was dead. 'Oh, shit.' She phoned him back immediately, turning her body away from a gust of cold wind that cut right through her. It went straight to his voicemail. 'Bollocks.' With numb hands she wrapped her cardigan tighter around her and returned indoors.

Still deep in thought she put her mobile on a nearby table top. When she'd gone through the remainder of the box, having got Sarah to take some copies of anything she thought might be important, she replaced the photos and box. Grabbing her things, she picked up her shoulder bag and headed into Sarah's office.

'That's me away.' Glancing at the original photos lying by the side of the copier, she said, 'Do you want me to—'

'Don't worry. I'll put them away.'

Fletcher gave Sarah her business card and said goodbye. Retracing her steps back downstairs to the front door, she ran her hand over the fading ancient flock wallpaper as she went, feeling like a naughty schoolgirl. She liked the texture of the raised surfaces of the wallpaper and noted the deterioration in places from the oils and acids of human touch. The whole building reeked of history and she hoped that when it was converted in to a house its uniqueness wouldn't be lost.

The weather had changed. A light drizzle starting to fall. The air was feeling a few degrees warmer than it had in the morning. Glancing at her watch she decided to retrace her steps to the boiler house where the second body had been found.

It was a five-minute walk from Old Braids. Buttoning up her coat, she threw her bag over her shoulder and set off on the tarmacked road behind the Pink Building. Within a couple of minutes she had taken a right on to the coarse stony path that led to the cluster of graffiti-covered boiler houses. By the time she'd reached the first, the drizzle had turned in to a steady rain. Cursing, she turned her collar up against it. She walked past the rhododendrons and ugly elders to the entrance of the boiler house where the man's body had been discovered.

The more she thought about it, the more she felt that not only were the two deaths connected, but that they were both connected to Braidwood's troubled past. She thought back to the photograph. What had Chief Superintendent Bob Marshall been doing at Braidwood? He had been wearing his uniform. What official business would have brought him to the home in 1973?

There was an eerie silence in this place where death had caught its prey. The only noise or colour the police tape fluttering in the wind. Casting her mind back to her last visit she saw the murder scene as it had been then. Saw everything. Every last detail. Replayed it, wondering if she had missed anything. The legs of the deceased sticking out from the shed. Dr Mackie leaning over the torso, glasses perched on the bridge of his nose. Blinding flashes of white light, like strobe at a nightclub, as Liu, nimble footed as ever, took his series of photographs. She took a step back and heard a twig snap like a gunshot. Frowned.

The sound had come from behind her, not underfoot.

She whipped round. Nobody there. Must have been an animal. Still, she started to feel uneasy. Watched the rain dripping off the elder trees making pools on the ground. The place felt bleak and unloved, the smell of decay earthy and pungent.

Another twig cracked right behind her. Before she had a chance to swing round she felt a painful blow to the side of her head. Everything went black. Woozily she staggered, trying to clutch the stone wall beside her – dimly aware of a shadowy dark figure. She heard the far away calling of a woman's voice. But the blow was too forceful, the darkness closed in and she fell.

***

'Andie, what the hell happened? Are you OK?'

Carruthers was sitting by her side in the hospital, his eyes searching her face, taking in the plaster over her right eye. He swallowed hard. She looked so small and pale in her hospital bed.

Fletcher tried to sit up but her movement was slow.

'Don't try to sit up.'

'Don't worry. Looks worse than it is. It wasn't a hard whack but I gashed my head on a rock as I fell, apparently. They're keeping me in overnight for observation. I guess it's because it's a head wound.'

'Are you up to talking? I won't stay long. The nurse has only given me a couple of minutes with you.'

'I'm a little groggy, that's all. And I feel as if I've got half of the Man United team stomping around in my head… but yeah, I'm OK to talk. Just got a blinding headache. No worse than when I drink tequila.'

Carruthers smiled at her trying to be so brave. 'Wayne Rooney with hobnailed boots. Not a pretty image. Well, talk me through what happened from the moment you arrived at Old Braids.'

Fletcher struggled to sit up. 'My bag. Got something important. Need to show you.'

Carruthers leant over and gently restrained her by laying a hand on her shoulder. 'Take it easy.' He stood up. 'I'll ask one of the nurses for your bag. No moving until I get back.' He left the ward and flagged down a passing blonde-haired nurse.

'No, I'm sorry. I was here when your colleague was admitted and she didn't have a bag on her. It's certainly not here in the hospital.'

'I just heard,' said Fletcher when Carruthers walked back in. He sat back down in the visitor's chair. 'Must have been after what was in the bag.' She turned to Carruthers. 'How could they have known? Unless they followed me into the building. Who found me, Jim?'

'Sarah Harrison. Apparently, you left your Blackberry up at Old Braids. She came after you.'

'I thought I heard a woman shouting. That was the last thing I remember.' Fletcher winced as she reached over to the table for a glass of water. Carruthers helped her half sit up and angled the straw towards her. She took a sip and, with Carruthers' help, lay down against the pillows once again. 'I'll have to thank her. She might have saved my life. I'm surprised she left the building. Told me she doesn't like being outside on her own.' Fletcher let out a sigh.

'Are you in pain?' Carruthers asked.

'Yes, but that's not why I sighed. Just trying to remember what else I had in my bag.' Her face brightened. 'Credit cards were in my other bag. Thank goodness. Car keys, but I've got another set in the house.' Fletcher groaned. 'My police notebook was in the bag. Shit!' She turned to Carruthers. 'Mostly they were photocopies that I had in the bag. The original documents and photos are with Sarah.'

'Not any more. Whilst she was waiting with you for the ambulance, someone sneaked into the building and took the originals.'

Fletcher groaned. 'I left them by the photocopier. Sarah said she would put them back. Oh shit.' Again Fletcher tried to ease herself in to the seated position. She winced.

'Stop trying to move.'

'Jim, what have you found out? Any developments your end? Then I'll tell you about the photographs.'

'Well, yes, Bingham's agreed to me flying out to Iceland to interview Paul Fraser.'

'How did you wangle that? You know what he's like about budgets. How did the interview with Henry Noble's widow go?'

He shook his head. 'Too heavily sedated to talk. Waste of time me being there.'

'Jim, I need to tell you about the photographs—'

'Look, Sarah Harrison is here at the hospital. She's come to see you. Don't worry. I can get a lot of the information I need from her. I'm going to interview her here, and then, if you're up to it, the nurse said that she could just pop in for a few minutes and say hi.'

'No, don't go. She's an archivist, not a copper. I need to tell you myself.' She was tugging on his sleeve. He knew not to try to stop her when in full flow. He sat back down. 'I found a photograph… similar to the one picked up at the home of Ruiridh Fraser. Same era. Same dark-haired boy. Another man in the group. An H Noble.'

Carruthers' ears pricked up.

Fletcher continued. 'It could be a coincidence but we need to find out if Henry Noble worked at Braidwood. The names of the people in the photo were marked on the back. William Rutherford, head of the children's home and Chief Superintendent Bob Marshall, alongside H Noble, with two boys. It was during the time the place was a children's home. Marshall was in uniform. What was Marshall's connection to Scott and the children's home, Jim? Oh fuck.' She struggled again to sit up. 'The interview.'

'What interview?'

'I'd set up a meeting to interview a man called Angus Dawson. Seven tonight at the Braidwood Gardens Hotel. In 1976 he was a reporter for *The Fife Courier*. Responsible for running the story about the alleged abuse at Braidwood, until it got pulled by the editor-in-chief.'

Carruthers retrieved his mobile out of his jacket pocket. 'You won't make the meeting. I'll phone Gayle. See if she can make it.'

'He lost his job over that piece he wrote. Angus Dawson. Told me on the phone, abuse took place, that it wasn't a one-off incident. Said he got threatened, told to issue a retraction. Felt he had no choice.'

Fletcher grabbed Carruthers' sleeve. 'Also, said he had evidence. Evidence of abuse that took place at Braidwood.'

Carruthers leant in to Fletcher, kissing her on the cheek. He then got up and started to walk away from her. 'I'd better make the call to Gayle,' he said. 'Tell her to drop everything and make that meeting a priority. Then I need to pack.'

CHAPTER EIGHT

The flight from Glasgow to Iceland's Keflavik International Airport was just over two hours. Carruthers spent most of the journey listening to music and going over his notes on the Fraser case. Was wondering when he'd find the time to ring his brother, let alone visit him. Or get his cholesterol tested.

As the plane began its descent he gazed curiously out of the window. What he saw beneath him was a darkening frozen wasteland of ice, snow, sea and sky. The ocean a cobalt blue surrounded by a flat desert of snow. A dusky pink streak of sunset sat low in the sky.

Navigating passport control he headed out of the exit with his hand luggage to join the taxi rank. The cold air hit him full in the face. Like opening the freezer door. His cheeks felt pinched; hands raw. Although he was thankful for his black down jacket, his blue jeans were no match for the Icelandic winter. Jumping into a taxi with legs that felt as if they'd spent half an hour in the freezer, he headed towards Reykjavik.

He noticed that on either side of the arrow straight road out of the airport the countryside resembled an apocalyptic scene from a sci-fi movie, with its modern functional warehouses and barren lunar landscape. He marvelled that, as it grew darker, the earth with its glare of snow, became lighter than the sky. An eerie yet exciting experience. His ex-wife hadn't been a great traveller. They had mainly holidayed within Scotland so they could pop in and see her parents. Now that marriage had ended he'd promised himself that he would do more travelling.

Within forty minutes he was approaching Reykjavik's bright lights. Found himself virtually on the edge of his seat, excitedly straining against the seat belt like a dog on a lead. Pulling up at his hotel he climbed out of the taxi, noticing an enormous futuristic-looking church of stone and stained glass on the other side of the road. He was surprised at how beautiful such a modern religious structure could be, with its clean angles and perfect symmetry. Hoped he would be able to make time to find out what the interior was like.

Having checked in, he dumped his hand luggage in the small but functional white bedroom then set out on foot to explore the city. He managed to pick up a guidebook from a still open bookshop. His time was his own until his appointment with Fraser's son at ten the next morning. He felt frustrated that he couldn't get the meeting organised any sooner but Fraser's son had been out of town. As he walked, he noticed how the capital city was a mix of futuristic concrete and glass buildings, oddly placed between the historic timber houses of the old town.

He wandered down to the harbour. It was bitingly cold. He saw the warehouses looming out of the darkness, imagined the hulking whaling ships of the past. The wind whipped across his face, stinging his already cold cheeks. He reckoned the wind chill factor must be at least minus twenty. Carruthers glanced at his watch. Approaching 7pm. Fast losing the feeling in his gloveless hands he shoved them deeper in to his jacket pockets. Feeling peckish he decided to make his way the few minutes back to the picturesque old town where there were a number of cafes and restaurants. They were still quiet. The night was young by Icelandic standards: most people, especially at weekends, didn't venture out until the wee hours of the morning. Carruthers knew that the high price of alcohol meant that they tended to drink at home first and hit the town later.

Instead of going to one of the cheaper cafes, he decided on one of the decent restaurants that served authentic Icelandic food. He looked through the windows in a couple and finally settled on one whose attractive old weather-board frontage entranced him.

Inside it was warm and had a wonderfully rustic charm. The wooden tables were bedecked with red tablecloths and candles and there were old-fashioned wooden skis attached to the walls. He was seated at a small table near the window by a young man in his twenties with a shock of blond hair and the bluest eyes Carruthers had ever seen.

Carruthers read the menu with interest, surprised to see whale meat on it, although he knew that the Icelandic government had made a controversial decision to resume hunting these beautiful creatures. The national dish, however, was fermented shark, which was also on the menu. He decided to give it a wide berth, thinking it sounded disgusting. Also, he noticed there were such delicacies as reindeer, the expected salted cod and guillemot. He was coming to realise that Icelanders were a hardy and resourceful bunch whose food had traditionally been more about necessity than luxury, although that was starting to change. In the end he settled for the reindeer and a glass of red wine. Even if he hadn't been working the next day, the prohibitive prices would have stopped him from having too much to drink. Deciding that was a good thing, he settled back in the chair with his guidebook.

After a second glass of wine and a surprisingly good meal he made his way back to his hotel. He was surprised to see he had five missed calls, one from Andie, one from his mum and three from Gayle Watson. Anxiety gripped him. Despite his tiredness he rang his mum back straight away. The phone was engaged. He then rang Gayle.

'Where have you been? I've been trying to get hold of you.' She sounded edgy, nervous.

'Sorry. I was travelling and then having a meal in a restaurant. I didn't have mobile reception. What's up? How did your meeting with Angus Dawson go?'

'That's just it, Jim. I didn't have it. I turned up to find there'd been a RTA just outside the hotel. Looks like a hit-and-run. I was the first on the scene. I did what I could but he was already dead.'

'Well, look, I'm sure if you explain it to Dawson, he'll understand. Get him on the phone and set up another meeting.'

'I can't. That's what I'm trying to tell you. Dawson was the hit-and-run victim.'

'Jesus Christ.'

'Jim, I don't know what's going on. With Andie in hospital… and now Dawson dead…'

'Were there any witnesses? Was it an accident?'

'It was no accident. According to witnesses, a car pulled out of a space, driver put his foot down hard on the accelerator deliberately smashed into Dawson as he was crossing the road. At least two witnesses say it was almost as if the driver was lying in wait. Third witness doesn't remember the parked car starting up. Just saw the accident. Ditto the fourth. All the witnesses saw the driver get out of the car once he'd run the victim down and pick up what looked like a satchel from the victim's body. He then jumped back in to his car without even checking the victim was alive and sped off.'

'Christ. Did anyone get a number plate?'

'No. All said it looked like a dark car. Two thought it was maroon. Maybe a Mondeo.'

'Look Gayle, I've got a meeting set up with Paul Fraser tomorrow morning. I'll get back as soon as I can. OK? Just keep me informed. Does Andie know?'

'I haven't told her yet.'

'Ok. Look, I need to speak with her anyway. I'll tell her. Just keep in touch.'

'Aye, boss.'

Carruthers hung up. He rang his mother a second time. Still engaged. His anxiety was beginning to build. He tried to ignore the tight feeling in his own chest. Christ, he hoped nothing had happened to his brother. He listened to the message from Fletcher. She had been released from hospital and was convalescing for a couple of days. Knowing her, she would be working from her laptop at home. She wanted to know how things were going with him. He debated calling her back, then decided against it.

They both needed a good night's sleep. He'd call her tomorrow. Too tired for a shower, he stripped off, climbed into bed. But he couldn't sleep and in the end tossed and turned for what seemed like hours. He eventually fell asleep at 4am to the sound of breaking glass and the loud raucous laughter of some drunken Icelanders leaving a bar outside.

***

'I don't know what Jim's going to think,' said DS Watson. 'You're supposed to be recovering at home. I don't want you to have a relapse. I could have taken Dougie with me.'

That's probably exactly what she wants, thought Fletcher, *for me to have a relapse. It would leave the way clear for her.* She glanced at Watson. The stockier woman was immaculately dressed as ever wearing a smart shirt and tie and black trousers over which she was sporting a black woollen overcoat. Fletcher had phoned Watson and suggested they interview Agnes Noble together. Watson had sounded unconvinced but in the end had agreed. They were in the station car park, walking towards one of the pool cars. Watson drove out in silence towards the home of Agnes Noble.

The wind had started to pick up, buffeting the side of the car. Watson found a place to park and angled the car in to the space. To Fletcher's embarrassment a gust of air had caught her car door and had partially closed on her. *God, what is it with me and car doors,* she thought. Watson had walked round to Fletcher's side and held the door open for her. Without looking at her Fletcher thanked her and they both started walking across the road.

'Are you sure you're OK? asked Watson.

Standing on Agnes Noble's doorstep Fletcher rooted around in her shoulder bag for some paracetamol. Popping two from the blister pack, she threw them in to her mouth. She washed them down with a couple of gulps from the bottle of water she was carrying. 'I'm fine to work. It's just bruising, not brain damage. If it makes you feel better, you take the lead.

'Thanks,' said Gayle evenly, 'I will, but I wasn't worried about your ability as a cop, I was worried about your health.'

'I'm fine. Really.'

'OK.'

Fletcher wondered why she'd told Watson to take the lead when she'd wanted the lead herself. Had she felt guilty about excluding Watson from the earlier interview, or did she feel insecure questioning Agnes Noble in front of her more than capable colleague? She wasn't sure. One thing she did know though – this self-doubt was both alien and unwelcome.

Gayle looked as if she were about to say something more, but the door was opening, and it was time to get to work.

A spindly elderly lady introduced herself as 'Joan, Agnes's next-door neighbour'. She tutted when the two police officers showed her their ID badges, almost as if having the police call round was an inconvenience.

'I know this has come as a terrible shock,' said DS Watson wiping her feet on the mat and following the woman into the living room, 'but we do need to ask Mrs Noble some more questions.' She directed her next question to the woman sitting in an armchair with a tartan travel rug round her legs. 'Are you up to answering them now?'

Agnes Noble nodded. Her face was pinched and she looked all of her eighty-two years. Her neighbour, who was a similar age to Agnes Noble, started fussing around her. 'I dinnae ken why you have to ask her these questions now. Still looks groggy to me.Must be the shock. Doctor's given her something.'

'Believe me,' said Fletcher, 'we wouldn't, if it wasn't important.' She took a seat on an uncomfortable armchair opposite Mrs Noble. She had taken off as many layers as she could without causing the old dears offence but, with both the central heating and gas fire full on, it was still oppressively hot. Her head was throbbing. Watson sat on the far end of the couch, angling her body so she was able to look at Mrs Noble.

Watson leaned forward, making contact with Agnes Noble's clouded eyes. 'How long had you and your husband been together?' she asked.

'Oh dear. Is this relevant? Are you going to trawl through her entire life history? Why aren't you out there catching the murderer?' Mrs Noble's elderly neighbour started fussing with her hair pins, managing to drop one on the floor. 'Oh, now look what you made me do.'

Watson leant over and picked it up for her.

'Look Joan,' Mrs Noble turned to her neighbour, 'I'm sure the police are only doing their jobs. Why don't you go back to your house now. I'll see you later.'

'Well, if you're sure.' Mrs Noble's neighbour sniffed then with difficulty stood up and walked off on her spindly legs.

'Thirty-seven years. I married late in life. Henry had been married before. We met in 1978 and got married in 1980.'

Fletcher paused from scribbling in her notebook and looked up once more at Mrs Noble. 'What did he do for a living?'

Agnes Noble sniffed. 'A handyman when we met.'

Fletcher listened carefully and saw an opening.

'And before you met?' She found she was holding her breath, which was no bad thing. Apart from it being oppressively hot the room had the faint smell of mothballs that some older people's homes have.

'A care worker.'

Fletcher exchanged a glance with Watson.

'Do you know where he used to work?' said Watson.

Fletcher's heart was in her mouth.

'Up at Braidwood.'

Fletcher got to her feet, fishing her mobile out of her bag. Agnes Noble looked up. 'Just going to make a call to the station.'

Agnes Noble nodded.

'Did he continue to be a care worker after you got married?' Watson asked.

'No, the care home shut down. He became a handyman. Self-employed.'

'Did he talk much about his time at Braidwood?'

'No.'

Fletcher shut the door on the conversation, interested that Noble had never talked about his time as carer. She punched in the numbers, gave the station the update, finished the call and re-entered the room putting the mobile back in to her shoulder bag.

'So… he never told you about his work there, the boys, the other care workers?' said Watson.

'I've told you, no.'

'Is his ex-wife still alive?' Watson continued.

'I have no idea.'

Fletcher noticed Agnes Noble was making quick darting movements with her fingers as she scrunched the tartan rug on her lap.

'Have you any idea why they split up?' said Watson.

'Henry said that she never understood him.'

'So you have no idea at all where she would be now, if she's still alive or how we would find her?' continued Watson.

Agnes Noble jerked her head up sharply and stared at Watson. 'Why would you want to do that?'

'Your husband was murdered, Agnes,' said Fletcher. 'At Braidwood. This is the second body we've found there. We believe the deaths may be linked to the site and perhaps to its time as a care home. Did your husband know a man called Ruiridh Fraser?'

'Doesnae sound familiar.'

'Are you sure?' asked Watson.

'Quite sure. Is he the other dead man?'

'Aye. Have you heard of a man called Angus Dawson?'

Agnes Noble shook her head. Fletcher kept scribbling in silence, reminding herself that she had given the lead to Watson. But she wanted to ask the woman if she had felt she'd had a close relationship with her husband. The heat was now starting to make her feel woozy and her head felt as if it was being pierced by a needle. She licked the salty sheen from her top lip.

'Did your husband own a computer or a mobile phone?' asked Watson.

There was no answer. For a moment Fletcher wondered if the old lady had nodded off. Eventually she lifted her head and answered, but Fletcher could see that the strain of answering so many questions about her husband so soon after his death was taking its toll.

'Aye but he doesnae have the mobile anymore. Told me he had no need for it.'

'So he got rid of it?'

'Aye, that's right.'

'When?'

She sniffed. 'Couple of months ago.'

'We're going have to take away your husband's computer,' said Watson.

'I dinnae ken why you'd need his computer but if that's what you need to do…' She shrugged. 'I cannae use one so I have no need for it.'

'What was your husband's mood like on the day he died?' asked Watson.

'Well, now you mention it, he'd been a wee bit crabbit recently.'

'Any idea why?' Watson stretched across to pick up the tartan rug that had once again started to slip off the old woman's knees.

'None. Just thought it was old age. He had some mobility problems.'

'How long had he been a bit, er, crabbit?' said Fletcher, using the Scots word.

'A couple of months.'

'And you have no idea what was bothering him?'

'No.'

'Do you happen to remember your husband's mobile number?'

'Aye, I've got it written down.'

'You said your husband was in the habit of going for a short walk.'

'Aye.'

'Was it always the same route every day?'

'More or less. Aye.'

'Ever to Braidwood?'

'Never.'

'I'll take that mobile number now if you've got it?'

Grabbing the tartan rug, Agnes Noble reached over to the low coffee table in front of her for her glasses and put them on. Watson passed her a pen and a piece of paper she had ripped out of her notebook. Mrs Noble scribbled the number down for her. Watson took it, looked at it long and hard before passing it to Fletcher. There was something about it that looked familiar. She would have to check back at the station but she was pretty sure she had seen it before.

'What sort of man was your husband?' asked Fletcher.

'What do you mean?'

'Was he sociable? Did he go out much? Have friends? Was he a drinker?'

'He had a couple of pals.'

'Anyone he'd know a long time? Anyone from his Braidwood days?' said Fletcher.

'I think his pals were more recent than that.'

'You do know Agnes, that at the time your husband worked at Braidwood, there were allegations of sexual abuse?'

Agnes Noble took her glasses off and holding them with her right hand, said, 'What does that have to do with Henry?'

'Some of the boys made complaints against some of the staff, the care workers.'

She carefully put her glasses back down on the coffee table. 'I still don't see what that has to do with Henry. And it was over thirty years ago. What relevance has it got now? The care home's closed, boys are all grown and have, no doubt, moved away. Got on with their lives. I'm assuming there was nothing in these allegations, otherwise arrests would have been made… Are you saying you think my Henry was one of the staff members who abused the boys? That is nonsense. Look, this isnae helping. I dinnae feel well. I think you should leave.'

Watson stood up. Fletcher followed suit. 'We didn't mean to upset you,' said Watson, 'And I'm not accusing your husband of anything. Look, we'll see ourselves out.'

Agnes Noble said nothing and, as the two police officers walked towards the door that led to the hall, Fletcher stole a glance back at Agnes Noble. Shaking her head and muttering she looked like a troubled woman alone with her memories.

***

'What do you reckon to Agnes Noble?' asked Fletcher, gulping in the fresh air like she'd had a plastic bag over her head.

'I'm not sure,' said Watson. They both walked to the parked car. 'I can't believe she never spoke to her husband about his time at Braidwood. My gut feeling is she's holding something back. But then she's still in shock about his murder, so who knows.'

Fletcher remained silent.

Watson wrenched the door open. 'Something isn't right. It's almost as if she's in denial. She didn't seem to find it odd he didn't talk about his previous life at all. Not his work. Not his first marriage.'

'I agree,' said Fletcher.

'Maybe she didn't know. If he had something to hide about his past he wouldn't want to talk about it, would he? Perhaps she accepted the fact he had a past he didn't want to talk about. It doesn't make him a paedophile. We all have secrets. And let's face it, we all have a past and baggage, especially the older we get.'

***

Carruthers awoke to the sound of the guests in the next room going down to breakfast none too quietly. Rolling over he looked at his watch. It had already gone eight. He got up and headed for the small bathroom. Gasping as he stepped under the piping hot shower, he wrinkled his nose at the sulphurous smell that poured from the jets. He'd read that Icelandic homes were heated by hot water from the natural springs; Iceland being the first country using geothermal power, and wondered if all bathrooms in Iceland smelt as bad as this.

Carruthers managed to grab a seat on the end of a shared table with a group of young Germans in the breakfast bar. It was self-service so he got himself a coffee from the percolator, a continental breakfast and grabbed some cutlery. Sipping his bitter coffee, he pushed thoughts of the dead journalist out of his head to focus on his interview with Fraser's estranged son.

He wondered if Fraser's son had an alibi for the time of his father's murder. How would he feel about his father's death, and how willing would he be to open up and share his private thoughts about his father with a complete stranger? What had been the cause of the estrangement? Carruthers put the scalding coffee to his lips, breathed in the vapours and took a long sip whilst he stared out of the steamed-up window in to the pitch darkness. But his thoughts kept coming back to Angus Dawson and the hit-and-run. Deciding against speaking to Fletcher before his interview, he got the hotel to call a taxi and waited in the foyer.

Paul Fraser lived with his girlfriend in Hafnarfjörður, a suburb of Reykjavik. It was a short but expensive taxi ride. According to the guidebook, Hafnarfjörðurhad once been a separate town but was now part of the fast-growing and sprawling capital. It still had a lot of the old tin-clad wooden houses that Carruthers was beginning to like so much.

The taxi driver located the address and pulled up at a block of modern flats beside the old Maritime Museum. Carruthers paid the driver and stepped over an icy puddle to get to the front door. He looked up at the buzzers and selected the one marked Fraser/Gunnersdottir. He pressed it and waited.

The door buzzed and opened and Carruthers started climbing the stairs with long athletic strides. Paul and Anna lived in a second floor flat in the immaculately presented block. Paul Fraser was already by the open door with an outstretched hand. It was a friendly gesture but Carruthers noticed there was no smile in greeting. His eyes had a suspicious, almost defensive look about them. Carruthers judged him to be mid-to late-forties. He had a slim build, short dark hair and round glasses.

'Anna's at college,' Paul said, once the introductions were out of the way.

'Oh, does she teach?'

'She's gone back to studying. Training to be a nurse.'

'That's OK. I don't need to speak to her.'

Paul immediately seemed more relaxed. Carruthers sensed relief. He was curious as to the reason why. There must be things in his background that Paul didn't want his wife to know. Perhaps in some ways he was very much his father's son – secretive.

Paul took him in to a light and spacious living area that was dominated by a sculpture of a woman and child in the centre of the mantelpiece. There were a couple of striking and colourful art works of Icelandic landscape scenes on the wall but apart from this, the colours in the room were muted – all cream and beige. The feel of the room was one of simplicity and elegance. Carruthers thought it had a distinct woman's touch.

'Look,' said Paul, 'I'll be honest with you. I don't know why you've come all the way over here. I've already been informed of my father's death by the local police. I'm sure we could have conducted this over the phone.'

Carruthers was surprised by this piece of news. He hadn't said anything on the phone about Paul's father's death and expected to have to tell him in person. But it was true that he had liaised with the local police in Reykjavik prior to his visit.

'This is a murder investigation, Paul. In fact, it's now a double murder investigation.'

Paul looked up shocked. 'A second body's been found.'

'A double murder?' Paul looked momentarily shaken but then shrugged. 'The problem is that I haven't seen or heard from my father in more than thirty years. I doubt I can be much use. I know nothing of the last three decades of his life.'

'But that's not actually true, is it?' said Carruthers.

'What do you mean?'

'You wrote him a letter. Your father. Recently. One of my team found it in a box of your father's things. I've read it. It was a pretty threatening letter. What I want to know is, why did you write it? Had he written to you?'

Paul Hunter looked away from Carruthers and stared at the bare wall. 'I don't want to talk about this.'

'You're going to have to. You're currently the prime suspect for his murder.'

Paul swivelled round to face his unwelcome guest. 'But that's stupid. I haven't seen him in over thirty years.'

'Why did you write to him?'

'He wrote me a letter. Wanted to "make amends".'

'What did you take that to mean?'

Paul Hunter shook his head. 'You said there was a second man murdered. Where was he killed?'

'At Braidwood. Like your father.' Carruthers noted that Paul tensed. 'We found out this second man worked at Braidwood when it was a children's home in the seventies. His name was Henry Noble. Does that name mean anything?'

Paul Fraser shook his head. Carruthers looked at Paul to see if there was any hint of recognition in his eyes, but there was nothing.

'I appreciate this must be difficult for you.' Carruthers gave it the obligatory moment's respectful silence before continuing. 'Can you tell me why you were estranged from your father?' Uninvited Carruthers took a seat on the cream sofa. 'As you said, you've barely had contact with him for thirty years, yet we're starting to believe the seeds of this murder may lie in his past. And that his murder is in some way linked to the place of his death.'

Paul looked uncomfortable. Carruthers pushed on. 'Look Paul, we know next to nothing about your father. We need you to fill in some of the gaps for us. And if you know something that might help us in our investigation you must tell us. Otherwise I'm going to think that you are the murderer.'

Carruthers could sense a shift in Paul. It was almost as if he was weighing up whether to tell him something. Something important.

'You think both people were killed by the same person?'

'Yes.'

Paul glanced outside in to the pitch darkness. 'You know, it doesn't get light in the winter here until about half eleven. I've been here eight years and you'd think I would've got used to it by now, but I haven't.'

Privately Carruthers found himself thinking that he would struggle to get used to it too, but he recognised avoidance tactics when he saw them, so pressed on. 'What brought you over to Iceland?'

Paul's face softened. 'Anna.I met her when she was on holiday in Scotland.'

'Have you been together long?'

'Ten years.'

'Yet you're not married and you don't have kids.'

'No.'

Paul didn't elaborate and Carruthers sensed his reluctance to speak about his personal life. He tried a different approach.

'If you don't mind me saying you don't seem very upset by the news of your father's death.'

'I'm not. There were times I could have killed him myself. He got what was coming to him.'

'Why do you say that?'

Paul looked away again. Out into the darkness. 'You don't know what he was like.'

'What *was* he like, Paul?' This question was greeted with silence. 'You know there were allegations of child abuse around that time. It looked like they centred on the children's home.'

Paul remained silent but a flicker of something came in to his eyes that Carruthers found hard to interpret. He tried a different tack. 'What age were you when you left home?'

'Sixteen.'

'Why did you leave?'

Carruthers was starting to have a good idea of why Paul had left but he needed to hear it from him. In a lot of ways, he was hoping he was wrong.

Paul continued to stare out of the window. He seemed lost in his own thoughts. 'No, I haven't got used to the pitch black, but there's something rather reassuring about the darkness, don't you think? Perhaps it goes back to us being inside your mother's womb. You feel safe.'

'Why would you need to feel safe, Paul?'

Paul didn't answer but continued to stare into the inky blackness.

'Do you know what your father's connection to Braidwood was?' Carruthers pushed on. 'We know there was one.'

Paul was still looking out of the window, not making eye contact with Carruthers. Then suddenly said, so quiet that Carruthers wasn't sure he'd heard him right, 'He worked there.'

Carruthers, who'd been holding his breath, finally expelled it in one long sigh. From his point of view his visit to Iceland was vindicated. He had got the information he needed. He had established the link the two men had to their place of death. Thank Christ for that. He could just imagine Bingham's reaction if he'd come back empty-handed.

'When?' he asked, a little sharper than intended.

'Back in the 1970s.'

'When it was a children's home?'

'That's a joke. Children's *home*.'

The bitterness was stronger than Carruthers had expected, but he tried not to let his shock show.

Carruthers pushed on. 'Did his work there have anything to do with why you left home?'

Paul suddenly slumped forward. He put his head in his hands. Carruthers observed that his chest was rising and falling with great rapidity and when he spoke, his voice came out in great shuddering breaths. 'He deserved to die.'

'Paul, have you had any recent travel back to Scotland? Where were you between 6pm and 9pm on 15th January?'

'I didn't kill him, if that's what you're getting at, although I imagine if others knew where he was living, there would be a whole queue of people.'

'Others?'

'The boys from that so-called care home. His special boys.'

'His special boys?'

'That's what he called them. "My special boys."'

Carruthers stomach was turning. He was starting to feel sick.

Paul eventually lifted his head making eye contact with Carruthers. He had a haunted look about him. Carruthers had seen that look before. It was the same look as had been in the eyes of the boy in the photograph Fletcher had shown him.

'He brought them home, you know. To abuse them.'

Carruthers looked up sharply. 'Who?'

'His special boys. Sometimes he used to bring them home. He made mum and me leave the house but we knew what he was doing with them. He used to use the spare room.'

'Your mother *knew*?'

'Yes.'

'She didn't try to stop him?'

Paul shrugged. 'What could she do? She was scared of him. We both were. Don't get me wrong. She did what she could. When she found out what he was up to, she turned the guest bedroom into a utility room. Got rid of the bed when he was at work one day and set up an ironing board instead.'

'How did your father react?'

'He was furious. I think he hit her.'

'But it didn't stop him?'

'No. He started to use my room instead. I used to come home to find the bed, well, you know…'

Carruthers felt disgusted. 'How old were you?'

'Fifteen.'

Carruthers took a deep breath. 'And how old were you when he started abusing you?'

Paul turned his head away from Carruthers so he was staring out of the window again. His features were set like granite and his expression was unreadable. Carruthers wondered what he saw out there in the darkness. He couldn't imagine the images were pleasant. Without looking at Carruthers he said, 'How did you know?'

'I've dealt with abuse cases before, Paul.'

'I was eleven or twelve.'

'How long did it continue?'

Paul shrugged. 'Until I was fourteen.'

'You moved out at sixteen. Why did it stop at fourteen?'

'I put a growth spurt on. I was bigger than I used to be. I started to fight back. Besides,' he said picking at the skin round his nails, 'he was working at the children's home by then. He used to leave me alone.'

'You said sometimes he used to bring them home. When he didn't bring them home, where did he take them?'

'There was a hotel they used. He thought we didn't know. He used to rent rooms. On a Sunday night. They all did.'

'All?' said Carruthers, his heart sinking.

'Yes, some of the other men at the children's home.'

'Would this include William Rutherford? Head of the home?'

'Yes, I think so. And there was a policeman. He was pretty senior. I think he was a superintendent.'

'Superintendent Bob Marshall?'

'Yes, he came to the house once and I heard them talking. They thought I was up in my room playing music. They were discussing which of the boys they were going to take to the hotel. Poor blighters. My father had a particular favourite. Marshall liked him, too. I saw him a few times. I'll never forget him.'

'Do you remember his name?'

'Mal. I don't know his surname. It's funny what you remember, isn't it?'

'What did he look like?'

As he gave his description, Carruthers's could feel himself growing colder than the icy lakes around Reykjavik, despite the central heating in the flat. Being given a physical description of the boy somehow made it more real to him. He could now picture him in his mind's eye. It was an image he didn't want lodged there. Very gently he laid a hand on Paul's shoulder. 'I could do with a coffee. Would you mind?'

Paul shrugged again. 'OK.'

'Whilst you're fixing up the coffees, I just need to make a phone call.' Paul disappeared in to the kitchen. As soon as he had left the room Carruthers retrieved his mobile from his pocket and called the station.

When Paul reappeared Carruthers asked, 'Does your girlfriend know?'

'That I was abused as a boy by my own father? No. I've never told anyone. The only person who guessed was my mother.'

'Yet she still stayed with him after you had left?'

Paul remained silent and Carruthers could sense that he was starting to shut down. 'Where were you when your father was murdered?'

'I was on a break to the Westfjords with my girlfriend and her parents. You can check.'

'I will. I have to, I'm sorry. I'll need to get the details from you. Just out of interest, have you heard of a man called Angus Dawson?'

'No. Who's he?'

Carruthers wondered how these early years of abuse had affected Paul. Had he found it hard to trust? To form relationships? To banish the demons that must have plagued him? How had he felt leaving his mother with his father? Carruthers glanced over at Paul who was still picking at the skin around his nails again. They were starting to bleed. Suddenly he felt claustrophobic. The room, despite its initial bright, airy feel suddenly appeared too small for the both of them. He felt utterly depressed that man's selfishness and depravity could have such long-term consequences – could blight lives and wreck futures.

'Paul, I forgot to ask – what do you do for work?'

'I'm an artist.' Paul indicated the art works in the room.

'You did these? They're very good. You manage to make a living from it?'

'A modest income, but yes, enough to live on.'

So he had been wrong about whose taste had furnished the room. It was likely to have been Paul's. Carruthers suddenly heard a noise behind him as a key was turned in the front door. Paul leapt to his feet. He looked agitated.

'Paul, I've had to come home. I've got one of my head— oh. You've got a visitor?' The woman who stood in front of him was a striking girl in her thirties. She had jet-black hair cut in a long bob, and blue eyes. She spoke English with a strong Icelandic accent. 'Sorry, I didn't know you had anyone coming round. I'm Anna Gunnarsdottir. Paul's partner.'

Carruthers thought quickly. Paul obviously hadn't told her of his visit. He wondered if he'd told his girlfriend of his father's death.

'Jim Carruthers. I'm in Reykjavik for a couple of days.'

'We had a bit of unfinished business. Work. It's finished now though,' said Paul.

'Oh, are you an artist too?' asked Anna.

'No, I'm not.'

Carruthers put his hand out and Paul shook it. Carruthers noticed that Anna had a questioning look in her eyes but he kept silent. He looked over at Paul. 'I'll be in touch if anything else crops up.'

As Paul spoke, Carruthers could see that the shutters were back down. 'It won't. I'll see you out. Won't be a moment,' he said to Anna. 'Look,' he turned to Carruthers once they were out of earshot of Anna. 'I've moved on. All that's in the past and I've worked hard to make sure that's where it stays. Hopefully now that the old bastard's finally dead, I'll get some closure. But that part of my past is behind me.'

'If it is, then I'm glad,' said Carruthers, privately doubting that it was. All he could hope for was that Paul found some solace in his art and his relationship with Anna. 'But if your father has been murdered for the part he played in what is sounding like a paedophile ring, then there's somebody still out there for whom the past is much more recent. And with two people dead, we need to catch the killer before he strikes again. I'll need you to give me the names of all the people you can remember who were connected with the care home and with your father. I'm staying at the Hotel Leifur Eiriksson, near the Hallgrimskirkja.'

'I know it.'

Carruthers gave Paul his business card. 'My flight leaves at 8am tomorrow. I'll need to meet you tonight.'

Paul remained silent.

'You might have moved on Paul, but there's somebody out there who hasn't, and they're dangerous. You have to do this. Imagine, if next time he strikes, he gets the wrong man.'

'You think he's likely to kill again?'

Carruthers wasn't sure but it certainly looked as if he might have a serial killer on his hands.

Suddenly Paul spoke. 'Do you know the Cafe Loki? It's on Njardargata street, just down from your hotel. It's run by a man name of Gunnar Arnason. He's a friend. It's late opening and quiet. Meet me there at 9pm tonight. I'll have a list for you.'

'Thank you. You will be there, won't you? If not, I know where to find you.'

'I've said I will. Now go. I don't want Anna to ask any awkward questions.'

'You should really tell her, Paul. About the abuse.'

'That's my choice. Not yours. I may not have had any choice about being abused as a child, but as an adult I have a choice about how I deal with it and who I decide to tell and when.'

Paul was right, that as a child he had had no choice about a great many things, but as an adult, things were different, but only to a degree. Carruthers understood that finally having choices was important to Paul and the many other survivors of abuse. 'But Paul, I am going to catch who did this and when it goes to trial, you may no longer have the choice of anonymity. I'm sorry.' Carruthers suddenly remembered Ruiridh Fraser's post mortem. 'By the way. Your father. He was dying. Heart disease. Perhaps that's why he wrote you a letter. Making amends?'

'You and I both know that was never going to happen,' said Paul.

***

Carruthers left the apartment and hailed a taxi in the street. After an agonisingly dark morning it was now light and the sky was streaked with different hues of blue. By the time he got back to his hotel it was well past lunchtime and his stomach was growling. He found the cafe Paul was talking about at the end of his street. Its inviting lights indicated it was still serving lunch, so Carruthers entered and took a seat facing the window. He looked at the menu. He couldn't quite stomach the flatbread with sheep's head jelly, turnip and salad so he instead he ordered rye bread with eggs and herring and a coffee. As he waited for his lunch he took out his notebook and started to make notes. He decided that later he would head back to his hotel room and check Paul's alibi.

Carruthers didn't doubt for a minute the truth of Paul's admission that he had been abused by his own father, but this in itself gave the man a strong motive for murder. If, on the other hand, his alibi checked out, and he hadn't murdered his father, then who had? His money was on the killer being one of the many boys who'd been abused. How many other victims were out there? How many knew where Ruiridh Fraser had lived? Most crucially, why had the murderer waited forty years to commit the murders? What had been the trigger?

'It just seemed the most likely scenario that a former victim would be the murderer. But if that was the case where did Angus Dawson fit in? If he had been about to expose the paedophile ring why was he killed? Surely not by a child abuse victim. Carruthers was starting to form an idea in his head and it wasn't one that he very much liked. Could it be possible that there were two murderers out there? Two murderers whose lives were connected in some way but who had very different motives. The first had killed the two men but then there was a second, one who had bashed Andie and killed Dawson?'

His thoughts turned to the Hunters. Fletcher was most probably right. Perhaps the old man's attention had turned to Jordan Hunter. That would certainly account for the boy calling him a paedo. But Jordan had an alibi for the night Fraser was murdered. He had been away on a school trip to France. Where had his father been that night, Carruthers wondered? Away on one of his many business trips? How easy would it have been for him to slip back and murder his next-door neighbour? They had noticed how defensive he'd been of the boy. It had even been recorded in the original notes taken by Brown and Harris.

Carruthers was starting to feel uncomfortable. He was also starting to kick himself that he'd forgotten to ask Paul for a list of the names of any of the boys his father had brought back to the house. He was unlikely to know surnames but he might remember first names and vague descriptions.

His thoughts turned to Angus Dawson's sudden death. Four witnesses to say it hadn't looked accidental. Then there was the fact the killer stopped at the scene, not to check on the man he'd just knocked down but rather to pick up what looked like a satchel from the body. You couldn't get much more cold-blooded than that. He sighed, picked up his mobile and phoned the station, then Paul.

***

Carruthers got back to the hotel, had a quick shower and changed clothes. He'd phoned the hotel where Paul and Anna had been staying with her family and, as luck would have it the receptionist, who spoke near perfect English, had been working on the day of their arrival and remembered the party of four. Paul had used his own credit card to pay for the stay so there was record at least that he'd been there at the start and at the end when they had checked out after their four nights. The dates he claimed to be on holiday were the very dates over which the murders had taken place. On the surface, it looked as if he was off the hook. Carruthers knew, though, that they would have to have a much more comprehensive check before they could rule him out.

He decided to eat before meeting Paul that evening. Choosing a busy noodle shack within walking distance of both his hotel and the café, he settled on beef noodle soup with extra chillies. After eating traditional Icelandic food he felt like something hot and spicy. He ordered a coke to go with it. He still hadn't phoned Fletcher. Knowing her, the news would have her out of bed and straight in to the station. He decided to put it off for as long as necessary. Fletcher had no more information to give him and Watson was a capable officer.

He spent an enjoyable half hour people watching. The cafe had drawn a lot of young people to it and, despite its proximity to his multicultural hotel, Carruthers had the impression it was very much a local's hang-out. A number of the young men had beards and long hair. In their bearded faces and unkempt locks, Carruthers could quite easily see forefathers wearing helmets and brandishing swords, getting into their Viking longboats. His English teacher had always said of him that he had a vivid imagination that would get him in to trouble. He was sure that if he voiced these current thoughts, it probably would.

With time on his hands before meeting Paul, Carruthers took a short wander back to the impressive Hallgrimskirkja. He was pleased to see that, even at this late hour, it was still open to the public. He brought out his guidebook to see what it said about the building. At seventy-four metres high, tall enough to double as a radio mast, which had been the intention of its creator, it dominated the city skyline. From its ribbed tower clad in granite, which was an echo of Iceland's basalt rock formations, to its vaulted ceilings and columns flanking the nave, it was a study in both beauty and simplicity. Carruthers was unsurprised to learn that it had taken forty years to finish, having been started at the end of the Second World War in 1945 and finally completed in 1986.

At this time of evening the chapel was quiet. Most tourists would more than likely be in bars or eating their evening meal in restaurants. Carruthers slipped inside and took a comfortable seat at the end of one of the wooden benches. After gazing at the illuminated altar, he bowed his head in reverence and quiet contemplation. He was awestruck by the church's beauty, and not for the first time moved that the human race that could produce murderers and paedophiles could also create something so exquisite.

Carruthers was suddenly aware that someone had slipped in to the pew beside him. He heard a familiar voice. 'Peaceful, isn't it?' Carruthers looked up. It was Paul. 'I was early for our meeting,' Paul said. 'Thought I'd come in here for a few minutes. Do you find that strange?'

'No, not at all. I had the same idea. I wanted to see what it looked like from inside.'

'I've got that list for you.'

'Thank you.' Carruthers took the folded sheet of paper from him. He opened it up.

'It's only what I can remember. There may be more.'

'Were you ever—'

'No, just by my father. I suppose I should be thankful for small mercies.'

The only two people who had been in the church at the same time as Carruthers were just leaving. He and Paul were now completely alone.

Carruthers scanned the names on the sheet. There were seven in total. Apart from his father's name there were only two he recognised – those of Marshall and William Rutherford. Noble wasn't one of them.

'How sure are you of these other men?' Carruthers asked.

'Pretty sure. Let's just say my father wasn't discreet. He must have felt he was untouchable. And he was, wasn't he?' Paul Fraser added bitterly.

'So you heard all these names mentioned by him in phone conversations?'

'Yes, all except Marshall. As you know, he visited.' Paul went on, 'All these boys were just kids. Just like me. Who would have believed them? And we all know kids and teenagers have strong imaginations, can sometimes be fantasists.'

'It did get reported though, didn't it?' said Carruthers. Given that Paul was a suspect, there was no way Carruthers was going to tell him about the call from Angus Dawson and his subsequent sudden death. 'It got into the papers. Although I do remember reading in a follow up article that the case was dropped by the police. The paper made it very clear there'd been no wrong-doing by the care workers.'

'We all know why it was dropped. Pressure from on high.'

'Marshall?'

'Not just him.' Paul pointed to another name on the sheet of paper of the alleged abusers. 'John Whitelaw. He was editor of *The Fife Courier* at the time.'

Silence stretched between them.

'I do remember being interviewed by a young police officer,' Paul mused.

'You were interviewed by the police? You never said.'

'Must have slipped my mind.'

'So your mother did report it?'

'No, no she didn't. One of the boys in the home had cited my father as being one of his abusers. The police wanted to interview him in connection with that. I was in the house at the time. I was asked to come in to the living room. The policeman asked me if I had ever seen any of the boys in our house.'

'What did you say?'

Paul hung his head. 'I said "no". I was interviewed right in front of my father. I was only thirteen.'

Carruthers inwardly swore.

'You have to remember that I was terrified of my father. We both were.'

'I'm not judging you, Paul. Do you remember the police officer's name?'

Paul took a sharp intake of breath and let it out slowly. 'You're talking over thirty years ago.'

'I know. Think, man. It's important.'

'But as it happens I do remember it. Just by pure chance he had the same name as my maths teacher. And you never forget the names of your teachers, do you? It was PC McBride.'

'First name?'

Paul shook his head. 'No, sorry. I don't think I ever got told his first name.'

'Thank you, Paul.' Carruthers shut his notebook.

When Paul spoke again, his voice was a just a whisper but also full of emotion. 'If I had spoken out, perhaps I could have prevented those boys from being abused.'

Carruthers placed his hand on Paul's shaking shoulder. 'You would probably have just made things worse for you and your mother.'

Carruthers watched Paul leave the church. He brought his mobile out of his pocket, realised he'd had another missed call from his mother. Phoned her as he walked.

'Jim, where've you been? I've been trying to reach you. It's Alan. He's in hospital.'

Carruthers' heart leapt in to his mouth. 'Mum, I'm in Iceland with work. What happened?'

'He was having chest pains.'

'Oh Christ.'

'Look, I'm sorry to give you this news on the phone. He needs a triple heart bypass.'

'Triple? I thought it was only two arteries that were blocked? What about the stents?'

'I'm afraid all three are blocked. The artery that had the stents put in – well, it's not coping well. The procedure hasn't worked.'

'Jesus. Have you got a date for the bypass?'

'Not yet. They need to do more tests. Find out if he's even a candidate.'

Carruthers found that the lump in his throat at the start of the call had now grown to the size of a golf ball.

Look, Mum, I'll be back in Scotland tomorrow. I'll give you a call as soon as I get back. Give him my best.'

Carruthers finished the call and wiped a freezing tear from his face. Arriving back at his hotel room he started packing.

CHAPTER NINE

As soon as the flight landed Carruthers called his mother. His brother was stable. He asked if he should drive straight to the hospital, to be told there was no point, his brother would be undergoing tests all morning and they would be unable to spend much time with him. Perhaps he could come through the night before Alan's bypass? Carruthers agreed.

Driving to Fife with his head full of his brother and the twists and turns of the investigation, Carruthers barely registered the flakes of snow beginning to fall on his windscreen and the leaden sky above. It was only when he reached the M80 with the onset of a blizzard he noticed the worsening conditions. He cursed as he was forced to slow his speed to a crawl. The flakes were falling thick and fast. The car in front ground to a halt. Carruthers braked and thumped the steering wheel. He connected his phone to the hands free and called his brother but there was no reply. Perhaps he was having a sleep.

The traffic finally started to move again. Ten minutes later he was able to see the cause of the jam when he passed a silver Audi that was at an angle across the road. Once past, he managed to pick up a little speed, but for the next ten miles progress was painfully slow.

By the time he got to the Kincardine Bridge the blizzard had stopped. There was the occasional break in the sky allowing a silvery sun to peek out on to the melting snow and wet roads. Carruthers blasted his horn long and hard when the driver of an articulated lorry with Italian plates in front of him opened the window and threw out his rubbish.

It had been an early start. By the time he arrived at the station he was dog-tired. Gratefully, he accepted a coffee from Fletcher.

Sipping it, he realised that she'd had the foresight to go for a double shot of espresso.

'Jim,' this from Watson who had just entered the room, clutching a sheaf of papers. 'I checked the number Agnes Noble gave us for her husband's mobile against Ruiridh Fraser's phone statements. One of the numbers Andie said appeared several times—'

Fletcher looked up. 'It's Henry Noble's?' she asked.

'Aye, it is.' Watson looked from Fletcher to Carruthers. 'Proves the men knew each other and were in touch as recently as three months ago.'

'Good work. We're starting to get somewhere now. Let's take this into the brief.' Standing up Carruthers grabbed his notebook and the three of them left his office.

'Right, let's have some quiet,' shouted Bingham.

The caffeine was doing the trick. Carruthers was already starting to feel more human. As for the sight and sounds of Iceland, they were fast becoming a distant memory.

With all leave cancelled there was a full complement of staff. Carruthers glanced over at Fletcher, taking a closer look at her as she took a seat. Immaculately dressed as ever, she wore close-fitting dark grey trousers with black-heeled boots and a black V-neck tank top over a crisp white shirt. She had her hair loose around her face and looked a lot younger than her early thirties. The bandage round her head was gone. The only sign she'd been in the wars was her pale complexion and the cut and bruising above her right eye. No doubt she could feel a bump on the back of her head too, but it wasn't visible. Carruthers was concerned about her. He thought it too early for her to be back at work after such an attack.

'We've got a lot of ground to cover,' said Bingham. 'Jim, over to you.'

Carruthers walked to the incident board. 'Right,' he said, 'this is starting to move fast. We've managed to establish a link between these two men,' he said, pointing at the photographs of

Ruiridh Fraser and Henry Noble. 'They were both care workers at Braidwood in the mid-seventies.'

'We dinnae ken if they're both paedophiles, though,' said Harris.

'No, that's true,' said Carruthers carefully. 'Although Paul Fraser says he was sexually abused by his father. He's also produced a testimony to say that his dad was part of a wider paedophile ring that centred on abuse at Braidwood. He's given us these names.' Carruthers pointed at several names on the board including those of Superintendent Bob Marshall, William Rutherford and editor of *The Fife Courier*, John Whitelaw.

'It goes to the very top,' said Fletcher, shaking her head, and then wincing. 'All we need is a politician or two and we'll have the full set. No wonder the allegations were dropped. I mean, if it's true, between the police super, the head of the home and the newspaper editor, those poor kids never had a chance. No wonder the investigation didn't get going. Marshall wouldn't want his activities made public.'

'We may well find this investigation grows arms and legs. This could be just the tip of the iceberg. Look, let's not kid ourselves,' said Carruthers. 'If these allegations *are* true, and I have no reason to disbelieve Paul Fraser, then this could be massive. And it'll send shockwaves right across the country. However,' he held up his hands, 'We need to focus on the present. As repulsed as all of us are, we're not here to round up paedophiles. We need to leave that to the experts. What we have are two murders to solve, a nasty assault on Andie; and now a suspicious death of an ex-reporter.'

There were murmurs of agreement.

'Did the same person who killed those old men, also assault Andie and run down the newspaper guy?' asked Brown.

'Well, that's the question, isn't it?' said Carruthers. 'We believe there may be a link with the hit-and-run. Andie's stolen bag contained her diary, which had details of the meeting she'd set up with Angus Dawson. The man was killed before the meeting took place.'

'And whoever ran him down,' said Watson, 'was calculating enough to stop the car and retrieve his satchel before driving off. The big question is, of course, how did the killer know the man crossing the road was Dawson?'

There were murmurs of agreement. Fletcher hung her head. 'I'd scribbled down Dawson's mobile number and home address.'

'So,' said Carruthers, 'it is possible that the killer located where he lived and followed him from his home—'

'But that also means he must have been following me,' said Fletcher. 'It can't have just been a coincidence he pitched up at Braidwood the same time, and even if he did, how would he know I'd got the photographs in my bag?'

'OK,' said Carruthers carefully, 'so let's say the assailant follows Andie, presumably from the library on Braidwood Road, up to the resource at Braidwood Campus.'

Fletcher turned to him. 'When I spoke to the librarian at the public library she said two other people had been in recently asking questions about Braidwood in the seventies.'

'There must be something we're missing here,' said Watson. 'Why follow Andie? Unless it was a coincidence they were at the campus at the same time or they just happened to be in the library.'

Fletcher shook her head. 'I didn't see anyone else up at the campus. A few parked cars in the car park. But that was for the staff on site.'

'But why Andie? We're all involved in this investigation,' said Watson.

There was a moment's silence until Fletcher broke it. 'The community meeting,' she said. 'I appealed for information at the meeting about the development. There were about fifty people in that room. I gave out my telephone number and told them which station I was attached to.'

Carruthers scratched his chin. 'So in all likelihood, it's someone who attended the meeting.'

'And before you ask,' said Fletcher, 'there was no signing-in book so no record of who attended.'

'Pity,' said Carruthers. 'OK, we need someone to go to Angus Dawson's house. Take it apart. See if we can find the evidence he said he had, unless, of course it was with him when he was killed.'

'We'll go, boss,' said Watson, pointing to herself and Fletcher. 'We'll head over there after this meeting.'

Carruthers nodded. He privately thought it a good opportunity for them to spend some time together. 'OK, great, but Andie, only if you're up to it. Gayle, what have you got?' he asked.

'The two men, Fraser and Noble, would have definitely known each other at Braidwood. More than that, we've found out they'd been in contact with each other recently. That disconnected mobile phone number on Fraser's statement belonged to Noble.'

Carruthers scratched the stubble on his chin again. Again, the partying in Reykjavik had kept him awake till the early hours and he hadn't woken almost until check-in time. In his haste to catch his flight he hadn't had a chance to shave.

'Even though Agnes Noble told us she'd never heard of a Ruiridh Fraser, it proves the two men clearly knew each other,' continued Watson.

'OK, but we've got no evidence Noble was part of a paedophile ring,' said Carruthers. 'He doesn't appear on Paul's list. And his wife was horrified when she thought we were accusing him of being a kiddy fiddler. However, we've got to remember she wasn't married to him in the 1970s. She's his second wife. And, let's face it, she didn't know about his connection with Fraser.'

'You've got to wonder how much she knew her husband at all,' said Watson.

'And how much she wanted to know,' chipped in Fletcher.

'Yeah, but not every husband and wife tell each other everything. Some are barely on speaking terms,' said Brown.

'So you didnae ken that I've been shagging yer wife then, eh Brownie?' said Harris.

'Yer welcome to her. She's been frigid for years.'

'Christ, will you two shut it,' said Carruthers. 'We've taken Noble's computer away for analysis. We've got the IT boys working on it now. John's back from leave. So perhaps that'll tell us something.'

'We've had a look at Fraser's phone statements going back over five years and Noble's mobile number only appears on it within the last few months so it looks as if contact has only been recently established. Why?' asked Fletcher.

'Well, something's been going on. According to Agnes Noble her husband was becoming increasingly bad tempered and edgy. His change in mood seems to have started around the time of his renewed contact with Fraser,' said Watson.

Carruthers cleared his throat. 'OK, let's have a look at suspects for a moment. The obvious one is Paul Fraser. According to him, he was away with his girlfriend and her parents in a hotel in north east Iceland. Speaking to the reception staff at the hotel he was there in person to check in and was definitely present to check out. Paid by credit card.'

'What about the two days during the trip?' asked Brown.

'In terms of flights from Iceland I don't think there's any way he could have conceivably done it. Not in those two days,' said Carruthers.

'No chance he could have got a ferry?' Fletcher asked.

'I don't think so. I still want us to contact the UK Border Agency, also check with the airlines and ferry companies – anyone else who might have an official record of his comings and goings. If the trip was a prepared alibi he would've taken steps to ensure the alibi was backed up. Gayle? Can I put you on to that?'

Watson nodded.

'Let's turn our attention to the Hunters,' continued Carruthers. 'The kid, Jordan Hunter, was on a school trip at the time of Fraser's murder. That checks out. However, I want us to focus our attention on the father, Malcolm Hunter. What do we actually know about him?'

'Works in the pharma industry,' said Fletcher, referring to her notes. 'Travels away a lot. Wife and two kids. Over-protective of his son. If Ruiridh Fraser was making advances towards Jordan it certainly gives Hunter Senior a motive for disliking him. But murder? That's a hell of a leap.'

'He's got a temper on him,' said Carruthers.

'So do a lot of people,' said Watson. 'But it doesn't mean he's capable of murder.'

'I reckon most people are capable of murder given the right incentive,' said Fletcher.

'What's Malcolm Hunter's alibi, Andie?' asked Carruthers.

'Away with work. We're checking the details.'

At that moment the door to the incident room opened behind Carruthers and a man in his late twenties with a receding hairline and glasses popped his head round.

'Boss, it's Speccie Techie,' said Harris, referring to their resident IT expert, John Forrest.

Carruthers swivelled round. Catching his eye, Carruthers followed him out of the room calling over his shoulder as he did, 'Won't be a minute.' He shut the door behind him.

Carruthers leant in close to John. 'Be quick. What have you got for us?'

'You're not gonna like it. Kiddy porn. Hundreds of images. Present day but there's also some photos going back to the 1960s and seventies by the look of the collars and haircuts. All boys. Age range seven through to about sixteen.'

'Christ almighty.' Carruthers scratched his frowning forehead. 'Good work. Can you get a print-out for us of any of the boys going back to the seventies? We only need to see their faces. Oh, and any of the most recent images, too.'

'It's gonna take some time. Like I said, there's hundreds of images on that computer.'

'Work as fast as you can.'

Carruthers re-entered the incident room to be greeted by a fug of stale warm air. Tension stretched like an elastic band.

'We've got it. Kiddy porn's just been found on Noble's computer. John thinks some of it dates back to the 1970s.What we need is to try to find a list of all the boys who passed through Braidwood during that time. There's got to be one somewhere. We also need to try to trace them all.'

'Christ, that'll take fucking weeks,' said Harris.

'We don't have weeks, Dougie.'

Fletcher shook her head. 'When I spoke with Sarah she wasn't confident any such list exists. There certainly wasn't in the boxes I found the photographs in.'

'There must have been a list at one time,' said Carruthers. 'It's got to have been kept in a log book or file.'

'Perhaps it's been destroyed,' said Fletcher.

'Do you reckon the murderer could be one of the abused kids?' asked Brown.

'It would make sense if he was,' said Fletcher. 'What better motive for murder than abuse?' She paused. 'But then if the hit-and-run was no accident, why would a victim of abuse be wanting to keep the story from seeing the light of day?'

'Unless we're dealing with two murderers,' said Carruthers, slowly. 'Two murderers with two opposite motives.'

'The first killer has revenge as the motive, the second maybe self-preservation,' said Fletcher. 'Christ, you might be right.'

'Look, it's just an idea I'm floating about,' said Carruthers. 'We need to keep an open mind.'

'Why now, though?' Harris asked. 'If it is an abused kid seeking revenge, and I wouldnae blame the wee bugger, why now? Why wait over forty years?'

'That's a good question; and that's what we need to find out. We also need a list of everyone who worked at Braidwood, right down to the ground staff.' Harris groaned. 'I also want the names of any other reporters working on the original story until it got axed, and the names of any of the cops involved in the original investigation. Dougie, I want you to check for a PC McBride connected to the Fife Constabulary mid-seventies.

The likelihood is that it was Superintendent Marshall who axed the investigation, but there would have been other, more junior cops involved in the information gathering. We already know McBride was one of them. Let's find out who's still alive and take it from there.'

'Boss, I think it might be worth our while to bring in a psychologist,' said Fletcher. 'You know, find out a bit more about the long-term effects of child abuse on the adult. It's not a subject any of us are experts in.'

'A psychologist?' said Harris. 'Ye dinnae half talk a load of shite. What the fuck do we need a psychologist for? We already ken that anybody who's been abused as a bairn is gonna be screwed in the heid. Dinnae need a psychologist to tell us that.'

'Why not?' said Carruthers. 'Can't hurt. Get it set up, will you Andie? I'll square it with Bingham.' He sounded more confident than he was. In light of the recent changes within the Scottish police he knew budget restrictions were even tighter. However, he also knew he could be persuasive when he wanted to be.

Harris snorted and turned his head away in disgust. 'Waste of fucking time,' he said under his breath.

Carruthers watched Fletcher catch Watson's eye. They exchanged a smile. Carruthers felt relieved. Fletcher was clearly thawing towards Watson.

'Right, that's it. Brief over. I'll be in my office.'

'Jim,' said Fletcher putting her head round a few minutes later. Carruthers looked up, taking in Fletcher's pale face and dark shadows. 'Is it OK if I leave early today? I need to get home?'

'Feeling OK?'

'Yes, nothing like that. I have a locksmith coming round. That's all.'

Carruthers felt a knot of tension in his stomach. 'Mark's not causing any trouble, is he?'

'Nothing I can't handle. Actually, he was waiting for me when I got back from yours the other night. I never had a chance to say.'

'Oh, Andie.'

'It's OK. Just made me realise what a plank he is, and that I'm better off without him.'

Carruthers didn't say anything but he took in the too-bright eyes and downcast mouth.

'What time you thinking of heading off?'

'I'll probably leave straight from Dawson's. Just before 5pm if that's OK? I'll set up the meeting with the psychologist first. That's the other reason I wanted to see you. Will you be available tomorrow if I can get it organised?'

His desk phone started to ring. 'You might have to handle it yourself. Depends what comes in.'

'I'll ring you later,' she said and shut the door as Carruthers leaned over a pile of paperwork to try to find his phone.

***

Watson and Fletcher stepped through the splintered door in to the hall. A painting was hanging at a precarious angle, the coat stand overturned. The doors to both bedroom and living room thrown wide open.

'Jesus. I'll call this in,' said Watson pulling her mobile from her jacket pocket treading between coats. 'I'll take the bedroom,' Watson said to Fletcher.

'Be careful, in case whoever's done this is still here,' said Fletcher.

Fletcher entered the living room, taking in the books and paperwork that were wantonly strewn over every inch of the carpet. Her eyes travelled to the now empty bookshelf. Whoever had ransacked the place had pulled every single book out. Everything was covered in a fine film of white feathers. She stared at the three-seated grey sofa, which had three long gashes in its cushions. Someone had similarly taken a knife to the matching armchair whose cushion was lying at an angle half on and half off the chair. Its foam interior was heaped in piles like guts next to it. But when Fletcher saw the fireplace her heart almost stopped. The living flame gas fire had been dismantled. Coal by coal.

She retreated from the living room, meeting Watson in the hall. 'Bedroom's a mess,' Watson said.

'Same with the living room. Even taken the gas fire apart.' They both moved up the staircase to the upper rooms. A second bedroom and bathroom were on the upper floor. Both ransacked.

'Whoever's been here has long since gone,' said Fletcher.

Watson turned to her. 'Aye, but did they find what they were looking for?'

***

'Boyfriend trouble?'

Fletcher remained silent.

'It usually is,' said the dark-haired locksmith.

Fletcher couldn't help but smile. 'You an expert on relationships then?'

'Me? Nah.' He turned back to the door, tools in hand. 'You'd be surprised how many call-outs I get after a break-up, though. Relationships can be messy. Don't tend to have them myself.'

'Well, I think I'll steer clear myself for a while.'

'Got a broken heart on my hands, have I?' He turned round, giving her a sympathetic smile. 'Rule number one. Never give them a key. As soon as they're given a key, they get their feet under the table.'

'You the love 'em and leave 'em type, then?' asked Fletcher, warming to the easy banter between them.

'Been known to break a few hearts in my time.' He looked slyly at her. 'Doubt I'm the only one though.'

Fletcher watched him working on the door. 'Do you want a cup of tea, or something?' she asked.

The locksmith turned round. 'Whoever he was, he's made you miserable. Plain to a blind man. You look like you've got the weight of the world on your shoulders. Christ, you should have some fun. What are you? Mid-twenties?'

'Early thirties.'

'You don't look it. You're young enough to make a few mistakes and still be able to start again. I envy you that. Gorgeous girl like you… he must need his head read. If you're making a cup of tea, I'll take mine with milk and two sugars. By the way, I couldn't help but notice, you've had a nasty accident.' He motioned towards her head.

'Accident at work.'

'Shit. I'd take them for all they've got if I were you.'

'Not as easy as that in my place of work.' She smiled and walked away from the front door towards the kitchen. 'Won't be a minute.'

She was standing by the window dunking her tea bag in her mug of hot water when he walked in to her kitchen. Fletcher couldn't help but notice the man's bottom encased as it was in his overalls. In fact she couldn't help but notice his whole torso was rather appealing.

'Hope I didn't offend you earlier. I was just teasing.' Giving her back the empty mug he threw her an easy smile. 'Right, that's me away, hen.'

'Already?'

'Aye, that's you. Safe and secure. No need to thank me. It's my job.' He turned and smiled at her again.

The locksmith caught Fletcher staring out of the window and came and stood behind her.

'Reckon there's more snow on the way,' he said. He was standing close enough that she could feel his hot breath on her neck. She felt a shiver of excitement at being this physically close to an attractive man who wasn't Mark.

'D'you reckon?' she said turning round.

He wasn't tall but he was broad shouldered. His short dark hair was thick and wiry and she was close enough to smell the lingering effects of his aftershave. She felt a rather surprising pull in her groin.

She watched his wide mobile mouth as he spoke. Every so often her eyes would stray to his. They were sea green.

'Is there anywhere I can wash my hands? That was my last job of the day.'

She felt a sudden pang that she would be spending her evening on her own. Suddenly she wanted company.

'Do you want to stay for a drink? asked Fletcher. 'I've got beer, wine.'

'A beer would be good, thanks.'

She pulled open the fridge door. Grasped a beer.

'Now all we need is a bottle opener,' she said.

'You were going to show me where I can wash my hands? Or you can show me the way to the bedroom if you like? I'll wash my hands first though.' He leant in and gently kissed her on the lips. She didn't pull back but nor did she respond. Her heart was hammering in her chest. Just as she was trying to decide what to do, he took the beer out of her hands. Set it down on the kitchen table. Putting both hands on her shoulders, he drew her closer to him then kissed her again but this time deeper. She found herself responding in a way she hadn't responded to a kiss in a very long time. She led him to the foot of the stairs. 'Bathroom's top of the stairs first left.'

His eyes locked on hers. He stroked her cheek setting all her nerve ends on fire. 'And bedroom?' he asked.

'Next door.'

***

Fletcher lay back in the crumpled bed sheets. A lazy hand trailed a finger between her breasts and down to her stomach. His warm palm rested there and she could feel the heat from it permeating her still glistening skin.

'You're beautiful, do you know that?' he said, taking a strand of her dark hair and winding it round his calloused finger. She couldn't remember when Mark had last told her she was beautiful. He inched towards her and angled his lean body so it was touching hers. She smelt his sweat and aftershave and found the combination a powerful turn on. He kissed her nipple and tugged on it as he took it in his mouth. All the while his right hand cupped the other breast. She arched her body and he moved on top of her. There was a sudden noise as hailstones pelted the bedroom window.

CHAPTER TEN

'Thanks very much for making time to meet with us at such short notice. I'm DI Jim Carruthers and this is DS Andie Fletcher.'

'You're welcome.' The man had to stoop when he walked into Carruthers' office. 'Dr Greg Ross.' he said, shaking hands with them both, his appreciative gaze lingering on Fletcher just a little too long. 'I believe you knew my predecessor, Amy Toye? I understand you're investigating child abuse in a children's home in the 1970s?'

'Well, not exactly,' said Carruthers pulling up a chair and indicating for Ross to do the same. 'But we are interested in child abuse from that period as it may relate to an on-going investigation.'

Dr Greg Ross sat down and put a black leather briefcase on the table from which he took out a pen and a notepad. 'OK, what would you like to know?' He removed the leather case from the table and tucked it under his chair. He smiled at Fletcher and she could see him trying not to look at the plaster over her eye.

His accent had a hint of Scots and Fletcher judged him to be well-to-do-Edinburgh. Perhaps public school. He used his hands a lot when he spoke. It made him seem lively, vital somehow. Fletcher liked his open face with its smattering of freckles.

'We're specifically wondering what effects child abuse can have on the victim in later life,' she said, joining the conversation and making a serious effort to put any memories of last night's no-strings sex out of her mind. She felt like blushing when she thought about it.

Gripping his pen, Ross said, 'And this is child abuse that takes place in a children's home?'

'Well, yes, a children's home, but also in a family environment,' said Carruthers.

Fletcher suspected that Carruthers was thinking of Paul Fraser.

'Perhaps you can give us a bit of background,' said Carruthers. 'There's been lot of press coverage about former children's homes where abuse by staff on the kids took place. What I want to know is how widespread it was and what effect growing up in an abusive environment would have on the child in later life.'

Greg Ross clicked his pen. 'OK, unfortunately there's a growing body of evidence to show that child abuse in children's homes was much more widespread than anyone would have believed. We may well be seeing just the tip of the iceberg with places like North Wales and Kincora Boys Home in East Belfast coming to light. In fact, the report into the scandal surrounding the homes in North Wales has resulted in changes in policy in how authorities deal with kids in care. We're now able to build up a picture of the most likely homes in which abuse took place.'

'Go on,' said Carruthers.

'Interestingly abuse was much more likely to happen in homes placed in the middle of nowhere, run by men. Up until the 1960s most of the care workers were women. Often it was women whose husbands had died in the war or who had never married due to a shortage of men. Of course, caring was seen as women's work and naturally it was low paid.'

'Naturally,' said Fletcher.

Carruthers looked up. 'What changed in the sixties?'

'A lot of these women retired. They were replaced by men. The work was still low paid and, back then, there were no checks made on the people who were employed to staff the care homes. Most were unqualified. A lot of the men were disciplinarians and it appears that the homes where abuse was most likely to occur were run in a military way. But the seclusion seems to be a recurring factor through which abuse was able to flourish.'

Fletcher's eyes narrowed. 'What are the long-term effects of being abused as a kid?' she asked.

'Certainly in some cases, but not all, those who've suffered abuse can start to suffer from post-traumatic stress disorder or PTSD.'

'How might it manifest itself?' asked Carruthers.

'The symptoms of PTSD can be quite general,' said Dr Ross. 'And can mimic other disorders: depression; anxiety; insomnia; eating disorders or alcohol and drug problems.'

'Could a victim have outbursts of anger?' asked Fletcher.

'Irritability, anger; violence,' said Ross. 'Many have problems in their relationships and with trusting another person again.'

'You said that an abused child doesn't always go on to develop PTSD. What, in your view, determines whether a child in later life goes on to develop it?' said Fletcher.

'There's a good number of factors. Some professionals believe younger kids may be less at risk of long-term PTSD.'

'Why's that?' she asked.

'It's thought younger children are less likely to intellectually understand and interpret the effects of a traumatic situation. Another factor is the level of support the victim has in his day-to-day life. Guilt is yet another. If the child feels somehow responsible for the attack, they're more likely to go on to develop PTSD. And of course, how resilient the child is will have a huge bearing. Research indicates it's generally girls that tend to suffer from PTSD but I certainly wouldn't rule out a boy suffering from it in later life. There's also another couple of factors you should be aware of.'

'Which are?' asked Carruthers.

'By the time a child is put into care he or she may already have been the victim of abuse in the family home. Sometimes kids are put in to care *because* they've already suffered abuse at home. Unfortunately, a survey commissioned by the NSPCC shows that kids who had been sexually abused in the family home were more likely to be victims again in care.'

'You said there were a couple of factors? What was the second?' said Fletcher.

'Don't assume abuse that takes place in a children's home is done solely by the employees. I'm afraid some of the abusers are other kids.'

'Like the Jamie Bulger case? I think I remember reading that one of the child abusers of the toddler had himself been abused,' said Fletcher.

'Dreadful case. Different circumstances of course. But like I said it's not uncommon for victims of child abuse to go on to be abusers. It's all they've known. Of course, it throws up all sorts of interesting moral questions about culpability when the child's very young, but,' he glanced at Fletcher before adding, 'I'm getting off track here.'

Fletcher felt queasy. Dr Ross crossed his legs. 'What you need to remember is when we talk about abuse, whether it's in care or at home, in a lot of cases it's not just about these kids being sexually abused.'

Fletcher glanced over at Carruthers to see him raising an eyebrow. 'Although that's terrible in itself,' Ross continued, 'it's much broader than that. It's about the removal of basic human rights. Quite often the abuse that occurred in these homes went hand-in-hand with a systematic process of humiliation.'

'What sort of thing?' asked Fletcher.

'Well, to give you a few examples, there's shocking reports of the kids being made to wear nightwear all day with bare feet, having no access to writing or reading materials or TV, sometimes for weeks on end.'

'That sounds like a form of torture to me,' said Fletcher.

'Exactly right,' said Greg Ross. 'Perhaps this doesn't sound so awful in itself but what it amounts to, especially if it went on for several weeks, is a form of sensory deprivation that, as you rightly said, did amount to torture and illegal imprisonment. It was all about intimidation, coercion and, as I said, a denial of basic human rights.'

'I'm not sure how this is going to help our case but it's useful to know. Thank you,' said Carruthers, leaning back in his chair. 'I've got one final question for you. What's likely to happen if a child abuse victim comes in to contact with their abuser in later life? Say thirty to forty years later?'

Greg Ross shook his head. 'One couldn't say with any degree of certainty. Again, it would depend on the specific circumstances and the individual child. It would certainly bring back a lot of bad memories. The victim may feel anger; hatred; despair. There could be a whole range of emotions ranging from internalising the anger–'

'You mean engaging in self destructive behaviour?' asked Fletcher.

'Yes, maybe drinking to excess or even self-mutilation.'

'Even suicide?' said Fletcher.

'Yes, it's a possibility. Sadly there's a number of victims of child abuse who do go on to commit suicide. Or the victim may externalise the anger.'

'When you say "externalise the anger" you mean they could be driven to commit violent acts?' asked Fletcher.

'It's possible.'

'Including murder?' asked Fletcher.

Ross thought about this for a moment or two. 'The longer the abuse continued, the higher the risk of causing severe symptoms, so yes, it's possible.'

'OK,' said Carruthers standing up. Fletcher and Ross followed suit. 'This has been really helpful. Thanks for coming in to see us here. It's much appreciated. Sorry we couldn't make time to meet you in a more informal setting.'

'I understand. It's been my pleasure,' he said looking at Fletcher. She blushed. 'Here's my card,' he said, giving it to her. 'If you think of anything else you need to ask me just give me a call. Perhaps next time we can meet over a bite to eat and a drink. Even the police have to wet their whistles once in a while, if you'll pardon the pun.'

***

'What are you thinking?' asked Fletcher a little while later when they were on their own. They'd gone back in to his office. She laid her mobile down on his desk.

Carruthers turned to her smiling, 'Amongst other things that Dr Greg Ross has the hots for my DS.'

'Don't be ridiculous,' she said reddening again.

Carruthers stole a glance at her. 'Did you get the locks changed OK yesterday? Everything alright?'

'Everything's fine. Locks changed and I'm moving on with my life.'

'Good.'

'What do you make of Dawson's flat being ransacked?' said Fletcher. 'Done by the same person who ran him down?'

'Could just be a coincidence,' said Carruthers, clearing up his notes. There's been a lot of burglaries in that area recently.'

She looked in to his blue eyes. 'Is that what you really think? Different MO to the other burglaries, Jim. The place was taken apart. Even the coals from the fire were removed. If someone was prepared to go to that much trouble, then they were looking for something pretty desperately, which they obviously didn't find when they ran him down,' Fletcher added.

The long silence was finally broken by Carruthers. 'The question is, did they find what they were looking for, or is the evidence still out there somewhere? Look, I'm heading for a coffee. Do you want one? I'll treat you to a doughnut. I need the sugar rush.'

'Yes please. If you get the doughnuts I'll chase up John Forrest,' she said. She picked up her mobile. 'See if he's got any printouts for us.'

***

Fletcher put her head round the canteen door. She spotted Carruthers having a word with a colleague. Managing to catch his eye she said, 'I've just spoken to John. He's heading over.'

Clutching his bag of doughnuts Carruthers said, 'I'm on my way.'

***

With a hammering heart, Fletcher spread a mass of photographs John had given them in front of her. They had commandeered an interview room. It was more private. The photographs covered every square inch of the table. She took a slurp of her steaming coffee and flinched as she burnt her tongue.

Pouncing on the photographs, Carruthers said, 'Right, what have we got?' said Carruthers.

'Look,' said Fletcher, picking up one particular photograph. It had been taken from the inside of a bedroom. There was an old-fashioned bed in the centre upon which a naked boy of about ten years old lay. There was a window behind the bed. In the background was an eo Gothic looking Victorian building. It looked familiar.

Fletcher pointed at it. 'Isn't that building Queens Braids up at Braidwood?' she asked.

Carruthers peered at it. 'Yes, I think it is. So if Queens Braids is seen from the window of that building that means the photograph must have been taken from—'

'Old Braids. I can't imagine a boy's dormitory looking like this, Jim. It must be one of the care worker's rooms.'

'Jesus, look at this one.'

Fletcher moved one of the photographs to a more prominent place on the table. As well as a naked thirteen-year-old boy, the picture showed a man in his forties. Her stomach lurched.

'Isn't that Bob Marshall?'

Carruthers picked up the photograph and examined it closely. 'Hard to see from that angle. If it is him, I'm surprised he allowed himself to be photographed. After all, he would have laid himself wide open to blackmail.'

'Probably thought they were untouchable,' said Fletcher.

'That's what Paul Fraser said. Pity a lot of these players are dead. I'd really like to be the one to take them down.'

Fletcher picked up an assortment of other print-outs and passed them to Carruthers. All of them were either of naked boys or various men committing indecent acts on boys. The youngest boy in any of the photographs looked to be about ten years old. Her stomach lurched for a second time. She was embarrassed to find it was making gurgling noises. She wondered how Carruthers was coping with seeing such obscene images.

'Do you recognise any of the men in these pictures?' he asked.

'I don't know. It's hard to get a clear image.'

'Of course, we've no idea who any of the boys are.'

'It's a pity there wasn't a photograph of all the kids together with their names underneath,' said Fletcher.

'Like a school photograph, you mean? That would be too easy, wouldn't it?

Fletcher sighed and fanned her hand over the remainder of the photographs.

'This job's really hard sometimes. It's not easy looking at these images knowing you can't go back and change the past.' She picked up a photograph of a small naked boy of about ten. 'Look at his eyes. They're so sad. They almost seem to follow you about. I wonder what happened to all these kids?' She picked up a doughnut but found she had lost her appetite. The sweet smell of the sugar made her feel sick. She put it down again. 'It was such a long time ago. What if the abusers are all dead? What good will it do the victims? What justice can they ever have?'

'Then perhaps it'll be about a public acknowledgement of what the victims have been through,' said Carruthers. 'We can only hope these sorts of crimes are never allowed to happen again.' He took a swig of his coffee.

'It'll always happen,' said Fletcher. 'There'll always be paedophiles. Look at the amount of information shared over the internet now.'

Carruthers put a hand on her arm. 'Andie, this must be really hard for you. How are you doing?'

'It's OK. Feeling much better. Like I've turned a corner. You don't have to be worried about me.'

'It will take a while to get over what happened – to get over Mark.'

Fletcher was slow to answer. 'I think it will take longer to get over the miscarriage than it will to get over Mark.' As she said this the realisation hit her that throwing herself into these investigations was just what she was needing. And that she'd meant it when she told Carruthers that she was starting to feel better. They weren't just empty words. She hadn't thought about her anxiety since she'd been at Agnes Noble's house. She was even starting to thaw towards Gayle Watson. Perhaps she'd misjudged the woman. She started to leaf through the photos. And yes, she was definitely over Mark. Her thoughts turned to her locksmith. She could feel her cheeks burning again.

'What aren't you telling me?'

She glanced sideways at Carruthers and an embarrassed look spread across her face. 'Let's just say the locksmith did more than just fix the locks.'

Carruthers threw his head back and laughed. 'You didn't? You floozie. I take it from the look on your face you had a good time?'

Fletcher just raised her eyebrows. The self-satisfied look on her face said it all. 'A lady never kisses and tells. It's strange though. It's not like me. I don't do casual sex. And I would have thought it would have been too soon after the miscarriage. I think my emotions are all over the place to be honest.'

'Perhaps it's what you needed,' said Carruthers.

Picking up a couple of photographs she said, 'Those IT boys have worked fast.'

Carruthers agreed. 'Speccie Techie's done a good job.'

'Does he have any sort of life outside work?'

'Of course not. He's an IT geek.'

'He's probably still a virgin, then.' They both laughed.

'Do you really think there could be two murderers?' asked Fletcher.

'At this stage I have absolutely no idea,' said Carruthers. 'Wait a minute. What's this?' Carruthers picked up a photograph that had slipped between two others. It was different from the other photos. More recent.

They found themselves staring at a photograph of a boy in a shower. He was unaware he was being photographed. The picture had been taken with a long lens camera from another building. The youth had jet-black hair and looked about fifteen years old. Jordan Hunter.

'Jesus Christ,' said Carruthers. They exchanged glances. Fletcher's heart was beating just a bit quicker. 'So not just watching him, but taking photos as well. Looks like Fraser's taken this from his flat, and of course it now means both he and Henry Noble were sharing images.'

'Not the easiest if Fraser didn't have a computer. I wonder how Noble got the image?'

'Perhaps he got sent the photo in the post and scanned it. Or by mobile phone. We can check with Speccie.'

'What should we do now, boss?'

'We need to talk to Agnes Noble and the Hunters. Think we also need to speak to Jordan Hunter again. In fact, I wouldn't mind having a word with Jordan and Anne Hunter whilst Malcolm's not around.'

'Do you think Jordan might have been abused?'

'Doubt it. Hunter and Noble were old men. Jordan's a strong wiry teenage boy. Wouldn't do any harm finding out from Jordan just how far their interest in him went, though.'

'Plenty to keep us busy, then.' There was a knock on the door. DS Gayle Watson entered the interview room.

'Boss, just to let you know I've checked with the UK Border Agency as well as the ferry companies and airports.'

'And?' said Carruthers.

Watson shook her head. 'There's no way Paul Fraser would have been able to travel over from Iceland to commit the murders.'

Carruthers turned to Fletcher. 'That leaves us with Malcolm Hunter. Gayle, chase up Hunter's alibi, will you? Oh, and what are Dougie and Willie doing now?'

'Organising the tracking down of all former care home workers and boys at Braidwood. Boss, we've discovered that over a ten-year period, Braidwood housed approximately 120 boys. At any one time they had beds for twenty boys. It's going to be a huge effort to try to find a list of all their names, let alone trace what's become of them all.'

'I'll talk to Bingham about drafting in more support staff,' said Carruthers. *Christ,* he thought, *good luck with that one*. It was hard enough to get him to agree to pay for a psychologist for an hour.

'Aye aye, boss.' With a sharp salute and her trademark grin she was gone.

'How are things between you two?' Carruthers asked turning to Fletcher.

'Fine, much better. I've realised that we don't have to be fighting all the time.'

'Good. Like I said, there's room for both of you. Any more problems with Mark?'

'No, thank goodness.'

Fletcher put her coffee down. 'Jim, can you give me two seconds? I just want to talk to Gayle.' Fletcher followed Watson out of the door running to catch her up.

'Gayle, look I was wrong about you. I just wanted to say sorry.'

'Don't worry about it. I'm not trying to take your place, Andie.'

'No, I know that now. Like I said, I just wanted to apologise. Best get back,' she said, returning to the office where she'd left Carruthers.

She found him draining his coffee. 'Right, grab your coat,' he said.

'Where we going?'

'To interview Agnes Noble again. Tell her what was discovered on her husband's computer. Reckon she's going to be in for a nasty shock.'

***

'I still can't believe Agnes Noble knew nothing of her husband's activities,' said Fletcher after their interview with her. She and Carruthers were back at the station in Carruthers' office poring over some more indecent photographs. 'What did she think he was doing on the internet all that time? Playing patience? He must have spent hours on it, if the number of photographs the IT guys found were anything to go by.'

'His computer was in his study,' said Carruthers. 'Did you notice it was very much a man's room? He could have shut the door and kept her out. Couples need their own space. Remember they're of a generation where men and women had much clearer roles. A lot of men of his generation and my dad's can't cook. Perhaps he never ventured in to the kitchen. Maybe the study was his domain, the kitchen hers.'

'Maybe. I still can't believe she didn't have an inkling, though,' said Fletcher.

There was a tap at the door. Watson's head popped round. Carruthers glanced at her, photo in hand.

'C'mon in. Got some news, Gayle?'

'Aye, some very interesting news,' said Gayle still standing at the door. She seemed reluctant to enter. 'You know how Malcolm Hunter claimed to have been away with work during both murders?'

'Claimed to be?'

'He lied. I called his work. Moncrieff Pharmaceuticals.'

'And?'

'Made redundant just before Christmas.'

'Was he now?' said Carruthers, putting the photograph he'd been holding down on his desk.

'He hasn't been in work for the last month.'

'Perhaps he's managed to pick up another job?' said Fletcher.

Watson shook her head. 'I've already checked. No, he's still out of work.'

'OK, I want you to invite him in,' said Carruthers. 'Now. We'll use interview room two.'

'Right boss.'

'Hunter's got motive *and* opportunity,' said Carruthers to Fletcher after Watson had left. 'This isn't looking good for him.'

'True, but we don't have any evidence he's committed a crime.' Fletcher was still riffling through the latest photographs.

'Yet. Looks like we've got another man with secrets. I'd also like to know where he was when you got assaulted.'

Her hand lay motionless on a photograph as she turned to her boss. 'You don't seriously think he was the one who did it, do you?'

'Well, it was done by someone who's desperate for us not to see any incriminating photographs.'

'That's not going to be Malcolm Hunter, then. Christ, maybe you're right. Maybe there are two murderers.'

She carefully moved one particular photograph out of the way to see the one underneath. 'There's a lot of different kids here, Jim.' She picked up the next. 'Surely it's more likely to be one of the paedophiles that bashed me rather than the murderer? I don't really think I'd recognise an adult now from the photo of a child, would you?'

'You're forgetting we don't know what he or she was after. You're still assuming our murderer was an abused child.'

'Well, it's most likely, isn't it? I mean the link is obviously Braidwood. Why else would two former care workers, who've been implicated in a paedophile ring, be murdered?' Her stomach rumbled, and she felt her cheeks redden.

'Why indeed?' said Carruthers. He stood up. Fletcher followed suit. 'Get yourself another coffee and a sandwich,' he said. 'It could be a long day. No more doughnuts, though. Don't want you to end up looking like Dougie.'

Fletcher snorted. They left the office together. Fletcher headed for the canteen, Carruthers to the coffee machine. Carruthers fixed himself another coffee and took it back to his office. He sat down at his desk thinking, as he took a sip, that he was drinking far too much of the stuff. He couldn't remember if caffeine had a negative effect on the heart. He resolved to find out when Harris appeared at the door. His oversized frame was straining against his taut white shirt. Two of his buttons looked like they were about to pop and Carruthers had an unappealing view of his hairy white belly.

'Boss,' he said.

'For Christ's sake, Dougie. Smarten yourself up a bit, man. Get your wife to buy you some bigger shirts. Staring at your hairy belly is putting me off my chocolate digestive.'

'Nothing wrong with my shirts except they shrank in the wash.'

'Aye, that would be shining bright,' said Carruthers.

Harris sniffed. Still lurking at the door he said, 'We've tracked down the cop who interviewed Paul Fraser. He's still alive and living in Glenrothes.'

'Good work. You got an address for him?'

'Fourteen, Etive Drive. It's on the north side of toon.'

'OK, I want you and Andie to go over there and interview him. You'll find her in the canteen. We'll also pull in Malcolm Hunter. Myself and Gayle will interview Hunter.' Harris turned and left. A couple of minutes later there was a further tap on the door. 'Christ, it's like Piccadilly Circus in here today.' This time it was the IT guy. 'What you got for us, John?'

The young man pushed his glasses back from the bridge of his nose and handed Carruthers a large packet. 'Thought you might want to see these. Most recent pics on the computer. These were scanned in about six months ago.'

***

As Harris pulled up in a convenient space, Fletcher looked skywards towards the post-war flats on the opposite side.

Etive Drive was in the north side of Glenrothes, about ten minutes' drive from the city centre.

'D'you reckon he'll be at home this time of day?' asked Harris.

'Only one way to find out,' said Fletcher.

They locked the car and crossed the road, weaving between the traffic slowing for the red light at the cross roads.

'I think I've seen movement in a window of a second floor flat,' said Fletcher. 'C'mon.'

Fletcher reached the main door first and buzzed McBride's flat. There was no answer. She tried each buzzer in turn until the second to last buzzer and within seconds the main door opened.

'C'mon. We're in.' They climbed the stairs without speaking. By the second flight Harris was panting like a long-haired dog in a heat wave.

'Christ, you're unfit,' said Fletcher taking two stairs at a time. She reached the door and knocked on it. There was no answer. She knocked again.

She crouched down and peered through the letterbox. She narrowed her eyes so she could focus on the dim interior of an unlit hall. Just as she was about to stand upright again and let the letterbox ping back she saw a flash of black jeans and white shirt as a shadow flitted past. She turned to Harris. 'He's in. I've just seen him.' She banged on the door and called through the letterbox.

'Mr McBride. Police. Open up, please. We know you're inside. We just need to ask you a few questions with regard to a couple of incidents.'

The door inched open. 'What's this about?' asked Lenny McBride, hand on doorframe.

'We're conducting an investigation in to a double murder over at Braidwood,' said Fletcher, taking in the stocky appearance and florid complexion.

'What's this got to do with me?'

'Look, can we come in please?' asked Fletcher.

Reluctantly McBride opened the door wider and they followed him through the hall in to his study.

'I believe you used to work for the Fife Constabulary? Ever been to Braidwood?' asked Fletcher.

'Not that I recall,' he said, over his shoulder. 'Look, like I said, what's this about? I'm busy.'

'So I can see,' said Fletcher, looking over McBride's shoulder to the online poker game on his laptop.

He shut the lid. 'Look, aye, I used to work for the Fife Police, but I've long been retired.'

'Look, dinnae take the piss with us,' said Harris. 'You ken how things work on the job. We ken in the mid-1970s you interviewed kids over at Braidwood about alleged child abuse.'

'Jesus, that was over forty years ago. You don't expect me to remember every interview I conducted?'

'Not every interview,' agreed Fletcher. 'But you'd probably remember conducting interviews with kids about alleged child abuse that centred on a children's home. We know there was a paedophile ring in operation, Lenny. We know it was widespread. We also know your boss, Superintendent Bob Marshall, was involved.'

'That's shite. And you shouldn't talk ill of the dead. Yer both scum. You internal complaints?' He sniffed.

'No. Like I said, we're currently investigating the murder of two men at Braidwood Campus,' said Fletcher.

'And like I said, what's that got to do with me? Look, Superintendent Marshall was a great boss. And from what I remember, there wasn't a case to be made. Those kids were attention-seekers and troublemakers. No point in following it up. Christ, they were in care. Couldn't believe a word they said.'

After staring at his now shut laptop, Fletcher said, 'we've got evidence Superintendent Marshall was involved, Lenny. But now, after talking to you, we're wondering what part you played in all this.'

Fletcher noticed McBride's eyes narrowing. 'What do you mean?'

'Were you part of the ring? Taking boys to hotels? Buggering them for your own sadistic pleasure? Wrecking their childhoods? Ruining their futures?' she said.

Lenny McBride turned paler than a waxing moon but resolutely said nothing.

***

'I demand to know why you've brought me to the station. I need to go back into work. I just came home to collect some papers.'

'You're free to go any time. You haven't been arrested.' Malcolm Hunter made to move towards the door of the interview room but Carruthers put his arm out, barring his path. He shook his head. 'I don't think you'll want to go home just yet.'

'What do you mean?' Hunter's eyes narrowed as he looked from Carruthers to Watson.

'I need to ask you if you want a solicitor present? We can arrange for one to be here with you,' asked Carruthers.

'I don't need one. I haven't done anything wrong,' said Hunter.

'OK, if you're sure, we'll begin the interview then. He leant over and pressed play on the recorder. After introducing everyone in the room he said, 'I don't think you went home to collect some papers, Malcolm,' said Carruthers. 'Do you DS Watson?'

'No, I don't.'

Hunter reddened. 'Now look here—'

'No, you look here,' said Carruthers leaning forward. 'We know for a fact you didn't go home to collect some paperwork because you don't happen have a job to go to, do you?' There was a silence. 'Well, do you? You were made redundant at the end of last year.'

'I—'

'We called your company, Malcolm. You might as well come clean. Why've you been lying?'

Hunter was silent.

'Look, I can understand you lying to your family. After all, you're the breadwinner. Your wife expects to live a particular lifestyle, which your money provides.'

Two red spots appeared in Hunter's cheeks. 'You leave my wife out of this.'

'It's humiliating, isn't it? Being made redundant.'

Hunter looked away.

'Embarrassing, even. You feel worthless. All those years at work. All the loyalty you've shown them… then wham! Suddenly you're not wanted anymore. No, I can understand why you lied to your family because you didn't want to lose face. There's one problem though.'

'What's that?'

'You lied to us. You told us you were away with work when both murders were committed. You see the problem? We now know you weren't, which means you have no alibi. Where were you, Malcolm?'

Hunter sniffed, leant back in his uncomfortable seat and put his hands behind his head.

'I think I want a solicitor now.'

'Where were you on the dates they were murdered?' Carruthers stared Hunter down. 'We're waiting.'

Hunter put his hands on the table and sat over it hunched. He remained silent but was the first to look away.

'I'm only saying this once more,' said Carruthers. 'Where *were* you?'

'I *said* I want a solicitor.'

'Legally I am obliged to get you a solicitor if you request one but we'll have to stop the interview.' Carruthers glanced at Watson and nodded. She passed a slim A4 envelope to him.

Carruthers held the envelope. He looked from the envelope to Hunter. 'You may not want me to stop the interview until you've seen this.'

Hunter looked puzzled. 'What is it?'

'Take a look,' said Carruthers.

The stalling tactic had worked. Hunter took the buff envelope from Carruthers and took out the contents. It was a series of photographs.

'Take a look at them,' urged Carruthers. Not yet understanding what he was looking at, frowning, Hunter glanced at the top one.

When he saw its contents his hands bunched in to fists, scrunching the photographs up. The veins stood up and his knuckles went white.

'Careful,' said Carruthers.'That's evidence.'

Hunter looked first at Watson then at Carruthers. 'Where did you get this?'

Carruthers answered with a question of his own. 'Can you confirm these photos are of your son, Jordon?'

Malcolm thumped his fist on the table. 'You know they are.' He stood up abruptly, knocking his chair over. 'Where did you find these photographs?'

'On the computer of the second murder victim, Henry Noble. We think the photos were taken by your neighbour, Ruiridh Fraser and that he passed them on to Noble. You've heard of paedophiles sharing photofiles?'

'The bastard. The filthy bastard. If he wasn't already dead I'd fucking kill him.' He scrunched up the photos.

'We have an admission by Fraser's own son that his father used to abuse him. Fraser's been implicated in a paedophile ring that centred upon Braidwood when it was a boys' home. According to Paul Fraser some of the boys were bought back to his house or taken to a nearby hotel.'

Suddenly a roar escaped Hunter's throat, low and primitive. He knocked all the photographs flying, picked up his chair and hurled it at the window. It bounced off and landed on its side on the floor. Carruthers stood, then calmly placed the chair upright in front of Hunter.

'Sit down, Mr Hunter,' said Carruthers. 'I can understand your anger at your neighbour taking photos of your son in the shower, but you need to calm down. We need to continue this interview.'

'If you weren't at work when the two men were being murdered, where were you?' said Watson.

'I'm saying nothing until my lawyer gets here. You can't keep me here.'

'You're not under arrest. You're helping us with our enquiries. Now, I'm going to ask you one last time. For a start where were you between 6pm and 9pm on 15th January?'

Malcolm Hunter sat back and folded his arms. He stared at the wall behind Carruthers's head.

Watson and Carruthers exchanged glances again.

Carruthers scratched his wrist. 'How did you find out both Fraser and Noble were part of a paedophile ring in the seventies?'

Silence.

'You just lost it, didn't you, when Fraser started to look at Jordan,' said Watson. 'You already knew what he was, what he'd done, but when Fraser started to look at your son, you lost it. What we want to know is, how did you know what he was? And at what point did you decide to kill him?'

Silence.

Watson continued, 'When did you find out Fraser was sharing photographs of your son with Noble?'

Hunter looked resolutely at the wall.

'OK,' said Carruthers, 'we're getting nowhere here. I've got another question for you. What was your childhood like?'

Hunter looked up puzzled. 'What?'

'Your childhood. What was it like?'

Hunter fidgeted in his seat. Not making eye contact with either officer he said, 'Like any other.'

'Where did you live?' asked Carruthers.

'Here in Fife.'

Picking up a pen and opening his notebook, Carruthers said, 'Address?'

'Cupar.'

'Jesus. It's like getting blood out of a stone. Where in Cupar?' asked Carruthers.

'Thirty-five, Main Street.'

'We can check,' said Watson as Carruthers scribbled down the address.

Hunter looked uncomfortable. 'Go ahead.'

Suddenly the door opened and Brown's head appeared. 'Boss, you've got a phone call.'

'I'm in the middle of an interview here, Willie.'

'It's important.'

Carruthers sighed.

Watson and Carruthers left the room together. 'What do you think?' asked Carruthers.

'He's no' giving an inch. Something's not right, though. Did you notice how uncomfortable he was when we asked him about his childhood? I want to know what's making him feel so uncomfortable. What is it about his childhood he doesn't want us to know?'

'Boss,' said Brown. 'The phone call. It's Dr Mackie. Says it's urgent.'

Carruthers nodded at Harris. 'Gayle,' said Carruthers striding away from her towards his office, 'I need to take that call. I won't be long.'

CHAPTER ELEVEN

'Frustrating how unhelpful he was,' said Fletcher, as she and Harris walked back towards their car. A horn sounded as Fletcher opened her door.

'What's the matter with that bawbag?' said Harris. 'You could drive a bus through that space. Numpty,' he shouted. Turning back to Fletcher, he said, 'McBride obviously heard about the murders. My bet is he didnae want to get involved.'

'That's the impression I got. He also didn't want to hear a bad word said against Marshall. You've been in the force a long time. Did you ever meet Marshall?'

Harris put the key in the ignition and started the engine. 'Na. I'm no' that old. But I'd heard about his reputation. He wasnae a man you stood up to, by all accounts. Big fella, too. I imagine if he told you to drop something you would drop it, nae questions.'

'And if you didn't?'

Harris started manoeuvring out of the space. 'Probably ran you out of the force. Policing was a lot different back then. It was a man's world. You started at the bottom, put in the graft and if your face fit and you were good at your job you climbed to the top. None of these bum-fluff graduates being fast-tracked.'

'When you say "bum-fluff graduate", I take it you're referring to me and Jim?' Fletcher said, feeling her face redden.

Harris shrugged. 'S'pose Carruthers is a good detective. Bit too touchy-feely for my liking. Heard his brother's had a heart attack. How's he doing?'

'OK, I think.' Fletcher didn't want to say too much.

'What about Gayle?'

'What about her?' asked Fletcher, noticing the sly look on Harris' face.

'Has she made a pass at you yet?'

'No. I doubt I'm her type. Anyway, just 'cos most men go for anything with a pulse, doesn't mean women follow suit.'

'Follow suit. I like it.' Harris pretended to hold his sides laughing.

'Oh shut up, Dougie. I'm starting to get sick of your sexist shite. Gayle's OK.'

'You two best buddies now, then?'

Fletcher remained silent.

'I still find it hard to believe Marshall was part of a paedophile ring, though,' said Harris.

Fletcher checked her mobile as they pulled out in to the road. The lights changed to red. 'I still want to know why the investigation got dropped. Mind you, investigations in to child abuse weren't taken as seriously in those days, especially when the victims came from children's homes. Somehow they were seen as being less important.'

'Aye, poor wee blighters,' said Harris. 'Yeah, look at the fuss they've made over Jimmy Saville and what he got up to in the seventies and eighties. Mind you, I always thought he was a weirdo. You just had to look at him to see he was a freak. I dinnae see the point in pursuing it now, though. He's deid.'

'It's not just about him though, is it? Although it's seems to have become a real witch hunt.'

There was a sudden shower. Harris switched the wipers on. 'Cannae help but feel sorry for some of those old boys like Stuart Hall. See he's been dragged in and questioned.'

Fletcher turned to look at him. 'You feel sorry for people like Hall?'

'Well, they cannae all be guilty, can they?' He wiped his nose with his sleeve. 'Like you said, it's become a witch hunt.'

'Well, women have obviously made complaints against him otherwise they wouldn't be questioning him,' said Fletcher.

'Is this red light ever gonna change? Look,' said Harris putting his foot down as the light finally turned green. 'If you were a teenage lassie visiting the BBC, meeting some of your idols for the first time, I'm sure you'd drop your drawers willingly. Some of them must have done.'

'Well no, I wouldn't. Those girls were still underage and it sounds like some were coerced into sex if not downright raped. Come to that, what's the difference between coercion and rape? Anyway, look we're getting off the subject.'

'Different era,' said Harris. 'If he'd been threatened, no' that I'm saying Marshall did threaten him or anything. But it was nearly forty years ago. How are we supposed to find out what really happened now?' He turned to Fletcher. 'What's up with you? You've got a face that would turn milk sour.'

'I just felt he wasn't telling us everything, that's all.'

'Mebbe he was scared. After all, there's some loony tune nut job of a murderer on the loose. Mebbe he didnae want to be the next victim.'

Fletcher laughed. 'I like your turn of phrase, Dougie. Come on. Let's get back to the station.'

***

'Ready to talk yet, Malcolm?'

'It's after 6pm.You can't hold me against my will. My wife will be worried. I want to see my kids.'

'You're free to leave any time you choose,' said Carruthers, knowing perfectly well he couldn't hold Hunter. Malcolm Hunter stood up. 'And we could bring in a solicitor for you but it's only going to delay you getting back to your family. Carruthers sat tapping a pen against the desk. 'It will also look better for you if you co-operate. We need to know where you were when Ruiridh Fraser and Henry Noble were being murdered. It's a simple question. We know you weren't at work. You got made redundant less than a month ago. Not long to find another job.' Carruthers sat back, interested to know what Hunter would say.

Malcolm Hunter sat back down slowly, rolled his shirtsleeves up and leant back in his chair. He made eye contact with Carruthers, holding his gaze. Shook his head and expelled a long even breath. Put his hands behind his head.

Carruthers picked up his pen. 'We're listening.'

Hunter leant forward and put his hands palm down on the table. 'You're right. I wasn't at work. I did get made redundant and I haven't told my wife.'

'Finally,' said Carruthers, looking over at Watson, 'we're getting somewhere. Well?'

'I was with another woman.'

'You mean you're having an affair?' said Watson.

'Well, not an affair exactly. I just meet women for sex. One woman actually.'

Carruthers and Watson exchanged glances.

'And you were with her when Fraser and Noble were being murdered?' asked Carruthers.

Malcolm Hunter stood up. Gathered his coat from behind the back of the chair. 'Yes, I was. So you see I do have an alibi. But you can also see why I didn't tell you. I don't want my wife to find out. We have a good family unit. She loves me and I love her and the kids.'

'Then why?' asked Watson.

Hunter shrugged. 'There's no sex. Anne isn't interested anymore.'

'Sit down,' ordered Carruthers. 'You've already lied to us. The least you can do is give us a proper explanation this time. And it had better be the truth.'

Hunter sat back down.

'And this other woman,' said Carruthers. 'She'd be willing to back you up?'

'Yes, she would. She won't like it, but I'll ask her.'

'Why would she be reluctant? Does she not know you're married?' asked Carruthers.

'She's married.'

A look crossed Carruthers' face, a look not lost on Hunter.

'I can tell you disapprove,' said Hunter, 'but you have no right to judge me or anyone else in the same position. How can you possibly know what goes on in someone else's relationship? What an individual's needs are? Whether they're being met?'

Hunter turned to Watson. 'Is he always this sanctimonious?'

'We'll need her name and the address,' said Watson.

Hunter took a deep intake of breath and shook his head.

'You don't have a choice,' said Carruthers. 'We need to corroborate your story. We'll try to be discreet.'

As Carruthers listened to the details of the married woman Hunter had been seeing, his mind was already racing ahead. They were none the wiser about who had bashed Fletcher or killed Angus Dawson. Had it been the murderer of Fraser and Noble, or someone else? Who else would have wanted to get their hands on the historical material from Braidwood? He also wondered how Fletcher and Harris had got on interviewing the one remaining cop from Marshall's time. He hadn't had a chance to talk to Andie about giving Gayle the Hunter interview. He knew by rights it should be Andie's. He hoped she wouldn't bite his head off when she next saw him.

***

'How did you get on with Lenny McBride, Andie?' said Carruthers, drinking from a bottle of fizzy water. Too much caffeine was starting to give him a headache. As for the number of doughnuts he'd been eating lately, all that sugar was making him feel bloated and sick. Carruthers and Fletcher were back in his office. He'd set up a short informal meeting with her and Watson, but he'd asked Fletcher to come five minutes earlier than her colleague.

She shook her head. 'I'm not happy with the way it went. I'd like to pull him in, but we don't have anything concrete on him. Reckon he's got something to hide. Just haven't found out what it is, yet.'

'Look, I hope you don't mind me giving the Hunter interview to Gayle. I know it should have been yours.'

'I wasn't happy about it,' said Fletcher, 'but now I've interviewed McBride, I think he could be a major player in all this.'

Carruthers took a gulp of water. 'What did McBride say about the allegations into child abuse being dropped? He did admit to being involved in the case?'

'Well, first he denied ever going to Braidwood. Later admitted he'd been involved but said at the time he started the initial investigation, he didn't realise Marshall was going to be named as one of the abusers.'

'Did he say Marshall put pressure on him to drop the investigation?'

'No, he said he didn't believe the allegations, especially when he heard Marshall was named. Got the impression a bit of hero-worshipping was going on. Told me Marshall gave him his first big break.'

'What else did he say?'

'Wasn't keen to discuss the case. Said Superintendent Marshall was an outstanding cop and it must have been lies. That there's no way he would have been a kiddy fiddler. Was very defensive of him.'

'Does he remember interviewing Paul Fraser?'

'Yes, he said Fraser told him his father hadn't abused him and that boys didn't go back to the house.'

'Did he admit to conducting the interview in front of the boy's father?'

Fletcher stared open-mouthed.

Carruthers continued, 'And did you tell him that Paul has since made a statement he'd been abused by his own dad?'

'I did tell him but he didn't seem to want to talk about it.'

'There's a fucking surprise. Seems to be a recurrent bloody theme in this case.'

Fletcher played with her file. 'Do you think he could have been one of them?'

'What? A paedophile?' said Carruthers, looking at Fletcher sharply. 'We've got no evidence he was in that ring. I'd hate to think the whole Fife Constabulary were either abusers or accessories. I'd like to think Superintendent Marshall was the one bad apple. Afraid the evidence against him is now starting to look undeniable.'

There was a tap on the door and Watson walked into the office eating an apple. 'Is this Lenny McBride you're talking about?' she said.

'Andie wants to pull him in but we don't have anything on him,' said Carruthers.

'It's just possible he may be the man who attacked me,' said Fletcher as Watson pulled up a chair.

'Did you recognise him?' asked Watson.

'No. I never saw him. Got attacked from behind, remember? But he fits the general description of one of the two men the librarian said was enquiring about Braidwood.'

'Well, if it was Lenny McBride, why would a former police officer attack you?' asked Watson, throwing her apple core in the bin.

'I can think of two reasons,' said Fletcher. 'If he really did hero worship Marshall, he's trying to prevent his name being besmirched by allegations of child sexual abuse coming to light now.'

'It's a bit extreme, attacking you, isn't it?' said Watson.

'True. Or there's another reason. He was a member of the paedophile ring.'

'In which case, he would have a lot more to lose,' said Carruthers.

'We've been thinking that our murderer is a former abused child,' said Fletcher. 'Well, what if he's a former abuser instead? Think about it for a minute,' said Fletcher. 'That there aren't two murderers. Just the one. But he's starting to unravel. That's why not all their actions aren't making sense to us.'

'Why would he kill other members of the paedophile ring?' said Watson.

'Perhaps he found out Fraser was up to his old tricks. Discovered he was sharing photos of a local lad with Henry Noble? Thought they'd get careless and slip up.'

'And the subsequent investigation would lead the police back to their time at Braidwood as supposed "carers", which would mean the whole ring would get exposed,' said Watson.

'It's possible. I don't think it's likely though,' said Carruthers.

'Think about it,' said Fletcher. 'Look at Operation Yewtree in the Jimmy Saville case. Big names being exposed over thirty years later and arrested. They'll realise from that case they won't be exempt from prosecution just because it happened decades ago.'

'I've got a few calls to make,' said Carruthers. 'Report back when you've got anything on Hunter's mistress, Julie Coutts, will you?'

'Sure boss.'

'And Andie? Don't overdo it. This is starting to get complicated. I need you with me. You too, Gayle.'

As soon as Watson and Fletcher had left his office he picked up the phone and dialled Jodie's number.

'Hi, it's me.'

She sounded pleased to hear his voice.

'How's it going?'

'Pretty hectic. How's everything with you?'

'Good. I've had a day off today.'

'I remembered. That's why I've rung you.'

'Any chance of us meeting up again, Jim?'

Carruthers felt a warm glow. 'I'd love to see you, Jodie. I just don't know when. Things are starting to really intensify here. My brother's not well, either. I'd hate to make arrangements and then have to cancel.'

'I'm sorry about your brother. Well, you've got to eat. Do you want to come over to mine? I'll cook?'

Carruthers hesitated, glancing at his watch, wondered if he had time.

'How about I come over to the station?' said Jodie, 'pick up your house key and cook you a meal? If you get delayed then you can just give me a call. I can always put the food in the fridge and you could heat it up later.'

It was almost as if Jodie had read his mind. But for some reason he couldn't fathom he felt reluctant to agree. He knew it was a wonderfully unselfish gesture on Jodie's part but he felt some disquiet about giving her his house key. He couldn't work out why, when he knew he wanted to see her again.

'I couldn't ask you to do that.'

'You're not.' She laughed. 'I'm sensing a little reluctance here. Do you think it's too soon to be given your house key?'

'No. well, maybe. Sorry.'

'No, you're right. I'm sorry. Far too early days. Don't know what I was thinking. Forget it.'

'Jodie, do you like camping?'

'That's come out of left field. Why do you ask?'

'I just wondered if you'd like to go camping with me sometime. When the weather gets warmer, of course.'

'I've never been camping before but I'd give it a shot.'

'Atta girl.' Suddenly Carruthers felt absurdly happy.

He finished the call then dialled his mother's number. Found out his brother was doing OK. His mother sounded relieved. Hospital had told them Alan was a candidate for a bypass after all. They were just waiting on a date. Resolved once the case was over and his brother was on the mend to spend more time with him.

***

'What have you found?' Carruthers asked Fletcher a short while later. 'I can tell just by the look on your face you've got something for me.'

'You look happy,' said Fletcher. 'Have you just spoken to Jodie?'

'I don't know how you do that Andie, but it's scary.'

'I think she'll be good for you. I just wanted to say we've tracked down Julie Coutts.'

'Fast work. I'm impressed.'

'Says she's willing to give Hunter an alibi on both nights, so long as we keep her name out of it and we don't tell her husband.'

'Shit. I was so sure it was him.'

'Still could be. She could still be lying.'

'Why provide a false alibi? There'd be too much at stake for her.' Carruthers steepled his hands under his nose. 'With Paul Fraser already ruled out… there's got to be someone else. Someone we've completely missed.'

'You really don't think it was Fraser? He had motive.'

'But no opportunity,' said Carruthers.

'Could have paid someone to kill his old man. Wouldn't be the first.'

'Shit, who knows? This is becoming so complicated. I agree with Gayle though. I think we need to interview Lenny McBride again.'

'Now?' asked Fletcher.

Carruthers glanced at his watch. 'Christ. I didn't realise the time. It's the back of nine. After we pay a visit to Mrs Anne Hunter. Get yourself home, Andie. We'll do that first thing in the morning.'

His thoughts turned to Jodie. Here was an attractive, intelligent woman showing an interest in him. He liked her. Really liked her. Yet, something was holding him back. He couldn't work out what it was. He sighed. Went through his 'to do list' in his head. Still hadn't managed to speak to his brother. He picked up the phone, dialled Alan's number. He picked up.

CHAPTER TWELVE

'Grab the car keys. We're going over to Cellardyke,' said Carruthers the following morning. He was standing over Fletcher's desk. He'd had a sleepless night. Knew it showed on his face. He'd seen the lines and shadows in the mirror that morning. His eyes felt gritty. Speaking to his brother had been even harder than expected. He'd heard the fear and anxiety in the faltering words, the breaking voice. The cocky man who'd never smoked, the fitness freak, the competitive runner who had in the past competed in the Highland games. What did his future hold now? Carruthers wondered. And why Alan? It hadn't been a long call, but it hadn't needed to be. Carruthers told his brother he would be there for him. And he meant it.

'What right now, this minute?' asked Fletcher, breaking into Carruthers' thoughts. 'You OK?'

'Yes fine, and no time like the present.' Carruthers threw Fletcher her coat and grabbed his mobile. If truth be told, he was feeling more than a little guilty. He wished he'd managed to find time to visit Alan. Not just ring him. He could try blaming it on work but knew that wasn't the reason. After all, he'd still managed to find time for Jodie.

Over the last couple of days the weather had changed dramatically. The snow and ice had melted leaving conditions mild but wet and windy. The weather front was pushing in from the west. A bonus of living on the east coast was that it tended to be drier. If there was one thing Carruthers couldn't stand it was the relentless rain that reminded him of Glasgow.

'Boss, that's Malcolm Hunter just leaving the house now,' said Fletcher as she saw Hunter appearing at his front door. 'I've got to hand it to him. He's certainly managing to keep up the pretence.' She watched him, as, briefcase in hand, he climbed into his car and drove off.

'Bang on time.' Carruthers opened his car door. 'Right, let's go. I want to speak to Anne and Jordan Hunter on their own. There's a lot more to Malcolm Hunter than meets the eye. He's lied to us. Lied to his family. Just wonder how many more secrets he's keeping.'

'Wait,' said Fletcher. 'How are we going to play this?'

'What do you mean?' said Carruthers, getting out of the car and slamming the door.

Fletcher hurriedly got out of the car too. 'Are we going to tell her that her husband's been made redundant?'

Carruthers could already feel the wet rain on his face. 'I want to play it by ear.' He waited for a car to go past before crossing the road, stepping back smartly as the dirty spray from the tyres smattered his black boots. Cursing he walked up to the house. Rang the bell and waited. The door was finally opened by a harried-looking Anne Hunter.

'What are you doing here?' she asked. 'I'm in the middle of my exercises.' She was wearing a pale pink lycra top and stretchy black gym trousers.

'Do you mind if we come in?' asked Carruthers. 'We need to ask you and your son some further questions.' A smell of garlic and spices wafted out of the front door. He wondered if it was the smells from last night's meal. Carruthers thought he could also detect cumin and ginger. He sniffed appreciatively.

'I know about the photographs that pervert was taking of Jordan, if that's why you're here. Malcolm told me.'

'We'd like to speak to Jordan,' said Carruthers.

'He's not here.'

'Can we come in please, Mrs Hunter?' asked Fletcher.

Anne Hunter stole a glance both left and right up the street then opened the door wider and stepped back. She had a look of resigned impatience on her face. She led them in to the living room.

Carruthers was already unbuttoning his coat but remained standing. 'We want to ask you some questions about your husband. For example, how well you know him?'

Anne Hunter turned to the two police officers. 'What sort of question's that? I've been married to him for over twenty years.' She shook her head. 'Oh my God, you don't think he killed Ruiridh Fraser, do you? That's absurd.'

'We don't know what to think at the moment, Mrs Hunter,' admitted Fletcher. 'All we know is that two men are dead and not by their own hand.'

'Malcolm told me those two men had been sharing photographs of Jordan.' She shuddered and looked away. 'I can't believe I didn't know what was going on. Right under my own nose. But I still don't really understand why you're here. Their deaths have nothing to do with us.' She didn't offer them a seat and they both continued to stand.

'I can understand you being upset,' said Fletcher. 'But we feel your husband isn't telling us the full story.'

'You already have his alibi. He was at work.'

'That's just the problem, Mrs Hunter. He wasn't. He was made redundant at the end of last year. We spoke to his company who confirmed it.' As he said this, Carruthers looked over at Fletcher who nodded.

'But I don't understand. Are you now saying he doesn't have an alibi?'

Carruthers chose his words with care. 'He told us where he was on the two dates in question and we're double-checking.'

'Well, where was he if he wasn't at work? I can't believe he didn't tell me he'd been made redundant. Where the hell has he been going every day if it isn't to work?'

She walked over to the bay window and stared out sightlessly. Carruthers noticed the rain was continuing to fall. The sky was leaden and the darkness and gloom made the street appear narrower than it was. There was a whooshing noise as a silver car drove past through the wet streets.

He joined her at the window. 'That's a question you need to ask him, I'm afraid. The thing is, we're wondering just how well you know your husband? To us he's a bit of a mystery. We just need some background information.'

'What sort of background information?' she asked. Her voice was flat and carried no emotion.

'Well, for example, what do you know of his parents? His childhood?'

'Why on earth would you want to know about his childhood?' She faced Carruthers after making an exasperated clicking of her tongue. The question seemed to bring her back to the room with them. The frown marks that Carruthers had noticed when she'd opened the front door suddenly seemed deeper. The crow's feet around her eyes appeared more noticeable too. The dark shadows under her eyes told their own story.

'Is everything alright?' Carruthers asked.

'No, of course it's not alright,' said Anne Hunter. 'We've just found out we've been living next door to a paedophile who's being taking photographs of my son. The man's now been murdered. And to cap it all I've just found out my husband's been made redundant, didn't tell me and has lied to the police. God, I've just signed the consent form for my daughter to go on a school skiing trip. How can we afford it?' She started wringing her hands.

Well, when you put it like that, thought Carruthers, *who would be OK?*

Fletcher walked across and joined them at the window. 'Have you had a proper talk with Jordan?' she asked. 'He didn't ever get,' she hesitated before using the next word, 'touched by Fraser, did he?'

Anne Hunter shook her head but remained silent.

'We'll need to talk to him ourselves,' Fletcher continued.

Anne Hunter ran her hands through her long blonde hair. 'No, no. We both sat him down. Nothing like that, thank God. But I can't believe I didn't know about it. I mean, I knew Jordan was talking to Malcolm about something, but I didn't ask. There's always been a special bond between them. There usually is, isn't there, between father and son?'

Carruthers thought it was usually between father and daughter, and mother and son but he kept silent.

'Look,' he said, 'don't beat yourself up. Let's just be grateful Jordan didn't get abused. Looks like Fraser's heyday for being a serial abuser, if that's what he was, was back in the seventies when he worked at Braidwood. He may still have had the inclination but he clearly no longer had the physical strength for anything else. And, of course, he no longer had the opportunity he'd had then.'

'I think all sex abusers should be hanged,' she said, staring out of the window again.

Carruthers didn't know what to say but it wasn't his place to express an opinion. He always saw himself as pretty liberal but there were moments when he felt the same way – usually when he heard of or had to deal with a terrible crime.

Anne Hunter let out a deep sigh, turning away from the window. 'What did you want to know about Malcolm's past?' she asked finally indicating for them both to sit down. They sat on the couch.

'You understand it's just procedure to look in to someone's past in cases such as these,' said Fletcher.

Anne Hunter nodded and took a seat facing the two officers in a lime green arm chair.

'Where your husband's concerned, we don't seem to know much about him,' said Carruthers.

'Look, Malcolm's always been a closed book when it comes to his past. He said that before he met me his life hadn't been particularly happy.'

'Do you know what he meant by that?'

'Not really. I just assumed he hadn't enjoyed his childhood or school. He certainly wasn't close to his parents. That much he said. He's always kept his cards close to his chest. I wish he was a bit more open sometimes but he's a great dad and a good husband. I've had to accept him for the way he is, just as he's had to accept me, faults and all.'

Carruthers couldn't imagine her having too many faults. She seemed too perfect. Was perfection a fault? He didn't know. 'You mentioned his schooling. Did he ever tell you where he went to school?'

'It was in Fife but other than that I don't actually know the name of it.' She frowned as if trying to recall exactly what he had said.

'Did you ever meet his parents?'

She shook her head. 'No, they died before we met, and he had no siblings.'

'Do you know where he grew up?' asked Fletcher.

Anne Hunter once again shook her head. 'Not the address, although he did tell me he grew up in Cupar.'

Well, that tallied with what Hunter told us, thought Carruthers. *Perhaps for once he'd been telling the truth.* Stretching out his long legs Carruthers said, 'Do you have any photographs of him when he was a kid?'

'I've only ever seen a couple. He said that his parents didn't take many.'

'Would you be able to show us one of him as a child?'

Anne nodded. 'I don't know why you want to see it, but yes.' She got up and moved over to the bookshelf. 'We keep the photo albums on the second ledge down.' Carruthers wondered why she had chosen to tell them this. Perhaps she was nervous and uncomfortable talking in this way about her husband. She selected one and opened it. After flicking through, she showed them a black and white photograph of Malcolm Hunter when he was a boy. Carruthers took it from her and studied it. It showed a little boy about the age of eight wearing shorts and an Aertex T-shirt. He had an angelic baby face. But when Carruthers looked closer he could see that the T-shirt the boy was wearing was too large for him and his hair was unbrushed. His shorts were dirty, as was one of his knees. His feet were bare and grubby. He passed it on to Fletcher. It could mean nothing but still…

He thought back to his own childhood. Playing football in the street. Could still hear his mother's angry words, when one day he had come in, football still under arm, trailing mud on to her newly washed kitchen floor that always smelled of lemon pine. He'd managed to rip his shorts and had got a smack for that. Being dirty and tearing your clothes were part and parcel of being a young boy. Nothing unusual in that. He remembered he'd worn Alan's Rangers top that day. Sleeves almost over his hands and top so long it nearly covered his knees.

He swallowed the lump in his throat as he thought about those carefree days, pushing all thoughts of his sick brother out of his mind, promising himself he'd make it up to him. Looking at the photo Fletcher passed back to him he thought about kids up and down the country messing about, getting filthy. No, in itself the photo didn't mean anything, but it was useful to have.

'Can we keep this for now?' he asked. 'We'll give it back in due course.'

Anne shrugged. 'I've no idea why you would want to, but yes, as long as I get it back. He's not in any trouble, is he? You did say he had an alibi for Fraser's murder?'

'Yes, he's given us an alibi.'

'Well, are you going to tell me what it is?' asked Anne Hunter.

'Best you ask him yourself. Thank you for the photograph.' He stood up. Fletcher followed suit. 'We'll see ourselves out. Just one last thing,' said Carruthers. 'How would you describe Malcolm?'

'Describe him?'

'Yes, you know – quiet, talkative? Does he like to be on his own or does he have a wide circle of friends?'

'More of a loner I'd say. He's always been quiet. He can get moody but I know a lot of moody men. He suffers from sleep problems – always has, but then a lot of us do. And it's not always easy with kids. There's always something to worry about. But he's also generous, funny and, like I said, a good husband and dad. Does that answer your question?'

Fletcher and Carruthers both stood up. 'Yes, thank you,' said Carruthers. 'Does he take any medication for his insomnia?'

'Yes, he's been prescribed zopiclone.'

'Who's his GP?' asked Carruthers.

'Dr Bill Taylor at Anstruther Health Centre.'

'Thank you, Mrs Hunter. Like I said, we'll see ourselves out.' Carruthers hesitated. 'Would you mind if I used your bathroom before we leave?'

Anne Hunter pushed a stray lock of blond hair that had fallen over her face. 'Upstairs, first on the left.'

Carruthers left the two women standing in the living room, made his way up the stairs and opened the bathroom door. Shutting and locking it carefully behind him he took a look round the room. Noticing a small stainless steel bathroom cabinet above the sink, he opened it and had a nose around. Alongside an assortment of plasters, paracetamol and mouthwash he found the box of zopiclone. Taking the box out he read the label. They had indeed been prescribed to Malcolm Hunter.

He flushed the toilet and made his way downstairs. 'Thank you, Mrs Hunter.' Turning to Fletcher said, 'Ready to make a move?' She nodded. They left a very troubled-looking Anne Hunter standing on her own at her front door.

'I wasn't sure whether we were going to tell Anne Hunter about her husband's redundancy,' said Fletcher.

The rain had momentarily eased off and a watery sun was trying to appear from behind the clouds. It caught the pools of water in the road so that they glinted. There was a smell of damp in the air.

'I wasn't sure either, but it just seemed the right thing to do.'

'I find it difficult to follow your lead if I don't know where you're going,' admitted Fletcher.

'You have to trust me, Andie. As a cop, you've great instincts but you need to trust more. We're part of a team.'

'I'm not sure we did the right thing telling Anne Hunter about her husband's redundancy, that's all.'

'If Hunter is the murderer, we may've just forced his next move,' said Carruthers.

'But we're already advancing the investigation. Isn't it dangerous trying to force his next move?'

'It's a calculated risk. Anyway, we're not advancing it fast enough. I don't want Bingham breathing down my neck. I've got enough to think about.'

'Is he breathing down your neck, Jim? Does he realise just how much legwork's involved?'

Carruthers put his hands up. 'He's giving us more support staff but wants to see results. It's my neck on the block if we don't deliver.'

'I just don't like the fact you seem to have set the Hunters against each other, that's all. They seem like a decent family.'

'Is that what you think I'm doing?'

'I felt sorry for Anne Hunter. She knows her husband's been keeping secrets from her. And then there's all that stuff with Jordan. She's really beating herself up about not noticing anything was wrong. I just think the news about the redundancy should have come from him, not us.'

'Look, this is a murder investigation. We can't always play nice. Sometimes we have to do things we don't want to do in order to get results.'

'And will we? Get results, I mean?'

Carruthers sidestepped a grey puddle of water and unlocked his car. He climbed in just as the rain started. As he sat in the driver's seat he watched the rain making patterns on the glass as it smattered on the windscreen.

'Yes,' he said simply. 'Whatever it takes.'

Fletcher turned to him. She tucked an unruly lock of dark hair behind her ear. Looking at the beads of rain clinging to her face and her eyes as blue as cornflowers he felt a sudden rush of affection for her and thought she had never looked lovelier. He was so grateful she was OK.

'Good. Well I hope for all our sakes you're right because I reckon we'll have some explaining to do when Hunter finds out what we've done.'

'Yeah, well, don't worry about Hunter. He's in a whole heap of shit just now and having illicit sex is just one of his worries. If his alibi doesn't pan out he could be on a murder charge.'

'For that you'll have to find some evidence.'

'Believe me, if he's the murderer, I will.'

CHAPTER THIRTEEN

'I'm not sure interviewing Julie Coutts during her shift in a busy pub is the best idea,' said Fletcher, bringing her tonic water to her lips. She watched as rain lashed the grimy windows.

'Well, what would you have us do?' Harris asked. 'The boss wants answers and she wasnae at home to question.' He shrugged.

They were sitting in the King's Arms in Glenrothes. Fletcher looked around her at the no-frills pub. It was a working man's pub, a real spit and sawdust place.

Harris sat, legs astride, admiring his pint of Guinness before taking a long thirst-quenching swig. He smacked his lips and set the glass down on a wet, dog-eared mat with a satisfied belch.

'Anyway, it's lunchtime and I'm hungry. A man's gotta eat.' He wiped some of the frothy head from his upper lip. 'Slips down nice and easy, just like a prossie's drawers.' He picked up the torn and dirty menu. 'Think I'll have the steak pie. What you gonna eat?'

'The soup. Need something to warm me up.'

Harris took his packet of Marlboro out of his pocket saying, 'I'm away for a fag. I'll order the food whilst I'm at it. Want another drink? I'm getting one. Thirsty work catching murderers.'

'We haven't actually caught one yet, so go easy on the booze.'

Although the banter was still a bit edgy, they had come to an uneasy truce of sorts. She took a sip of her drink and played with one of the tatty coasters. In a lot of ways Harris was the worst of the seventies-style cop – sexist and aggressive – the sort to act first and ask questions later, but at least you knew where you stood with him. He was also useful to have on your side if things turned nasty. He wasn't afraid of putting himself out there and, unlike some of the cops she'd met, he didn't seem to be on the make. *Definitely a product of his age and class though, that one.*

She wondered how his job choice had been greeted by his family. She sensed a strong loyalty in him. No, he wasn't all bad but she hoped his breed was dying out. Nothing wrong with being tough and working class but as far as she was concerned there was no room for the old-style cop in today's force.

'She's due to start her shift in five minutes,' said Fletcher looking at her watch as Harris settled his large frame back on to the stool. He traced his thumb up the side of the cold glass to catch some liquid that had slopped over. Just at that moment a spotty youth lurched towards them spilling some of his pint over their table.

'Watch it, ya wee radge,' said Harris. The youth mumbled something as he tried to look at them through unfocussed eyes. He was listing as badly as a ship in a storm. He hesitated then stumbled off, spilling his pint as he went.

'Classy joint,' said Fletcher.

Harris wiped his nose with his hand. 'Drink's cheap. That's all I care about.'

Fletcher took another sip of her drink as the front door opened. In walked a voluptuous red-headed woman in her mid-forties. She walked straight round to the back of the bar shaking out her umbrella and unbuttoning her close-fitting purple coat. Under the coat she was wearing a tartan mini skirt with knee-length boots and a low-cut cream blouse.

'Ya beauty,' said Harris. He drained his first pint in one go, belched loudly and said to nobody in particular, 'That looks like our girl to me. What a looker. I'll be right back. Grab another chair, DS Fletcher. We're gonna be having company.' Then in her ear he hissed, 'My money's on Hunter being off the hook. I'm no queer or anything but he's no bad looking and, let's face it, naebody could resist tits like that.' And with that he sauntered off to the bar.

***

'Christ, I know cops when I see them. What d'you want now?' asked Lenny McBride, as he opened the door to Carruthers and Watson. 'More shitting questions? And where's Morecombe and Wise?'

'Just one question to start with,' said Carruthers walking through the door, flashing his ID. He bent down to pick up McBride's post. 'Heard you weren't very helpful. The question is, why?'

The man shrugged. 'I don't want to get involved.' He held his hand out for the post, which Carruthers rifled through. The detective's eye caught a familiar looking leaflet.

'What's this?' he asked McBride. McBride made a grab for the leaflet but he wasn't quick enough. Carruthers stared at it. 'Thought you'd never been to Braidwood before? Isn't that what you told my colleagues?'

'I told them I couldn't remember ever having been to Braidwood,' he said.

'Well, if that's the case, what are you doing with a leaflet from the Friends of Braidwood?' asked Carruthers. 'It's a bit out the way from here, is it not?' He turned the leaflet over, his eyes scanning the bulletin-type points. 'Says here the developers have got their latest plans in to the council, and the community have until 31stJanuary to register objections.' Carruthers turned to McBride. 'Now why would that interest you?'

'What are you doing with their leaflet, Mr McBride?' asked Watson.

'I'm interested in the environment,' he replied.

'My arse, you are,' said Carruthers, making a mental note to ask the Friends of Braidwood what areas their leaflet drop took in. He doubted it extended this far. He turned to Watson. 'What do you think, DS Watson? Does Mr McBride here look like an environmentalist to you?'

'I can't say he does, no.'

'So what if I am interested in the work of the Friends of Braidwood? Doesn't mean anything. Folk support the RSPB without going to all the bird sanctuaries.'

Carruthers turned back to McBride. 'I know you don't want to be involved, but you already are. And maybe up to your neck. Now, are you going to invite us in properly or do we have to conduct our business on your doorstep? Your choice.'

'Do I have a choice?' McBride said with a sigh as he led them in to the small living room. Uninvited, they took seats on opposite ends of the sofa, like a couple of bookends. McBride remained standing. Carruthers noticed that the room was spartanly furnished. There were no ornaments or photographs cluttering the mantelpiece. Nothing of a personal nature.

'Look, what happened was a long time ago. I never believed the allegations, if that's what you want to know. Marshall was as straight as a die,' McBride said.

'There's a growing body of evidence to suggest he was an abuser, Lenny. I'm afraid you not wanting to believe it doesn't make it any less true,' said Carruthers.

'He taught me everything I know.'

'That's what worries me.'

McBride was silent but all colour drained from him.

Carruthers picked up a book from the coffee table in front of him. He glanced at the cover. It was a James Patterson novel. 'Like mysteries, do you? We're here because two men, maybe three, have been murdered within days of each other. You'll have heard all about the first two. It's been plastered all over the papers.' He put the book back down again.

'I don't watch TV or read the papers. Too much bad news.'

'Ruiridh Fraser and Henry Noble. Ring any bells?' said Carruthers.

'Na.'

'Here's the interesting bit. Both men worked at Braidwood in the 1970s.'

'So?' McBride shrugged but looked uneasy.

'So both turn up dead at the very place they worked some forty years before. Coincidence? I don't think so. Do you DS Watson?'

'No, I don't boss. I don't believe in coincidences any more than you do.'

Carruthers turned to McBride. 'And with your police background I'm sure you don't either. Fraser's son told me recently his dad abused him when he was a kid. He also confirmed the man had abused boys from Braidwood back at his house. We've found out that, prior to their murders, both men had been sharing child porn.'

McBride folded his arms. 'Nothing to do with me. I can't help you. You said three men. Who's the third?'

'Can't or won't?' asked Carruthers ignoring the question.

'Can't,' said McBride, walking over to the glass drinks cabinet and helping himself to a bottle of whisky. He poured a liberal amount in to a crystal tumbler and downed it in two gulps.

'Bit early for a drink, isn't it, Lenny?' said Watson.

'I'm retired now. I can drink when I want. Look, what do you want?' he said, turning to Carruthers.

'We want to know, Mr McBride, why the case of alleged sex abuse against boys at Braidwood was dropped. And how far this paedophile ring actually goes?' said Watson. 'And thirdly, and most importantly for us, what Braidwood's recent history has to do with two brutal murders.'

McBride remained looking at them through narrowed eyes. He poured himself another glass of whisky. He swirled the amber liquid around the glass without taking his eyes off Carruthers.

'Don't think you're off the hook because this happened some forty years ago,' said Carruthers. 'Irrespective of the two murders, if you've buggered boys in that home or been an accessory to it, I'll find out and I'll have your balls on a platter.'

'Christ, another moral crusader.' He took a swig of whisky. 'I've done nothing wrong.'

Carruthers grabbed the glass out of the man's hand and set it down on a coffee table. 'Then you won't mind answering a few questions, then, will you?' said Carruthers. 'First of all, what was your relationship with Ruiridh Fraser?'

'Who?'

'First victim.'

'No idea who you're talking about. I don't know him.'

'You interviewed his son, Paul, during the initial investigation into child abuse. Paul would have been about fifteen at the time.'

'I remember him. Small for his age. Bit of a runt. No case to answer.'

'Any reason why you'd interview a victim about alleged abuse with the alleged abuser present? Seems odd. That's all. Boy's hardly likely to open up with his abuser present.'

'That's not why I interviewed him. I interviewed his father as one of the boys from the home had made a complaint against him. Paul was present at the time of the interview and I asked him if he'd seen his father with boys from the home. I then asked him if his father had ever abused him.'

'With his father present? Paul was terrified of his father. Fraser sent Paul and his mother out of the house when he brought boys back. He raped boys in Paul's bed, man.'

McBride stood by the drinks cabinet as still as a statue, glass to his lips. The only sign the man was under pressure was the fact his knuckles were turning white. 'Boy said his father hadn't abused him and he'd never seen boys from the home brought back to the house. I believed him. I'm telling you nothing like that went on at Braidwood, whatever you say. It was just a care home for unruly wee neds. Not worth bothering about, if you ask me. Christ, I wouldn't be surprised if half of them hadn't ended up on the streets or in a life of crime.'

'And if they had, whose fault would it have been?' asked Watson. 'The system that failed them? Or perhaps, for the unlucky ones, the paedophiles who abused them?'

McBride pulled out a packet of Marlboro from his front shirt pocket, and slipped one of the cigarettes into his mouth. He stooped to pick up a box of matches from the coffee table. With the cigarette still dangling unlit he said, 'Waste of space, the lot of them.' He then struck the match. Watson watched the flame flare. There was a smell of sulphur in the air.

'You really are all heart. OK, let's move on,' said Carruthers. 'You told my officers there was no point looking for your archived police interview notes as they'd all gone missing soon after. Is that right?'

'Aye, that's right.'

'Convenient. What happened?'

'To the notes?'

'No, in the interview.'

'Look man, it was forty odd years ago. I can't remember that far back.'

'Yet you remembered the notes had gone missing. Interesting. Useful having a selective memory. So what did happen to the notes?'

McBride shrugged. 'We were in the middle of moving offices at the time. It happens.'

'It's surprising just how much paperwork conveniently goes missing when there's an investigation in to child sex abuse,' said Watson.

'And talking about files going missing where were you at approximately 3pm on 20th January? Anywhere near the library at Braidwood, Lenny?'

'Why would I be? I've never been to the library at Braidwood. I might have a James Patterson novel in my home but I'm no' a great' reader.'

'Really? Only a witness puts you, or someone looking very like you, at the library at Braidwood on the day my DS gets assaulted.'

'I wasn't aware that going to a library was a crime.'

'The person in question was asking some interesting questions about information relating to Braidwood when it was a children's home. Don't you find that odd, Lenny? Later that afternoon DS Fletcher sustained a nasty injury to her head when someone relieved her of some files she was carrying.'

'I haven't assaulted anyone.'

'That's good to hear. So back to my original question. Where were you when DS Fletcher was assaulted and Fraser and Noble were murdered?'

'Christ, first you accuse me of being a frigging paedo. Now you think I'm the murderer. Make your mind up. What possible reason would I have to kill two old men?'

'I haven't even started accusing you of being a paedo yet. You could be both. Murderer and paedo, for all we know. If you had been an active paedophile in the 1970s you would have had every reason for wanting them dead.'

'Why?' He drew on the cigarette and let out the smoke through his nostrils.

'We have no doubt these two men have been murdered because of their past involvement in Braidwood. They'd been in touch with each other recently. Ruiridh Fraser had been taking indecent photographs of his next-door neighbour's teenage son and sharing them with Noble. There's nothing like shitting on your own doorstep. You could have found out. Panicked. Worried they would slip up and your part in the ring would be exposed.'

'What part in the ring?'

'As a paedophile, Mr McBride.'

McBride's face was starting to look pinched and had taken on an unhealthy sheen. He opened his mouth, cigarette dangling precariously.

'If it comes to light you were part of that ring of sex abusers it will mean a prison sentence, and let's face it – I can't think of much worse than being put in prison as a paedophile and a former cop. Can you?'

'Doesn't bear thinking about,' said Watson, shaking her head. 'You wouldn't want to go anywhere near the showers for a start.'

'Now, I'd get your diary, if I were you, and start talking. Do you have alibis for the nights Fraser and Noble were murdered, or not?' said Carruthers.

***

'Look,' said Julie Coutts, showing her cleavage to a drooling Harris, 'I'm at work. I cannae talk long. Aye OK, I've been sleeping with Malcolm Hunter. It's sex, pure and simple but I'm married and so's he. It's no' an affair. He's no' leaving his wife for me and I'm no' leaving my husband for him. It's an arrangement and it suits us well.'

'We don't need the details, Mrs Coutts. We just need to know if you were with Malcolm Hunter on the dates we've given you.'

'Aye, I was.'

'Both dates?' asked Harris, never taking his eyes off her breasts.

'Aye, I've said, haven't I?'

'Where were you?' asked Harris.

'At a wee pub in Dunfermline called the Travellers Arms. Stayed both nights. Breakfast wasnae bad but we were in a different room the second night, and look at this,' Julie pulled up her top to display a well-preserved midriff, the only blemishes being three angry looking itchy red weals. 'Bed bugs,' she whispered. 'Shuggie, my husband, wanted to know where I'd got them from. I had to tell him the cat had fleas.'

'Where did your husband think you were?'

'Oh, at my sister's in Dunblane. She doesnae like him so she's happy to give me an alibi. Bit too useful with his fists.'

'Has he ever hit you?' asked Fletcher.

'A few times. Put me in hospital once.'

Fletcher knew better than to ask Julie Coutts why she hadn't left an abusive husband. The reasons were often complicated.

'And Hunter stayed throughout the night with you?' Fletcher checked. 'He didn't slip away for a few hours?'

'He was definitely with me all night. Trust me, I'm a light sleeper. I would've noticed.' She patted her auburn hair with a manicured hand.

'How did you two meet?' asked Harris.

'Right here in this pub. Came in for a drink after work. He'd had a meeting with some doctors in Dunfermline. I served his table. We got talking. There was an instant attraction. You ken how it is. He asked me if I'd stay and have a drink with him after my shift finished. I didnae have to hurry home. My husband was working nights.' She sighed. 'I suppose I should consider myself lucky. Shuggie's no' interested in me like that anymore. I'm sure he has his affairs. I'm no' interested if he does. I just need a roof over ma heid and a man to tell me I still look good once in a while. Shuggie does the first, Malcolm does the second for me. Makes me feel good about myself. He's a real gentleman. It's no' much to ask for, is it, wanting to feel good about yoursel'?'

Fletcher was staring at Julie Coutts. She almost felt sorry for her. It didn't sound like much of a life. If Julie had found a little happiness, albeit temporarily, who was she to judge her?

She looked over at Harris who had finally managed to drag his gaze away from the barmaid's cleavage and was staring in to an empty pint glass. He looked as bereft as if someone had told him his grannie had just died.

***

'This doesn't add up,' said Watson as they walked back at the car. The rain had come on again and the wind had picked up, blowing litter across the street like tumbleweed. Carruthers looked across at her. 'Lenny McBride killing Ruiridh Fraser and Henry Noble,' she said. 'I know we've said it before but if you were going to silence somebody to keep them from exposing you as a fellow paedophile, you'd hardly kill them at the very location the alleged abuse took place.' Watson dipped in her shoulder bag for her mobile. She checked her messages. Glanced up at Carruthers. 'I still think the murderer's got to be someone who wants the abuse scandal uncovered, which means it's not going to be an abuser. Or maybe it's a family member of someone who's been abused. The choice of location is deliberate, Jim, just as the cloth at the back of the men's throats is meaningful.'

'It's interesting McBride's got no alibi for either murder,' said Carruthers. 'And he's definitely hiding something.'

'And what's he doing with a leaflet from the Friends of Braidwood? Do you believe that rubbish about being into the environment?'

Carruthers shook his head. 'Na. Not for a minute.'

'Pull him in?'

'Not yet. We don't have enough on him.'

Suddenly Carruthers' mobile trilled. 'It's Andie.' He put it close to his ear. 'How'd it go?' Watson looked across, eager to hear how Harris and Fletcher had got on.

Carruthers' eyebrows shot up and he scratched his stubble. He made eye contact with Watson. 'So Coutts is willing to give Hunter an alibi. Both nights? Right, OK. You've got her statement? Anything else? What's she like – this Coutts?' There was a pause as he listened. 'OK, see you back at the station.' He put his phone away and drummed his fingers on the steering wheel.

'Looks like Hunter's off the hook then,' said Watson.

'Or Julie Coutts is prepared to lie for him.'

'Why would she? She doesn't stand to gain anything by it. It's not as if Hunter's prepared to leave his wife for her.'

'Maybe she's hoping he will. She's just done him a huge favour, after all. Puts her in a strong position.'

Watson's stomach rumbled. 'Well, whilst Dougie has been having a liquid lunch, I'm starving.'

'I wouldn't mind meeting this Julie Coutts myself,' said Carruthers.

'What are you thinking?' Watson gave him a curious look.

'Get on to the pub will you? Find out her rota. I might just pay the King's Arms a visit.'

'Before or after lunch?'

Carruthers laughed. 'You've made your point. We'll grab some sandwiches. Don't want you to fade away.'

'You got a hunch, Jim?'

'Maybe.'

'What about Paul Fraser?'

'Well, we've found there's no earthly way he could have travelled over to Scotland and back in the time he was away from his girlfriend.'

'He could have paid someone to kill his father.'

'Maybe. The problem is, my gut is telling me he didn't do it. Right. Let's get that lunch.'

He started the car, yanked the brake off and with one deft movement slid the car into a break in traffic. They both sat gazing at the windscreen in silence waiting for the lights to change. The drizzle had turned Kirkcaldy sepia, the only colour being the red of the lights.

CHAPTER FOURTEEN

'OK, when you asked me for a drink, this wasn't quite what I was expecting.'

Carruthers turned to his date. 'Sorry.' It hadn't helped that they'd collided with an abusive drunk leaving the pub.

'Why have you brought me here? It's not exactly salubrious.' Jodie frowned and wiped away a lipstick smudge from the top of her glass. It wasn't one of hers. 'I'm interested in your choice of venue. First date, The Dreel Tavern, Anstruther. Second, King's Arms, Glenrothes.' She brought the newly cleaned glass up to eye level and inspected it. 'Hmm. Think they should invest in a new dishwasher.' She turned to Carruthers. 'Anyone would think you were trying to get rid of me.'

Carruthers put down his pint of Belhaven Best and gazed at her. 'God, no, not at all. Far from it.'

'Are we eating here?'

'No, no, of course not. Let's just stay for a couple then head off somewhere else for food.'

'OK.' She looked relieved. Carruthers couldn't blame her. He'd already visited the gents'. It had been disgusting.

As she nursed her coke, he sat watching the bar staff and customers. 'What sort of day did you have in the end?' she asked.

'Busy. How about you?' Carruthers had his eye on a group of young lads at the bar. Was wondering if they were old enough to be served and whether the barman had bothered to ask for ID. Then again, the bartender hardly looked old enough to be pulling a pint himself.

'Are you OK, Jim? You're not being very communicative.'

'Sorry. Just tired.' Carruthers watched the staff and customers, whilst trying to keep his mind on their conversation.

Jodie stood up with a sigh. 'I'm away to the toilet. Back soon.' He almost wished her luck but thought better of it. He caught her hand as she brushed past him and squeezed it. She let it go almost immediately. He was starting to regret his choice of venue. It had been a stupid idea. Just went to show that it didn't always pay to try to kill two birds with one stone. But he'd been so desperate to see her again; she'd been free that night suggesting they meet for a drink. He'd known Julie Coutts was due to work the evening shift. It all seemed to just slot in to place. At least in theory.

'Double shift?' he asked with sympathy as a voluptuous red head sailed past his table carrying a tray of empty drinks. The woman stopped and frowned.

'Were you in at lunchtime? I don't remember seeing you,' she asked.

'They work you hard here.'

'I need the money.' She fixed him with a hard glint. 'Did you want something? I'm busy.'

Carruthers noted the lined, lived-in face of someone who'd once been a real beauty, before real life and broken dreams had too soon come crashing in. She was still a stunner though, if you didn't get too close. She had an easy sensuality about her, which seemed at odds with the suspicious, calculating look she was giving him. He wondered what she liked in bed, and if he'd ever go there.

He deliberated how to continue the conversation and then made the decision. 'How badly?'

'What?' she asked.

'I said how badly do you need the money?'

'Who are you?' Her eyes had narrowed.

'Enough to provide Malcolm Hunter with a false alibi?'

He looked up quickly and caught the momentary fear in her eyes before it vanished. 'I havenae provided anyone with a false alibi. Are you police? Your lot were in earlier. I explained everything then. Leave me alone,' she hissed. 'I'm at work.'

'DI Carruthers. I'd show you my badge but don't think it would go down too well in a place like this.' He eyed up a couple of locals at the next table who were throwing him dirty looks over their shoulders. 'I'm not ready to be run out of town by the local vigilantes.' He picked up his pint glass and inspected it. 'Glasses aren't too clean though. And the toilets are bogging, no pun intended.' He looked at her. 'If we find out you've lied, you'll have broken the law. Giving someone a false alibi in a murder investigation is a serious matter.' Noticing Jodie fast approaching he clammed up.

'That was an experience I'd rather not repeat.' Jodie carefully put her handbag on another chair rather than the floor, which was sticky with spilled drinks. She sat down on her ripped stool. 'What's going on?' she asked, looking from Carruthers to Julie Coutts. Coutts turned to Jodie.

'Your boyfriend's hassling me, that's what.'

Jodie frowned. 'How? And he's not my boyfriend.'

'No doubt he'll tell you he's making enquiries.'

'Just making polite conversation.' Carruthers gulped the rest of his drink down quickly, hurt at Jodie's last remark.

Jodie looked at Carruthers with a wounded look in her eye. 'Police business on our date? Why didn't you say, Jim?'

Carruthers was aware that they were starting to attract attention of the wrong kind. A few of the locals sitting nearby had tuned in to the conversation and were talking in low mumbling voices. Carruthers didn't like the look of them. Then again, he didn't like the look of anyone in the pub. Suddenly the place seemed hostile and he realised the folly of bringing someone like Jodie in to this environment. He could have kicked himself for being so selfish. He put his desire to see her above her safety.

Somebody sniffed loudly. 'Does anyone else smell bacon in here. I do.'

'Aye. Distinct whiff of pig.' There was a laugh.

'Have you got someone under surveillance in here? Is this why you chose the place?' hissed Jodie.

Several pairs of hostile eyes looked over at them. 'Well if I did, I don't anymore.' He stood up abruptly and grabbed Jodie's hand. 'We're leaving.'

***

Fletcher padded into her kitchen to make herself a cup of herbal tea when she heard her front door bell. She slipped on her pink mules and looked through the spy hole. There on her front door step was the locksmith. She let out a deep breath and turned round so that her back was against the door.

'Shit, shit, shit.' She looked down at her dressing gown covering not much else and her mules. Of all the days to have an early night. Her newly washed hair was swathed in a towel; her pink face devoid of makeup. She momentarily wondered if she should apply some lipstick then decided that, given that it was pretty obvious she was just out the shower, it would look absurd. Slowly she opened the door a few inches.

'Well, you're a sight for sore eyes,' he said taking in her revealing bathrobe. Feeling embarrassed Fletcher pulled the robe tighter around her.

'Are you going to open the door a bit wider so I can actually see you? I'm not going to bite. Anyway, let's face it, it's nothing I haven't already seen.'

'Look, what do you want?' she asked. 'I'm not in the habit of standing on my door step with nothing but my robe on.'

'Don't forget the towel round your head.' He reached in and in a deft movement took the towel away from her head. Her damp dark hair curled round her ears. He threw the towel at her playfully. She caught it and tried to feel annoyed at him for pitching up uninvited but couldn't. He looked gorgeous in his black leather jacket and checked shirt.

'Well, are you going to let me in? It's cold out here.' He pretended to shiver.

She opened the door wider and as he closed it quietly behind him with his heel, he'd already undone the belt of her bathrobe. It fell to the floor discarded. He took her in his arms and kissed her.

'What is this?' she asked.

He shrugged. 'I don't know. Why don't we find out?' He kissed her again. 'Why do you women always have to analyse everything? Why can't you just go with the flow?'

He took a step back to gaze at her then whistled. 'Now that's what I call a sight worth seeing.' He closed in on her and traced a finger over her collarbone and over the swell of her breast. He shrugged himself out of his jacket, which went the same way as the bathrobe and laughing, caught her in an embrace. He had his hand on the top button of his jeans and as he unzipped himself she heard her phone ring in the living room. Briefly she wondered who it was, but within moments had forgotten she'd heard the phone at all.

***

Jodie walked ahead of Carruthers to her car. He could hear the heels of her boots clicking on the pavement. The rain had finally stopped leaving behind pools of dirty grey water.

'Jodie, wait up. Wait.' He started to run to keep up with her. 'Look, I'm really sorry. I know tonight's been a disaster. Can we start again? I made a mistake. It was stupid of me.' He caught her up and made a grab for her arm. She brushed him off.

'I'm not interested in your excuses.' She turned to face him. 'Is it always going to be like this? Always a hidden agenda? I don't do complicated. If you want to go out to keep a suspect under surveillance, then you can do it without me. Don't ask me out for a drink when it's clearly something else.'

'Look, I made a bad call. I wanted to see you. It meant I could do both at the same time. That's all. There's not enough hours in the day. I'm sorry but this is a murder investigation. We're all under pressure at the station. Trying to fit in having a personal life at the same time isn't easy.'

'Don't you dare make me feel guilty for taking up your precious time. You asked me out, remember? And do you not think I have a busy job?'

'I didn't mean—'

'Anyway, I'm not sure I believe you about wanting to spend time with me.'

'What do you mean?'

Jodie stood just inches from him. Of a similar height to him, she looked him straight in the eye. 'You needed someone, Jim. A woman on your arm. To look less conspicuous. It would have looked obvious, wouldn't it? You coming in on your own asking questions of the staff.'

She turned away and started to walk away from him. 'You used me.' She stopped and turned round. 'You also embarrassed me. Do you think I didn't notice you watching the customers and staff. I never had your full attention. Not for a minute. You were keeping up the pretence of having a conversation, but all the while you had your police head on. You were eavesdropping other people's conversations.'

'That's not true.' Even as he said it, he knew deep down that Jodie had a point. He had missed some of her conversation because his mind had been elsewhere. She shook her head and started walking away from him. Carruthers didn't know whether to let her go or catch her up. He stood dithering, feeling useless. In the end he watched her walk away, listening to the angry staccato sound her heeled boots made. 'I would never use you,' he shouted. Carruthers was appalled that she could even think it. 'What about us? Can I see you again?'His voice was carried away on a sudden gust of wind. She didn't answer him. He watched her as she climbed in to her silver Mazda and sped off. Shoulders sagging, he turned to walk to his own car. As he approached it, he noticed a dent in the driver's door and saw that the driver wing mirror was at an angle, ripped out of its position.

'Fuck,' was all he said as he bent over and kicked the tyre.

***

Fletcher stretched out her bare arm, luxuriating in the afterglow of sex. She watched as her lover snoozed, enjoying watching his chest rise and fall and the contours of his glistening muscles. Her work mobile, which she had left on her dresser when she had gone for her shower, suddenly trilled.

'Shit.' She reached across him to pick it up.

He started to stir. 'Do you have to answer that? I must have dozed off. What time is it?'

'Yes I do. It's work.'

'You're not at work now. You're in bed with me.' He traced a lazy finger down one arm, grabbing her at the wrist in an attempt to pull her towards him.

She shook him loose and made a grab for the mobile.

'Detective Sergeant Andie Fletcher.' It was out before she had time to think about what she was saying. She realised that she hadn't told him what she did for a living. There'd been no need. After all she never thought she would see him again. Worse than that she couldn't actually remember his name. Had he told her his first name? How embarrassing.

She was aware that he'd tensed beside her, and had started to tune in to the expected conversation. She leapt out of bed, looked around for her dressing gown and then remembering that it was still on the floor somewhere on the stairwell, yanked open a cupboard and grabbed a towel which she managed to wrap around herself.

'Give me two minutes,' she mouthed then she left the room closing the bedroom door quietly behind her. She put the mobile closer to her ear. 'Sorry. I didn't catch that. What was it you said?'

'I have some information relating to the Braidwood murders.' The voice was male. Fletcher detected an anglicised Scottish accent. The man wasn't young, perhaps middle aged or older.

'Who is this?'

'My name's Simon Wallis. I don't want to talk on the phone though. Can we meet?'

'Where are you?'

'London.'

Fletcher gripped the phone tighter as her towel started to unravel. She grabbed it. 'I can't just drop everything and head to London. You'll have to give me a bit more. You said you had information?'

'Look, I was a police officer back in the day when Braidwood was a care home. I started working on the case of sexual abuse at the home before I was told to drop it.'

Fletcher's ears pricked up. Perhaps it might be worth meeting up after all. They had been tasked with trying to track down former police officers who had been around at the time of the alleged abuse. 'Who told you to drop it?'

'I told Superintendent Marshall I was going to go public with the information I had because I felt nobody was prepared to take it seriously. I knew kids were being abused.'

'Did Marshall threaten you?'

'Not Marshall. His nephew, McBride. I got told to lay off so I started to do some investigating of my own, in my own time. I ended up wishing I'd never started.'

'McBride as in Lenny McBride? You're saying Lenny McBride is Superintendent Bob Marshall's nephew?'

'That's him. Is he still kicking around? If he is then I doubt he'll be helping you with your enquiries.'

'Why do you say that?' Fletcher tried to keep her voice low. The last thing she wanted was the locksmith to be listening in to police business.

'There's a lot I know about Lenny McBride, and Superintendent Marshall come to that. I'm done keeping their dirty little secrets.

I'm not going to do it anymore. I don't need to, you see. I'm dying. I've got cancer, but before I die I want to make amends for not speaking out when I should have. It's something I've always regretted. Then I heard about the murders at Braidwood. It just seemed the time was right.'

Fletcher decided she'd better toe the line. There was no way she would get permission to journey down to London to talk about the abuse that did or did not occur some forty years before. Reluctantly she said, 'I'm sorry about the cancer, Mr Wallis, but we're not the team who will be dealing with any child abuse claims. I can pass on another number. I don't want to sound harsh, but we're currently dealing with two suspicious deaths. Unless you can help us with those I think you'd be better placed going to the other department.'

'I can't say for sure, but what I know might have something to do with the deaths. I don't want to just see you about the allegations of the Braidwood child abuse. Look, I'm saying too much on the phone, but it's also about a child from the home that went missing at the same time. The thing is, I think he's buried on Braidwood.'

Fletcher drew in a sharp intake of breath. 'Give me a bit more,' she said. 'What's the connection with McBride?'

'The boy was with Lenny McBride when he disappeared. And I know McBride's responsible for the boy's death.'

'Go on,' urged Fletcher.

'McBride was taking the boy by car to a hotel to be abused by Marshall, amongst others. Like I said, I don't know what all this has to do with your murders, but I think it might be all linked. Look, make your own decision. As far as I'm concerned, I've come clean about what I know. Like I said, it's haunted me all these years.'

'Why didn't you come forward before?' In the background she could hear movement in her bedroom.

'I didn't have a choice about leaving the force and even after I left, I still had threatening phone calls. Anonymous of course. I'm pretty sure Marshall or McBride were behind them. I decided to get right away and start again. That's why I moved to England. I didn't have any more problems from them after that. Look, you might hate me for being a coward, but trust me when I say that the abuse of these kids was real, but it also went to the highest level. And I'm not just talking about a superintendent. I'm talking about politicians, judges and lawyers. If I had gone to the newspapers I would have been hung, drawn and quartered by these bastards. I'm not even sure that the editor of the local newspaper wasn't himself involved. Now do you understand?'

Fletcher understood only too well. And what Simon Wallis said certainly backed up what they had found out. It was the same with the Hillsborough scandal. Individual police officers being forced to change their statements so that any blame was diverted from the force for mistakes made. Blame instead that was wrongly directed at the innocent Liverpool fans. Fletcher felt herself grow cold. In this case, it wasn't mistakes being covered up though. It was cold-blooded child sex abuse. And possibly murder. If that was the case how did it relate to the deaths of the two care workers? She thought on her feet. It was close to midnight just now. She'd missed the sleeper. She could be on a train to London first thing. 'Give me your details. I'll meet you tomorrow. It'll have to be lunchtime and close to King's Cross.' She brought the mouthpiece closer, bringing her voice even closer to a whisper. 'And don't talk to anyone else about this. I'll explain why when I see you.'

She finished the call and climbed the stairs to the bedroom. She opened the door to find her bedfellow pulling on his jeans.

'You never told me you were a cop. CID no less.' He whistled.

'You never asked. Does it matter?'

He pulled on his shirt, then his socks and shoes. She sensed he seemed to be in a hurry. She wondered if it was to do with her job. Wouldn't be the first time. She turned to him. 'I need to have a shower and get some stuff ready for tomorrow.'

'Don't let me stop you. I've got to get home anyway. Wife will be wondering where I am.'

Fletcher swung round. 'Your wife? You mean you're married? But you're not wearing a wedding ring. You told me you didn't do relationships.'

'You're right. I don't do relationships. Too risky. But I never said I was single. You just assumed.' He gathered the remainder of his things, his watch, his gold chain, stuffed them in to his jeans pocket and headed out of the bedroom. As he passed her, he bent down and kissed her on the cheek. Incredulous, with tears pricking her eyes she tried to slap him. He caught her arm mid-air.

'I wouldn't do that if I were you. After all, that could be seen as assault. You don't want to be up on a charge for assaulting a member of the public.' His eyes twinkled and his easy smile was back.

'You—'She was lost for words.

He shrugged. 'You enjoyed it, so what's the problem?' He started to bound down the stairs whistling. He paused to scoop up her abandoned knickers, which he threw at her. 'For the wash basket. And by the way the name's Barry.' He placed his hand on his heart in a theatrical manner. 'I'm hurt you didn't ask.' He winked at her and with that he was gone.

CHAPTER FIFTEEN

Fletcher was sitting in the quiet carriage. They'd just passed Newcastle. Having sent a text to Carruthers she then put her mobile on silent. Placed the phone in front of her on the table. The message had been short. 'Following lead. Back later today.' She knew that he would hit the roof when he found that she'd made her travel plans without consulting him, but it had been late and she hadn't been in the mood the evening before to discuss it with him.

'Tea, coffee, any refreshments?' asked the jaunty dark-haired girl with the Geordie accent. Fletcher shook her head and watched the buffet trolley pass through the carriage. She'd been up since the crack of dawn, driven to Leuchars and caught the London-bound train from Aberdeen.

Feeling sick with tiredness that not even a cup of hot sweet tea would cure, she had lain awake most of the night castigating herself for her stupidity. Her stupidity and lust. She had never knowingly slept with a married man before, but the fact that she had been kept in the dark about his marital status didn't make her feel any better about herself. She also hated being taken for a fool.

She managed to doze after they left Newcastle but awoke with a start when the train ground to a halt just north of Northallerton. After ordering a cheese sandwich from the buffet car she walked back to her coach where she devoured it, washing it down with a cup of coffee. She absorbed herself with her case notes until the train pulled in to London.

She had arranged to meet Simon Wallis in a café in Holloway Road, two stops north of King's Cross. As an Arsenal fan it was an area she knew well. As she came out of the tube station and turned right she was assailed with the vibrant and dirty sounds and sights of North London and felt a moment of nostalgia. She found the café he had recommended with little difficulty. Ordering a pot of tea and a bottle of water she settled herself at a table by the window so she could gaze out in to the busy street, which was right across from the tower block of the London Metropolitan University.

***

Simon Wallis had the look of a trendie leftie, from his multi coloured scarf down to his Dr Martens. Definitely not the look of an ex-cop. He had a shock of white hair and lively grey eyes. He caught the waiter's eye and ordered a white coffee.

'I like this café,' he said. 'It reflects all walks of life, don't you think?' He glanced over at the table to their right where three men of what Fletcher judged was Middle Eastern origin had just settled themselves with cups of strong black coffee. To their left was a West Indian woman in brightly coloured robes having a cup of tea with her little girl. Fletcher tried to push away the sudden terrible feeling of loss that threatened to overwhelm her.

Feeling bleak she turned away from the little girl, took a deep breath and said to Wallis. 'What did you do when you left the police?'

Wallis paused, as the café owner, another Middle Eastern man, brought over a cup of coffee and set it on the table in front of him.

Wallis laughed. 'I became a social worker.' He jerked his head towards the window. 'I studied at the Polytechnic of North London, as it was then.'

'The building across the road?' Fletcher asked, watching a group of black girls, arm in arm, walking past the café and crossing the road. They walked up the stone steps and in to the university building.

'No, over at Ladbroke House, Highbury Grove.'

'I know it,' said Fletcher. 'Right by the old Arsenal ground.'

'You know the area?'

'Only because of the football club.'

'A Gooner, eh?'

Fletcher smiled. ''Fraid so.' She brought her cup of tea up to her lips, blew on it and took a sip. 'I bet social work was a far cry from being in the police.'

'You might be surprised. Different environments. And political affiliations back then of course. Glad I came out when I did.' He took a sip of his coffee. 'Especially after Thatcher came to power.' He smiled. 'You'll be too young to remember that but there was a sizeable number of people who thought Britain was starting to resemble a police state back in the 1980s.'

'Still,' said Fletcher. 'One helluva change of career. From police officer to social worker.'

'Let's just say I was never cut out to be a police officer, especially back in that era.'

Becoming serious Fletcher suddenly said, 'What can you tell me about the boy who went missing?'

Scratching the stubble on his chin, he said, 'Tommy Kelly. I remember he was twelve. Been put into care because he was a handful.' He took another sip of his strong coffee. 'That was the official story anyway.'

'And the unofficial?'

'He'd been bullying his younger siblings. When I interviewed him myself—'

'You interviewed him officially?'

'Aye, before Marshall got wind of what I'd done and put the kibosh on it. The boy told me he'd been abused by his stepfather.'

'Did you believe him?'

Simon Wallis nodded. 'I didn't think there was any reason to disbelieve him. I saw some of the other kids around him.' Wallis stirred his coffee. 'They were wary of him. One in particular. It made me wonder if he'd turned bully himself. It happens.'

Fletcher nodded. That sounded all too familiar. She thought of the meeting with the psychologist who'd said much the same thing. Fletcher said, 'Other than that, what sort of boy was he?'

Wallis drew a deep breath in through his nose. 'Hard to say. Only interviewed him the once. But I felt something wasn't quite right. Got the impression other boys kept their distance from him. He seemed a bit cruel.'

'What makes you say that?'

'During the interview a butterfly flew in to the room. It was damaged. I remember its wing was torn. Tommy Kelly pounced on it and ripped the wings off. Right in front of me.'

Fletcher shuddered. 'Was he the sort to fight back if someone abused him, in your opinion?'

'Aye possibly.'

'Enough to get him killed?'

Wallis shrugged, scratched his left ear. 'Mebbe.'

'And you say he disappeared? How long had he been in the home before he went missing?'

'Around eight months, I think. It was June 1975 when he went missing. I left the force three months later.'

'So,' said Fletcher glancing at her notes, 'Tommy Kelly went missing in June 1975, eight months after he was placed in the care home.' She played with her glass. 'I'm just trying to make sense of all this. How this kid's disappearance may be linked to the deaths of Ruiridh Fraser and Henry Noble.'

'Look, if there's any chance of nailing Lenny McBride, I'd like to help. If he killed the boy, that is.'

Fletcher looked sharply at Wallis. 'You really think McBride had something to do with his death? Could the boy not just have run away? Or if he was killed, wouldn't it be more likely to be one of the care home staff? Maybe an accident?' She paused, leaning in to the table. 'What do you remember about that day? I need you to tell me everything. Anything you can think of, anything at all.'

Wallis looked round the café to make sure he wasn't being overheard before resuming talking. He leaned forward too, hands palm down on the table. 'On the day the kid went missing I saw McBride driving off with two kids in the back of his car. One was Tommy Kelly. Like I said on the phone, McBride was one of the last to see him alive. I think he was taking them to that hotel they used, but there's more–'

'You sure it was McBride?' asked Fletcher.

Wallis nodded. He leant back in his chair and picked up his coffee cup.

'Which hotel would that be?' asked Fletcher.

'The Queen's Head, just outside Braidwood. It changed hands numerous times since. Became the Garter and Horse. Burnt down a few years ago. Word was it was an insurance job.'

Fletcher scribbled this down in her notebook. 'How do you know all this?'

White took a sip of his coffee. 'Still got family in the area.'

Which kids did McBride have in his car?'

'Kelly and the second boy was a wee dark-haired laddie. I remember McBride lifting the second boy in to the back of his car. I think he'd given him something. A sleeping pill perhaps. They did sometimes, you know. Made them more docile.'

'Can you remember the second boy's name?' said Fletcher.

Wallis shook his head. 'Look, we're talking thirty-five years ago now. It's a long time. To be honest it's a miracle that I remember Tommy Kelly's name. All I remember of the other boy is that he had dark hair, slim build and had a bad cut on the chin as if he'd had a recent fall.'

'A cut?' she asked. 'The sort of cut that would leave a scar?'

Wallis nodded. 'It needed stitches. Aye, might have scarred. Certainly seemed deep enough.'

It was a long shot. Fletcher tried to calculate Malcolm Hunter's age. How old would he have been in the mid-1970s? He was early fifties now, which by her reckoning would make him about twelve in 1975. Give or take a year, same age as the boy.

'Any idea how he received the cut?' she asked. 'Did he have any other injuries?'

Wallis shook his head. 'None of the care home workers I spoke to seemed too bothered about where he got it. What did one say? "Boys will be boys." Kids are always getting themselves in to scrapes, aren't they? Especially boys.'

'These are serious allegations, Mr Wallis. You have to be sure of what you're saying. There's no physical evidence and it's a long time ago.'

'I know what I heard. And what I saw. It's my belief Kelly is buried up at Braidwood.'

'What makes you think that?'

'I overheard McBride talking to Marshall back at the station later that day. They didn't know I was there. There was nobody else around. It was towards the end of a quiet shift. I ducked down behind a cabinet. Of course, there's nothing that can be proved, but I heard McBride telling Marshall the boy had died. Marshall was angry, asked McBride where the body was. McBride saying it was in the back of his car in the station car park. Marshall telling McBride to wait till dark then bury the body in the woods up at Braidwood.'

Fletcher felt herself grow cold. 'You heard all that? What did you do? Did you confront them?'

For a moment, Wallis put his head down. Stared in to his near empty coffee cup. When he lifted his head Fletcher sensed a range of emotions in his eyes. Sadness, regret? Yes, definitely regret. And guilt.

'Christ, no. I hadn't long been in the force. I thought about it, wanted to, but Marshall was a powerful man. If they could kill a child, even accidentally, and bury his body, imagine what they could have done to me. They could've just made me disappear too. You have no idea what they were capable of. And nor did I, until that moment.'

'But you definitely remember hearing McBride telling Marshall the boy had died. Not that he'd killed him.'

Simon Wallis leant forward. 'That's right.'

Fletcher glanced around the café. The West Indian woman was busy paying her bill and the Turkish men were engaged in a noisy board game.

'Will you make a statement to that effect?' asked Fletcher.

Wallis nodded.

Making a calculated decision based on an instinct to trust this man, she bent down and fished in to her black briefcase bringing out a brown A4 envelope. 'Would you mind if I showed you some photos? They're not very pleasant, I'm afraid. We're just trying to put names to faces. Perhaps looking at them might trigger some more memories. I'd like to start with one in particular. I want you to take a good look. Was this the second boy in the car with Tommy Kelly?'

She brought out the photograph Anne Hunter had given them of the young Malcolm Hunter and passed it to Wallis.

***

'What made you think you could just waltz down to London without running it by me first?' Carruthers demanded from behind his desk. He was standing, hands on hips, glaring at Fletcher. 'I bet you've not even filled out a travel requisition form.' Stress about his brother and the fact Jodie hadn't returned any of his calls, had put him in to a bad mood. And now this.

'Oh for God's sake, Jim. I didn't have time. I had to make a snap decision. It was bloody midnight when I got that call. Look, if you're going to put me on a charge, just get on with it. Then we can talk about what I've found out.'

Carruthers sighed. He'd spoken to his mother and they still hadn't been given a date for his brother's bypass. All this waiting had made his mother really stressed. She'd burst in to tears on the phone. He couldn't blame her. Dragging his focus back he said, 'I'm not happy about this. For Christ's sake call me next time. Preferably before you board the train.'

'Yes, boss,' Fletcher grinned.

'Right, tell me everything you've found out. And I mean everything,' said Carruthers.

Fletcher pulled up a chair and started to talk. Every so often Carruthers would interrupt with a question. Finally, he said, 'Right, what we need to do now is to find out if Malcolm Hunter's ever been in care.'

'Easier said than done,' said Fletcher. 'He's hardly likely to tell us.' She paused for a moment before speaking. 'Wallis couldn't say for sure whether the photo I showed him of Hunter as a boy was the same kid as the one in the back of McBride's car.'

'Pity,' said Carruthers.

'It was a long time ago, Jim.'

'So Simon Wallis thinks Lenny McBride may have killed Tommy Kelly?' said Carruthers.

'Wallis overheard McBride discussing the fact the kid had died. I'm assuming either in the car or at the hotel. Something obviously went wrong. Wallis thinks they were taking him and the second boy to a hotel they used. Apparently, they drugged the boys sometimes. He thinks the second kid was asleep when he was carried to the car. Probably drugged.'

'But Kelly wasn't?'

'No, according to Simon Wallis he was awake.'

'So it could have been an accident?' said Carruthers.

'Could have been. Like I said on the phone, Kelly went missing in 1975. Body's never been found. Imagine if Hunter did spend time in care at Braidwood. He may well have been abused. And if he was, just imagine how he feels when he realises he's living next door to his former abuser?'

'Unless he tracked him down with the intention of killing him,' said Carruthers. 'Perhaps the move next door was deliberate.'

'Would you really go to the effort of moving next door to your former abuser?' asked Fletcher. 'But think about it, Jim. Fraser, the former care worker, starts showing an interest in Hunter's own son, Jordan. Think about how you'd feel if it was your son. You'd flip, wouldn't you? Imagine the feelings that would get stirred up. Say we're back in June, 1975.Malcolm Hunter wakes up to see Tommy Kelly dead beside him. Or he finds out Tommy's died. Of course he would have also been one of the last people to see Kelly alive, too. What sort of questions would you ask as a lad? Would you ask any? Or would you be too scared and keep quiet? Imagine if he did start asking some awkward questions. It's possible he was told he was to blame for the boy's death in some way.'

'Jesus,' said Carruthers.

'Well, you wake up from being drugged to find the boy next to you is dead. What are you going to think? You then have an adult telling you you're responsible, that you killed him. It would stop you pointing the finger at anyone else. Perhaps McBride is so sick he even enlisted Hunter's help to bury Tommy Kelly's body.'

'Whoa,' said Carruthers. 'You don't think you're running away with all this?'

'Look, I know it might sound a bit farfetched, but we already know Kelly had been abused at home. At least that's what he told Simon Wallis. We're assuming this made him vulnerable to further abuse in the home. But what if he was the abuser not the abused? We also know from Wallis that he got put in the home for bullying a younger sibling so he already had history. What if he bullied Malcolm Hunter? And that's why Hunter believed McBride when he was told he'd killed the boy?'

'We have no evidence, no corroboration of Wallis' story. Simon Wallis may have his own agenda. He may be lying. Have you considered that?'

'Thing is, I believe him, Jim. What we need to do is find the body. Or extract a confession from McBride.'

'The latter's hardly likely to happen. There is another scenario, Andie.'

Fletcher looked up. Carruthers continued. 'That Malcolm Hunter murdered Tommy Kelly and Lenny McBride covered it up with Marshall's help. Well, they would've had to. Otherwise it could have exposed their paedophile ring. If I'm right then we may well be looking at Malcolm Hunter being a killer from adolescence.'

'I didn't think of that. What's our next move, Jim?'

'We need to track down the parents of Tommy Kelly.'

'After all this time? How the hell do we do that? They may not even still be alive.'

'Good old-fashioned leg-work. Get a meeting set up, will you? I want as many willing hands as possible.'

'What do you want us to do about Lenny McBride? Bring him in?'

Carruthers sat chewing his pen, thinking. 'It will come down to his word against Wallis'. McBride's an ex-cop. And wily. Let's face it, if there *is* a body buried somewhere in Braidwood, where do we even start looking?'

A stray lock of hair had fallen over Fletcher's face. She tucked it back behind her ear. 'I've never dealt with a case like this before. Any point in bringing in the sniffer dogs?'

'I'll need to check that out. But even if we do find some old bones in that wood, even with the advancements in forensics, it may not lead to our murderer.'

'So he's going to get away with it?'

Carruthers snapped his head up, looking at Fletcher, a new zeal in his blue eyes. 'No, we're going to be clever and flush him out, instead.'

Fletcher curious, 'I'm listening.'

'I have a plan. I want you to phone Alison Stephens from the Friends of Braidwood. See if she's prepared to meet or at least talk to us on the phone.'

'Why?'

'I want her to devise a new Friends leaflet and put it through Lenny McBride's door. We may even get her to do a bit of cold calling and speak to him.'

'I'm not with you.'

'She's to tell McBride, and this is what the leaflet will say, that the developers have got the council's permission and reactivated an old consent to build and that they will start working in the woods within forty-eight hours.'

'We put a tail on McBride? Will Bingham agree? Can we even spare the manpower?'

'For a potential sex abuser and serial killer? He'll agree. Although I haven't decided if we put a tail on him or stake out the woods. After all, there's only two car parks from which you can access the woods.'

'And let's face it. It may not be McBride who turns up,' said Fletcher.

'Well, it will be if he's the only one who knows about the developers reactivating an old consent to build.'

'Perhaps put it out to a wider audience?' asked Fletcher.

Carruthers nodded. 'We'll see if Alison can send out an email. Perhaps she's got it on Facebook or Twitter. Just to widen the circle. We already know she must have McBride's address from the mailing list.'

'Then we wait?' said Fletcher.

'Then we wait,' agreed Carruthers.

CHAPTER SIXTEEN

Carruthers sat in his cottage, long legs encased in blue jeans. He had a glass of Highland Park in one hand and his case notes in the other. He was just contemplating putting on a Johnny Cash CD when there was a tentative knock at his front door.

He wasn't expecting company and, as he pulled himself out of his battered brown leather sofa with a sigh, he couldn't imagine who it might be. Fleetingly wondered if it was Jodie but deemed it unlikely. She still wasn't returning his calls. He sighed, wondering if he had blown it spectacularly. Then his thoughts turned to Fletcher. But why would she be pitching up? He replaced his cut crystal glass on a coaster and in just a few long strides, was opening the front door. The woman who greeted him was the very last person he expected to see. She had been crying. Of that there was no doubt. She'd made an attempt to wash her pinched face before leaving the house but it was blotchy and her blue eyes red-rimmed.

'Can I come in?' she asked.

'How did you find out where I lived?'

'It wasn't that hard. Anyway, we're practically neighbours.' Anne Hunter looked up at him with imploring eyes, her face framed by her long fair hair. 'I need your help.' Then she burst into tears.

Carruthers faced a dilemma. It was against all police policy to invite this woman in to his house so they were alone together. She was the wife of a suspect, perhaps even a suspect herself. He would have the book thrown at him. And yet he wanted to know why she was on his doorstep late at night crying. He made his decision, opened the door wider and stepped aside.

She took a seat on his sofa as he set up the tape recorder. He sat on the bucket chair opposite. She was wearing a moss-green knee-length woollen dress. Her long legs were encased in black leggings that fit in to her black knee-length leather boots.

'I'm not sure how I can help you,' he eventually said, breaking the silence that stretched between them.

'Just tell me what's going on with my husband. You know. Don't you?'

'Know what?'

'That he's in some sort of trouble.'

'Trouble? You mean because he lied to the police?'

'Well, not just that. Do you know who he's got himself mixed up with?'

'I'm sorry. I don't follow.'

'It's why he lost his job, isn't it? He hasn't been made redundant at all, has he? He's been dismissed. For stealing money.'

Carruthers was completely lost now. He was feeling in need of another whisky but would have to make do with a soft drink. He stood up.

'I'm going to get myself a Diet Coke. Do you want a soft drink or a cup of tea?'

She brushed a strand of highlighted blonde hair out of her face. She was make-up free and looked as young as a teenager in the light thrown by the lamp in the corner of the room. A teen with a blotchy face who's just discovered her boyfriend's not all he appears to be.

'I'd rather have a whisky.'

'Just soft drink or tea, I'm afraid.'

She sighed. 'Oh, OK, a Diet Coke please. Have you got any ice?'

'Coming right up,' he said. He went in to the kitchen. Rooted around in the cupboards for two cans of coke and a glass and then in the freezer for some ice cubes. He plonked a couple of cubes of ice in the glass. He took the two cans and glass back through to the living room and gave her the glass with the ice and a can.

'I think you should start at the beginning,' was all he said, as he pulled the tab. The coke made a fizzing noise.

'I don't know where the beginning is exactly. I'm worried he's got a gambling problem.'

'What makes you think he might?'

'He's had a bit of a problem in the past. And today my bankcard got declined in Aldi of all places. It was so embarrassing. I got a mini statement from an ATM. Found there's money missing from our account.'

'How much money?'

'A lot of money. Three thousand pounds.

Carruthers' ears pricked up. 'And when you say missing, do you mean withdrawn? As in taken out in cash?'

'Yes.'

'You think it's your husband?'

Anne Hunter looked puzzled. 'Well, who else could it be?'

'Have you asked him about it?'

She shook her head. 'Not yet. I thought I'd speak to you first. This on top of everything else. I just don't know what to do. Look, he won't tell me where he's been when he was supposed to be at work. When he was supposed to have an alibi for the murders.'

I bet he hasn't, thought Carruthers.

'Can you tell me where he was when he's not been with us and he's not been in work? I'm going out of my mind with worry here.' She sat with her face in her hands, the picture of dejection. She looked up at him as she said, 'I started to think that it might be another woman.'

Carruthers remained silent as Anne Hunter gulped the rest of her coke back. She choked.

'Hey, go slow,' he said taking the glass out of her shaky hand and setting it down on the coffee table.

'I need to know what sort of man I married. I've got the kids to think about. Who does he owe money to and why? Is that why he lost his job – because he's gambling?'

Carruthers was in a fix now. He didn't know how much to tell her. He was starting to have major concerns himself about where the money had gone. Didn't think it had gone to pay gambling debts, however. He was starting to form a hunch about what the money had been used for, and he hoped to God, for Anne Hunter's sake, he was wrong.

Perhaps he hadn't been far off the mark when he'd accused Julie Coutts of giving Hunter a false alibi. She'd said herself she was working a double shift because she needed the money. Well, if she had been the recipient of £3,000 cash, would she have banked it, stuck it under the mattress or spent it? Would there be a paper trail? Most likely, if she needed the money, she would have spent it without banking it first.

He grimaced.

'Anne, could I ask to see your bank statements?'

Anne Hunter shook her head. 'My husband deals with all the finances. I'm not even sure where he's filed them so I wouldn't know where to start looking.'

'And you don't do on-line banking?'

She shook her head.

Carruthers felt a moment's frustration with this beautiful woman.

'OK, could I ask you for details of at least who you bank with? If you could get me the sort code and account number, it would be a start.'

She nodded. 'I don't have them on me but I'll text them to you when I get home. They'll be on my card.'

Fresh tears pricked at her blue eyes. 'You must be able to tell me something.' She picked up her glass and held it out to him. 'Are you sure I can't have a whisky?' she asked.

He took the empty glass from her and laid it down on the table for a second time. 'I've already had one drink tonight,' he said. 'I think we'd both be better off with coffee. I know I would. Can't afford a hangover.'

'Fine. Decaff if you've got it. Are you always this sensible?'

Carruthers raised his eyebrows. He stood up. 'I'll be back in a few minutes.' He hesitated momentarily before leaving the room. 'Look, Mrs Hunter, Anne. I don't know what's going on myself. I don't have all the answers. I only wish I did. I don't think your husband's job loss was anything to do with stealing money if that makes you feel any better. I think it is a case of redundancy.'

She expelled an audible breath. 'Well, that's something I suppose. But what's he needed £3,000 for?'

'Now that, I don't know. Look, will you do me a favour? I'm trying to help you here. Will you help me?'

She looked up at him.

'Don't tell him you know about the missing money. At least not yet. Not for a couple of days. Let me make some enquiries first.'

Anne Hunter remained silent but nodded.

They finished their coffees in silence. Carruthers stood up. 'I think we need to get you home.'

***

That night, after Anne Hunter had left his cottage, Carruthers couldn't sleep. Thoughts were spiralling around in his head. When he wasn't thinking of his brother his mind was going in to overdrive about the case. It would be true to say that as murder investigations went, they'd made a lot of progress. A breakthrough was always vital in the early stages of any investigation and it had taken a while to get their first. But really, were they any closer to catching the murderer? Yes, Carruthers was now satisfied that they could rule out Paul Fraser and Jordan Hunter but that still left Malcolm Hunter and Lenny McBride. And what of Lenny McBride? Had he really had a hand in the disappearance – and possibly murder – of one of the boys? Carruthers had half the team working on trying to find the parents of Tommy Kelly, assuming he had actually existed of course.

Carruthers thumped his pillow for the umpteenth time. His thoughts then turned to the reason for Anne Hunter's visit. At

2am, giving up all of pretence of sleep, Carruthers switched on the bedside light. Making a snap decision he picked up the landline phone on his bedside table. The recipient of his call would be less than happy to hear from him at this late hour but then again, he was one of the few people Carruthers knew who might still be awake. And he was the only one at this hour who might be able to help. He punched in the number.

'John Forrest.'

'John, it's Jim Carruthers here. Look, sorry about the lateness of the hour. Did I wake you up?'

For the wee hours of the morning the voice down the phone sounded very bright. 'How late is it? Shit. It's 2am.'

'Have you not gone to bed yet?' Now he really did feel like a parent.

'Been playing computer games.'

That figures, thought Carruthers. 'Listen, John, a big favour to ask. Are you still in contact with Big Ron over in the Financial Investigation Unit?' He thought of the obese officer who was well known as Forrest's Dungeons and Dragons partner-in-crime. 'If I give you a bank account number can you get the FIU to access the last six months of statements for me? I'm looking for any large withdrawals, especially of cash.'

'Jesus, I hope you're joking me. It's the middle of the night.'

'No,' said Carruthers, 'I'm deadly serious.'

'It's only a few more hours till morning. If you wait till then I won't have to put my career on the line. Will a few hours really matter that much? But you know as well as me this sort of enquiry normally takes several days if not weeks.'

'We don't have weeks. Christ, John, you know what red tape is like. Not to mention all the bloody admin that goes with the job. We need to nail this guy before he strikes again.'

There was a long pause. 'As it happens, Big Ron owes me a favour. I'll give him a call. But I'm doing this legally. In the morning. Trust me. You'll thank me.'

Carruthers sighed. 'Shit. I know you're right. Sorry.' It was Carruthers' turn to pause. 'Don't know what I was thinking. OK. But first thing in the morning.'

'Scout's honour.'

Carruthers replaced the phone but he knew all sleep had deserted him. He pulled on a pair of jeans and padded downstairs. It was whilst he was waiting for his decaff coffee to percolate that he heard a soft knocking at his front door. He frowned and bare-chested walked over to door. He opened it several inches to see Anne Hunter on his doorstep. Before he had a chance to speak she thrust some scrolled up papers in to his hands.

'I found them. Our bank statements. Six months worth. I brought them straight over. Malcolm's working away tonight. You need to look at these and tell me what's going on.' With that she turned on her heel and, with a flash of blond hair, was gone.

Carruthers walked over to the kitchen still holding the statements. He poured himself a black coffee and placing his glasses on the bridge of his nose, sat in the bucket chair and started reading.

CHAPTER SEVENTEEN

'Tommy Kelly's parents are both dead,' said Fletcher passing Carruthers a sheet of paper. Carruthers was sitting at his desk, glasses perched on his grey head. Fletcher sat down opposite him. 'The boy was placed in a care home in 1975,' continued Fletcher. 'He has five other siblings, four of whom are still alive. None of them had any contact with him after he was taken into care. I can't find a marriage or death certificate for him and he doesn't appear to be on the electoral register. He seems to have just disappeared.'

Carruthers' guts twisted. Perhaps there was something in Simon Wallis' theory after all.

'Excellent work, Andie,'said Carruthers. 'I expect you haven't had time to contact Alison Stephens yet?'

Fletcher nodded. 'Yes, I have. She's willing to do it.' Carruthers debated whether he should tell Fletcher about his unexpected visitor the night before but decided against it. He'd only get a row for not following procedure, which would be somewhat ironic given his recent talk with her. Still, he was pleased with Fletcher. Of late she had started to look more like her old self. She was clearly enjoying being back in to her work, which was just as well since she was an invaluable member of his team.

'Alison Stephens,' Fletcher continued, 'is going to give us a hand by writing a leaflet that looks like it's been sent from the Friends of Braidwood. It's going to alert the community and all those who care about the site that the developers have been given permission to start digging in the woods. The leaflet will say that the digging is due to start within forty-eight hours. It'll be popped through McBride's door.'

'Great stuff, Andie. We've already put the shits up McBride. Well, if he is our man, he'll have a seizure when he hears that.'

'If he did have a hand in the murder of Tommy Kelly and he thinks we may be on to him, what's the betting he'll try to dig up the bones and move them off the site? That is, if he can remember where the boy's buried. It's a long time ago. So, do we stake out McBride or Braidwood?'

Carruthers shook his head. 'I'm banking on him wanting to get those bones, but he's not going to do anything during the day in full potential view of the public. With two murders already on site, it's too risky for him. He'll have to have some sort of spade with him. Being seen with that would attract far too much attention from an already nervy public. My reckoning is he'll leave it till dark. We'll get Bingham's permission to get a watch near Braidwood.'

'OK, boss, but do you think it'll work?' said Fletcher.

Carruthers ran his hand through his short grey hair. 'Only one way to find out.'

'The thing is,' continued Fletcher, 'after all this time there may be no DNA linking McBride to the body, *if* there is a body, that is, and *if* we find it. Surely it's less of a risk for him than digging for the body in the woods. I mean, let's face it, even at night, there's still a risk of being caught.'

There was movement in the doorway behind Fletcher. John Forrest pushed his glasses back on to the bridge of his nose. He nodded at Fletcher as he walked in to Carruthers' office.

'I called in that favour,' said Forrest. 'They're going to get on to accessing those statements straight away.'

'Statements?' said Carruthers, all thoughts of having asked John Forrest for the information he'd eventually got from Anne Hunter gone from his head.

'Bank statements for Malcolm Hunter? The ones you asked for only a few hours ago?'

'Jim, I'll see you a bit later,' said Fletcher standing up. She walked towards the door.

'OK,' said Carruthers to Fletcher. He turned to John Forrest. 'Christ, John, I'm sorry, I've managed to get hold of them myself.'

The IT expert's eyebrows shot up.

'Legally,' said Carruthers. 'It's been so crazy I forgot to let you know. How busy are you at the moment? I've got another job I need doing.'

'Was afraid you might say that.' Forrest sighed. 'Go on then. What is it?'

'More of the same I'm afraid. Bank statements for a Ruiridh Fraser and Henry Noble. If you can get copies for the last six months.'

'You know technically this isn't my job? It'll have to go back to the Financial Investigation Unit,' said Forrest.

'I know this is highly irregular but can you call in another favour from your contact there,' said Carruthers handing him a piece of paper. 'There's one more thing. I don't have her bank account details but here are the details I do have for her. Julie Coutts. Home address and pub where she works. I'm needing bank statements for her as well.'

Forrest's brows knit together. 'I thought you said one job. This is three.'

'Welcome to my world,' said Carruthers. 'I want them all cross-referenced. We're looking for withdrawals from Hunter's account and deposits into any of the other three. I want highlighted anything else out of the ordinary as well. Tell them I'm not wanting council tax direct debits or electricity payments. And John?'

Forrest looked up.

'Tell them it's urgent.'

***

For the next couple of hours Carruthers busied himself catching up with his paperwork. Every so often thoughts of Jodie or his brother would crowd his head but he pushed them away. Truth was, when it came to his brother he was feeling guilty that he hadn't been the one who'd had the heart attack.

Fletcher approached. 'I've just run into Speccie. Definitely working like a demon. He's come up trumps, too. Looks like we've got what we want. Two cash withdrawals going out of Malcolm Hunter's account,' Fletcher said, handing over the slip of paper Forrest had given her to pass on to Carruthers. '£3,000 on the 13th January and same amount for 15th November last year. A tidy sum.'

'We need to know what he's been doing with that money. He's obviously been taking out cash so it can't be traced.' Carruthers already knew about the missing sums of money from the statements Anne Hunter had given him. After she'd left his cottage he'd sat up an hour puzzling over them.

'Think we may already know what he's been doing with it. Take a look at this.' Fletcher handed over a handful of bank statements.

'What's this?'

'Take a look at the name of the account holder. I reckon this is a bit more than a strange coincidence but regular deposits have been going into the account of Ruiridh Fraser every couple of months – approximately 15th of the month. The deposits started the same time as the withdrawals made by Hunter. Deposits are all cash.'

Carruthers looked at the statements, at the lines someone had highlighted. 'Deposits for £1,500. Four of them.'

'Brings the total to £6,000,' said Fletcher. 'Is it enough for a search warrant?'

'There's still no proof Hunter was being blackmailed or even that he was taking out the money for Fraser. There's nothing that directly links the money between them.'

Carruthers' desk phone rang. He picked it up. 'Jim, Mackie here. The forensic results are in and we've found something pretty interesting.'

'Go on,' said Carruthers. 'I'm all ears.'

'You will be when you hear this. We've found a large quantity of sleeping pills and tranquilisers in the systems of both Noble and Fraser.'

Carruthers' pulse quickened. 'Zopiclone?' There was a hopeful edge to his voice.

'No. Lorazepam. You may have heard of it,' Dr Mackie continued. 'It's a benzodiazepine. Benzodiazepines are used for their sedative and anxiety-relieving effects. They work by acting on receptors in the brain called GABA receptors—'

'OK, doc. In layman's terms, what do I need to know?'

'There was enough in both men's systems to knock a racehorse out.'

'Cause of death?'

'No, but enough to render both men unconscious. Thought you'd want to know. Oh, one other thing which you might find useful. Lorazepam has a strong sedative effect.'

'I know zopiclone is used for short-term sleep problems,' said Carruthers. 'Is lorazepam also indicated for insomnia?'

'It's more commonly prescribed for anxiety but can be used for sleep problems where the insomnia is caused by anxiety. But the interesting thing about lorazepam is that it's sometimes used for criminal purposes in a manner similar to GHB. It's also tasteless and can be crushed.'

Carruthers thanked Mackie and hung up. He sat in contemplation, stroking the whiskers on his chin. He needed a shave. Frowning, he turned to Fletcher. 'I'm going to speak to Bingham about getting a search warrant for the Hunter place.'

'What are we looking for?'

'We've already found the zopiclone he uses. I want to know if he's got a prescription for lorazepam.'

Fletcher raised her eyebrows.

Carruthers turned to Fletcher. 'Both men have tested positive for lorazepam which means they were drugged before they were killed.'

***

Carruthers rapped on the door. 'Is your husband in?'

Anne Hunter shook her head.

'I'm sorry, Anne. We've got a search warrant to search the property.'

'I can't believe you people are back to do this to me again,' she said. 'What this time?'

'Can you please step aside.' Carruthers gestured for Harris and Watson to go ahead.

'You didn't answer my question,' she asked.

'Dougie, take the upper rooms,' directed Carruthers. 'Start with the main bathroom. Go through it and the bedrooms carefully.'

A while later Harris reappeared. 'It's clean. Nothing, boss.'

Anne Hunter stood, hands on hips at the foot of the stairs. 'I don't know what you're expecting to find. Look, the kids are going to be home soon, and I don't want them to find the police here again. How long are you going to be?'

Unsmiling Carruthers said, 'I know this isn't easy but it will take as long as it takes.'

'That's not an answer.'

'We don't always have all the answers, more's the pity.'

Watson popped her head round. 'Nothing downstairs, but there's a shed in the garden, access through the kitchen.'

Carruthers turned to Anne Hunter. 'Where's the key for the shed?'

'Hanging with the others in the utility room. I might as well just give you people a spare set of keys.' She flashed him a furious look. 'Just a moment.'

She disappeared, just to reappear a few seconds later holding a heavy brass key which she handed to Carruthers. He threw it over at Harris. Anne Hunter directed her next remark to Carruthers, 'There's nothing in the shed but garden tools.'

'Gayle,' said Carruthers, 'go with Dougie, will you? I want a word with Mrs Hunter. Anne—' He led her in to her sitting room.

'What the hell's going on?' she demanded.

'We've uncovered some information about your husband's past. We think he spent some time in care at Braidwood.'

'Surely he would have told me.'

'I think there's probably a lot about your husband you don't know. What other drugs is your husband taking?'

'Just zopiclone.'

'Not lorazepam?'

'No.'

'You sure about that?'

'Yes. Why?'

Suddenly there was a shout from the garden. It was Watson. 'We've found something. You'd better have a look at this, boss.'

Carruthers turned to Anne Hunter. 'Excuse me.' He strode through the kitchen, out in to the garden with a worried looking Anne Hunter trying to keep up with him.

Watson was kneeling on the ground prodding around in some charred wood and ash. 'Boss,' said Harris, appearing from behind the shed and indicating to where Watson was kneeling. 'There's been a recent bonfire. Still bits of cloth in the ashes. Nothing round the back of the shed though. I've checked it out.'

'Gloves on,' said Carruthers. 'Help Gayle sift through the ash. Cloth might've been used to wipe the knife.' Carruthers turned to Anne. 'Does Malcolm normally light fires in the garden in winter?'

'Well, he might if he'd been doing a big garden clear up.'

'In the dead of winter?'

Carruthers could tell Anne Hunter was torn between trying to defend her husband and washing her hands of him after all his recent lies. Her loyalty to her family won.

'It's not uncommon.'

'No, not uncommon if you're trying to get rid of evidence of murder,' said Carruthers.

'I don't know what you think you've found but he hasn't murdered anyone. He hasn't got it in him.'

'You sure about that?' asked Carruthers.

'He's not a killer.'

Carruthers took a walk to where the remnants of the fire had been. Taking a pair of latex gloves out of his pocket, he slipped them on and knelt by the charred embers. He, Watson and Harris worked in silence, sifting through the debris.

Harris picked up a piece of blackened material and held it up to Carruthers to inspect. The end of the material was untouched by the fire. It had been white cloth. He sniffed it. 'Doesnae look like he's burning garden waste to me.' He pointed to a stain on the cloth. 'Looks like a blood stain.' He bagged the remnant.

Anne Hunter opened her mouth to speak, but, hearing the house phone ringing from the living room, she cursed and hurried back inside. Still watching for signs of her re-emerging through the kitchen door, Carruthers said, 'We'll get it to forensics as soon as we're done here.'

'I'll call it in,' said Watson standing up and taking her mobile out of her pocket.

Still sifting Harris said, 'What about Hunter?'

'Once we've found him, we'll invite him in for questioning,' said Carruthers.

'Who'll interview him?' said Harris.

'I will,' said Carruthers. 'I'll get Andie to sit in with me.'

'Aye,' said Harris, stripped off his gloves. 'She's a good detective, even if she is English.'

'There's no place for that sort of prejudice here, Dougie. You know that.'

Harris shrugged. 'She'll have heard a lot worse.' Still on his knees he lifted his head jerking it towards Watson. He sighed. 'Anyway, just when I've got used to Andie now I have a dyke to contend with.'

'I'm sure you'll manage.' *How they manage to contend with you is another matter,* thought Carruthers.

Watson finished her call. 'We'll get the cloth remnants off to the lab for analysis, boss. Dougie and me can take them in.'

'While you do that I'll swing by the station, pick up Andie,' said Carruthers. 'I have a hunch I know where Hunter is.'

Anne Hunter turned to Carruthers. 'What's going to happen now?' Carruthers watched as Watson and Harris walked towards their car.

'We're going to need to bring your husband in for questioning. Any idea where he is?'

Anne Hunter shook her head. 'None.'

Carruthers believed her.

'You can't bring my husband in for questioning,' said Anne Hunter. 'He hasn't done anything.'

'We have no choice,' said Carruthers. 'I'm needing to head off now, Mrs Hunter,' he said. He started walking towards his own car.

Walking away back to the house Anne Hunter shouted, 'I'm going to phone my solicitor. I want him in the interview with Malcolm.'

'That's fine, Mrs Hunter, Anne,' Carruthers said. 'Your husband is allowed representation.'

'I trusted you,' she shouted as Carruthers climbed in to the driver's seat. She had the hurt look of a ten-year-old whose birthday party has just been cancelled.

'Perhaps you're trusting the wrong people,' said Carruthers, half to himself. He shut the car door smartly and drove off. He looked in the rear-view mirror to see her hurrying back indoors, presumably to make that phone call.

CHAPTER EIGHTEEN

'Any idea where Hunter is right now?' asked Fletcher. 'We need to find him before his wife can warn him and he does a bunk.'

Carruthers replaced his mobile in his pocket having assured himself he had no new messages. Looking up he said, 'there's only one place I can think of where his wife couldn't reach him. Let's head to Glenrothes. We'll take a pool car.'

Unlocking the doors of one of the cars Fletcher jumped into the driver's seat. Jim slid into the passenger seat beside her. His door was hardly closed as she shot out of the car park and down the road, the car tyres spitting up gravel behind them.

'Any idea when forensics will have the results for us?' she asked.

'You know how long they take, but they're going to fast-track it and get started as soon as Harris and Watson drop the items off. With a bit of luck, whilst we're still interviewing Hunter.'

'You're very confident we'll pick him up at Julie Coutts'.'

'Where else would he be?'

As soon as they'd left Castletown behind and were in the open country, Fletcher picked up speed.

'Slow down. I want us to arrive in one piece.' A lesser man would have been gripping the handle of the car door at the sight of a young woman driving like a demon. For all that, Carruthers had to admit Fletcher was an excellent driver, even if she did drive a little too fast for his liking. She was much better behind the wheel than most of the men Carruthers knew. Harris was the worst. He had the tendency to speed up when he saw a pedestrian crossing the road in an attempt to give them a fright.

'Hunter must know we're getting closer. Coutts would have told him about your visit to the pub. By the way, do you think it was such a good idea to give Hunter the heads-up we're on to him?'

'I'm starting to think nothing about that evening was a good idea.'

Carruthers saw Fletcher glancing at him. She had a questioning look.

'Let's not go there, eh?' he said, staring out at the wide-open green space and vast expanse of sky.

'Oh my God. You didn't.'

He turned back to look at her. 'Didn't what?'

'Take Jodie there on a date. You did, didn't you? I take it it didn't go well? Shit. What do they say? Never mix business with pleasure.'

Keen to change the subject Carruthers asked, 'How's the locksmith? Seeing him again?'

'No. Turns out he's married.'

'Shit, sorry, Andie.'

'Just shows appearances can be deceptive. Anyway, I don't want to brood about it. What's done is done.'

'They do say that people come in to your life for a reason. Either their purpose is to teach you something of value or you're there to teach them something,' said Carruthers.

'What a load of bollocks. What could that shit of a locksmith have possibly taught me?' she asked.

Carruthers shrugged. 'I don't know. That you're over Mark, perhaps? Ready to move on?'

Fletcher sighed. 'I already knew that. Talking of people not being what they seem… Malcolm Hunter. I think he must be emotionally very disturbed. Maybe even starting to unravel.'

'I'd have to agree with you. But that makes him dangerous. I don't know how he's going to react when cornered.'

'It's very unusual for an abuse victim to turn killer though, isn't it?' said Fletcher. 'Isn't the anger usually internalised?'

Carruthers looked across at her. 'Self-harm, you mean?'

'Well, look at everything the psychologist told us. The greatest surprise, if Hunter has been a child abuse victim, is how well, at least externally, he appears to have coped. He got married, had a family, held a job down.'

'Hey, let's not jump ahead of ourselves,' said Carruthers. 'We still haven't found the murder weapon.'

They arrived at Julie Coutts' flat, found a parking space across the road and got out. Walking across the road, they weaved in between the slow-moving traffic.

'Hope your hunch is right,' said Fletcher sidestepping a skinny teen on a skateboard. 'Otherwise this has been a wasted journey.'

'Only one way to find out.' As Carruthers pushed the doorbell he found he was holding his breath.

They waited on the doorstep for what seemed like an eternity.

'Shit. Doesn't look like anybody's in. Now what do we do?' said Fletcher.

Carruthers stepped up to the doorbell, put his finger on it and held it for ten seconds.

Suddenly the front door was wrenched open. 'What the fuck's all the noise aboot?' A dishevelled redhead stood there wearing nothing but a garish bathrobe, which had fallen open at the front, revealing her breasts. She grabbed the robe tighter around herself with one hand, keeping the other on the frame of the door. Carruthers dragged his eyes away from her cleavage.

'Is Malcolm Hunter here?' asked Fletcher.

'Keep yer voice doon. My husbands' been working nights. He's asleep. She jabbed a finger at Carruthers and looked at Fletcher. 'You're not welcome here.'

Carruthers peered over her shoulder to see a movement darting behind her in the dim hall.

'He's awake now. We'd like a few words with him.'

'He's no' had a decent sleep. Come back later when he's had a few more hours.' She tried to shut the door, but Carruthers had got his foot in the way. The woman's bathrobe started to unravel again and she let go the door to put it tight round her, doing the belt up as she went. Carruthers didn't need a better opportunity. He slipped in past her.

'Get out,' she shrieked. 'You cannae just come barging in to people's homes.'

'We can when we're conducting a murder investigation,' said Carruthers grimly as he darted in to the bedroom. As his eye adjusted he took in the dishevelled bed sheets, the used condom abandoned on the carpet and the pungent smell of sex and cigarettes. His eye travelled to the lit cigarette in the ashtray whose smoke was spiralling in to the air. He recognised the smell. He saw the packet of Camel on the bedside table. There was only one person he knew who smoked that brand.

'Where is he? I know Hunter's here.' Fletcher had entered the bedroom followed by Julie Coutts who was raining blows down on her. Her bathrobe had unravelled itself completely and she seemed neither to notice or care.

There was a sudden flash of movement as Malcolm Hunter, wearing nothing but a pair of blue jeans made a dash for the bathroom door. He slammed the door shut and Carruthers heard the bolt being dragged across.

'Malcolm, come out. It's futile. There's nowhere to go. Don't make this harder on yourself.'

A few minutes passed then the door was prised open and Hunter made a streak for the front door.

Carruthers leapt after him bringing him down in a rugby tackle. He pinned him to the ground.

'Nice to know rugby's good for something,' said Fletcher, adjusting her blouse. Coutts stood next to her in silence, arms wrapped protectively around her chest, a sullen pout on her face.

Carruthers turned to Malcolm Hunter. 'Malcolm Hunter, we're taking you in for questioning in relation to the murders of Ruiridh Fraser and Henry Noble.'

CHAPTER NINETEEN

Carruthers left Malcolm Hunter awaiting his solicitor in one of the interview rooms with Fletcher to keep an eye on him. Meantime Carruthers had gone in search of Brown.

He caught sight of Brown coming out of the gents'. 'I want you to organise a stake-out of Braidwood.' said Carruthers. 'For tonight. Soon as it's dark.' He filled him in.

'Do you no reckon this is a bit of a long shot?' Brown said.

'We don't have enough to arrest McBride,' said Carruthers. 'Yes, we could pull him in for questioning but he's been a cop for long enough. He's not going to talk.'

'There is another way,' said Brown, smoothing over his balding head with his right hand. 'Why no' invite him in for questioning and have him "accidentally run in to" Malcolm Hunter? See if the two recognise each other.' He paused. 'It's a thought.'

Carruthers stroked his stubbly chin, hoping he didn't look as tired as he felt. He was surprised at Brown's initiative. He wasn't usually known for his ideas. 'Have to admit that isn't something I've considered,' he said.

'It might be the first time they've come face to face in nearly forty years,' said Brown.

'Hunter was just a boy then. Would they even recognise each other?'

'Who knows,' said Brown. 'The other scenario is that they've been in touch more recently. If McBride was part of the paedophile ring in the 1970s and still lives in the area, then maybe he's been in contact with Fraser and Noble. Maybe he's been involved in the blackmail.'

Carruthers shook his head. 'There's no evidence McBride was still in touch with the two dead men or involved in blackmail. He lives in Glenrothes. It's not that close.'

Brown shrugged. 'Up to you. Might be worth a punt though. Nothing like raw emotion to unlock a secret. That's what I'd do, rather than waste valuable time staking out a wood nobody might visit.'

'Well, look, I'm about to conduct the interview with Hunter,' said Carruthers. 'We're just awaiting his solicitor. I'm going on a hunch. Let's do it my way for now, and if this doesn't work, we'll try it your way. Get somebody ready for tonight, will you? As soon as it's dark. We'll need a rota and we need to be discreet. I'd also like someone to keep an eye on McBride.' Brown turned to go. Carruthers caught his arm. 'And if there's any movement at all I want to know about it. Especially if Lenny McBride turns up. If he had anything to do with Kelly's murder, we need to catch him red-handed.'

***

Carruthers opened the door to the interview room. 'You'll be wondering what you're doing back at the cop shop,' he said, taking a seat opposite a hastily dressed Malcolm Hunter. Carruthers sat back, stretching his arms behind his head, noticing that in his haste, Hunter had the buttons of his shirt done up wrong. 'I'll give you a clue. You're not here because you're shagging another bloke's missus.'

Carruthers nodded at Fletcher who produced copies of Hunter's bank statements out of a buff file. The relevant withdrawals had been marked with a yellow highlighter pen.

'Have you got a lighter?' asked Hunter. He picked up his cigarettes.

'Even if I had one, you couldn't smoke in here,' said Carruthers. 'You know the rules, although I think you'll probably need one when you know the new evidence we have against you.'

Hunter, who'd already placed a cigarette between his lips with his left hand, let it droop as he said between clenched teeth, 'What new evidence?'

Carruthers took the cigarette out of Hunter's mouth and placed it back in the packet. Carruthers leaned over the table and pressed the record button on the tape recorder. 'For the purposes of the tape interview starts at 1900 hours. Present is myself, DI Jim Carruthers, DS Andrea Fletcher, Malcolm Hunter and Malcolm Hunter's solicitor, Toby Snedden.'

Carruthers paused before speaking again. 'I never noticed you were a left-hander before, Malcolm. Fraser and Noble were both stabbed to death by a left-hander. The similarities in their deaths indicate it was done by the same person.'

Hunter shrugged. 'So? It's no secret I'm left-handed but then I'm not the only one.'

'We also know you've been in care, at Braidwood.' Carruthers knew this was a stab in the dark but it was a punt worth taking. Hunter remained silent. 'You're a very secretive man, Malcolm. Even your wife didn't know.' Carruthers leant forward eyeballing him. 'I don't like overly secretive people, Malcolm. Especially in my line of work.'

Hunter broke eye-contact first, looking away from Carruthers to Fletcher and then finally back to Carruthers again. 'You haven't got anything on me. Why would you have? I didn't kill them.'

'You were at Braidwood the same time Fraser and Noble worked there, which proves you will have known them,' said Carruthers.

Hunter shrugged. 'What if I did? So did scores of others.'

'Let's stop pissing about, Malcolm,' said Carruthers. 'We've found the evidence. Whilst you were getting your end away with the voluptuous Mrs Coutts, the police were searching your property. In fact, they're still there.'

Malcolm Hunter turned pale, a twitch appearing at the side of his face.

'What evidence?'

Carruthers looked him in the eye. 'The two victims were killed by a knife with a serrated edge by a blow from a left-handed man. We're currently searching your property for that knife. We've also found bloodstains on the remnants of a cloth you were trying to burn. Not well enough, though.' Carruthers didn't yet know they were definitely bloodstains until he had the results back from forensics, but Hunter didn't need to know that.

Hunter's solicitor finally spoke. He was a thin, morose man with a dome of a bald head. He adjusted his glasses. 'Look, you haven't got anything on my client, otherwise you'd have arrested him. Well? Are you going to arrest him?'

'Yes, are you going to arrest me?' said Hunter.

'All in good time, Malcolm. The remnants of cloth we found in the ashes of the fire are with forensics as we speak. Considering we can keep you here for twelve hours with the possibility of an extension, well, I don't imagine you'll be going anywhere anytime soon.'

Malcolm glanced at his solicitor. 'You don't have to say anything,' the solicitor advised.

'Like I said,' continued Carruthers, 'I reckon it's just a matter of time now before we find the knife.'

After a moment's hesitation Hunter said, 'OK, let's say I did it. Why would I kill them now, over thirty-five years later? Especially as Fraser was living next door to me. I could have had a pop at him any time.'

'I must admit, that did puzzle us for a while,' said Carruthers. 'What we do know is that there's strong evidence of a serious paedophile ring operating around the time you were in that care home. I don't blame you for not wanting to talk about being in care, especially if you were abused.'

A momentary flicker passed Hunter's eyes and Carruthers watched his Adam's apple bob up and down as he swallowed with difficulty. Hunter shifted uneasily in his chair, his eyes settling on the forlorn cigarette packet.

Carruthers noticed there was a slight tremor in Hunter's hands. He was rattled. But the big question was – would he talk?

'You were abused in that care home, weren't you?' urged Carruthers. 'By a person or people you thought you could trust.' Whilst he was talking, Carruthers' eyes never left Hunter's face. Fletcher was silent, busy making notes, as was the solicitor. Malcolm Hunter too remained silent.

'I don't know what you're talking about,' he eventually said.

Carruthers noticed that the shakes were getting worse.

'Who else were you abused by, Malcolm? Apart from Ruiridh Fraser and Henry Noble?'

Malcolm Hunter shook his head, which remained bowed.

'Superintendent Marshall? Lenny McBride? He's still alive by the way, Lenny McBride, and not living a million miles away from you.' Carruthers paused before continuing. 'What about Tommy Kelly?'

Hunter snapped his head up. All colour draining from his face. In a fleeting moment he appeared to have aged ten years. Carruthers watched his chest rise and fall with great rapidity and hoped he wasn't about to have a heart attack right there in front of him.

'You knew him, didn't you Malcolm? Tommy Kelly. There's no use denying it. We've got a witness who's willing to testify that you hung round together. An ex-policeman, actually.'

Hunter remained silent, staring at the cigarette packet, his thin lips looking no more than slashes in his face.

'You don't have to say anything, Malcolm,' cautioned his solicitor.

Hunter was silent.

Carruthers continued to press. 'He went missing, this boy, didn't he?' There was no answer from Hunter.

For the first time Fletcher spoke. 'We think he was killed, Malcolm. There was a cover-up. Unsurprising, given the amount of sexual abuse that was alleged to have been going on. He was murdered, wasn't he? And his body dumped at Braidwood. It's still lying there even now, undisturbed in the woods after all these years. The only surprise is, he wasn't murdered by a paedophile or care worker. But by another boy. And that boy was you. We're just not sure why you killed Angus Dawson.'

Malcolm Hunter looked confused. 'Who?' he asked.

'This is outrageous,' said the solicitor, taking his glasses off and vigorously cleaning them on a handkerchief he brought out of his breast pocket. 'I won't have you making unsubstantiated accusations about my client in this way.'

Hunter tore his eyes away from the cigarette packet, eyeing Carruthers as if the police officer were the lion in the arena and he the gladiator. 'OK, so I knew him. I got bullied by him but it doesn't mean I killed him. I don't know what happened to him. One day I got up and just didn't see him again.'

Carruthers recognised the first small victory. This was the first time Malcolm Hunter had admitted to being a resident of Braidwood, of knowing Tommy Kelly and of being bullied by him. It was a start.

He hurried on sensing an opening. 'You must have been really worried when you found out the land had been sold to property developers who wanted to build two hundred and fifty new homes on protected green space. You wouldn't want the bulldozers digging up the remains of Tommy Kelly, would you?'

Hunter didn't respond.

'You said Kelly just disappeared,' said Fletcher. 'No questions were asked of his disappearance, were they? His parents were encouraged to have no further contact with him. And let's face it, the running of the home was at best shambolic, at worst criminal. Braidwood, like many other homes at the time were staffed by untrained, low-paid male staff. A veritable breeding ground for paedophiles, if you think about it. But it let you commit the perfect murder, didn't it? Nobody was going to want police looking into the disappearance of one of the boys. Might mean the abuse was uncovered. Of course, even that was sewn up too, wasn't it? Superintendent Marshall was part of the ring.'

'You only had one problem,' said Carruthers.

Malcolm Hunter looked in to his face. 'What was that?'

'How to dispose of the body. For that you needed help. After all, you were just a kid. And that's when you got into bed with the devil, to coin a phrase. You turned to Ruiridh Fraser.'

Hunter turned to his solicitor. 'All of this is untrue,' he said.

'It took me a long time to work out all the details,' said Carruthers. 'Only you know what really happened the day Kelly died but this is what I think happened. Likely self-defence. After all, he was sexually abusing you, wasn't he?'

'No, that's not true,' said Hunter. He wiped his hands on his trousers.

'He was older and bigger than you and, like I said, you needed help burying the body,' continued Carruthers. 'Fraser or Noble stumbled across you. They helped you dig a grave. It was to be your little secret. I can't imagine what it must have been like for you. Being in debt to a paedophile. Let's face it, you were never going to get off paying that debt, were you? What did Fraser want from you? Did you become his errand boy? Picking out other boys for him?'

'No, that never happened.'

'Anyway, fast forward thirty odd years you've built yourself a family, finally left all that behind you. But it never leaves you, does it? The past? All those nightmares. No wonder you're on pills for insomnia. Then you find yourself living next to Fraser. That was the other thing we couldn't work out. Was that planned? Or just coincidence? Did you deliberately move next door to him? Because if it was deliberate that can only mean one thing. You planned to murder him and your every move was calculated. But horror! He takes an interest in your teenage son, Jordan. I bet that wasn't planned.'

Hunter said nothing.

Carruthers continued. 'He blackmailed you, didn't he? He wanted you to pimp out your own son to him in exchange for his silence. But when you refused he upped the ante. Started to demand money. He was sharing the information he had on you and the photos of Jordan with Noble. You found out.

You knew he would bleed you dry, you'd never be free of him and all the while he's threatening you with going public with the Kelly murder. You had to get rid of him and Noble. You used lorazepam to sedate both men. After all, why would your wife suspect it's being used for anything other than your sleep problems? But what puzzles me is, how did you get the two men to Braidwood? After all, according to neighbours, Fraser rarely left his house. Did you lure them there with the promise of a good time with your son?'

Hunter shook his head. 'You're disgusting.'

'You managed to administer the lorazepam, somehow get them to Braidwood and then you killed them.'

'I already told you. I didn't kill them and I've never even heard of lorazepam.'

'Don't forget,' said Carruthers, 'we've got the remnants of the bloodied cloth. What's the likelihood it's going to test positive for Fraser or Noble's blood? If that cloth was used to wipe the knife that murdered Fraser and Noble and we find either of their DNA on it – we've got you.'

Hunter let out a massive sigh. He clamped his hand over his nose and mouth and rubbed his face.

'Malcolm, I'd come clean now if I were you,' said Carruthers. 'After all, most folk will think you've done the world a favour by getting rid of two paedos. However, I would like to know what happened to Kelly and where he's buried. His family have a right to know. He was just a kid. He deserves a proper burial.'

Hunter drew in a deep breath. 'He may have bullied me, but he never abused me. And I didn't kill him.'

Fletcher opened her mouth to speak but Carruthers put up a warning hand. They were finally on the verge of getting Hunter to talk. Hunter caught the movement and clammed up. Carruthers cursed.

The solicitor carefully put his glasses back on the bridge of his nose and his handkerchief in his pocket. 'If you're not going to charge my client, I think you'd better let him go.'

Carruthers banged his fist down hard on the table. Even the solicitor got a shock. 'What happened the day Tommy Kelly went missing, Malcolm? Don't you think his family have a right to know?'

'I didn't kill him,' he said.

'Who did?' asked Carruthers. 'I have all day and you're not going anywhere.'

'I honestly don't know. All I remember is being told to wait with Tommy in one of the rooms at New Braids. We knew we were going to go to the hotel. It had happened before. Tommy started to get agitated. Started to kick and scream. I'd never seen him like that before. The staff tried to calm him down but he just got worse. Suddenly I felt a hand over my mouth. I don't remember anything else until I woke up in the car.'

'Whose car? Malcolm? Was Tommy with you?'

'The policeman's car. No, I was on my own. I never saw Tommy again.'

'I don't believe you,' said Carruthers. 'You murdered Tommy Kelly. Ruiridh Fraser and Lenny McBride helped you cover it up.'

'I didn't kill him.' Malcolm Hunter had started to shout. 'I didn't kill him!'

Carruthers watched Hunter carefully, noticing a flicker pass over his eyes. 'There's something you're not telling us, Malcolm. What is it? You're not telling us the whole story.'

'I don't remember how Tommy Kelly died,' he said eventually.

Carruthers leant forward across the desk. 'Don't know or don't remember? They're two different things. You started off by saying you don't know. Now you're saying you don't remember. Which is it?'

As Carruthers straightened up, Hunter leant forward, elbows on table, buried his face in his hands and wept. After a few moments he sat back. Wiped his eyes and his nose with the back of his hand.

'OK? I got told I'd killed him but I don't remember. I don't remember killing him.'

'Who told you you'd killed him?' asked Carruthers.

In a tight voice Hunter said, 'Lenny McBride and Ruiridh Fraser.'

Suddenly there was a knock on the door and Brown put his head round. 'Sorry to interrupt, boss. Phone call. You'll want to take it.'

Carruthers excusing himself, silently cursing, left the room and took the phone from Brown. 'This better be good,' he said.

'It's Gayle,' said Brown as he handed it over.

'Have you found it?' Carruthers found he was holding his breath.

'We've got it Jim. Knife with a serrated edge, still bloodied. Hidden in the shed under some loose floorboards.'

'Good job. Get it to the lab.'

'Already on its way.'

Carruthers put the phone down and hurried back to the interview room.

'For the purposes of the tape, DI Jim Carruthers is re-entering the interview room at 2000 hours. Game's up Malcolm. The knife we think that was used to murder Ruiridh Fraser and Henry Noble's been found at your property. What have you got to say for yourself?'

Hunter looked up. He spoke directly to Carruthers. 'I didn't kill Fraser or Noble. I have no idea where that knife came from. Must have been planted.'

Carruthers' face broke in to a smile. He turned to Fletcher. 'Oh he's good, isn't he? Knife's been planted. Next you'll tell me it was planted by one of our lot.'

Hunter wiped his nose with his shirt sleeve. 'Well it's a bit of a coincidence I found the knife in the shed just after your first house search.'

Carruthers turned to Fletcher, 'What's he talking about?'

'No idea, boss. Why don't we ask him?'

'Ask my wife. I wasn't there… One of your lot came round to search the property. Turned the place upside down. Even went in to the shed.'

Carruthers shook his head. 'When was this supposed to have happened?'

'Couple of days ago. I never told Anne I found a knife. I'm the only one who uses the shed. Found the blood-stained knife wrapped in a cloth. I panicked. Wouldn't you? Turns up just after the police come round. What would you do?'

There was a knock on the door. Brown appeared with a note in his hands. He gave it to Carruthers who read it and passed it to Fletcher. Lenny McBride was on the move. Carruthers stood up and followed Brown out of the interview room. He caught up with him in the hall.

'We'll despatch someone to follow him, boss. Don't worry,' said Brown. Carruthers put his hand on the older man's shoulder. Lowering his voice he said, 'I'm following a hunch here. Can you organise for Gayle to go to McBride's flat. Get her to take a couple of uniforms and conduct a full search.'

'But—'

'I'll square the paperwork later and I take full responsibility.'

'What are they looking for?'

'Anything that might incriminate McBride in a murder.' As Brown walked away, Carruthers shouted, 'A recent one.'

If Hunter wasn't the murderer there was only one other person Carruthers could think of who had both motive and opportunity. And that man was Lenny McBride.

Carruthers stepped to one side, and steeling himself for what was ahead, dialled Bingham's home number. The man wasn't happy about being disturbed, but Carruthers' track record for not making unnecessary out-of-hours calls at least got Carruthers a minute. It was tight to explain what was in his head and the silence from the other end of the line when he had finished tied his guts into knots. 'Judge Moran's usually sympathetic to cases against paedophiles:s he might be worth a call.'

Another two seconds passed, they felt like decades to Carruthers.

'OK. If you get Judge Moran on-side you have my permission to search the property of Lenny McBride.'

CHAPTER TWENTY

'Now about this man who came to the house—'said Carruthers.

Hunter suddenly stood up. 'I need the toilet.'

Carruthers looked at Fletcher. 'Get a PC to take him, will you?'

'Yes, no problem.'

Fletcher walked down the corridor with Hunter in silence. Glancing at him, she wanted to say something, anything, to let him know she understood, in so far as she did, but couldn't find the words. She didn't know what to say. And she didn't understand. How could she? She hadn't been through what he, or any other child who'd suffered abuse at the hands of an adult, had been through.

He'd had a horrific childhood, a childhood that for most people was totally unimaginable. She had every sympathy with the tough start he'd had. However, although outwardly normal with a happy family life, he'd gone on to kill two, maybe three people. Calculated, planned, murdered. Perhaps four, if he had a hand in the death of Tommy Kelly, whose remains were likely lying in a make-shift grave undisturbed for nearly forty years. In a sense, they were all victims – Tommy Kelly; Paul Fraser; Malcolm Hunter. But only one had turned killer. She wondered what the truth of Tommy Kelly's disappearance was and whether they'd ever find out.

Approaching the gents' she spotted a male colleague walking towards her. She started to call him over. Hunter turned to her. 'I want to go in alone. I won't have any privacy in prison. It will be like Braidwood. You're living by somebody else's rules; being told what to do, when to do it. It was the lack of privacy I couldn't stand.'

'Prison can't govern your thoughts,' said Fletcher, but even saying it she knew it sounded trite. She turned to Hunter. 'I'm sorry. I can't let you go in alone.'

She turned to the uniform. 'Escort him back to interview room three when he's done, will you?' The PC nodded. As she walked away from the gents' she wondered what sort of future Hunter would have in prison. She knew many care leavers ended up there, failed by a system supposed to protect them. How could they survive in the real world? Given little or no responsibility in care and then suddenly out in the big world with no continuing support. How would they keep a roof over their head? Pay bills? Get a job? Perhaps for some – they needed the security of prison, couldn't function in the outside world, had literally become institutionalised. However, others, Malcolm Hunter being one, led lives; had families; held down jobs. For him, life inside would be unbearable.

She met Carruthers outside the interview room. He was watching Hunter's solicitor through the glass. He turned round.

'We've got him, Jim,' she said.

Carruthers shook his head. 'I'm not so sure.'

'What do you mean?'

'I've despatched Gayle to McBride's flat. He's on the move.'

'We don't have a search warrant,' said Fletcher.

'I've squared it with Bingham and managed to get hold of Judge Moran.'

'Why would you do that? Tell me you don't believe Hunter?'

'It's something Anne Hunter said when we were at the property conducting the search, do you remember?'She said, "I can't believe you people are back to do this again."'

'I don't get it,' said Fletcher.

'I took that comment to mean I don't believe you people are back to bother me again. What if she meant "I don't believe you people are back to *do* this again" – to conduct another search.'

'Surely you can't mean—'

'And then she said something about giving us a second set of keys. It didn't make any sense at the time. Lenny McBride's been a police officer for long enough to be able to impersonate one. And if he's claiming to be CID he wouldn't need a uniform.'

'Oh come off it, Jim. That's a helluva leap.'

'Think about it, Andie. Just think about it for a moment. Lenny McBride kills Tommy Kelly back in 1975. Ruiridh Fraser's present. Malcolm Hunter is drugged. When Hunter wakes up he gets told he's killed the boy. He can't remember but assumes he is somehow responsible for his death.'

'OK, but—'

'Malcolm Hunter finds nearly forty years later he's living next to one of the men who abused him as a kid, and that man then shows interest in his teenage son. He tells Fraser to stay away from his son. Fraser holds Tommy Kelly's death over Hunter and starts blackmailing him.'

'Which means Hunter has the perfect motive for murder,' said Fletcher.

'Yes, he does, but then so does Lenny McBride.'

'I'm not with you.'

'Somehow Lenny McBride finds out Fraser and Noble have been getting up to their dirty little tricks and sharing obscene images of boys. Perhaps he finds out about the blackmail. Hold that thought, Andie.' Carruthers pulled out his mobile and punched in a number. 'Has Brown left yet? He hasn't? Good. Get him to take John Forrest with him, will you? I want to know what McBride's got on his computer.'

He turned to Fletcher.

'You think McBride's killed Fraser and Noble, as well as Kelly?' she asked.

'I think it's a definite possibility. If he killed Tommy Kelly, then he's one desperate man. The circle's closing in around him. Fraser and Noble's recent activities may have just put the frighteners on him. If one of them slipped up the whole historic paedophile ring could get exposed and with it McBride's part in Kelly's death.'

'You're going to be in a whole heap of shit if nothing's found at McBride's flat.' Fletcher suddenly glanced at her watch. 'Christ, where's Hunter?' she said. A terrible thought entered her head. Carruthers and Fletcher looked at each other at the same moment. They both ran down the corridor towards the gents'. Carruthers, arriving slightly before Fletcher, wrenched open the door of the toilets. Looked around wildly. Fletcher could see the uniformed PC lying on the floor groaning. *Shit*, thought Fletcher. Nobody at the urinals. The door of one of the cubicles was shut. Another was open but Fletcher noticed that a sizeable piece of formica had been torn off the cubicle door. She looked at the shut door. 'Malcolm,' Fletcher called. But even as she called his name she saw it. A darkening pool of blood appearing from underneath the cubicle door. Then the sickening smell hit her. The metallic smell. She tried to push the door open but it was locked. Carruthers shoulder-charged it. It didn't budge. He told Fletcher to stand back then kicked it in. The lock splintered and broke. She saw it all as if from a great distance. Hunter fully dressed sitting on the toilet, head lolling to one side, arms out in front of him, blood running from his wrists. A jagged piece of formica in his clenched right hand.

'Get an ambulance,' shouted Carruthers. The uniform, struggling to get to his feet, shouted he was on to it.

Fletcher went over to the basin, chest heaving. Looking behind her shoulder she saw Carruthers trying to stem the bleeding. She ran to the nearest first aid point out in the corridor and yanking the box off the wall, grabbed the gauze bandage and hared back to the gents'.

***

They had got to Hunter in time. He was alive and in hospital under police guard. If he'd taken the formica to his neck, it would have been a different story. Fletcher was sitting with head down. The mood was still sombre at the station when the call came in.

It was the call they'd been waiting for. Lenny McBride had arrived at the nature reserve.

Carruthers frowned as he looked at his watch. It had just gone eight. 'He's earlier than I expected. Perhaps he needs to do a recce. If he has buried Kelly, he'll want to try to remember exactly where the kid's buried. Would you remember after forty years?' Fletcher shrugged, seemingly disinterested. All the fight gone out of her. Carruthers looked at her. 'Don't blame yourself,' he said.

'He was in my care.' She looked up. Tried to smile.

'If he was hell-bent on trying to kill himself, he would have found a way. Look, get yourself a strong coffee. It could be a long evening. We need to head to Braidwood.' He glanced at Fletcher's shaking hands. 'I'll drive,' he said. Fletcher looked at him gratefully.

'How the hell did he manage to tear off that piece of formica? Have you heard any more news from the hospital?' she said.

Carruthers shook his head. 'Not yet. His wife's with him and we've posted a uniformed officer there. At least he's alive.'

***

'OK, so now what do we do?' asked Fletcher.

Carruthers cut the engine. 'Now we wait.'

They were parked up outside the entrance to Braidwood, orders having been given not to use either car park for fear of arousing suspicion. Carruthers took his mobile out of his pocket. Listened to his messages.

Fletcher tore her gaze away from the inky darkness back to Carruthers. 'Any news from the hospital?'

'You only asked me twenty minutes ago, Andie. Wounds are deep, especially the cut to his right wrist, but he's still alive.'

'I know he may be a killer, Jim, but a lot of folk would probably say Fraser and Noble got what they deserved.'

Carruthers looked at her pained face. 'I don't doubt it, but there are others who would say the case deserved to go to trial and that what they deserved was long prison sentences. Anyway, we're still waiting to see what Gayle finds at McBride's flat.'

Fletcher reached for the Thermos by her feet, unscrewed it, pouring some steaming liquid in to a cup. She blew on the strong coffee, took a tentative sip and sat cradling the cup with her hands.

'One way of keeping warm,' she said. 'It's a cold night tonight.' She sat staring out through the glass of the car window, craning her neck skywards. 'Lot of stars in the sky.'

Suddenly Carruthers' mobile started to trill. He answered it with a few terse words, then turned to Fletcher. 'McBride's started to dig.'

Fletcher opened her car door.

Carruthers laid an arm across Fletcher's shoulder. 'Not yet. We need for him to find the body first before we go in.'

She shut the door with a clunk and they sat in silence. She passed him the coffee cup.

'I'm not very good at waiting,' she said.

'Who is?' He took a long drink from the cup and passed it back to her. Thought about his brother's wait for a bypass.

'How are things between you and Jodie?' asked Fletcher. 'Have you managed to talk to her yet?'

Carruthers shook his head. 'I think it's over. She's still not responded to any of my calls.'

'Have you tried apologising?' Fletcher asked.

'Bit hard when she's not talking to me, like I said.'

'You could leave a message on her answer machine.'

'To go with the other five? I don't think so.'

Fletcher shut up.

Time stretched once more between them. They sat in silence until Fletcher said, 'How's your brother?'

Carruthers silently stared out in to the inky darkness.

'It might help to talk about it,' she said.

'Not good. He's needing a triple bypass. All three arteries are fucked. The stents didn't work.' Carruthers opened his car door. 'I'm getting out for a pee.'

He walked away from the car and road in to the side entrance to the woods. As he unzipped his fly he heard the high-pitched child-like scream of a fox. The hairs on the back of his neck stood up. Fletcher was right about the stars. As he stood, feet apart, he stared up in to the deep blue sky that was punctuated by twinkling stars. The cold cut into him even in the short time he was outside. As he did his fly back up with numbing hands his mobile rang. He cursed the unnatural sound, which disturbed the quiet of the woods, prayed that McBride wouldn't have heard it. Briskly he walked back to the car, cutting through a gap in the stone wall.

He returned the call. Nothing important. They sat for a further hour mostly in silence until suddenly Carruthers said, 'I still can't believe he's had a heart attack. He's so fit. I'm the unhealthy one.'

Fletcher encouragingly said, 'You need to get this off your chest. I'm listening.' She reached out and covered her boss's hand. She squeezed it before letting go. 'And by the way, you're not that unhealthy.'

Suddenly Carruthers found himself opening up, talking about his brother in a way he hadn't done for years. 'We used to be close,' he summed up, 'Christ, I don't know when we stopped. Maybe when we were teenagers. I miss it.'

'It's not too late,' said Fletcher.

'You can't turn the clock back,' said Carruthers. He found himself craving a cigarette.

'Perhaps not. But it's not about turning the clock back. It's about going forward.'

'Sorry, I don't know where all that came from,' he said a bit later, embarrassed. 'But, well, you did keep pushing. It felt good to get it—'

Suddenly Carruthers' phone started to ring again. Fletcher looked up expectantly.

'It's Gayle,' he mouthed to Fletcher.

'Jim, we've got him,' said Watson.

'Gayle, what have you found?' said Carruthers.

Watson's voice came out tinny, distant. Carruthers strained to catch her words. 'We've taken his flat apart,' she said. 'Found a blood-stained shirt in a cupboard under the sink and what we think is Angus Dawson's satchel in his attic.'

Thank God, they'd managed to get the warrant. 'Great work. Keep searching.' He spent another couple of minutes listening and talking. He cut the call and turned to Fletcher.

'They've found a blood-stained shirt. What's the betting the blood will match either Fraser or Noble?'

Fletcher looked like she'd been punched in the gut. 'I was so sure it was Malcolm Hunter,' she said. 'It all fit. He had motive, opportunity, he was being blackmailed, for Christ's sake.'

'McBride wanted us to think it was Hunter. Clever bastard. Gayle's even found the lorazepam used to sedate the two men. It was in a drawer in McBride's bedroom.'

Fletcher knelt with her head in her hands. 'Instead of bringing in the right person for questioning we brought in the wrong person. And now he's tried to top himself. In police custody. The press will have a field day. How in God's name did McBride find out about Fraser and Noble's recent activities?'

'Perhaps we'll learn more when we get in to McBride's hard drive,' said Carruthers. 'Speccie's still trying to get access.'

Just at that moment Fletcher's' mobile rang. The call was short. Fletcher opened her car door, throwing the half cup of coffee out. 'That was Dougie. We're to make a move. Think he's found the body.'

Within moments they were out of the car and walking in through the gates of the park. The old university buildings loomed up eerily out of the darkness, their parapets and spires piercing the darkness. The clearness of the night was slowly being obliterated by a thick band of cloud, which was blotting out the stars, one by one.

In darkness, except for the beam from Carruthers' torch, they walked across the orchard with its handful of dying apple trees, their gnarled branches clutching the sky. Making their way past the Pink Building they reached the gap in the old stone wall which they squeezed through. Carruthers, who was ahead of Fletcher, turned to her and in silence gestured for them to make as little noise as possible. He switched the torch off.

His eyes getting accustomed to the gloom, Carruthers could make out a faint but moving shadow up ahead by a large oak tree. He and Fletcher inched forward then each behind a tree, stood, waited and watched. They heard a grunt and the sound of a spade hitting the earth. Carruthers strained his eyes and ears. The bulk of the man ahead was half hidden by a large hole in which he was now standing. Carruthers couldn't see Harris or Brown but knew they would be watching from their vantage points.

The man disappeared from sight. Carruthers assumed he must be down on his haunches. The ground was too hard and the time too short to dig a hole that could completely hide him from view whilst standing. He heard a couple more grunts and then the man was standing upright again with what looked like an old blanket in his arms. A shout went up and Carruthers saw movement and light from behind other trees. Harris racing over, breaking his cover with a couple of uniforms. Torches shining in the face of the shocked man. The man dropped his bundle but before he was able to make a move, Harris, first on the scene shouted, 'Got ye, ye filthy nonce. Yer nicked.'

Carruthers stared in to the ruddy and dirtied face of Lenny McBride, noticing how, despite the cold, grimy sweat was pouring down his cheeks. From McBride he looked down at the pathetic bundle on the ground. What was left of a blanket was filthy, full of holes and mostly disintegrated. A thin, brown skeletal arm was hanging out. The final remains of Tommy Kelly.

EPILOGUE

'I just can't stop thinking about all those kids, the ones at Braidwood,' said Andie the next day. 'What their lives would have been like. How many ended up in prison? On the streets? Committing suicide? It's so fucking tragic.'

Fletcher hardly ever swore. Carruthers couldn't remember the last time she had used language like that.

'Is Hunter really going to be OK?' she asked.

'Physically he'll recover and he'll be offered counselling. It can only help. Perhaps the truth will finally come out at McBride's trial and Hunter'll be able to put the past to bed.'

'You mean about Tommy Kelly's death?'

Carruthers nodded. 'Let's face it, if Hunter was drugged when he was placed in that car, it's much more likely McBride killed Kelly. We've got Simon Wallis' testimony that he overheard McBride telling Marshall the boy had died whilst with him.'

'Yes, but not who killed him,' said Fletcher.

'Who would your money be on? A drugged twelve-year-old or a grown man and paedophile? Hunter's got a good family who love him.'

'If Anne stays with him,' said Fletcher. 'It's only a matter of time before she finds out about the affair.'

'Well, we won't tell her. Hunter's been through enough.'

'What will happen to Braidwood now?' she said.

'Well, the whole area is now a crime scene,' said Carruthers. 'There'll have to be an investigation. Depends on whether any other children went missing from that period. Probably be enough to hold the developers back from any imminent build. Meanwhile life goes on.'

Fletcher looked bleakly into her coffee cup. 'I think the buildings should be bulldozed.'

'I'm sure you wouldn't be the only one who thinks like that. I wonder how the locals trying to save the site will feel when they know its recent history. Will they still want to save it? But would you bulldoze the Pink Building? Didn't you tell me it dates back to 1537? Seems a shame. It has over four hundred years of history before it became a care home.'

'OK, I'd save the Pink Building and the land. It's a fantastic nature reserve.' She stopped for a moment thinking of the glorious open feel of the old sweeping orchard, the majestic line of rhododendrons and Scots pine. 'Oh and New Braids with its amazing hall. But I'd bulldoze the rest.'

'They will get to the truth of what evil went on there, Andie. There'll be prosecutions.'

Fletcher shrugged. 'Won't turn the clock back.'

Carruthers looked thoughtful. 'Maybe not. But places like Braidwood survive because of the secrecy surrounding abuse. The fact people don't want to talk about it. It's the elephant in the room. If we know the ingredients of what allows child abuse to flourish in places like Braidwood, then that's a start. And yes, there will still be abuse allegations coming to light all over the UK. We're just seeing the tip of the iceberg now, but I don't think we'll ever see widespread abuse on that scale again. We can't.'

'Thank God,' she said. She turned to Carruthers, looking thoughtful. 'Have you still got that leaflet from the Friends of Braidwood?'

He frowned. 'Somewhere. Why?'

'I feel I need to redress the balance. Do something positive in my own small way.'

'I'm intrigued,' said Carruthers. 'What did you have in mind?'

She smiled. 'I'm thinking of joining the Friends of Braidwood.'

'You know you can't do that. Don't want to face you across a picket line.'

Fletcher pulled a face.

'If you want to do something positive,' said Carruthers, 'why don't you do something positive for yourself first?'

'Like what?'

He slipped his hand in to the inside of his jacket pocket and brought out a card.

'Hunter's not the only one who needs it. Book yourself that appointment for counselling and don't tell me you've already done it. I know you haven't.'

Handing her the card he grabbed his jacket and mobile. She took it from him and smiled. 'Where you going?' she asked.

'Something I should have done weeks ago. Visit my brother.' And with that he was gone.

THE END

A NOTE FROM BLOODHOUND BOOKS

Thanks for reading Care To Die We hope you enjoyed it as much as we did. Please consider leaving a review on Amazon or Goodreads to help others find and enjoy this book too.

We make every effort to ensure that books are carefully edited and proofread, however occasionally mistakes do slip through. If you spot something, please do send details to info@bloodhoundbooks.com and we can amend it.

Bloodhound Books specialise in crime and thriller fiction. We regularly have special offers including free and discounted eBooks. To be the first to hear about these special offers, why not join our mailing list here? We won't send you more than two emails per month and we'll never pass your details on to anybody else.

Readers who enjoyed Care To Die will also enjoy

Robbing The Dead also by Tana Collins

Bad to The Bone by Tony J Forder

ACKNOWLEDGEMENTS FOR CARE TO DIE

A huge thank you to Bloodhound Books for their fantastic work in promoting my debut novel, *Robbing the Dead.* I was incredulous at its success and want to thank not only Bloodhound but also all the hard working authors and bloggers who participated in my blog tour and all those who made an effort to leave such positive reviews!

The biggest thanks for *Care to Die* must go to fellow writer Avery Mathers for the painstaking hours he selflessly put in to earlier drafts. Thanks must also go to my crime writing friends Alison Baillie and Sarah Ward who, along with Avery, were my first readers.

Thanks also to editor, Gail Williams, who helped whip my book in to shape before approaching Bloodhound. My success is in no small way thanks also to her. Thanks also to Clare Law, my editor at Bloodhound.

I want to thank all the crime writers and readers who have influenced and supported me along the way. What an incredibly supportive bunch you are!

All my family, friends and clients at Scottish Water and Leonardo for their enthusiasm and support of my writing. You know who you are! Particular thanks to Greg, Gemma, Anna, Mike, Chris, Vicky and Graham B for their enthusiasm and interest. Jane Amaku for cheering me on from her vetinary surgery, Amanda Selway for the fab friend she has become, Gill McLaren and Jacqui Fraser for the fab friends they have always been, best friend Bettina and lastly Henrietta whose enthusiasm is still as contagious as it was when we were six years old!

And finally, Ian, who has had to put up with me writing on every holiday we've been on in the last ten years!